Crestwood Lake 2

Satan's Revenge

TONI —

HOW WONDERFULLY
EVIL!

Mike R Npl

Crestwood Lake 2

Satan's Revenge

Mark R. Vogel

ISBN: 1722808616

ISBN 13: 978-1722808617

CreateSpace Independent Publishing Platform

North Charleston, South Carolina

To my dearest Yang,

I will always love you.

Acknowledgements

Once again, my foremost appreciation will always be to my wife, the most devout champion of my work, not to mention my life in general. She is unyielding in her support. She is my sounding board, my reality check, and my advocate. Quite simply, she is my everything. Thank you, my love.

Next, I would like to thank my professional editor, Jennifer Walkup, and my personal editor, my mom. Each provided invaluable feedback from missing commas, to the big picture, and everything in-between. Both Jennifer and my mom helped hone many facets of my writing.

I also wish to express my sincerest gratitude to my writing group, the HighlandScribes, certainly for their input on my three novels, but also for facilitating my development as a writer.

A big shout out is once again deserved for Oscar and Vivian of Imagining Concepts in Randolph, NJ, for my cover design and promotional materials.

Finally, I want to thank my good friends Dr. Scott Guerin and Laura Shally, for the numerous times I solicited their opinions on multifarious issues about my story.

The Pact

April 24, 1655

Ghastly screams of anguish sheared through Adriana's mind, jolting her awake. She jerked upright, gasping, reaching for her husband Franco, but he was gone. The screams continued. Adriana stumbled across the cold stone floor to the window. The sun was just breaking over the horizon. She gaped in horror.

The Duke of Savoy's army, quartered amongst the citizens of Torre Pellice, was slaughtering the populace: men, women, and children. Scattered homes were ablaze. The townsfolk ran wildly through the streets, chased by bands of soldiers. The lucky ones were killed forthwith; others were tied and tortured. In the square, three men were bound to stone pillars. Their French assailants slowly amputated their extremities until exsanguination bestowed the only mercy to be had. Women and girls were being violated. Heads and limbs littered the streets. In the distance, a squad of troops marched toward the square, their arms buttressing pikes, upon which sagged the bodies of impaled victims.

"Mama!" hollered Serafina, Adriana's twelve-year-old daughter.

Adriana bolted out of the room and peered over the edge of the sprawling marble staircase, down to the torch-lit first floor. A cadre of French soldiers awaited her. On the floor lay her husband Franco, gagged, bound, and bloodied. One soldier held her daughter, while a second restrained her eight-year-old son, Giacomo. The children whimpered.

At the base of the staircase stood the French capitaine in his pristine uniform, stern gray eyes, exuding dominance. "Come join us, Madame Barberi. Unless you prefer to watch me slay your family from your lofty perch."

Adriana flew down the stairs and rushed toward her children, but was seized by two soldiers.

"No!" yelled Adriana.

"Oh yes," snickered the capitaine. His smile faded as he snarled, "It's time for you, and all of your fellow Waldensian heretics to pay for your apostasy."

"We just wish to be left alone!"

The capitaine stormed toward Adriana and smacked her. "You are a blasphemer!"

Franco squirmed and grunted. The soldier next to him kicked him in the ribs. The children's whimpering escalated to a cry.

Blood dripped from Adriana's nose. "Please spare my family."

The capitaine grabbed Adriana's long dark-brown hair and yanked her face toward his. "It is *you* who has doomed your family. You have renounced your faith and taken refuge in this heathen stronghold."

"We came to Torre Pellice only to be near my husband's family—"

The capitaine smacked her again. "We know who you are Adriana Barberi. You are descended from the Borgias. You're worse than a Waldensian. You're probably a witch."

"I am not a witch!"

"Enough of this," said the capitaine. He nodded to the soldier standing over Franco.

The soldier swung his sabre, decapitating him.

"No!" shrieked Adriana.

"Papa!" squealed the children.

The capitaine approached Serafina. Around her neck was a dazzling sapphire amulet, supported by a thick gold chain. He yanked it off of her and said, "Take the boy away. The girl stays with me."

The soldiers pushed Giacomo out the door.

"Your daughter will keep my bed warm tonight," said the capitaine.

Tears streamed from Adriana's eyes. "I'll kill you—you worthless bastard!"

The capitaine chuckled. "I think not." He waved his hand at the soldiers holding Adriana. "Take her to the stockade. She'll be of use when I tire of her daughter."

A soldier struck Adriana in the back, knocking her to the floor. They tied her wrists behind her back, clutched her arms, and dragged her toward the French garrison, ignoring the mayhem surrounding them. More houses were afire, as well as people, burning at the stake. Screams—endless screams—pierced the air from all directions: victims being raped, tortured, or murdered. The streets were filling with corpses. The soldiers draggled Adriana through pools of blood, before arriving at the stockade.

"Lock her up," said one of the soldiers to the guards.

The guards jostled Adriana toward a staircase descending to the cellar, then shoved her onto her back. They grabbed her ankles, and yanked her down the stairs, allowing her head to bounce off each step. They threw her inside the cell, slammed the door, and left.

The cell was dank, cold, and reeked of excrement. Windowless, it was morosely dark. Adriana, still bound, curled up into a fetal position against the wall and cried, and cried.

Hours elapsed. No one attended to her. Eventually the sounds of the massacre died down, but not Adriana's agony. Her mind was in a frenzy: a twisted turmoil of shock, gloom, and horrid thoughts. Could she bargain her way into saving her children? Were they even still alive? And if not?

Slowly, rage eclipsed her grief. The capitaine obviously had plans for her, or she would have been murdered by now. She would bide her time and find a way to kill him, even if it meant her own death. The hours pressed on.

Adriana remained curled up next to the wall. Necessity had forced her to urinate on herself. Her thirst was mounting, as was the pain in her back and arms.

A soft red glow, from no discernable origin, filled the room. Adriana twitched her head toward the center of her cell. A tall figure, in a black cape and hood, towered above her.

Adriana gasped and wriggled away.

"Have no fear, Adriana. I am here to help you." His deep voice seemed to reverberate from all directions.

"Who are you?"

He stretched out his hand toward the rock wall. Two slabs of stone slid out from it across the floor. He sat on one, motioned toward the other and said, "Sit."

Adriana struggled with her bindings.

"Allow me to assist you," he said, taking one of Adriana's hands. Her ties fell, the pain in her back and limbs dissipated, and her clothes were instantly unsoiled. Still holding her hand, he effortlessly glided her through the air, and onto the awaiting slab. He sat on the other and faced her.

"You're not of this world," said Adriana cowering, beguiled by his fathomless black eyes.

"Indeed I am."

"Not the mortal world."

"That is correct, my dear."

"You're a witch."

"No, I am not."

"What then?"

"The witches bow down before me."

Adriana slowly opened her mouth and leaned back. "You are Satan?"

He frowned. "I never approved of that term. It means adversary in Hebrew. I am not your adversary, Adriana."

"What do you want from me?"

4

"I told you. I am here to help you."

"My children?"

He shook his head. "I am very sorry my dear. It's too late for them."

Adriana wept and shook her fists. "Why? Why my children? They are innocent!"

"They have no regard for human life," he said.

"Then put me out of my misery. They will brutalize me."

"No, Adriana." He placed his hand on her knee. "*You* will brutalize *them.*"

"I don't understand."

He tightened his grip as his eyes grew even darker. "I can feel your hatred. You do wish to avenge your family, do you not?"

"Yes."

"And your persecutors?"

Adriana felt a surge of wrath course through her body. "I want them to suffer. All of them."

"Good . . . very good. Then ally yourself with me. I will ensure you receive your retribution."

"But I am a Christian . . . and you . . . you are . . ."

"Christians?" he said, his voice rising. "Your people, your family, have been tortured and slayed by Christians, all because you don't recognize that pompous patriarch in Rome. Is this the religion you are defending?"

"And what of God?" asked Adriana.

"God? What God? I didn't see your deity come to the rescue when they stormed your home, butchered your husband, and stole your children. Where is your God now? Is this how he repays your loyalty?"

Adriana's mouth quivered.

"I am here! I will save you—I will give you everlasting life—and I will see to it that each and every *Christian* pays for the injustices inflicted upon you."

Adriana felt her rage returning.

"Unless you prefer to rot in this hole until they rape and murder you, thus allowing your children's deaths to go unpunished."

"No. I can't let that happen."

He extended his hand. "Then come with me but know this: from now on I am your master, not your so-called god who has ignored your plight. I reward allegiance, but I can be as merciless as the Christians should you betray me."

Adriana took his hand. "Agreed."

"Come," he said, standing, with a satisfied grin. "There is much to be done. Shall we start with the capitaine?"

The Portent

August 2016

Captain Butch Morgan and his best friend, seventy-five-year-old Gil Pearson, sat at the bar in Toby's, nursing their respective bourbon and rye whiskey, awaiting the start of the Boston Red Sox game. Morgan normally preferred to watch sports in the comfort of his own living room, but Vicki, now his wife, had to bartend this Sunday, and being close to her was more important.

"I'm putting my retirement papers in Monday morning," said Morgan.

"Finally," said Gil. "That's great. You and Vicki better start enjoying life now, before everything starts to hurt, and you smell like piss all the time."

"I'm only fifty-five."

"My point exactly," said Gil.

"I want to give Vicki a second honeymoon, the one she really wanted: Paris."

Gil chortled and took a sip of his drink. "Now there's an image for ya: Butch Morgan strolling through Paris." Gil held up his hand like a waiter supporting a tray, and in a cheesy French accent said, "Excusez-moi, Monsieur Cro-Magnon, do you require utensils, or will your hands suffice?"

"Don't be a douchebag."

Gil chuckled.

"What'd he do now?" asked Vicki coming within earshot.

"What he always does," said Morgan, "acting like himself."

"He told me about his plans to take you to Paris," said Gil.

"Paris? You're taking me to Paris!"

"You stupid shithead!" said Morgan. "I wanted to surprise her."

"How was I supposed to know?" Gil's blue eyes pleaded innocence.

"Is it true?" said Vicki. "You're taking me to Paris?"

"Yes," said Morgan.

"Then that means…?"

"Yes, I decided to retire. I'm letting the mayor know Monday."

"When's your last day, baby?"

"I don't have an exact date," said Morgan holding up his hands, as if trying to stop a dam about to burst. "I have to find and train a replacement, and clean up lots of other details, but I'm thinking before the end of the year."

"Yes!" said Vicki bouncing up and down, her long red hair bobbing wildly. "I don't know what I'll love better: having you around more, or going to Paris."

"Your answer determines whether we go or not," said Morgan.

"Of course you," said Vicki, stroking the back of Morgan's hand.

"Smart girl," said Gil.

"Let me get you boys another round." Vicki pranced away, stopped, looked over her shoulder at Gil, and playfully mouthed the word "Paris."

Morgan glared at Gil like he was about to rip out his innards.

"Butch, I didn't know."

"I was going to take her out for dinner next week after it was official and then tell her."

"Then why didn't you say something? Your species developed communication not too long ago."

"I was going to, but then Vicki came over. You'd think by now I would have learned to tell you to shut up first, and then tell ya what I have to say."

Vicki returned with their drinks. "You boys ready to order yet?"

"Just give me a burger and fries," said Gil.

Vicki turned to Morgan, "Let me guess . . . pastrami on rye with mustard—extra meat."

"That's why I love ya, darling."

As Vicki put in their order, Gil noticed a man entering Toby's. "Hey, Butch," he said, tapping Morgan's arm. "That's the guy buying my old house. I saw him there with the realtor the other day."

"You mean *Burke's* old house—he bought it from you."

"Whatever. We should warn him."

"Huh?" said Morgan.

"I feel guilty about what happened to Burke. I knew of the rumors."

"And that's all they were at the time—rumors."

"Well, now that we know they're true, I feel compelled to say something."

"Like what? Hi, welcome to Crestwood Lake. Your house is haunted."

Gil patted Morgan's shoulder and said, "Don't worry. Conscience development happens not too long after speech."

Morgan sneered.

"Here he comes." Gil waived his hand to the man and said, "Excuse me."

The man approached.

"Hi, I'm Gil Pearson and this is Captain Butch Morgan, the chief of police."

Morgan stood up to shake the man's hand.

The man had to raise his line of sight eight inches to meet Morgan's eyes. "Hello . . . I'm Pete Hadley . . . is something wrong?"

"No," said Gil. "We just wanted to introduce ourselves. You're buying the house at 214 Crestwood Lake Road?"

"Yes, I am."

"I live down the street. Number 106."

"Well it's nice to meet you."

"What do you do?" asked Morgan.

"Oh, I'm retired, but I used to be an editor at a publishing house."

"How old are you, Mr. Hadley? If you don't mind me asking."

Hadley tilted his head. "I'm . . . forty-eight."

"And you're retiring?"

"I have health problems, Captain."

"Sorry to hear that. Any family?"

"No, not really. My wife and I recently divorced and my daughter's in California at college."

"I see."

"So, I understand the house has been on the market for quite a while," said Hadley.

"Three years," said Morgan.

"I'm surprised no one bought it. It's a beautiful house—perfect location. And the price was unbelievable. I don't know why it was so low."

"I do," said Gil.

Hadley awaited Gil's answer.

"Mr. Hadley, I know how this is going to sound, but I have to say it. The house is haunted."

"What?"

"My family used to own that house. A number of people have died there over the years, including the last owner who I sold it to."

Hadley looked at Morgan.

"It's true," said Morgan.

"Excuse me, gentlemen, but is there some reason you don't want me to move into this town?"

"No," said Morgan, "it's nothing like that."

"Butch has lived here three decades," said Gil, "and I've lived here all of my seventy-five years. We know the history of that place."

"Which is . . .?"

"Like I said, a number of people have passed away in that house, and before they did, they had premonitions about their own death. They sensed—in one form or another—their own doom. The last owner complained that the house smelled like something died in it. I was there and didn't smell anything. Weeks later I found him dead, decomposing, stinking to high heaven."

Hadley darted his eyes and jiggled his head. "Why are you telling me this?"

"I felt I had to," said Gil, "since I used to own it."

"And what do you expect me to do? Just believe your ghost story, cancel the sale, and move away?"

"Look, Mr. Hadley," said Morgan, "I can vouch for the fact that an unusual number of people have died in that house. Something weird goes on in there. We're not trying to get rid of you. You're welcome in Crestwood Lake. Gil just feels obligated to give you a heads up since he was a previous owner."

"Well, gentlemen, I'm certainly not going to back out now, and start all over looking for another place, especially in my condition. Your ghosts and goblins will just have to accept that."

Hadley turned to leave when Morgan said, "Hold on."

"Yes, Captain?"

"Let me give you my card."

"Give him my phone number too," said Gil.

11

Morgan scribbled down Gil's number and handed the card to Hadley. "If you need anything, please call either one of us, OK?"

"Thanks," said Hadley walking away.

"Feel better now?" said Morgan to Gil.

"You'd better check in on him in a few weeks."

"I'm hoping all that shit is behind us," said Morgan.

Gil gently scoffed.

"What?" said Morgan.

"Nothing. Here comes the food."

Vicki dropped off their plates and said, "Enjoy, boys."

Morgan finished his drink, sunk his teeth into his pastrami, and moaned in satisfaction. After swallowing he said, "They make the best damn pastrami around here." He was masticating his second chunk when his cell phone rang. "Goddammit! Always when I'm eating."

It was Lieutenant Carl Edwards, calling from the station.

"What is it?" snarled Morgan.

"Butch, we got a robbery in progress at Metzler's! One of the employees called. Some psycho with a gun is emptying all the cash registers. He shot a woman and her baby!"

"He shot a baby?"

"That's what he said."

"Surround the place; I'm on my way."

"What's up?" asked Gil.

"Someone's robbing the supermarket and shooting people. Gotta go." Morgan raced out of Toby's, jumped in his pickup truck, turned on his lights and siren, and shot out of the parking lot. He got on the radio and contacted Edwards for an update. "This is Morgan, I'm almost there, what's happening?"

"Our units are en route. Last report from the store said the perp was still there."

"What's he look like?"

"Caucasian, long black hair, jeans and a blue shirt."

"Where's our cars?"

"They were either on other calls, or patrolling away from the center of town. The ambulance just arrived. Where are you?"

"I just pulled onto Main Street."

"You'll be the first cop there. Wait for the cavalry, Butch . . . Butch?"

Morgan darted in and around cars, careening into the store's parking lot. He heard a gunshot, then saw a man matching the suspect's description, carrying a pistol, running out of the store. Morgan was speeding right toward him.

The man assumed a firing stance and shot repeatedly at Morgan's truck.

Morgan ducked and floored it, slamming into the man, launching him into the air. He bounced off the back of a van and fell to the ground in a mangled, bleeding pile.

Morgan hopped out of his truck, picked up the gun, and approached the paramedics. "Don't worry about him—there's a woman and her baby shot in the store."

Morgan and the paramedics ran inside. A hysterical woman was holding a wailing baby, the bottom of her shirt wrapped around the infant's bloody arm.

"He shot my baby!" she cried.

The one paramedic took the baby and examined him. "It's only a nick," she said. "He'll be OK."

The other paramedic assessed the woman to make sure she wasn't hit.

Morgan said to the crowd, "Anyone else hurt?"

"No," said one of the customers.

"Get that baby to the hospital!" said Morgan.

The mother and the paramedics hurried to the ambulance.

Morgan followed them out. One of the paramedics headed toward the culprit. "I told you to forget about him. He's already dead. Now get that baby to the hospital now!"

The paramedics complied and sped away.

The man lay in an expanding pool of blood, choking out his last breaths.

Morgan approached.

"Help me," he wheezed.

Morgan bent over and stuck his index finger in the man's face. "Don't you *ever* fucking interrupt my lunch!" Then he casually sauntered back into the store.

~~~~~~

The next day Morgan was in his office doing paperwork, drinking his mid-afternoon coffee, when the officer at the front desk buzzed.

Morgan let out an annoyed sigh and picked up the phone. "What?"

"Captain, I got Dr. Wyatt on the line for you."

"Put him through."

"Captain?"

"Yeah, Doc, go ahead."

"I just finished the autopsy on the man who robbed the supermarket yesterday."

"And?"

"Remember that guy you shot on 91 three years ago? He had that huge tattoo on his back: an upside-down pentagram with a sinister ram's head in the center?"

Morgan's stomach fluttered. "Yeah."

"Same thing, Captain. This guy has the exact same tattoo, in the exact same place. You want to come here and check it out?"

"No, just e-mail me the pictures. Anything else about him?"

"Not much. Found a few needle tracks. Doesn't look like he was a regular user, but he's chased the dragon in his time. Otherwise, not much to tell. He's young, early twenties, no signs of disease. Oh I forgot, he does have genital warts."

"Jesus Christ," said Morgan. "Like I need to know that shit?"

"You asked if there was anything else about him."

"Goodbye, Doc."

Morgan took a long sip of his coffee. Then he took out his retirement forms, ripped them in half, and threw them in the trash.

Morgan pulled into the driveway of the home he and Vicki purchased last year. They had each sold their houses from their previous marriages, pooled their resources, and made a fresh start. Morgan had worked through his grief from his past wife's death, and Vicki just wanted to forget the abuse—and her fall from grace. They found a small cottage near the outskirts of town. Neither of them wanted to be on or near the lake, given the multiple deaths that had occurred there.

As soon as Morgan opened the door, Vicki ran over and gave him a big hug and a kiss. "Hey, baby. How you doing?"

"I'm OK, honey."

"Gil's inside. He said you told him to meet us here."

"Yeah, I gotta talk to both of you."

Vicki followed him into the living room.

Gil was sitting on the couch with a glass of rye. "It's five thirty; I thought you told me to be here at five."

"What time did you actually arrive?" asked Morgan.

"Five twenty."

"That's why I said five."

Gil smirked.

"Want a drink, babe?" asked Vicki.

"No," said Morgan. "I don't want anything. Sit down. We got a big problem."

"What's wrong?" said Vicki, sitting Indian style in the leather recliner.

"The guy who robbed Metzler's yesterday had the same tattoo on his back as the witch I shot on 91 three years ago—the one who almost killed me and Gil."

Gil's face sank. "If he's a witch, and you didn't kill him with holy water, he's going to return as a demon."

"I know."

"Butch," said Vicki, her voice tenuous and fragile, "You don't think *he's* back . . . do you?"

"I don't know, but it's not a good sign."

"Oh my God," said Gil.

Tears pooled in Vicki's green eyes. "It can't be."

"Honey," said Morgan, "I know it's the last thing you want to hear, but we have to consider the possibility."

Vicki looked like she was watching a horror movie in the distance.

"He could be rebuilding the coven," said Gil. "Little by little, converting local people, maybe bringing in witches from other areas, just like last time."

16

"Could be," said Morgan. "The perp didn't have any ID, but he wasn't from around here. Nobody recognized him."

"No, no," said Vicki. "It can't be. Maybe he was just passing through."

"And what if he wasn't?"

"No! I can't go through that hell again. I can't!"

Morgan held her arms and said, "Take it easy. Maybe it's nothing. But if it's not, I'm gonna need your help. We'll handle it together, honey, OK?"

Vicki nodded weakly.

"Now you tell me," said Morgan. "This could be the start of something, right?"

"Yes," said Vicki, starting to sob. "I've always been afraid he'd come back, especially for me."

"Why you and not me?" asked Morgan. "I'm the one who destroyed his coven."

"Oh, he'd want you too. But he'd have a particular grudge against me. It infuriates him when any of his converts defect. He can't tolerate betrayal."

"We better go see Professor Aaronson," said Gil. "Van Haden's not going to make the same mistakes this time, and we need to figure out a game plan. Aaronson will know what to do."

"If you go to see him," said Vicki, "I want to go too."

"No problem," said Morgan.

"Has there been anything strange going on lately?" asked Gil. "I mean other than the robbery yesterday? Anything like before?"

"No, nothing unusual." Morgan looked at Vicki, her eyes seeping desperation—clinging to the hope that it wasn't true. Then he said to Gil, "I don't want to go running off half-cocked. Let's see if anything else happens."

"Well, at the very least," said Gil, "you better get over to Saint Matthew's, get some holy water, and splash it on the robber's body."

"That won't work," said Vicki. "It's too late. If he's a witch, and already dead by conventional means, he'll have already begun his transformation. And he'll be back with a vengeance."

"Can you tell from his body whether he was a witch?" asked Morgan.

"No," said Vicki.

"If he was a witch, and becomes a demon—what happens to his body then?"

"Nothing. The demon is his spirit. The body will decompose like any other."

"We should still go to the church and get some holy water," said Gil, "just in case he or any other witches or demons appear."

"OK, slow down," said Morgan. "First, we don't even know that this guy was a witch. Second, even if he was, we don't know that they're targeting Crestwood Lake again. And third, what the hell am I gonna say to the new priest there, Father . . . what's-his-nuts?"

"Sean," said Gil.

"Yeah, Father Sean. How do I explain why I need all this holy water? If we're wrong, I'll look like a mental case."

"So what do we do?" asked Gil.

"We put our guard up and start investigating, but I want something more than a freak with a tattoo, before we go off on some wild goose chase."

"All right," said Gil. He finished his drink and stood. "We'll know soon enough." Gil bade them good night and left.

"Keep your ears open at Toby's," said Morgan. "Let me know if the townsfolk talk about anything strange, or mention their animals getting killed."

Vicki nodded. "So does this mean you didn't talk to the mayor about retiring about retiring?"

"I'm afraid so."

"You think we're in danger."

"Let's just say I want to be sure before I step down."

Vicki sighed and rubbed her hands against her thighs.

Morgan put his arm around her and said, "Honey, don't worry. I'm not going to let anything happen to you. He'll have to go through my corpse first."

"That's what I'm afraid of," said Vicki.

The Revenant

The last box was unpacked, the last picture hung, and the last check to my parasitic lawyer dispensed. Twenty grand to adjudicate what percentage of my assets would be remitted to my ex-wife, now playing house with my ex-best friend. This was a woman I loved—not one I abused, criticized, or embarrassed. This was a friend I trusted—not one I swindled, scorned or mistreated. And the coup de grâce was not my rapacious attorney (he was merely salt on the wound), but the alienation from my daughter, who was inevitably poisoned against me by her adulterous mother. My daughter even matriculated into a new college, solely to be closer to my betrayers.

With that final blow, I decided a new life was in order. I departed east, back to my home state of Vermont, purchasing a delightful waterfront house in the town of Crestwood Lake—delightful until Gil Pearson and Captain Morgan told me my house was haunted. Were they trying to scare me away? I could understand an old coot like Gil believing in the supernatural, but the chief of police? Did they object to me moving into their town for some reason? I was starting to feel as if the entire world was against me.

I would never admit this to anyone, but what really haunted me, was the possibility that such things could exist. My fear of the macabre began when I was five years old. The only advantage I had in life was my intellect, particularly my language skills. In kindergarten, my reading level was that of a third grader. One day I came across a horrible story on the front page of the newspaper. A woman and her father had pulled into her driveway and encountered a strange man. As they exited their vehicle, the man brandished a knife and—I still remember the exact words—"stabbed the father four times in the heart." The article was accompanied by one of those ghoulish police sketches of the culprit. To this day I cringe whenever I see one of those drawings. *Four times in the heart,* still resonates through my brain. Anyway, to make a long story worse, the newspaper report scared me, and I cried. My father, more concerned about my "effeminate" reaction than my terror, spanked me, thus compounding my anguish.

Not long after this trauma, I became afraid of the dark. It began as a vague uneasiness at nightfall, intensifying at bedtime. Then it morphed into something more ominous. I would wake up in the middle of the night, certain that someone had called my name. Twice I felt something grabbing my ankles and pulling me. In each instance my parents were asleep in their bedroom on the other side of the house.

Then I started picturing images in the blackness: a spooky tree throwing boulders at me, wild animals, dark figures lurking in my doorway, and the creepiest of all—one that only happened a few times, but one that I will never forget—the face of a scary old man coming straight at me. He wasn't gruesome. He didn't have fangs or distorted features, or anything like that. In fact, his impeccable white hair made him look distinguished. What terrified me was his eyes. Those piercing eyes! And his expression—like he wanted me dead. I would pull the covers over my head and shudder. I couldn't call out to my parents, lest I wake a different monster.

One day when I was about twelve, while my father was at work, my mother left me alone for a quick trip to the store. I was in the basement reading as I heard her close the kitchen door and pull out of the driveway. Moments later, the kitchen door opened, followed by a set of heavy footsteps stomping through the house. I called out "Mom," but no one answered. I looked out the basement window. The driveway was empty. I crept upstairs and found the kitchen door wide open. I ran back downstairs and called the police. With guns drawn they canvassed the house but found nothing.

The final ingredients in the evolution of my current phobias happened when my ex-wife and I were first married. I had just started an entry-level position with a small publisher, while my wife toiled in a menial clerical job. We rented a small apartment near a crime-ridden neighborhood. The building next to us was so close, that once on top of its roof, one could literally walk over to our kitchen window.

Twice we arrived home and discovered evidence of someone trying to pry their way in. The third time was the worst. I was in bed asleep while my wife was in the living room watching TV. Someone started coming in through the window. My wife screamed, and the intruder fled. But what horrified me was: what would have happened if we were both asleep? Would he have raped her? Killed me? Killed us both?

Since that time my neurosis about the dark has taken on two additional dimensions: As I walk through my house at night, I have visions of someone, or some-*thing*, lunging out and attacking me. Secondly, I can't come home without envisioning someone already inside my house . . . waiting for me. And that now happens even during the day.

I feigned dismissiveness with Gil and Captain Morgan, but in reality, they had burrowed right into my primordial fears. But what could I do? My young-onset Parkinson's was advancing, and would continue to do so, medication or not. Coupled with my chronic colitis, insomnia, and sundry other ailments, I was in no condition, physically or otherwise, to move again. Moreover, most of my life was behind me. What was the point?

Because of my physical limitations, I had hired people to perform the hard labor that the house required: painting, cleaning, yardwork, etc. Nevertheless, there were countless miscellaneous chores to attend to, which was fine with me. My doctors had recommended that I maintain a modicum of physical activity, and even an egghead like myself can't tolerate sitting around reading all day.

I was tinkering with a stuck window shade one morning when the doorbell rang. I opened the door to an elderly woman with long gray hair and large sunglasses, holding a plate of cookies.

"Hello. I'm June Perkins; I live up the street at 226."

"How are you? I'm Pete Hadley."

She extended her arms and said, "I just wanted to welcome you to the neighborhood. I baked these myself." She peeked over my left shoulder.

"Thank you," I said, taking the plate.

"Is there a missus I can say hi to?"

"No, just me. How about you?"

"Well, I let my husband stay with me . . . when he behaves."

We laughed.

"Where ya from?" she asked.

"I'm originally from Vermont."

"Oh yeah, where?"

"Burlington. Moved to California for many years while I was married. We recently divorced, so I decided to return to my home state."

"It's good to come back home," said June.

"Would you like to come in?"

"No," she said, "I see you have company."

I snapped my head back and then forward. "I don't have any company."

"Oh," she said, glimpsing over my shoulder again, "I thought . . ."

"You thought . . .?"

"Nothing, I thought I saw someone. Must be these damn glasses."

"So, would you like a cup of coffee?"

"No, that's OK, I have to be going. Welcome to the neighborhood and if you need anything, let us know."

"Thanks for the cookies," I said to her back, as she abruptly faded from view. I shut the door, dropped the cookies on the floor, and surveyed every room, looking out the windows as well. What the hell did she see? Then I had my ambush image again: some freak or monster leaping out and assailing me. I noticed my tremors increasing, so I took some valium and lay on the couch, listening for any strange sounds.

Two days later my colitis flared up. I was curled up in bed with abdominal cramps, running to the bathroom every fifteen minutes. As I lay there, hands trembling, stomach churning, my mind wandered to the dark side. What would I do when my Parkinson's became so severe I couldn't care for myself? I'd be forced to sell the house—probably end up in a nursing home. Maybe I'd die before then. How many years could I have left? Maybe I'd kill myself before I reached that point.

That's when I thought of the argument I had with my ex-wife, just before I caught her cheating on me. It was a day like today: marred by exacerbations of my medical woes. My wife and I were fighting—something about the family, and issues with our daughter. My pain was intensifying and finally I yelled "Maybe I'll just kill myself. Will that make you happy?"

Even now, her response still claws its way through my heart: "You mean you'd actually do that for us?"

I clenched my pillow furiously, imagining it was her neck, accomplishing nothing but aggravating my colon. I ran back to the bathroom, collapsed on the toilet, and punched the wall. Then I flinched—sensing a presence—much like when people say they feel like they're being watched. In-between spurts, I cupped my ear and listened, but heard nothing. I pulled up my pants and darted through the house, inspecting every room. I wrote it off as my illness and took a valium.

By morning my symptoms had eased, so I decided to reach out to my daughter. Every so often I'd call her. Occasionally she responded, almost always via a brief e-mail. The last time we actually spoke was months before the divorce was finalized.

My daughter lived in an apartment near her university. I had given her a large sum of money for living expenses when she was first accepted. Her mother and I split the tuition each semester. It was slowly draining what remained of my retirement funds after the divorce settlement. I no longer had a nest egg—I had an eggshell.

As I dialed her number, I breathed in and prepared for an altercation. She never answered when I called, and we hadn't had an outright quarrel in some time. Nevertheless, I always felt trepidation when trying to contact her.

It went to voice mail—of course. I left my plea: "Hey, honey, it's Dad. Just thinking about you. I'm settled into my new place. It's beautiful here . . . you'd love it, if ever wanted to come by. In the meantime, give me a ring when you can. I hope everything's OK at school. I love you." I placed the phone in its charger as a shadow skipped across the floor.

I spun around so fast I could almost feel my brain bounce off my skull. *Nothing was there.* What the hell? Maybe it was my own shadow. I looked at the floor again, but I wasn't casting one. I just stood there, like a deer in the forest that heard a suspicious noise. That's when I decided I needed a break from the house.

I had been contemplating taking a trip to Burlington to see my old stomping grounds. Who knows how many more times in my life I would do that. In addition to some shopping, I wanted to visit the local library to research my new dwelling and the town. I probably could do it from my home computer, but the library helped me believe I was going to Burlington for a real purpose, other than escaping my willies.

24

It was a peaceful two-hour ride to the city of my birth. Well, the drive itself and the scenery were peaceful, not my internal landscape. I was nervous about traveling so far. My latest intestinal bout seemed to be ebbing, but my colitis could return without warning—and with ferocity.

I thought about my health, my finances, my daughter, the house—you name it. I had hoped the trip would relax me. Unfortunately, the repetitious scenery, and the incessant drone of the engine, served as a blank screen for my mind. Upon it I projected all my underlying anxieties.

I arrived in Burlington, hit a few stores, cruised through my old neighborhood, and got some lunch. Then I went to the library. I told the reference librarian about my relocation to Crestwood Lake, and my desire to learn more about the town and my house. She gave me a strange look, but nevertheless escorted me to a computer. She showed me various websites, such as where to retrieve past newspaper articles, and the history of my property.

Three hours later I was sick to my stomach, and not from the colitis. The more I dug into the goings-on of Crestwood Lake, the queasier I became: suspicious fires, missing persons, mutilated animals, and rumors of witchcraft and devil worship. Most disturbing were the deaths—grisly deaths—like stabbings, and people found mutilated in the woods. Then there were the suicides: hangings, a nun who drowned herself, and a man who threw himself in front of a train. And as for my house—oh my God—Gil and Captain Morgan were right. The original owner, sixty-three years prior, shot his wife and himself. A number of other owners in recent years died in the house, including one woman poisoned by her husband. The man who owned it before me, three years ago, was found dead with an axe in his hand. Apparently, he went berserk and hacked away at the walls until his heart gave out.

I hurried out of the library and drove home. My mind was a tempest. What in God's name was I going to do? I just moved—I couldn't move again. My finances were strained, my body was breaking down, and I had no one—not one person in this world to turn to.

As my initial shock faded, I tried to get a grip on reality. I reminded myself that nothing tragic had happened in Crestwood Lake in three years. And while all the deaths were horrid, they were nonetheless *human*: real people taking their own or others' lives. Rumblings of the preternatural were nothing more than conjecture. I certainly wasn't going to uproot my life over events that occurred years ago. I just hoped I wasn't deluding myself.

25

But even my reorientation to sensibility could not vanquish my dreads. As I walked through my front door, thoughts of someone waiting for me, and images of someone attacking me, shot through my mind. Why do we mentally rehash our terrors? If we're so panic-stricken by them, why do our brains so eagerly replay them? Like that dubious little bump in your mouth that your tongue is hypnotically drawn to. Why can't we just concentrate on the good things?

I knew the answer to my own question. Negative experiences leave scars and pain, just like a physical injury. Our mental agonies are often unsettled issues. When conflicts remain unresolved, they are readily provoked, engendering aversive emotions. Thus, they continue to haunt us.

As if my Freudian falderal actually allayed my fears. My previous therapist told me I was an intellectualizer, someone who defensively reframes their troubles into intellectual paradigms to mitigate their emotional burden. I told him there were worse ways to cope—and right now I certainly could have used one of them.

I searched every room in the house, ensuring every door and window was locked. After nuking a frozen "crap-aroni" and cheese for dinner, I took all my medications. It was like a second meal. I watched a little TV and went to bed early, augmenting my pharmacological mélange with a sleeping pill and a valium. I *had* to sleep, and dozed off promptly . . .

"Peter."

I shot up in bed like a jack-in-the-box. I heard my name. It was just like the times during my childhood. I groped for the lamp, but my quivering hand knocked over the water glass instead. "Shit!" I found the light and scanned the room. Nothing. I got up, checked the rest of the rooms on the second floor, went downstairs, and fetched a roll of paper towels. Wiping up the water, I told myself it was just a bad dream, a side effect from my chemical cocktail.

I glanced at the clock; it was only 11:30. I was so agitated. Now what? If it had been at least three in the morning, I would have said screw it, made my morning coffee and relinquished any further rest. But it wasn't even midnight and sleep was the only respite I had left. I couldn't stay up all night, but there was no way in hell I could fall back to sleep now. So I took another sleeping pill—and another valium.

Slowly I came to consciousness—my tremors were the first confirmation. I felt hungover: a groggy headache accompanied by malaise. It was 4:41 a.m. I was done for the night. I lay there for ten more minutes, slowly feeling less fuzzy. I got up to make coffee, but momentarily lost my balance, bouncing off my dresser in the near darkness. My outdoor lights shone a faint glow through my bedroom windows.

A dark figure stood in my bedroom doorway, just like when I was a child. I gasped, jumped back, and tripped into my nightstand, frantically fumbling for the lamp, second glass of water splashing everywhere. Finally, I clicked on the light—to an empty room.

I rose and stared at the doorway, almost as if I were willing it to reappear. My mind ran amok: was it a person? A ghost? Something worse? Was it after me?

But I forced those thoughts from my mind and attributed it to my drug-induced haze. Or maybe the Parkinson's? The disease does destroy neurons, albeit ones related to muscular function. But who's to say that it couldn't affect other parts of the brain? I had an appointment with my new neurologist later in the week and would consult him. What wonderful options I had: evil spirits or hallucinations. I again tried to comfort myself by blaming it on the pills.

I headed downstairs to make coffee, unable to fight off the ambush images until the kitchen light was on. As the coffee pot perked, I again checked the entire house, even scoping out the basement. This was nuts—I couldn't live like this.

I was anxious the entire day. My rationalizations could not keep my apprehension at bay. What if my house *was* haunted? What if the whole damn town was haunted? Could all those tragedies that took place in Crestwood Lake really be a coincidence? And something was resurrecting my childhood horrors. Could it really just be my maladies and medication? It wasn't my illness that made June Perkins think she saw someone in my house.

For some reason, I thought about calling Gil. Maybe I just needed some human contact—an external source of validation that I wasn't going crazy. But, petty as this sounds, I didn't want to give Gil the satisfaction. Nor did I want to look like a pathetic fool. I rebuff his warning and then come crawling back like a frightened little boy? That was out of the question.

I tried to get lost in household chores but couldn't—I was too nervous. The tremors were getting worse, a combination of my disorder and anxiety. The stirrings in my bowels were sure to be another eruption of the colitis. I wished my daughter would call me back. I repeatedly checked my e-mail throughout the day to see if she responded in her typical manner. There's no better way to take your mind off one problem than by obsessing over another.

Evening approached. Still on edge, I decided to call Gil, but not reveal anything that was happening to me.

"Hello?" said Gil.

"Hi, it's Pete Hadley."

"Oh . . . uh . . . yeah, Pete. I didn't expect you to call. Are you OK?"

Why would he ask me if I'm OK, as opposed to just saying how are you? "Yeah, just wanted to chat with you about something."

"All right."

"I went to the library in Burlington yesterday. I uncovered all sorts of information about Crestwood Lake's past: murders, suicides, slaughtered animals. I also read about some of the people who died in my house that you mentioned."

"And . . ."

"I don't know, it just kind of gave me the creeps."

"Is anything happening in your house, Pete?"

"No . . . uh . . . no, I guess I was just curious about what caused all that mayhem in a quiet little town like this. You said my house was haunted. Do you really believe in the supernatural?" After a long pause, I said "Gil?"

A long pause.

"Gil?"

"Yeah I'm here. Uh, I do think there's something to the spirit world. Does that explain everything that transpired in Crestwood Lake? I don't know. But nothing new has happened in three years."

"Then why did you warn me about my house?"

"Pete, I'm glad you called, and I'm here if you need anything, but what's going on that *made* you call me?"

"Nothing . . . like I said, I read all that stuff yesterday and it freaked me out a little."

"You're sure nothing strange has happened in your house?"

"No."

Gil cleared his throat. "I'm not saying this to scare you, but if you ever need to just get out of there for some reason, you're welcome to come to my place. I don't care if it's the middle of the night."

"Thank you, Gil, that's very kind of you, but I don't think that will be necessary."

Another long, awkward pause. Then Gil said, "Why don't you come over right now and have a drink with me?"

"No, now's not a good time. Maybe later this week."

"All right. You know where I am."

"Thanks Gil, good night."

Gil undoubtedly knew more than he was willing to share. But then again, so did I. My conversation with him did not provide the reassurance I was seeking. It only made me more uneasy.

A sandwich and a can of soup comprised my dinner. I certainly didn't feel like cooking. I took a valium, but it didn't do much, probably because of my increasing tolerance. I tried to watch TV, but images of being waylaid by some creature or deranged person kept flashing through my mind. Every so often I'd get up, poke around the house, or peek out the windows. I debated when to go to bed, and how many pills I should take tonight. About nine thirty, sick of my jitters and the whirlwind in my head, I decided to turn in, popping two sleeping pills and one valium. It took me about an hour, but I eventually drifted off.

I slid down the bed, awaking as if trapped underwater, gasping for breath. Something had grabbed my ankles and yanked me. Again, like when I was a child! My feet were dangling over the edge of the bed. I scooted back toward the headboard and turned on the light. Nothing was there. This was *not* my imagination. Even a restless dream couldn't have dragged me across the bed. That was it! I had to get out of this house. Even if there was a rational explanation I would never be able to sleep here again. I'd run down to Gil's and spend the night there.

I jumped out of bed, threw on pants and a shirt, heard a sound, but ignored it. As I was slipping into my shoes, the phone rang. I looked at the clock. It was exactly 12:00 a.m. Who the hell would be calling me now? I checked the caller ID. My daughter! Was she in trouble?

"Jen," I said, my voice cracking.

"Hey, Dad," she said in a cool monotone.

"It's midnight, are you OK?"

"Oh yeah, sorry. I keep forgetting you're three hours ahead."

"Did you get my message?"

"Yeah, yeah."

"Are you all right?" I asked.

"I'm calling about school. They're saying there's still an outstanding balance for my tuition, and if they don't receive it within thirty days, I won't be able to register for the spring."

"I don't understand. It was a little late, but I sent them a check."

"Well they don't have it."

"I'm sorry. I can't deal with this right now. It'll have to wait till Monday."

"Well if you had sent it on time in the first place, we wouldn't have this problem."

"Well excuse me, but maybe if your mother wasn't shacking up with Jeff, I wouldn't have to go through all the shit I'm dealing with."

30

"Oh, so everything's her fault?"

"I'm not the one who cheated! My Parkinson's is getting worse, and I've got all sorts of problems with my new house."

"Dad, just send the school the damn check, OK?"

"Jen, wait—"

Click.

"Goddammit!" I threw the phone into the wall. I stormed toward the bedroom door—but something lunged out of the hallway—slamming me to the floor so hard I heard something crack. He pounded his fist on my face like he was hammering a nail, shattering my nose. I wailed in pain. He straddled me, pressing his knees against the inside of my elbows.

That's when he withdrew a large knife and held it above my chest. I gazed up through my blood splattered eyes. It was him! The same man from the police sketch when I was five! He looked exactly the same: sunken, crazed eyes, and stubby, gray hair. How was it possible? He clutched my throat and glared at me with an unholy rage. I couldn't speak. His grasp—the pain—the shock. I was thoroughly subdued, and at his mercy.

Then, another figure emerged from the hallway. A tall, elderly gentleman, in a black three-piece suit, with a flaming-red tie and pocket square. He stepped around us and stood over me, the tips of his black oxfords just inches from my left shoulder. It was him as well! The same face I saw coming at me in my childhood bedroom, with large, almost black eyes, boring through mine. I was so aghast—I couldn't even begin to comprehend what was happening.

"Good evening, Peter," he bellowed.

I was frozen in fright.

He turned toward the man on top of me and said, "Let him speak, Stan."

Stan eased his grip on my throat, but still wielded the knife as if he were about to strike.

"Who are you?" I whined.

"I am Luther Van Haden."

"How do you know me?"

"I've been following you your entire life."

"What? Why? How?"

"Sorry about your marriage, but Jeff and I had a deal. Business is business—nothing personal, mind you."

"Who are you?"

"Who am I? I can be your best friend, or your worst nightmare. In fact—it is *you* who will decide what I will mean to you."

My mouth was agape. I could feel my heartbeat.

"I can take away your pain, Peter. Your diseases, your sleeplessness, your fears. We could even avenge your ex-wife's infidelities. You'd like to see her suffer, wouldn't you Peter? Be honest with me—I can see into your heart."

"No, I don't want anyone to suffer."

Van Haden chuckled. "Oh, Peter. Now we know that's not true, eh? I am acutely aware of the darkness that has permeated your soul. And your daughter—oh the wrath you feel about her desertion."

"You leave my daughter out of this."

"Too late for that, Peter." Van Haden removed a check from his pocket and held it out. It was the check I had written months ago for my daughter's tuition. He tore it into bits, then sprinkled them over my face as he snickered. He crouched down, resting his elbows on his knees, his face two feet from mine. "Come join our coven. Rejuvenating your body will merely be the beginning. I can eliminate your ex-friend Jeff, return the love of your wife and daughter . . . whatever you want. All things are possible through me Peter—*all* things."

I glimpsed at Stan. He looked like a rabid dog and I was a piece of meat. I could *feel* his desire to plunge his knife into me. I turned back to Van Haden.

"I grow weary, Peter. I don't mind bargaining, but I don't have the patience for dithering. Do you want to transform your life or not?"

"You're the reason for all my suffering? My childhood nightmares, my sicknesses, my family's abandonment?"

Van Haden smiled with sickening satisfaction. "Yes, Peter. But it can all be undone. Now are you with me or not?"

I spit in Van Haden's face.

He stood up, wiped his cheek and said, "Damn. I really wanted you Peter." Then he turned his head and said, "Stan . . . if you please . . ."

Four times in the heart.

The Encounters

Morgan was leaving for work when he passed the bathroom and saw Vicki putting on her lipstick. He stopped, a subdued but satisfied smile on his face.

"What?" said Vicki.

"Nothing," said Morgan. "You're just beautiful."

Vicki gave him a cutesy smile. "Well, it helps when your clock's been turned back nine years." Vicki placed the cap back on her lipstick. "The best part is I get to relive them with you."

Morgan moved in to kiss her.

Vicki stiffened. "I just put my lipstick on."

Morgan wrapped his arms around her and gave her a firm, lingering kiss.

Vicki let out a soft moan and pulled him closer. Then she giggled. "Your moustache always tickles me."

"If I'm not too busy," said Morgan, "I'll stop by Toby's for lunch."

"Great. What are you doing today?"

"I'm gonna cruise around town, snoop around a bit. See if anything funny's going on."

"OK, baby. Hopefully I'll see you later."

"Let me know if you hear anything at Toby's," said Morgan.

"I will."

"I love you."

"Love you too, baby."

Morgan hopped in his truck and called the station. Lieutenant Edwards answered.

"Carl, it's Butch. I'll be out patrolling this morning. Just call my radio or my cell if you need me."

"*You're* patrolling? Is someone out sick?"

"No. I just want to patrol my town today. You got a problem with that?"

"No, no, not at all. Just a reminder, the mayor wants us to complete those yearly environmental and safety inspections on the station."

"Yeah? Well tell him I said he can inspect my ass. I'll get to it when I get to it."

"All right, Butch."

Morgan circled the perimeter of Crestwood Lake, stopping periodically to talk to residents he saw outside. Nothing was out of the ordinary. Just the usual "When's-the-town-gonna-fix-that-pothole?" and "Her-dog-keeps-shitting-on-my-lawn," kinds of complaints.

Morgan drove through the center of town, visiting businesses whose prior owners or employees had been part of the 2013 coven. Of course, the current proprietors were unaware of their predecessors' nefarious alliance. Most of the people who had knowledge of the Crestwood Lake coven were dead. The Satanists killed those who refused to join, and Morgan killed those who did—except for the few that repented. Nevertheless, if Van Haden was planning a revival, individuals with economic means and municipal clout, such as business owners, were prime fodder for hell redux.

Morgan strode into what used to be *Roses are Red*, a floral shop owned by Karen Gardner, a particularly sadistic witch who Morgan had dispatched with the utmost satisfaction. The shop, now transformed into a bookstore called *The Good Book*, was owned by Scott Guerin, a newcomer to Crestwood Lake. Morgan was always suspicious of newcomers. Karen Gardner had been one, and she turned out to be Lucifer's gal Friday. He'd check out this potential freak and then hit Toby's for lunch.

Guerin was a blue-eyed, clean-shaven, sixty-year-old. Perched on his rolling library ladder, he was rearranging one of the top bookshelves in the rear of the store when Morgan swaggered through the door.

35

"Hello," called Morgan.

"Be right with you, Captain," said a faint voice.

Morgan quickly looked around. No one was within eyesight.

Guerin emerged from the racks, smiling warmly and extending his hand. "Good morning, Captain. Welcome to my store."

"How did you know who I was?"

"I saw you pull up. Your gold badge gives you away."

"Saw me from where?"

"My back window."

"Your back window?"

"Yes. How may I be of service?"

"Well, I make it a point to introduce myself to new business owners in my town. I like to know who's who."

"Naturally, that's quite prudent. I am Scott Guerin and I am most glad to meet you."

"Where you from, Mr. Guerin?"

"I'm from Salem."

"Salem? As in Massachusetts?"

"Yes, that one."

"You a witch?" said Morgan half-seriously.

Guerin chuckled. "Far from it, Captain."

"Did you know the previous owner of this store?"

"Karen Gardner? No, I never met her."

"How did you come to acquire this place?"

"Well, according to the bank officer, Ms. Gardner disappeared mysteriously three years ago. The property eventually went into foreclosure and—as you must know—nobody bought it. I purchased it from the bank."

"So you know about Gardner?" said Morgan.

"I heard *she* was a witch."

Morgan's pupils dilated. "Oh really?"

"I'm not telling you anything you don't already know, Captain."

"Do you believe in witchcraft?"

"I've studied it extensively. I have an entire aisle devoted to it over there." Guerin pointed.

"You didn't answer my question."

"You ask as if it's something that demands faith."

"What do you mean?"

"Well, I wouldn't ask you if you *believe* that the world is round."

"So you're saying that witches actually exist."

"Captain, please. I know you are toying with me in an effort to discern my true identity and intentions."

Morgan opened his mouth, but Guerin cut him off. "I don't blame you. I am cognizant of the nightmarish acts that transpired in Crestwood Lake, including the attempts on your life. Naturally, you need to know who I am."

"Damn straight," said Morgan.

"Captain, I do not wish you, or your town any ill will. You'll just have to take that on *faith* for now."

"And just how do you know about what happened here?"

"People talk. Not to mention the newspapers."

"Why are you here, Mr. Guerin?"

"I got the property at a very good price, and as I told you, I study witchcraft."

"So you're saying that witchcraft is still going on in Crestwood Lake?"

"I'm afraid your town is an epicenter of evil."

"What makes you say that?"

"You're playing coy again, Captain."

Morgan reached in his shirt pocket and removed a vial of holy water.

Guerin smiled knowingly.

"Sorry about this, but it's necessary." Morgan splashed the water on Guerin.

"All that proves is that I'm not a witch," said Guerin. "And you know full well, Captain, that one needn't be a witch to ally with Satan."

"Well? Are you allied with Satan?"

"Would I tell you if I was?"

"Can I see some ID?"

Guerin retrieved his wallet and handed Morgan his driver's license.

"Your address is the same as the store?"

"I live upstairs, Captain."

Morgan scribbled down Guerin's license number. "You got any family?"

"No, it's just me."

"I'm going to run your info at the station. I trust you understand why."

"Absolutely, Captain. If I can be of any further help, please let me know."

Morgan left and walked around the back of the store.

It was windowless.

It was 11:30 a.m., and the lushes and early-lunchers were already moseying into Toby's. Vicki was frazzled. She had knocked over a tray of glasses, one of which had shattered into the ice bin. Emptying and replenishing the ice put her behind schedule, and now she was racing to get the bar ready. Vicki liked to have everything prepared ahead of time. She found it discombobulating to have to slice lemons or restock the beer with a bar full of customers. Moreover, she wanted to spend any free moments she had chatting up the locals for anything unusual.

Toby's had only a dozen tables surrounding the U-shaped bar in the center, but it was the most popular tavern among Crestwood Lake's three thousand inhabitants. Like every bar in the world, Toby's had its regulars.

Jed was waiting for his Budweiser and shot of Wild Turkey, Lottie for her Bloody Mary with lemon, *not* lime, Alan for his Scotch, and Ziggy . . . well . . . his order depended on what the voices were saying that day.

Vicki dispensed the drinks, took the lunch orders from those having a solid meal, and turned her attention to the overhead glass rack. She was sliding wineglasses through the slots when a man's voice hissed behind her.

"How ya doin' sexy?"

Vicki flinched, glasses shattering on the counter.

It was Derrick Larson, her fifty-year-old ex-husband. The last time she saw him, twelve years prior, he had broken one of her ribs and knocked out a tooth, the grand finale of years of abuse. Morgan arrested him and threatened to kill him if he ever returned to Crestwood Lake.

Vicki whipped around.

Derrick's fists pressed against the bar, accentuating his muscular forearms. He leered, his gray eyes reflecting lechery and contempt. A salt-and-pepper crew cut topped off his six-foot frame.

"What are you doing here?" quivered Vicki, her stomach tightening.

"I was in the neighborhood. Thought I'd check in on you. See if you're still a bitch."

Vicki pointed toward the door. "You get the hell outta here right now."

"I heard you married the cop. Is he your hero now, sweetie?"

"He sent you to prison once. You want to go back?"

"Why not. Maybe you and I could have conjugal visits."

"You leave me alone or else—"

"Or else what? You'll sick Johnny Law on me?" Derrick leaned in closer. "Tell me, sugar pie . . . do you think he appreciates your hot little coochie as much as I did?"

"Why don't you ask him yourself?"

Derrick's face slammed into the bar, blood spurting. "Motherfucker!" he growled, spinning around.

Morgan punched him twice in the gut, then uppercut him, sending him crashing onto the floor. Morgan stomped on his groin; Derrick wailed. He grabbed the front of Derrick's shirt with both hands, yanked him up, and walloped his jaw, once more introducing him to the floor. Derrick spit up blood and passed out.

Morgan attended to Vicki. "Are you OK, honey?"

Vicki was horrified and relieved at the same time. "Yes . . ."

"What happened?"

"He just showed up, took me by surprise . . . started asking sick questions. What is he doing here?"

"I don't know, but I intend to find out." Morgan's eyes swept the bar. Every single patron was staring at him. Morgan got on his radio and called for an ambulance. Turning to Vicki, he said, "How about a bowl of chili?"

The Unearthing

Bernardo Iannucci, curator of Castel Sant'Angelo, just outside Vatican City, lit his cigarette, inhaled its enslaving ecstasy, and sipped his espresso. He leaned back in his Nella Vetrina leather chair, plopped his feet on his black mahogany desk, and thought about his mistress Gina. She was the most gorgeous woman he had ever made love to: a twenty-three-year-old, slender, long-haired brunette. He took another drag of his cigarette, spun his wedding band with his thumb and pinky, and mulled the tantalizing scenarios in his mind. That's when the earthquake hit.

The entire building shook. Crashes, creaks, and shatters rebounded in all directions. Iannucci's paintings flew off the walls, peppered with shards from the exploding windows. He fell over in his chair, scrambled to his feet, and leapt toward his liquor cabinet—but not in time. It slammed onto his marble floor, shattering a fortune of Riedel crystal, but even more painfully, over thirty bottles of Barolo.

Iannucci flung open his office door and looked in all directions. It was 7:49 in the morning and the only people in the museum were employees. He saw one of the housekeepers on the floor, lying next to her upset cleaning cart. Iannucci wobbled down the trembling hallway, flailing his arms to keep his balance. He approached the housekeeper and shouted, "Are you OK?"

"Yes, sir."

As Iannucci picked her up, the lights went out. "Is anybody hurt?"

"I don't know, sir. I was by myself."

Iannucci guided her to a column. "Hold on to this. I'm going to check on the others." He stumbled down the stairwell, bouncing off the walls, until he reached the ground level. He darted into the center atrium. One security guard was holding on to a large stone desk, another to a door handle. Most of the windows had burst. The din of the earthquake and its destruction continued all around them.

Iannucci lost his balance and fell. The security guard behind the desk tottered over and helped him up. They both ran back to the desk and held on.

"Watch out!" yelled the security guard by the door, pointing overhead.

41

A large Renaissance-era painting broke free of its supports and came crashing down, five feet away from Iannucci.

And then it stopped. The three men stood there, hesitant, not yet convinced of their safety.

"Check the entire building," ordered Iannucci. "See if anyone's injured."

The guards took off in opposite directions. Outside, sirens blared in the distance.

Iannucci called his wife on his cell phone, hoping the quake hadn't affected the cell towers. The couple lived in the coastal town of Santa Marinella, sixty miles from Rome. It rang; she answered.

"Rosa, are you OK?"

"Yes, I'm fine, and you?"

"I'm all right. Did you leave for work yet?"

"No, I'm still home," she said.

"And the house?"

"Two of the windows are cracked, but I think that's all."

"OK, I have to go," said Iannucci. "I have to check on my staff. I'll call you later."

Iannucci headed for one of the main exhibit halls when a worker came running toward him.

"Bernardo! Hurry, go to the cellar. Antonio needs you."

"Is he hurt?"

"No, but he told me to tell you to come immediately. Here, you'll need this." He handed Iannucci a large flashlight.

Iannucci ran to the stairwell and down three flights to the museum's basement. As he entered he cried, "Antonio."

"Back here," echoed a voice from the far end. "Come quick."

Iannucci stepped over debris, boxes, and toppled shelves. "Where are you?"

"Over here."

Iannucci zeroed in on Antonio's voice. He reached the far corner of the basement and aimed his flashlight. "What the hell?" he said.

An extensive chasm had etched its way across the basement floor.

"Antonio?"

"Down here."

Iannucci shone his light into the ten-foot deep fissure.

The beam found Antonio, who pointed toward the ground and said "Look!"

Iannucci dropped to his knees and made the sign of the cross. "Holy Mother of God!"

The Familiars

I swallowed a Xanax, pressed my fingertips against my temples, and tried to use those stupid visualization techniques my therapist recommended. Yeah, right. Because *imagining* shit is how to deal with reality. What I needed was another pill, and something stronger to wash it down with. But it was 8:00 a.m., and I couldn't sit in my car any longer. I had to muster the strength to face the world again.

It was my first day as an LPN at Crestwood Manor. What a name—*Manor*—as if it were some kind of snooty estate, and not a dismal state-run nursing home and hospice. It was located in Concord, one town over from Crestwood Lake, where I had just rented a small house, if you want to call it that. I think hovel would be more accurate.

I made my way through the parking lot, and up the long, concrete walkway toward the main entrance, pausing to behold the building. It looked more like an insane asylum than a nursing home: three stories of muddy-red bricks and barred windows, capped by a weathered, gray dome, all surrounded by barren landscaping. The crab grass was the most vibrant thing in sight.

The interior was no better: institution-white walls, austere furnishings, and a grimy, nauseatingly speckled, tile floor. I approached the main desk and waited for the nose-ringed clerk to stop playing with her phone.

"Can I help you?" she said, her voice as apathetic as her face.

"Hi, I'm Lori Oliver. I'm starting work today. I'm supposed to be on unit two-west."

The clerk grabbed a clipboard and ran her finger down the page. "Oh yeah . . . you have to see Ms. Thorn. First floor, east wing, room 102."

I looked left and right.

"That way," she said pointing, with a surly tone.

As I walked to Thorn's office I wondered why she needed to see me again. She had participated in my initial interview, but as the director, would not be my immediate supervisor. That distinction went to Nancy Haddock, clearly the less human of the two.

Darlene Thorn was trim, and attractive for a woman nearing sixty. The vestiges of her erstwhile beauty were still detectable on her aging face. With her shoulder length blonde hair (obviously dyed), she reminded me of a mature Lauren Bacall. Hailing from money and private education, she comported herself with urbane formality tinged with hubris. She had recently assumed the directorship of the facility.

Haddock, on the other hand, was more like a goon: a stocky, forty-something-year-old RN, with cold, lifeless eyes, a disdain for anything warm-blooded, and the personality of a dial tone. She was the nurse in charge of the unit I'd be working on.

I knocked, heard Thorn's gravelly voice say, "Come in," and opened the door. Both Thorn and Haddock awaited me.

"Have a seat, Lori," said Thorn. She sat behind her spacious desk, a pair of cross swords mounted on the wall above her. "Good morning, and welcome."

"Thank you."

"It's ten after eight," said Haddock, not blinking. "Your shift starts at eight. I expect you to arrive on time."

"I'm sorry. Just a little first-day disorganization. It won't happen again."

"It doesn't get easier from here," said Haddock.

I wasn't sure what to say.

"What Nancy's implying," said Thorn, "is that the work here can be very demanding and emotionally taxing. We're understaffed and have elderly patients, many of them near death, with round the clock needs."

"Yes, that was explained in my interview."

"We just want to be sure," said Thorn, "that you're well enough to handle it."

"What do you mean *well enough?*"

Thorn turned slightly to Haddock, who leered at me like she was going in for the kill. "Since we offered you the job it's come to our attention that you've had some emotional difficulties."

"Emotional difficulties?"

"Yes—that you were hospitalized."

"That's none of your business."

"Oh I disagree. The health of our employees can affect the care they provide our patients, and that is distinctly my business."

I looked at Thorn, who said, "We just want to know if you're up to the challenge, dear."

I was fuming. How did they find out I had a psychiatric admission? And what gall they had to confront me about it. I was one brain cell away from telling them where to go, but the only thing stronger than my outrage was my desperation. There wasn't enough in my bank account for next month's rent. So, I suppressed my indignation and said, "I'm fine. I went through a rough patch, but I got help and I'm OK. I'm ready to get back to work."

"All right," said Haddock. "But I expect you to come to me if you have any problems, understood?"

Yeah right. I wouldn't entrust this woman with a goldfish, but I said, "Yes, of course."

Haddock escorted me to the unit, gave me a perfunctory tour, and introduced me to the staff, including Kim, a young, blonde LPN, ten years my junior, whom I would be shadowing for the first week. I found that a bit humiliating. I'm sure Haddock assigned me a babysitter because of my history, but what could I do? Funny how when you've been down and out in this world, you end up having to take even more shit. Speaking of which . . .

Being a newbie meant being given all the scutwork. It was my first day on the job and Kim had me emptying bed pans and wiping asses. This was the nurses' aides' job, but "we're understaffed and have to pitch in," was obviously the nursing home's mantra.

It was a little after three in the afternoon, and I had just finished washing a combative eighty-year-old Alzheimer's patient. During one of his attempts to smack me, he hit the bedpan, spilling piss on the floor. Of course, I had to clean it up.

I was standing outside the patient's room, rubbing my aching forehead, when Kim came by.

"You all right?" she asked.

"Yes, I just finished with Mr. Krause."

"How many times did he hit you?"

"I lost count. What's wrong with him—I mean other than dementia?"
"He's just an asshole. Family says he's always been that way. Dementia can amplify pre-existing traits."

"Yes, I'm aware, but why does he always have to—Agh!" Something brushed against my leg. I whipped around and was confronted by a hissing gray cat. Its piercing green eyes were even fiercer than Haddock's. "What the hell?"

"Oh that's Lilith. She belongs to Ms. Thorn."

"She has a cat in a nursing home?"

"Yeah. She says it gives the residents some company."

I grimaced at Lilith. She hissed at me again and ran away. "That has to be against the state health codes."

"I don't know," said Kim. "Everyone's big on service dogs and pet therapy now. Anyway, you want to be the one to confront the director about her cat?"

"What's her deal anyway?"

"Ms. Thorn?"

"Yeah."

"I don't know much about her; she just took over a month ago. I know she's loaded. Lord knows why she works here."

"What does her husband do?"

"He's dead. He was even richer. The rumor is she bumped him off to get all the dough."

"Are you serious?"

"And then, after he croaked—"

"I don't pay you girls to gab in the hallway" grated Haddock's voice as she marched toward us. She seemed to loathe us, and sadistically enjoy castigating us simultaneously.

"I was just explaining to Lori—"

"Mrs. Dawson needs her bandages and bedpan changed—now."

As we walked away Kim whispered, "If I didn't need this job so bad I'd empty a bedpan on that bitch's head."

I made it through the remainder of the day and headed home. I couldn't wait. Oh, did I need a glass of wine . . . or two. I didn't give a shit if it clashed with my medications or not. My new place still needed organizing, but that would have to wait. Tonight I needed to relax and process the day's events.

Coasting along, I thought about my house. I rented it from the Meyers, an elderly couple who lived in southern Vermont. It was an old, one-bedroom dwelling on a desolate road. My concern was that my closest neighbor was too close.

On the same lot as my house was an even smaller structure, fifty feet away. Apparently, it had once been a detached garage. The Meyers converted it into an apartment and rented it out as well, "To a nice young man named Rodney." Nice young man my ass.

Rodney was a thirty-something, uncouth, unshaven lowlife, with oily black hair, a teardrop tattoo below his eye, and the swagger of a pervert who just got off on a technicality. I still can't get past how he introduced himself when I moved in last week. With beer can in hand he said, "Hi, I'm Rodney, but they call me *Rod* for short, even though it's not—if you catch my drift." I wanted to crawl into my own stomach and throw myself up.

I pulled into my driveway hoping the sleazebag didn't notice. I heard 1970s disco music erupting from his apartment. *Do a little dance . . . make a little love . . . get down tonight.* I didn't even want to think about what he was doing in his lascivious lair.

Halfway to my front door, a large black dog came sprinting toward me. I froze in terror. It stopped just a few feet shy, growling, bearing its teeth. It looked like a pit bull, only larger. I didn't know what to do. My heart pounded. The dog maintained its ground, ready to strike.

Finally, my brain started to work. I reached into my purse and removed my mace. I aimed—the dog charged—I sprayed it right in its face. The dog sprang back, yelping, and then zipped across the street into the woods. I glanced at Rodney's . . . *Get down, get down, get down, get down . . . get down tonight baby . . . .woo woo woo woo woo woo woo woo woo . . .*

I rushed into my house, poured a glass of wine, and drank half of it in one swig. I called the police to report the dog. As it rang, I considered saying something about Rodney's music too, but decided against it. The officer blithely took the information and dispensed the standard "We'll look in to it."

I changed into my sweats, finished my wine, and filled a second glass. I lit some candles, turned on my elevator music, and nestled under a blanket on my couch. That's when the doorbell rang. Could it be the police? I was surprised they actually were looking into it.

I opened the door to Rodney—standing there in a Hawaiian shirt, holding a six-pack, and smiling like a pedophile in a playground.

"Hey, Lori baby. What's up? Saw your car." He held up the Budweiser. "Thought I'd bring you a house warming gift."

"Thank you, but I don't drink beer, and now's not a good time."

He peeked into my living room. It felt like he was peeking up my skirt.

"Uh, I'm sorry, I can bring you some wine instead. I'll bring a couple bottles. Then you and me can do a *tasting*." He licked the corner of his mouth.

"No thank you." I hated prolonging the conversation, but I had to ask. "Have you seen a large black dog around here?"

"Uh . . . no. Why?"

49

When I came home from work this big black dog came at me. I sprayed it with mace and it ran off. Does anyone around here have a dog like that?"

"Nah, girl, I haven't seen any dogs—"

"OK, thank you, have a good night."

I shut the door as he started to say something. I watched from my window to make sure he slithered back into his hole. Then I returned to my blanketed refuge on my couch, and stewed about my new job, *and* my new living arrangements.

The next day at work, I was sitting in our morning report. That's where the night staff give the day staff an update on the patients before the shift change. We were all seated in a circle, except Haddock, who stood, looming over us like the mutated progeny of General Patton and a vampire.

When the night nurse finished her report, Amy, one of the veteran RNs said, "Today's Dr. Stanley's birthday. I thought maybe I could run out, pick up a cake, and then we can present it to him at lunchtime."

"No," said Haddock. "We're too busy and too short-staffed for you to go shopping. If you girls want to do something for Dr. Stanley, do it on your own time."

"But he's so nice. One of the few doctors around here who treats us with respect."

"We don't have time for parties," snapped Haddock. "We have sick patients to take care of. Is that clear?"

I'm certain this woman has Voodoo dolls of every one of her employees. In any event, we went about our duties. Technically, I was still supposed to be shadowing Kim, but she assigned me my own patients, joining me whenever Haddock was lurking nearby.

I had to give Mrs. McGinty her medication. What a poor soul. She was ninety-three and had no breasts, one kidney, and two tumors. The cancer had spread to her liver and brain. The doctors still had her on chemo, even though it was hopeless. If it were my call, I'd up the morphine and let nature take its course.

50

As I walked into her room I saw Lilith standing on Mrs. McGinty's chest, both of their mouths wide open. The cat was making a sucking sound, as a hazy, white mist streamed into its mouth from Mrs. McGinty's. I just stared, flabbergasted. The stream ceased. The cat twitched its head toward me and hissed.

"Get off of her," I yelled, dashing toward it. The cat yowled and swatted me, inflicting four deep scratches into the back of my hand. "Dammit!"

The cat sprung off the bed and scurried out of the room.

Holding my bleeding hand, I turned toward Mrs. McGinty. She wasn't breathing. I hit the emergency button and checked her pulse. None. I bolted to the doorway. Two nurse's aides were hurrying down the hallway. "Get the crash cart!" I cried.

I ran back to Mrs. McGinty and started performing CPR, alternating breaths with chest compressions. Still no pulse. I glimpsed toward the door. Why wasn't anyone coming? I returned to the CPR. I pinched her nose, tilted her head, and placed my mouth on hers. Her breath tasted like how a funeral parlor smells. I gave her two breaths. Then back to the chest compressions. One—two—three—four—have to give her thirty before checking her pulse— sixteen—seventeen—eighteen—nineteen—

"Stop the CPR!" barked Haddock.

"She's not breathing. She has no pulse. I hit the button. Why didn't they bring the cart?"

"She has a DNR," said Haddock sternly.

"What?"

"D—N—R. Do not resuscitate."

"Yes, I know what that means."

"Then you should also know she has one."

"We're just gonna let her die?"

"Her daughter, who has power of attorney, has a DNR order. You should know this before caring for a patient. Now get away from her."

At that point Kim and Barry, a tall, Jamaican nurse's aide, pushing the crash cart, came into the room.

"The emergency's over," said Haddock. "She's DNR." Then she glared at Kim. "Where were you? Lori's supposed to be shadowing you, not treating patients on her own."

"She's not," said Lori. "I had to go to the bathroom."

Haddock noticed McGinty's medication on the bed and then faced me.

"I came to the room with her medication. I was going to wait for Kim to get back from the bathroom and let her dispense it."

Haddock glowered at the two of us suspiciously and then said to me, "You should still know she had a DNR order."

"Even if she didn't die of natural causes?"

"Meaning what?" asked Haddock.

"When I came in the room, that gray cat was standing on her chest. It looked like it was sucking her breath out. I scared it away." I displayed my bleeding scratches. "It attacked me and darted out of the room."

Barry had a concerned yet knowing expression on his face.

"Are you having trouble coping?" asked Haddock, squinting at me.

"No, I'm fine."

"Because we have a ninety-three-year-old with terminal cancer, and you're telling me a cat killed her?"

"Maybe the weight of the cat on her chest interrupted her breathing. All I know is my first instinct was to save her life."

"Your first instinct should be to know your job. And that includes knowing whether a patient has a DNR order. Do you realize if you did manage to resuscitate her and the daughter got wind of it, we could be sued?"

"Well that's the difference between you and me, Nancy. I care about people, not money."

Haddock's pupils dilated. In a forced, hushed tone she said to Kim, "Take care of the body and all the arrangements." She turned to me. "Clean that wound before you infect somebody, and then meet me in my office." She marched out.

"She's an Obeah-woman," said Barry. His Jamaican accent was thick and resounding. "And that cat is probably her familiar."

"What's an Obeah-woman?" asked Kim.

"A woman who practices sorcery," said Barry.

I didn't know how to respond to that, so I promptly disinfected my hand and went to Haddock's office. That bitch chewed me out again and wrote me up. My second day on the job and she gives me a written warning. That meant that the next infraction would be grounds for termination. She probably would have written Kim up as well if she had proof I wasn't being supervised. If it weren't for my finances, I would have quit there and then.

As I approached my house my ruminations switched from work to El Creepo. He better not ring my bell tonight. It was an unusually warm day for September and as I arrived, there he was, in a lawn chair, drinking a beer, smoking a cigarette, and listening to Donna Summer's "Hot Stuff" on a boom box. Was this freak stuck in a time warp?

I took a deep breath and stepped out of my car.

"Looking good, baby. Whatcha doin?"

"Nothing, I had a bad day. Just want to be left alone."

"No prob, sister. Maybe on the weekend if you're feeling better, I'll bring you that wine."

"Whatever," I said, heading directly into my house. I got inside and thought, why did I say that? This jerk will interpret "whatever" as: *oh yeah, get some wine, get me drunk and do me.* I should have been more emphatic about my disinterest. But being so exhausted, I couldn't deal with another confrontation.

Later that night, getting ready for bed, I took my antidepressant, a sleeping pill, and a Xanax. I just wanted to turn my brain off. Forty minutes later the growling started, right outside my bedroom window. A deep, menacing growl. That goddamned dog was back. I thought about getting up but was too wiped out. I had just enough energy to take a second Xanax. Finally, the chemicals overtook my apprehension and I zonked out.

In the morning I walked around the outside of my house. I'm not sure what I was looking for, but I didn't find anything that would incriminate a canine. On Rodney's side of my house, I found cigarette butts, beer cans, and a condom wrapper. Worthless degenerate.

Later that day, Kim and I were having lunch in the nursing home's cafeteria. It was even worse than hospital food. It reminded me of the MRE's we ate in the army during my tour in Afghanistan. MRE's or meal, ready-to-eat, were packaged rations used for sustenance by troops out in the field. We called them Meals Rejected by Ethiopians.

Kim spied Barry and waved him over. Barry was well over six feet and muscular. But he was a gentle soul with eyes that conveyed a unique mixture of warmth, worldliness, and melancholy.

"Hi, Barry," I said as he sat down.

"Good afternoon, ma'am."

"You don't have to call me ma'am. You can call me Lori."

"OK," he said with a friendly smile.

"So what exactly happened yesterday?" asked Kim.

"Well, basically what I said. I walked into Mrs. McGinty's room and that gray cat—"

"Lilith," said Kim.

"Whatever. *Lilith*, was standing on her chest, sucking some kind of— I don't know—a flow of something white out of Mrs. McGinty's mouth."

"Her life essence," said Barry.

54

"What?" asked Kim.

"Her life essence. The cat was sucking the life out of her."

"Are you for real?" asked Kim.

"I've heard of it," I said. "Isn't it supposed to be babies that cats do that to?"

"Can be anyone," said Barry.

"Wait a minute," said Kim. "This is folklore, right?"

I scoffed. "That wasn't folklore that I saw yesterday. Barry, you said Haddock was familiar with the cat."

"No, no. Not that she's familiar with the cat. I said the cat *is* her familiar. A familiar is a witch or demon in animal form, or an animal that's possessed by a witch or demon to do their bidding. In the West Indies, especially Jamaica, there be people who practice sorcery, some call it witchcraft. We call it Obeah. Animals are used for sacrifice. But some are used to do evil. Those are the familiars."

"And you think Haddock is a witch?" I asked.

"I don't know for sure. But it wouldn't surprise me. Especially after what you saw."

"Are you kidding me?" said Kim. "You really believe this shit?"

"Let's just say I seen things in the islands that I can't explain."

"But the cat belongs to Ms. Thorn," said Kim.

"Then maybe she be the witch."

"This is nuts," said Kim.

I pressed my index finger on the table and said, "Then how do you explain what I saw?"

"I don't know. Maybe Mrs. McGinty was dying and expelled something from her lungs."

"Into the cat's open mouth?"

"Maybe you were having a bad day and thought you saw it," said Kim.

"What did you say?"

"Nothing. I'm just saying that stress can affect us like that."

"So I'm hallucinating?"

"I don't know . . . Are you?"

"What the *hell* are you saying?

Kim just looked at me with her mouth half open.

"I am *not* crazy," I said, standing up. Staff at nearby tables gawked in my direction.

"You're acting a little crazy now."

"Aaaaagh!" I roared, shaking my fists, flashes of my mother slicing through my mind. And then in a loud voice, "People like you are all the same. You invalidate others—make them feel that their *real* experiences are crazy. Then when we react with appropriate frustration, you say we're acting crazy, when *you're* the ones driving us crazy!"

"Easy, Lori," said Barry. "Not everyone will understand what you saw."

I left my lunch on the table and stormed out.

Later in the day Kim gave me a half-ass apology. I could tell she just wanted to placate me. We still had to work together and I'm sure she was worried about me freaking out again.

The rest of the day was uneventful, except for how conversation stopped, and furtive glancing started, when I walked into a room. That was extremely unnerving. I can handle the patients, the physical work, cleaning shit, but I can't deal with being around people who think I'm a whacko. They either treat me like a child, ignore me, or coddle me. I can *feel* their uneasiness and that begins to unravel me.

56

After work I called my psychiatrist. I explained that my new job was stressful and making me feel off kilter. His solution, as usual, was to prescribe more medication: an antipsychotic, not because I was "actually psychotic," but because it would help me stay in control. Yeah, right. That's shrink-speak for: you're already a kook, and if you don't get a grip soon, you're gonna go totally bat-shit. I never filled the prescription.

Friday finally came. Thank God. The weekend was in sight. Two whole days to relax, and take my *own* kind of medication. I had cancelled plans to meet a friend on Saturday. Told her I was sick. All I wanted to do was hunker down in my living room until Monday.

It was about three in the afternoon. I was walking down the corridor when I heard it again—that sucking sound—a steady, low-pitched rush of air. I looked around but couldn't pinpoint the source. Two doors down, I saw Lilith scamper out of Mr. Ferguson's room. I ran to his bed. He lay there motionless, mouth open, his eyes ghastly. He wasn't breathing, no pulse. Oh no, not again. I checked his wristband: DNR. Another one? I hit the emergency button, sprinted into the hallway and called for help.

One by one, Barry, Kim, Amy, two nurses' aides—and Haddock—arrived.

"It happened again! That cat was in here and a patient's dead!"

"Did you perform CPR?" asked Haddock, ready to pounce.

"No, I didn't. But that's not the point. That damn cat was in here and Mr. Ferguson's dead."

Kim gently held my arm and said, "Lori, Mr. Ferguson was in the final stages of emphysema. His doctors didn't expect him to make it through the week."

I yanked my arm away. "Don't give me that crap. I know what I saw. That's two patients now who died because of that cat."

Amy and the two nurse's aides were staring at me.

"Don't look at me like that!"

"Enough," said Haddock. "Our patients are old, sick, and dying. Perhaps you can't handle it."

"I can handle death, lady. I was in Afghanistan. I've seen shit that you can't even fucking imagine."

"Not another word. Go to the nurse's lounge and pull yourself together. Then you and I will discuss your future here."

I wanted to punch Haddock right in her smug face, but Barry, with compassionate eyes, slowly shook his head, as if saying, "Don't do it." So I sneered at Haddock and went to the lounge, only because my purse was there, and I definitely needed a Xanax.

A thousand thoughts whizzed through my mind as I shoved open the lounge door. I withdrew my purse from the closet and swallowed a pill dry.

"Are you all right, dear?"

I twirled around. Standing in the corner was Thorn, in her black designer suit and red blouse. Perched on the table next to her was the gray cat. Thorn was scratching its neck. The cat was purring, but its eyes were fixated on me. I was agape. I realized that both Thorn's and the cat's eyes were the exact same shade of green. Strangely, while I was just on the verge of ripping off Haddock's head, in Thorn's presence I felt intimidated.

I took a few breaths and gathered my thoughts. Except for scratching the cat, Thorn stood motionless, unblinking, awaiting my response.

"Two patients have died this week, and in each instance that cat was with them. In fact, I saw it standing on the chest of the first one as she stopped breathing."

"Most of our patients are approaching death, dear. Lilith provides them with a modicum of comfort before they pass on."

The cat, maintaining its stare, switched from purring to a faint growl. I somehow found my courage.

"The only person that cat comforts is you."

"I don't know what you mean, dear."

"I think you do. And stop calling me dear. That thing has something to do with two patients' deaths and you just stand there nonchalantly."

Thorn stopped scratching the cat. Its back arched and its growling increased. Thorn's eyes darkened. "Watch yourself, young lady. It would behoove you to reconsider your impudence."

"What are you gonna do, fire me? For what? Caring that patients died?"

"No, for your behavior. As I feared, you may not be mentally stable enough to handle this work. Your little outburst a few moments ago suggests that."

"You fire me for my past emotional problems, and I'll sue you for wrongful termination."

Thorn smirked as if I had threatened her with a water pistol. "Lori, why don't you take the rest of the day off, with pay, and relax this weekend. I want you to reflect on this job, and your emotional health. Come back on Monday morning with a clear head, and we'll decide then whether this place is suitable for you."

"Fine." There was much more I wanted to say, but the chance to get out of there early took precedence. I grabbed my purse and opened the door. The cat hissed at me as I left.

Driving home, I thought about devil-dog and Rodney. I hadn't seen either in two days and hoped it would stay that way. I crept into my driveway, waited, and watched. No dog. I checked out Rodney's house. No music, lights, or other signs of life. Wonderful.

I made it to my front door when I heard something tear-assing toward me. I turned around—it was the dog—running fiercely from the woods across the street. Frantically, I fumbled for my key, jiggled it into the keyhole, pushed the door open, and slammed it closed, just as the dog plowed into it. He remained just outside the door, barking relentlessly.

I thought about calling the cops but said screw that. It was time to show this mongrel just who he was dealing with. I went to my bedroom, opened my night table drawer, removed my .45 semi-auto, slapped in a magazine of hollow-point bullets, and cocked it. I strode toward the front door. The dog was still barking. I held the gun in my right hand, grasped the doorknob with the left, and flung the door open . . . The dog was gone.

I stepped outside and scanned my perimeter. A branch was wobbling at the edge of the woods. I closed the door, returned the gun to my bedroom, and poured a glass of vodka.

I ate some salad, made a second drink, and plopped on the couch to watch TV. I wasn't even going to contemplate what to do about work tonight. Somewhere around eight my doorbell rang. Shit! It was you-know-who holding two bottles of wine.

"Hey, chicky. As I promised, these are for you."

"Rodney, that's very nice of you, but I don't need them."

"Well geeesh, I just wanted to give you a housewarming gift, and you said you didn't drink beer. Here, at least take one of them."

He handed me the bottle and I took it. Big mistake.

"Thank you, Rodney." I started to close the door.

"Aren't you gonna invite me in? Just for one glass?"

"I can't, but thank you for the bottle."

"Aw c'mon, girl, you're dissing me. I'm just trying to be a good neighbor."

I felt a twinge of guilt until Rodney said, "Ya know, chicky, I got some weed. Maybe that'll loosen you up better."

"Rodney, I appreciate your gesture, but I'm really not in the mood for company. I had a tough day and I'd rather just be alone. OK?" I thought I heard a growl.

"Well maybe tomorrow you might want to—"

"No. I have to go." I shut the door, retrieved my gun, and sat with it on my lap, sipping my vodka.

The next morning, I was in my kitchen drinking coffee, thinking about work. I considered Barry's supernatural explanations, but decided they were moot. It didn't matter if Haddock and Thorn were bitches or witches. I had to leave this job, but needed to find something else first. If I quit prematurely, I could easily end up evicted before being rehired, as there weren't many nursing opportunities in this part of the state. I couldn't handle that prospect.

My life had already been uprooted a number of times. Returning from overseas and acclimating back into society was overwhelming. Civilians don't understand what we go through in combat zones, or the struggles of readjusting back into the world. I had trouble sleeping, bad dreams, and felt on edge all the time.

A few years later, the depression came. As it worsened, so did my war trauma. I drank almost every day and felt suicidal. Sometimes I thought I was hallucinating, hearing or seeing things that weren't there.

One day I had it out with this woman at the supermarket. She saw my army cap and made cracks about "warmongers" and "baby killers." I went berserk. After I bashed her face into the soda machine, the police arrived and took me away. That's when I got committed to a psychiatric facility. It was a long haul climbing out of that hole.

So now, I finally had my own place again, and what I had hoped would be steady employment. As screwed up as my job was, ending up broke and homeless would be even worse. Even if I had to leave nursing and barely eke out a living, I would do it. But I had to stay put for now.

Throughout the day I peeked out my windows, checking for the dog. My intentions were clear. If I saw it again I'd blow its ass away. Nighttime came. I was trying not to drink. I had previously cut down, but now my nerves were frayed. I opened a bottle of wine and told myself I'd only have a few, wouldn't drink during the week, only needed it temporarily—all the usual bullshit.

Three glasses later the doorbell rang.

"Hey, mamasita, how's it hanging?" said Rodney, swaying, holding a bottle of Jack Daniels.

"Rodney, I don't—"

"It's Saturday night. Let's have a drink and welcome you to the neighborhood."

"No, I'm not interested."

61

"Aw c'mon, chicky, I'm just trying to be friendly. Just one drink."

"Rodney, this is the last time I'm telling you. No."

Rodney stepped forward and grabbed my arm. "Honey, I ain't got no diseases, if that's what you're worried about, and I always use a condom."

I shoved him with both hands, knocking him onto his back.

"What the hell?" he said.

I sprang to my kitchen counter, seized my .45 and hustled back to the door. Rodney had just stood up.

I pointed my gun at his head. "You get the fuck outta here right now or I'll unload in your face."

Rodney tripped back. "Jesus Christ, you're a psycho."

"If you ever bother me again, I'll waste your ass, understand?"

Rodney stumbled away. "Crazy bitch."

I finished my wine, opened a second bottle, and held my gun all night.

Sunday night I was getting ready for bed. I was proud of myself. I didn't drink that day, although I did pop a few extra Xanax. I rationalized that was better than alcohol, which is probably at least partially true. I didn't see or hear Rodney all day.

I curled under the covers, .45 on the nightstand. I had taken my usual bedtime pill-fest. As I lay there, I heard the growling again. It sounded like the dog was circling my house, stopping in front of my bedroom window with each pass. This time I decided to act. I got up, clutched my pistol, turned on my outside light, opened the front door—and heard nothing—saw nothing. I squeezed the gun so hard it went off, firing into the ground. Then I punched the wall and went back to bed. I slept like shit.

Monday morning, about to leave for work, I did something I've never done before: stashed my gun in my purse. I wasn't taking any chances of being caught off guard by the dog. I gulped the remainder of my coffee and stepped outside.

Sure enough, no sooner had I started walking to the car, the dog came charging at me from the woods. I withdrew my pistol, threw my purse to the ground and assumed a firing stance. "C'mon you prick," I snarled.

When the dog got to within fifteen feet I fired twice. The first bullet devastated its chest. The second blew off one of its legs. I ran up to it, ready to fire a parting shot, but it was unnecessary.

Now what do I do? Should I call the police, or just dispose of the body and hope no one noticed? I glanced at Rodney's house, but nothing was stirring. I went back inside and returned the gun to my drawer. No more need for it now. My anxiety was skyrocketing. My initial relief was giving way to a surge of panic.

I tried to think. I had no time to bury the carcass. If I was late for work, especially after Friday's events, I'd be fired for sure. So, I decided to just drag it around the back of my house and worry about it later.

I went back outside and gasped in horror. Rodney's naked body lay where the dog's had been! His chest had a gaping wound, his right leg was detached, and there was blood everywhere. I was losing my mind. How . . . how . . . how was this possible? I stepped forward to get a closer view. Images of Afghanistan flashed through my mind: soldiers with missing limbs, body parts, the aftermath of IEDs. I felt like I was going to have a heart attack.

Then I noticed a tuft of gray hair on Rodney's head. I picked it up and examined it. It looked like cat hair! Then I heard a hiss. I whipped around but saw nothing. The cat. Of course—it was the cat! That frigging cat caused all of this! Barry was right. It was a demon.

I had to kill the cat. I raced back inside, shoved my gun into my purse and sped toward the nursing home like a madwoman. I was gonna end this once and for all.

I zoomed into the nursing home parking lot, scraped two cars, jumped the curb, and parked on the grass next to the front door. I ran to my unit and shoved the two entrance doors so hard they slammed into their respective walls. I startled Haddock and a group of employees standing in the hall. "Where's that fucking cat?" I yelled.

Haddock stormed toward me holding up her hand. "What the hell do you think you're doing? Calm down this instant."

I reached into my bag, pulled out my .45 and shot her right in the center of her forehead. Her brains splattered everywhere as her lifeless body collapsed to the floor. God that felt good.

People started screaming and running in all directions. With my pistol blazing, I went from room to room, scouring each one for my quarry. Someone hit the fire alarm. I wove my way around patients in wheelchairs and assorted staff running for their lives. I saw Barry ducking for cover. He didn't even try to reason with me. All I wanted was the cat.

I searched every room to no avail. By that time all the staff had departed. Should I canvass the rest of the building or go directly to Thorn's office? Yes, that's what I would do. I'd go to the source. I left the unit and headed down the hallway. There were closets on either side along the way. I opened each door, just in case the beast was skulking inside.

"Freeze! Police!"

Two officers, guns drawn, were standing behind both corners of the end of the hallway.

"Drop your weapon or we'll fire."

Damn. I didn't want to kill police, but nothing else mattered now. I was about to shoot when the screeching cat lunged from a closet shelf, scratching my face with both claws, causing me to drop my gun. The police charged. The first one kicked my .45 away. Then they tackled and handcuffed me.

The cat hissed.

"That cat's the Devil! It's a witch! It's killing the patients! It's a witch!"

The officers ignored me and dragged me out. I hollered all the way.

Thorn came rushing over. "Officers, I'm Darlene Thorn, the director. She's obviously having a mental breakdown. She has a psych history. You must take her to the medical center in Berlin. She was committed there before."

"She's lying! She's a witch too! That cat belongs to her! They're killing people!"

Thorn raised her eyebrows at the officers as if saying, "Well?"

The officers nodded and took me away.

On the psychiatric unit, four staff members held me down and strapped my wrists and ankles to the bed. I was squealing and thrashing the entire time.

The psychiatrist walked in. "Lori, please calm down, we're trying to help you."

"There are witches at the nursing home! They're killing people!"

"We understand your concern. Just please try to calm down for now." He turned to the nurse and said, "Give her five Haldol and four Ativan stat."

"Four milligrams of Ativan?"

"You heard me. She's been on Xanax for a while; she has a tolerance. We must sedate her. You know she shot someone, right?"

"They were witches!"

The nurse came back with two needles. The other three staff leaned on me. The nurse pulled my pants partially down and injected my buttocks.

"OK, Lori, you're going to rest now," said the nurse, as everyone left the room.

The medication took effect in less than a minute. A wave of stupor rushed across my brain. I was plunging into unconsciousness. The last thing I remember was Lilith jumping onto my chest . . .

~~~~~~

"You've done very well, Darlene."

"I was hoping you'd be pleased," said Thorn.

"Let us drink to our future successes." He opened a bottle of Courvoisier XO Impérial Cognac and splashed it into two snifters. They clinked their glasses and sipped.

"It's too bad," said Thorn, "we didn't have the chance to enlist Haddock. She would have been useful."

"Indeed. She was delightfully inhuman. She would have made an exemplary witch. She might even have rivaled you."

"Oh, I don't think so."

"Yes, you're quite right," said Van Haden, unbuttoning her blouse.

There was a knock at the door.

"Who is it?" asked Thorn.

"It's me, Kim."

"C'mon in."

Kim bounced into the room and smiled, rubbing her breasts. "May I join you?"

"But of course, my dear," said Van Haden.

The Maleficences

Morgan was finishing his beef stew as Vicki sat across from him, holding her wine glass against her breast.

"You didn't eat much," said Morgan.

"I'm not hungry."

"Honey, I'm not going to let anything happen to you."

"What if Van Haden's back, and Derrick's one of his?"

"Let's not get ahead of ourselves."

"But what if he *is*?"

"He still ain't getting free."

"You don't know that," said Vicki.

"Honey, he's still in the hospital—under guard. I'm charging his ass with violating parole, violating the restraining order, and terroristic threats. As soon as he's patched up, he goes to the county jail. He won't get bail; he's an ex-con with new charges. From jail he'll go straight to prison. We just have to keep our stories straight about him threatening you."

"He *did* threaten me."

"Yes, but his vague threats aren't enough to warrant all the charges I want to press, let alone the beating I gave him. You have to say he actually threatened to kill you, and I gotta say I heard it, and thought he was about to act on it."

Vicki took a long sip of her wine. "If he's one of Van Haden's, prison won't stop him."

"We don't even know if Van Haden's back. You're just going to scare yourself more by assuming that."

"No, Butch! I'm not scaring myself. *Derrick* is! The man who beat me for years has returned. Do you have any idea how that makes me feel?"

"I just don't want you—"

"You threatened to kill Derrick if he ever returned. He knows what kind of man you are, and that we're married now. He knows coming after me will get him back in jail or dead. And yet he still has the balls to walk into Toby's, in front of witnesses, and harass me. For him to do something that brazen means Van Haden's backing him up."

Morgan opened his mouth to speak but—

"And I was part of the coven. I know how they operate. So don't tell me that I'm scaring myself."

Morgan went over to Vicki and held her. "I'm sorry. I was simply trying to ease your fear."

Morgan's cell phone rang; it was Gil. "What's up?"

"Butch, it's me. You home?"

"Yeah."

"Can you meet me at Pete Hadley's? I'm afraid something's happened."

"Like what?"

"I've been calling him, and knocking on his door every day this week, and he hasn't answered. And his car's been in the same spot the whole time."

"Awwww shit," said Morgan. "I'll be right over."

"What is it?" asked Vicki.

"Gil wants me to meet him at his old house. Something might have happened to the new owner."

"It's starting again, Butch."

"You gonna be OK?"

"Yeah, just don't take too long." Vicki refilled her glass.

Gil was waiting in his car, flipping through a *Playboy* magazine when Morgan banged on the driver's side window. Gil flinched, tossed the magazine onto the passenger seat, and got out of the car. "Why didn't you just break the glass?"

"Get your face out of the smut and tell me what's going on."

"Hadley called me about a week ago; he sounded funny. Said he checked out Crestwood Lake's history, asked me if I really thought the house was haunted. Anyway, he hasn't answered the phone or his door since. And except for the bedroom, there's been no other lights on. At least not when I came by."

"And you want me to just bust in and see if he's OK?" said Morgan.

"Yeah."

"And if he's in there minding his own business, I'm gonna look like a jackass."

"Something's wrong, Butch."

Morgan opened the screen door, pounded on the wooden, inner door and shouted, "Mr. Hadley, it's Captain Morgan, Crestwood Lake Police."

"I already did that," said Gil.

Morgan took a step back and threw his six-foot-five, 270-pound frame into the door, shoulder first. The door burst open like a bomb blast.

"Mr. Hadley," yelled Morgan.

Morgan withdrew his Ruger .357 magnum and ran his hand along the wall, finding a light switch. He and Gil went from room to room, flicking on lights and calling for Hadley, canvassing the entire ground floor.

Gil exhaled heavily. "You know where we have to go."

Morgan nodded. With his pistol leading the way, they headed upstairs to the bedroom. The very same bedroom they found Burke dead in three years prior—decomposing with an axe in his hand.

Morgan turned on the hallway light and peered toward the bedroom at the other end. "Damn," he said, noticing the smell. He charged toward the bedroom and turned on the light. Hadley's body lay on the floor, face up, in a dried pool of blood.

"Jesus Christ!" said Morgan.

Hadley's T-shirt and underwear had been ripped away from his body. There were multiple stabs wounds in his heart, and a jagged gash across his abdomen. His ears and genitals had been severed.

"His organs have been removed," said Gil. "You know what this means, right?"

"Yeah I do."

"They're back, Butch. They're collecting organs for their rituals."

"I just said I know."

"I gotta go back downstairs," said Gil, clutching his stomach.

Morgan called the station. Within minutes the police and other personnel were descending on Peter Hadley's house.

While the officers were inspecting the house, and Dr. Wyatt, the coroner, was examining the body, Morgan pulled Gil off to the side. "Get a hold of Aaronson."

"I'll call him tonight. How do you plan to find Van Haden, or whatever receptacle he's keeping all the souls in?"

"I don't know. He won't be hanging out in plain sight like last time. He'll be more careful."

"We need help, Butch. Allies, like Father Mark and Cassandra."

"They're dead."

"Yes, I know they're dead. I didn't mean them specifically."

"So, what do you want to do, take out a help wanted ad for a demonologist and a white witch?"

Gil smirked. "I'm just saying that we can't tackle this by ourselves."

"Let's meet with Aaronson first. He can help us come up with a game plan."

"How's Vicki?"

"She's pretty shook up. I've tried to play down the Van Haden angle to keep her fears to a minimum, but she knows better. When she hears about Hadley, she's gonna freak."

"You know Van Haden will be coming after the two of you."

"Yeah I know."

Dr. Wyatt approached. "Captain, can I talk to you?"

Morgan held up his hand. "Gimmie a minute, Doc."

Morgan turned back to Gil and lowered his voice. "Go home and call Aaronson now. I'll call you when I get home."

"I want to hear what the doctor has to say first," said Gil.

Morgan motioned to Wyatt. "All right, Doc."

Wyatt stepped forward.

"This is my associate, Gil Pearson. Anything you have to say can be said in front of him. So what's the deal?"

"He's been dead about a week. The cause of death was four stab wounds to the heart. Then, after death, they cut open his abdomen. His liver, spleen, and pancreas were removed. Then they amputated his ears and genitalia. A very sharp knife, six to eight inches in length. I'll know more once I've done the autopsy."

"Thanks, Doc. Call me."

"It's happening again, Captain."

"What?"

"The demonic tattoos, the viciously mutilated bodies, the missing organs . . ."

"Why does every-fucking-body feel compelled to tell me the obvious? Get on that autopsy as soon as possible. I need any info you can provide."

"Sure thing, Captain."

As Wyatt left, Morgan said to Gil, "Do me a favor. Go to my house; call Aaronson from there. Stay with Vicki. I'm worried about her being alone. I'll be home as soon as possible."

"No problem."

Morgan assisted his officers with searching Hadley's house, dusting for fingerprints, checking his computer and phone, etc. About a half hour later, Gil called him on his cell phone.

"Butch, I'm at your place with Vicki—"

"Is she OK?"

"She's a little frayed but managing. I called Aaronson and spoke to his housekeeper. He's in Italy."

"Italy? What the hell is he doing in Italy?"

"On some personal business is all she'd say. She wouldn't tell me where he's staying, and she didn't know exactly when he'd be back. I explained our circumstances were exigent and asked her to call him and let him know we needed him."

"Exigent? Does that mean urgent?"

"Yeah."

"So why didn't you just say that instead of being a douche?"

"Sorry, when I'm under stress I forget your multi-syllabic limitations."

"Just stay with Vicki until I get home. I won't be much longer." Morgan hung up before Gil could respond.

~~~~~~

Sammy Martin wiped the residual cum off his penis, flushed, and returned to work. He still had to replace the rear brakes on the Ford F-150 he was working on, and had promised the owner it would be done by five o'clock. He lit a cigarette and removed the rear wheels.

Sammy was a thirty-eight-year-old, pudgy, high-school dropout. His ex-wife was a drug addict and his estranged daughter was a stripper. "Sammy's Garage" was bequeathed to him by his father. Were it not for his inheritance, he would have never had the funds, nor the credit, to own a business. Sammy lived in the cramped, one-bedroom apartment above the shop.

Crestwood Lake was a small town but had more than enough mechanics. Business was sporadic at best, and Sammy was always playing catch-up with his bills. He occasionally performed odd jobs, such as snow-shoveling or junk removal, so he could at least stay within sight of solvency.

One of the drains on Sammy's finances was his hope to reunite with his daughter. A Burlington private detective offered to find her for five grand. Once located, Sammy intended to initiate contact, and offer her money to leave her profession and attend school. The whole idea was a long shot, but the cost was a sure thing. At his current rate of saving, it would be years before he could enact his plan. That's why Sammy decided to start selling marijuana.

A friend of a friend was a moderate-sized dealer, always hungry for local distributors. Sammy had to purchase a minimum of three pounds at a time. That meant all his other creditors had to get in line.

Sammy knew he was taking chances, but planned to cease his illegal enterprise once he had enough money. Recently, he had been augmenting sales by encouraging his customers to provide word-of-mouth advertising. This accelerated the attainment of his goal, but at the cost of escalating his risks.

Sammy's head was under the chassis when her red stiletto heels strutted into view.

"Excuse me," lilted a delicate voice.

Sammy ducked out from under the car. She was five-feet-one with dirty-blonde hair. Her one-hundred-pound frame was wrapped in a tight red sweater, black leather jacket, matching leather skirt, and black nylons that accentuated her slender legs. Sammy cursed his recent "bathroom break"—as if there was even a chance.

"Can I help you?" asked Sammy.

"Hi. My name's Carolyn. I'm looking for Sammy."

"That's me."

"Uh . . . hi. A friend of mine told me to see you about . . . ya know . . . getting some weed?"

"Who's your friend?"

"Amanda, at the diner."

"How much you want?"

"An ounce."

You could almost see the dollar signs in Sammy's pupils. "Five hundred."

"Five hundred?"

"That's right. It's good stuff."

"Is that the best you can do?"

"That's the price, honey."

Carolyn frowned and rummaged through her purse. "I didn't expect it to be so much. I only have four hundred." Carolyn sashayed closer to Sammy, tilted her head and slid her tongue across her bottom lip. "I'll give you the best head you ever had for the difference."

"Fucking A," said Sammy.

Carolyn knelt and parted her lips.

Sammy quickly dropped his pants.

Carolyn grabbed his manhood—her eyes turned bright yellow and her nails became talons . . .

You could hear Sammy's screams a quarter mile away.

~~~~~~

Morgan entered the police station carrying a large to-go cup of coffee when Lieutenant Edwards intercepted him.

"Butch, the mayor called. He ordered me to tell you to go straight to his office the moment you arrived. He sounded pissed."

"That's because he's a little pissant."

"No seriously, Butch, he said if I didn't send you over right away—"

"Yeah, yeah, yeah. I'll see what he wants." Morgan headed toward the far end of the municipal building, where the administrative offices were located, mumbling aspersions all the way.

Ex-car-salesman Clyde Burrows, the forty-one-year-old mayor of Crestwood Lake, had cajoled his way into office with smarminess and venality. He and Morgan hated each other and had numerous altercations over the years. Burrows would have already tried to fire Morgan were it not for the photos Morgan had of him with a prostitute. But now, having sold his soul to Van Haden, Burrows was aiming to regain his leverage.

As Morgan approached Burrows's office, the secretary said, "Hi, Butch. I'll let him know you're here."

Morgan ignored her, opened the door and barked, "Whadda ya want?"

"Damn you, Butch. This is my office and you don't just barge in here without permission."

Seated in front of Burrows's desk was the Essex County prosecutor, Wilfred Jameson.

"In case you didn't hear," said Morgan, "we're working on a murder. Now do you want to give me an etiquette lesson, or come to the point so I can get back to work?"

Burrows glared, then gestured toward Jameson. "You already know Wil."

Morgan nodded at Jameson, turned to Burrows and said "Yeah?"

"Sit down," said Burrows, barely moving his jaw.

Morgan sat, took the lid off his coffee, sipped it, and placed it on the desk.

"Captain," said Jameson. "Derrick Larson has retained an attorney, a good one, from the largest firm in Manchester. He's suing you personally, and the town, for police brutality. His lawyer wants you arrested for assault."

"Bullshit. He's an ex-con who violated a restraining order and threatened to kill my wife—his ex-wife—who he brutalized for years."

"He denies threatening her. Claims he was only there to apologize for the past and tell her that his father is dying."

"That's a crock of shit! He threatened her—I heard him."

"Even if that's the case," snarled Burrows, "you want to tell me how that necessitated breaking his nose and jaw, not to mention the rest of his bruises?"

"He fought back. I was defending myself. Ask Vicki."

"Well, Captain," said Jameson, "I wouldn't expect your wife to refute your story. We'll be interviewing the other people who were in the bar at the time. So will Larson's attorney."

"I don't give a damn who interviews who. That piece of crap broke the law the moment he set foot in Toby's. Then he threatened my wife."

"That doesn't give you the right to assault him, Captain," said Jameson.

"I'm suspending you until this matter is resolved," said Burrows.

"You can't do that," said Morgan standing up, sticking his finger in Burrows's face. "I know the law of this town and this state. You can't take me off duty based only on an allegation." Morgan looked back at Jameson.

"No, he can't, Captain, but that's not the only allegation."

"What are you talking about?" asked Morgan.

"Mayor Burrows claims that you tried to blackmail him with photos of him and a woman engaged in an intimate encounter."

"Intimate encounter," said Morgan sarcastically. "You mean paying a frigging hooker for sex."

"There was no money exchanged," said Jameson reaching into his briefcase. "I have the young lady's sworn affidavit right here."

"And by the way, Butch," said Burrows, "in case *you* didn't hear—my wife and I divorced, and I'm not running for reelection. So for all I care, you can tell the whole damn world about what I did or didn't do with that woman."

"I'm more concerned you tried to blackmail a public official," said Jameson.

Morgan clenched his fist and pointed with his other hand. "It's my word against his, and neither of you slimeballs can remove me from duty without proof."

"Be that as it may, Captain, if I were you, I'd hire an attorney."

Morgan stepped closer to Jameson. "Obviously you two are swapping spit. Well I got news for ya. I've come up against far worse than corrupt scumbags. You're gonna need more than an ex-con, allegations, and a manipulated whore to take me down."

"Are you threatening *me* now, Captain?" asked Jameson.

Morgan leaned over, a foot from Jameson's face. "What do you think?"

Jameson swallowed.

"That's it!" hollered Burrows. "Get the hell out of my office. You're on notice. We're going to investigate these allegations, and when they're found to be true, you'll not only be fired, your ass will be in jail."

Morgan took a step toward the door when Burrows said, "Take your damn coffee with you."

Morgan reached for it, knocking it over across Burrows's desk.

"You asshole!" said Burrows, coffee spreading in all directions.

"Always a pleasure, Clyde," said Morgan strolling away.

The Provocation

Vicki deposited Morgan's Coke and Gil's rye on the table, then her derriere in the booth next to Morgan, who planted one on her cheek. The only other people in Toby's were the regulars: Jed, Lottie and Alan. Ziggy was home, tinkering with his dead-windowsill-fly collection.

"Heard from Aaronson?" asked Morgan.

"No," said Gil. "He's still in Italy the last time I checked."

Vicki turned to Morgan. "The biggest problem is Derrick's charges against you. You know the prosecutor is going to be interviewing *them*." She bounced her eyes toward the bar.

"Why don't you talk to them first?" asked Gil.

"Wouldn't do any good," said Morgan.

"Why do you say that?" asked Vicki.

"Because discussing it with them makes it look like I'm nervous—like I got something to hide. Besides, I've known Jed, Alan and Lottie for years. They ain't got nothing against me. They all know Derrick's a scumbag, and what he did to you. And they weren't close enough to hear the conversation. They can't say for sure that Derrick didn't threaten you."

"And what if Van Haden got to one of them?" asked Gil.

"Well then it's even more pointless. There's nothing I can say to them that'll undo that. The issue isn't what the people at the bar saw. The real problem is Van Haden. Derrick and Burrows are just pawns in a bigger scheme."

"So now what?" asked Gil.

"Now we have lunch." Morgan turned to Vicki. "Wanna see if our burgers are ready, baby?"

Vicki let out a playful snort. Slapping Morgan's back as she got up she said, "The day you lose your appetite is the day I'll *really* need to worry about you."

Before she could walk away, Gil held up his empty glass.

"Isn't it a little early to be hitting the booze?" asked Vicki.

Gil looked at her quizzically and said, "No . . . I'm awake."

Vicki smirked. "You're an addict."

"That's not true—I've been drinking for over fifty years, and I never found it to be habit-forming."

"He's incorrigible, baby," said Morgan.

As Vicki walked away, Morgan leaned forward. "Have you seen the new store that took over Karen Gardner's old place?"

"No," said Gil.

"It's called The Good Book. This guy named Guerin owns it. I was there the other day to check him out."

"And?"

"He's like Van Haden."

"How so?"

"Same shit as when I met Van Haden. He knew who I was before I opened my mouth. Claims he saw me through the back window, but his store doesn't have one. He was smooth, mysterious, said he studies witchcraft."

"Oh, Christ."

"I threw holy water on him. Didn't do anything."

"That doesn't prove—"

"I know, I know."

"Butch, we have to do something. They're closing in all around us: Derrick, the mayor, possibly the prosecutor, the punk that held up the supermarket, now this book-store guy. They're probably all in cahoots."

79

"And what would you have me do? We don't know where Van Haden is. He's not hanging out in plain sight like last time. I can't just go around shooting everyone who might be connected with him. That's why I want to meet with Aaronson. See what he thinks about how to proceed."

"Well, I still say we need to see Father Sean at Saint Matthew's. He might be of help."

"And what if he knows nothing about this crap?" said Morgan. "Just because he's a priest doesn't mean he knows the truth about Crestwood Lake. Hell, most clergy don't even know that the Devil and witches actually exist. He'll think we're both fruit loops."

"Well, we can try to feel him out. At the very least we need more holy water—a lot more."

"And how do we explain that? Tell him I want to wash my ass and take a holy shit?"

Gil rolled his eyes. "Butch, religious people sometimes keep holy water for various purposes."

"Well, you'll have to be the saint, cause he damn sure ain't gonna believe it's for me."

Gil snorted. "I'll tell him you're the reason I need it."

"Ha ha. Well, think of some kind of excuse, 'cause we can stop by this week." Morgan turned around. "Here comes our food."

Vicki placed the burgers and Gil's drink on the table. "Need anything else, boys?"

"No, baby. Thank you," said Morgan.

A group of people shuffled in for lunch.

"Gotta go," said Vicki.

Morgan took a Neanderthal-size bite of his burger as his cell phone rang.

"Goddammit!" he growled through half-chewed meet. "Always when I'm fucking eating." He retrieved his phone and snarled "What?"

80

"Butch, it's Hank. One of your residents went psycho this morning and shot a nurse at Crestwood Manor. Name's Lori Oliver. We brought her to the psych unit at Berlin Medical Center. We're at her house now; four Woodlawn Road. We think she killed her neighbor too."

"I'll be right there." Morgan put his phone back in his pocket.

"What's up?" asked Gil.

"That was Hank Pemberton, chief of the Concord Police. Some woman named Oliver on Woodlawn Road shot her neighbor and an employee at the nursing home. They're at her house now." Morgan proceeded to wolf down his burger.

"Aren't you going?"

Morgan swallowed and said, "As soon as I'm done. They'll still be dead."

"Want me to come with you?"

"No. Stay here with Vicki. I know we can't guard her twenty-four-seven, but the more we can, the better I feel. Go sit at the bar, have a few drinks, sniff around a bit."

"I certainly will," said Gil, glancing at an attractive brunette.

"Not with your dick."

"Yes, Butch."

Morgan scarfed the rest of his burger and stood up. "Tell Vicki what's going on. I'll see you later."

Morgan pulled up to Lori Oliver's house. He had called the station to dispatch additional officers. Pemberton's men and state police were already inspecting the scene. Morgan got out of his truck, spit, and walked over to Pemberton, who was standing next to the shattered remains of Rodney.

"How ya doing, Butch?"

Morgan nodded.

"You look like you lost some weight."

"I took a dump and got a haircut."

Pemberton shook his head with a wry smile. "Same old Butch."

Morgan grimaced at Rodney's corpse and said, "What happened?"

"Well, based on what the nursing home staff, and the owners of the house told us, Lori Oliver, age thirty-five, army vet—did a tour in Afghanistan as a medic—rented this place like two or three weeks ago. Started working as a nurse at Crestwood Manor last Monday. This guy here, Rodney Depina, rented the small house right there." Pemberton pointed. "Anyway, we don't have ballistics yet, but all the shells are the same. Looks like she shot him first, then went to work and shot her supervisor—name's Nancy Haddock, from St. Johnsbury."

"You said you brought Oliver to the psych unit at Berlin?"

"Yeah. She was hospitalized there after assaulting a woman a few years back. Plus, she was losing it when we apprehended her."

"What do you mean?"
"She was out of control, thrashing, and ranting about witches."

"Witches?"

"Yeah, she kept hollering that the director of the nursing home and her cat were witches—some kind of crazy shit—and that they were killing patients."

"The director?"

"Yeah, this woman named Darlene Thorn. Her and her cat." Pemberton chuckled. "Funny thing is, the cat helped us take Oliver down."

"How so?" asked Morgan.

"My men had Oliver cornered in the hallway; she was still armed. The cat jumped out of a closet and nailed her in the face, made her drop the gun. I'm ready to deputize the son of a bitch."

"How were they killing patients?"

"What?" asked Pemberton with a contorted face.

"What did she say about how Thorn and this cat were killing people?"

"How does that matter?"

"I want to know," demanded Morgan.

"She rattled off something about the cat jumping onto patients in their beds, sucking the life out of them. The staff said after she shot her boss, she was combing the place looking to kill the cat."

"What's up with this cat?"

"I don't know, you want me to bring it in for questioning?"

"Nah, you'd probably knock it up."

"You're a piece of work, Butch."

One of Pemberton's officers approached, holding a radio. "Chief, we just got notified by the medical center. They found Lori Oliver dead in her room."

"From what?"

"They don't know yet."

"Goddamn. This is getting worse by the moment," said Pemberton.

Morgan waved his officers over. "Give Chief Pemberton here any assistance he needs, understand?" He turned toward Pemberton. "Call me with any updates." Morgan started to leave.

"Where ya going?"

"To the nursing home."

"Why?"

"I want to talk to the director."

"We already did that."

"*You* already did that," said Morgan. "I haven't."

"What's she gonna tell you that she hasn't already told us?"

Morgan continued walking away.

Crestwood Manor had four parking spaces designated for administration. A sign read: "Reserved parking. Violators will be towed at the owner's expense." Morgan surveyed the spaces until he came to one occupied by a black Mercedes S-class. "Hmmmph," he snorted in disgust. The placard in front of the car denominated: Darlene Thorn. Morgan called the station, ran the license plate, and confirmed it was hers.

Morgan marched in the front door and up to the desk as if he owned the place. Before Ms. nose-ring could speak he said, "Crestwood Lake Police. Where's Darlene Thorn's office?"

"First floor, room 102. Do you have an appointment?"

Morgan smirked and headed down the hall.

"You can't just go in there," she called.

The door to 102 was open. Morgan stopped about six feet from the doorway and observed. Inside Thorn's office, three feet from the door jamb, against the wall, stood a seventy-five-gallon fish tank. The lid was on the floor. Between the tank and the door jamb was an eye-level shelf, upon which perched the gray cat. Darlene Thorn scooped out a dead, six-inch fish, and offered it to Lilith, who snatched it with both paws, and ravenously tore its teeth into it.

Morgan also noticed a vase of yellow flowers. He squinted—it was wormwood. The same flowers that Karen Gardner used to brew her malevolent potions.

"You may come in, Captain."

Morgan's frame filled the doorway; his contempt filled the building. "And what's *your* explanation of how you knew it was me."

"My receptionist phoned and said a policeman was here. I saw you strutting down the hallway. You don't seem like an underling."

Morgan turned his head. Eighteen inches away, Lilith was voraciously devouring the fish.

"Nice cat," he said sarcastically.

Thorn half-smiled, smugly.

Morgan looked at the tank. "What kind of fish are those?"

"Piranhas."

Morgan scoffed. "Why don't you just slay a goat, light some candles, and chant?"

"Why are you here?"

"I'm chief of the Crestwood Lake Police."

"Yes, I know who you are."

"I'm sure you do."

"I've already talked to the Concord Police about the events of this morning."

"And now you must talk to *me*," said Morgan, thumping his index finger against his chest.

Thorn extended her hand. "Have a seat."

"I'm fine where I am."

"What do you want, Captain?"

"I want to know why Lori Oliver lost it and shot her boss."

"She was mentally unbalanced. She was hospitalized before for violent behavior."

"That's not enough of an explanation. Even if someone's mental, something usually sets them off. And why here? She could have gone apeshit anywhere."

"Have you ever heard of workplace violence? Unstable people, particularly incompetent employees who have problems with their supervisors, sometimes become unhinged and kill them."

"Lori Oliver was incompetent?"

"Yes. We were considering terminating her."

"I ain't buying it, lady. She was competent enough to handle a war zone, but she can't handle wiping old peoples' asses?"

Thorn's brow furrowed. "When she went to war, she wasn't traumatized yet. That's where the damage occurred. She then brought that psychological vulnerability back home."

"What exactly did she do wrong?"

"Well, aside from having an outburst in our cafeteria, she didn't follow proper procedure with a DNR patient."

"A patient that died?" asked Morgan.

"Yes, DNR means do not—"

"I know what it means."

"Then why did you ask if—"

"And just how did this patient die? Because my understanding is Oliver thought this beast of yours over here had something to do with it."

"She was mentally ill, Captain."

"She also thought that you were a witch."

"What part of mentally ill do you not understand?"

"That doesn't mean she was wrong."

"I think we're done here, Captain. I've had enough of your ludicrous implications."

"Do you deny being a witch, Ms. Thorn?"

"Have you lost your mind as well?"

"You didn't deny it."

"You're as crazy as she was."

"*You* are a witch," said Morgan pointing. "I know one when I see one."

"I will not be subjected to this."

"I suppose Van Haden gave you this cat."

"No—uh—who?"

"Ha! Too late, lady. Now the cat's really out of the bag."

"Get the hell out of my office."

Morgan turned and grimaced at the cat. It was chewing the backbone, fragments of fish guts speckled its face. The cat jerked forward and swiped Morgan, nicking his chin.

Morgan spit in the cat's face.

The cat yowled and lurched backward, falling into the fish tank in a frenzied splash.

"You bastard!" shouted Thorn.

The cat clawed its way out, stumbled over the side, and darted under Thorn's desk.

"I'm sure I'll see you again," said Morgan, turning to leave.

"Count on it!" growled Thorn.

Returning to the parking lot, Morgan called the towing company affiliated with the police. Then he waited in his pickup for them to arrive.

The tow truck driver pulled in and parked next to Morgan. "Whatcha got, Butch?"

"Hey, Vinny, how are you? See that black Mercedes? It's parked in the director's spot. Tow their ass to the county impound lot in Guildhall."

"But my lot's right in town. Guildhall's is almost twenty miles away."

"Exactly," said Morgan. "Oh, and one more thing." Morgan sauntered over to the car, smashed the taillight with the heel of his fist, and withdrew his ticket book. "Almost forgot the summons for the broken light."

The Visitation

Bernardo Iannucci was about to conduct a guided tour of Castel Sant'Angelo for a group of American college students, mostly art and history majors. The museum housed an eclectic mix of paintings, sculptures, military memorabilia and medieval firearms. Iannucci, being the curator, wasn't expected to function as a docent as well. But he relished lecturing about his passions, especially to curious young minds. It also kept staffing costs down, and that always made the board of trustees happy.

Iannucci had expedited the earthquake-related repairs. There was sporadic damage throughout the building, but fortunately, the only serious destruction took place in the basement. And while renovations were still ongoing, necessitating that visitors weave their way around work stations, the museum was open for business. They could not afford to lose thousands of Euros in admission fees each day.

Ambling through the late Renaissance period, the group came to a six-by-ten-foot painting of an enigmatic woman. She was beautiful: long, lush, wavy brown hair, with alluring, deep brown eyes. She wore a dark-blue gown that flowed, as if gently encouraged by a spring breeze.

Iannucci blocked the nameplate from view and said, "Can anyone tell me who this is?"

"My future ex-wife," said one of the young men.

Iannucci frowned, waiting for the chuckling to end. "It's Adriana Barberi."

"That's Adriana Barberi?" said a young, nerdy woman with long, frizzy red hair.

"You know her?" asked Iannucci.

"I've read about her, but never saw this image."

"What's your name?"

"I'm Kaylee."

88

"Well, Kaylee, I assume you can tell me who Signora Barberi is?"

"She was an Italian noblewoman, descended from the Borgias. She was killed during the Piedmont massacre. I think she was rumored to be a witch."

"Impressive," said Iannucci.

"She's a Borgia?" asked another woman.

"I think so," said Kaylee. "I'm not sure of the ancestral line."

"I trust you are familiar with the Borgias?" asked Iannucci, addressing the entire group.

A few heads nodded.

"The Borgias," said Iannucci, "were an Italian-Spanish family who rose to prominence during the Italian Renaissance. They became instrumental in political and religious affairs, begetting two popes. Numerous members of the family were suspected of multifarious crimes: bribery, murder, incest, to name a few. Poisoning was supposedly their preferred form of homicide. And yes, they were also suspected of witchcraft.

"Lucrezia Borgia, probably the most notorious of the clan, and rumored to be an avid poisoner, had a son by the name of Francesco d'Este. He had an illegitimate daughter named Bradamante d'Este, who in turn gave birth to a daughter in 1595 called Camilla, who was Adriana's mother.

"Adriana lived in Torre Pellice, in what is now modern-day Piedmont, with her husband, a Waldensian nobleman. She had a son named Giacomo and a daughter, Serafina. Torre Pellice was a stronghold of the Waldensians, a Protestant sect, repeatedly persecuted by the Catholics. In 1655 the Duke of Savoy's army slaughtered seventeen hundred Waldensians in an event now known as Piedmont Easter. Adriana Barberi's body was not amongst the dead, and she was never reliably seen again"

"What do you mean by *reliably*?" asked Kaylee.

"There have been a number of unsubstantiated sightings of her throughout the years, almost inevitably when some kind of tragedy or villainy occurred."

"Throughout the years?" asked another student.

"Yes. Her husband and children were killed in the massacre. Allegedly, she sold her soul to the Devil to save herself—and inflict vengeance on her enemies. According to the legend, Lucifer made her his senior witch, bestowing her with immortality." Iannucci turned and stared at her painting. In a dour voice he said, "It's claimed that she still wreaks pain and suffering on humanity to this day."

Only the sound of distant workers could be heard.

Iannucci turned and clapped his hands together. "Who's ready for some Michelangelo?"

The group perked up.

"This way," he said, extending his hand.

After the tour, Iannucci returned to his office. He checked his messages and his e-mails, then poured himself a glass of Recioto della Valpolicella, a sweet red wine from Italy's Vento region. The phone rang.

"Hello?"

"Bernnnnnie . . ." a sultry voice cooed.

"Ah, Gina my dear. Good to hear from you."

"Whatcha doin' tonight?"

"I'm sorry, love. I have plans with the wife." He could feel Gina's pout. "Why not come by this afternoon? I have an hour or two."

"No, I'm at the salon. Besides, I don't want just an hour. When will you make some time for me?"

"Tell you what; I'll arrange something this Saturday. I can always say I'm needed at the museum because of the repairs. We'll spend the whole day together; I promise."

"You better, Bernie."

"I will. I'll call you. Ciao bella."

"Ciao."

Iannucci picked up his wine and stepped to the window. He gazed at the people, and the vendors lining the Sant'Angelo Bridge, spanning the Tiber River. He observed a street actor, dressed as the grim reaper, attired in a black robe and skull mask, waving a scythe. At his feet was a blue tip basket.

"Pay the reaper now—or later!" the actor cried to the passersby.

Iannucci scoffed, then got lost in thought. What to do about Gina? He loved her, but loved his wife too, and hated lying to her. How long could he sustain his subterfuge? Maybe he should just end the marriage. But would he have a future with Gina? She was so young. And what if she eventually decided—

"Good afternoon, Bernardo."

Iannucci spun around, dropping his wine and his jaw.

"I heard you talking about me today."

Iannucci was a block of stone.

"You accused me of some horrid deeds."

He lunged to his desk, yanked open a drawer and rummaged frantically.

"Looking for this?" asked Adriana, holding a vial of holy water.

Iannucci gawked.

The vial burst into flames and vaporized.

"What do you want?" he asked.

"You know what I want. Where are they?"

"I don't know what you're talking about."

"Don't you dare feign ignorance with me. I will make your death so much more painful."

91

"They're not here. They've already been removed. I *don't* know where; I swear."

"That's quite unfortunate for you, Bernardo."

In the fenced-in courtyard below, two security guards were grumbling about a drunken American they had to eject, when a resounding crash startled them. Looking up, a body came hurling out of a window, plummeting in a screaming crescendo onto one of the fence's metal spikes.

Impaled through the hip, coughing up blood, Iannucci wheezed and choked.

"Good God!" said one of the security guards, reaching for his radio.

The other looked back at the window. His and Adriana's eyes met . . . until he went blind.

The Conclave

San Pietro in Vincoli, otherwise known as the Church of Saint Peter in Chains, is a Roman Catholic basilica in Rome. Built in the fifth century, it is renowned for housing Michelangelo's statue of Moses, but even more importantly, a reliquary containing the purported chains that bound Saint Peter while imprisoned by the Romans in Jerusalem.

Behind the altar, in the back of the vestry, was a large closet, the side wall of which contained a hidden passage. It opened into a circular staircase, which descended three flights into an underground chamber composed of stone and marble. The walls were lined with torches, innumerable crucifixes, and bronze sacrariums every six feet, filled with holy water.

In the center of the room stood a large, rectangular table made of heavy oak, further illuminated by two candelabras. Two bowls of fruit and various bottles of wine completed the offerings.

Seated around the table were Cardinal Rossi, from Italy, Cardinal Salvador, from Spain, Bishop Mwamba of Botswana, Rabbi Azaria from Jerusalem, Maharaj Magesh, a sadhu from India, British archaeologist and demonologist Nigel Poole, and Professor Doug Aaronson.

Cardinal Rossi, the group's prefect, called the meeting to order.

"Cardinal," said Poole, "How's Iannucci?"

"He was in surgery for hours yesterday. They expect him to survive, but he'll be left with permanent injuries. The spire grazed his spine but shattered his hip. He'll need more operations and long-term rehabilitation. He'll never walk normally again."

"Who did this?" asked Bishop Mwamba.

"As they rushed him to the hospital, he kept mumbling, 'Adriana.'"

"No," said Cardinal Salvador. "It can't be."

"I'm afraid so," said Cardinal Rossi. "Two security guards were in the courtyard where Bernardo landed. The one looked up at his office window and saw a woman with long, brown hair, and then went blind."

"God save us," said Mwamba.

"We must assume she is here for the artifacts," said Magesh.

"No shit," said Poole. "Of course she's here for the bloody artifacts."

Cardinal Rossi sneered at Poole, then turned to the group. "The issue before us now gentlemen, is how to protect them. Unquestioningly, Satan knows they have been discovered and are close by."

"We must relocate them as soon as possible," said Mwamba. "They are definitely not safe in Europe. Perhaps my church in Botswana."

"No," said Cardinal Salvador. "With all due respect, Bishop Mwamba, your country, indeed your entire continent, is too unstable: civil unrest, military uprisings, terrorism. Not to mention the alarming number of practitioners of the black arts in your part of the world."

"I must agree," said Cardinal Rossi. "Africa is out of the question."

"So is Israel," said Rabbi Azaria. "For some of the same reasons."

"So where then?" asked Poole, reaching for a bottle of wine.

"I know exactly where they must go," said Professor Aaronson.

The Gambit

Morgan strode into Prosecutor Jameson's office as humbly as his impudence would allow. Jameson prevailed behind his behemoth desk as if on a throne. Clyde Burrows dragged a large armchair next to the desk and sat, armed with as much disdain as Morgan. The walls were bedecked with framed newspaper headlines, each one proclaiming Jameson's conviction of a prominent figure. Morgan glimpsed at the Yale law diploma and snorted "hmmmph" under his breath.

"Have a seat, Captain," said Jameson, gesturing toward a couch against the far wall.

Morgan grabbed the other armchair, hoisted it up like a dumbbell, and dropped it directly in front of the desk. It creaked as his weight descended upon it.

Jameson pressed his tongue against the back of his bottom teeth.

Morgan locked eyes with Burrows and didn't retreat until Jameson said, "Let's get right to it, Captain. You said you wanted to meet to discuss a plea deal."

"That's right," said Morgan, followed by an awkward silence.

"Well?" said Burrows.

Morgan looked at Jameson. "I'll plead guilty to use of excessive force and resign. You can put me on probation—but no jail time." Then he scowled at Burrows. "You get what you want—me off the force."

"Plus the fines," added Jameson.

"And you can kiss your pension goodbye," said Burrows.

"Agreed," said Morgan through gritted teeth.

"And," said Burrows, pointing at Morgan. "You make a public statement acknowledging your guilt. You're not just gonna slink away. You're gonna quit in shame."

"On one condition," said Morgan.

"What?" said Jameson, narrowing his eyes.

"Derrick Larson goes back to prison. He violated the terms of his parole by walking into Toby's and harassing Vicki. Even *if* I gave him an unjustified ass-whipping, he still violated parole."

Burrows eyeballed Morgan suspiciously. "This ain't like you to fold. You got some kind of angle, even if I can't see it."

"You could have eyes up your ass and still couldn't see shit. So what's it gonna be?"

Jameson motioned toward Burrows. The two of them leaned over and whispered to each other.

"C'mon, Clyde," said Morgan, "I don't have all day. You want to get rid of me, or do you want to protect your kissing cousin?"

Burrows finished murmuring something to Jameson, then turned to Morgan and said, "OK, you have a deal."

"And Derrick?"

"Fuck him," said Burrows. "A small price to pay for your arrogant ass."

Morgan faced Jameson. "I suggest you expedite Derrick's court date. I'll step down the day he's returned to prison."

"I'll draft the paperwork for your plea bargain," said Jameson. "I can't legally include that it hinges on another man's prosecution. But the day Derrick is reincarcerated, you either fulfill your end of the deal, or I'll prosecute you to the fullest extent of the law—and you *will* do jail time. Not in some cushy, white-collar facility, but in the state pen with all the cop-loving psychopaths."

Burrows had a wicked grin on his face. "They'll shove it so far up your ass, Butch—you might even switch teams."

Morgan ignored Burrows and said to Jameson, "Then we have a deal?"

"We do, Captain."

"Before I go, I just want you to know something, off the record. Between you and me, Derrick *did* threaten Vicki and came at me. My actions were justifiable."

"I don't give a rat's ass," said Jameson. "I get credit for putting a hardened criminal back in jail, and a wayward cop off the force." Jameson pointed to an empty spot on the wall. "You're my next memento, Captain. I'll remember you when I win the governorship."

Morgan ignored Jameson's threat and left the antagonistic encounter without a snarky retort. He walked back to his pickup, drove a mile away from the county courthouse, pulled over, and unbuttoned his shirt.

"Cocksuckers," he said, peeling the wire from his chest.

The Cacodemons

The two couples exited the car and wended their way toward the trees. Chrissy repeatedly clicked on her flashlight and shined the light behind her.

Mike placed his hand on Chrissy's shoulder. "Will you just chill out? There's nothing to be afraid of."

"I don't feel safe in the woods."

"You'll be fine once we smoke a few doobs."

"Do you remember what happened here three years ago?" asked Chrissy.

"What happened?" asked Devin, sliding his hand in and out the back pocket of Blair's jeans.

"Before you moved here," said Mike, "this kid got murdered in the woods."

"*Murdered*?" said Chrissy. "He was mutilated. And that woman. They found her ripped open too."

"Ripped open?" said Devin, his eyes bigger than his lenses.

Blair pulled Devin's hand out of her pocket. "In the fall of 2013, a senior named Brian Delmore and this woman—don't remember her name—were found dead in the woods. They were slashed opened and had organs missing."

"Holy shit," said Devin. "Did they catch the guy?"

"No," said Chrissy.

Mike rolled his eyes. "That was three years ago, and nothing's happened since."

Devin took Blair's hand and asked her, "Are you OK with partying here?"

"Yeah, I don't think the killer's been sitting here for three years waiting for us."

Mike tapped Chrissy's shoulder. "See, why can't you be cool like her?"

"Why can't we just go behind the old barn, or under the bridge?" asked Chrissy.

"Because there's more chance of getting caught there," said Mike.

"He's right," said Devin. "I can't get busted for pot in my senior year. If I screw up getting into college my parents will kill me."

Mike turned to Chrissy. "The woods is our best option. No one goes in there anymore."

"Gee, I wonder why?" she said.

"Aw c'mon. You gonna ruin the whole night because of one freak event three years ago? We're already here." Mike motioned to the trail that led into the forest on the north shore of Crestwood Lake. "There's four of us, we got flashlights, I got a knife—nothing's gonna happen."

"Tell ya what," said Devin. "Let's go in the woods, smoke a few joints, and leave. We'll go hang out in my basement and order pizza."

Mike looked at Chrissy wide-eyed and said, "Cool?"

Chrissy nervously ran her fingers through her blonde highlights and droned, "All right."

It was after six o'clock and sunset was approaching. There was just enough light for the foursome to navigate what Crestwood Lake teens used to call the "party-path," now perversely dubbed the "psycho-path."

After trekking a half mile, the foursome came to a nine-foot-wide clearing, encircled with rocks for sitting. In the center was a smaller ring of rocks, the enclosure for years of substance-inspired campfires.

"Check it out," said Mike. "The last people left a bunch of firewood. Awesome, now we don't have to find any."

"You're going to make a fire?" asked Chrissy.

"Of course."

"But we're only staying long enough to smoke a few."

"Well go ahead and light up, I'll do this in the meantime."

As Devin lit a joint and passed it to the girls, Mike scooped up a batch of dried leaves and plopped them inside the stones. He added twigs and firewood, then lit the leaves with his matte-black Zippo.

"Gimmie some of that," said Mike, reaching for the joint from Chrissy. He took a deep hit, suppressed a cough, and passed it to Devin. By the time Mike exhaled, the kindling was ablaze. "C'mon, let's sit by the fire."

The three of them complied, although Chrissy did so warily. "Won't the fire make it easier for people to see us?"

"What people?" asked Mike.

"I don't know, whoever. And how are you going to put the fire out?"

"Devin and I will piss on it."

"Guys are so gross," said Blair, passing the joint to Chrissy.

Devin lit a second. "This is good shit."

Chrissy exhaled and restlessly looked over her shoulders.

"Will you chill out?" said Mike. "Don't have another wig-out on me."

"Another wig-out?" asked Devin.

"I didn't wig out!" said Chrissy.

"Couple months ago," said Mike, "we were getting stoned and Chrissy got all weird."

"I was having an anxiety attack."

"You were frigging paranoid. Every car that came by, you thought it was a cop."

"Sometimes that happens," croaked Blair, holding in the smoke.

Chrissy took a toke and handed it to Mike, who took a drag and passed it on to Devin.

Mike put his arm around Chrissy's diminutive waist and flicked her crotch with his fingertip. "How ya feeling now?" a mischievous glimmer in his eyes.

Chrissy smacked his hand. "Behave."

"He is behaving," said Blair. "He's behaving like he always does."

"You're up," said Devin to Mike.

Mike pulled out his cigarette pack and lit a third joint.

Blair was twirling her forefinger through a lock of her long auburn hair. "Put some more wood on the fire," she said to Devin.

Devin tossed a few more sticks, and a handful of leaves into the flames. The fire's glow enveloped the group, its radiance fading seamlessly into the night.

Halfway through the fourth joint Chrissy looked like she was watching the inside of her eyeballs.

Mike leaned over and said, "On a hot summer night, would you offer your throat to the wolf with the red roses?"

"Sure, baby."

Mike and Chrissy started making out.

Devin turned to Blair. "What's he talking about?"

"It's a line from a song."

"What song?"

Mike slipped away from Chrissy. "It's Meatloaf, man, from the 70s."

"How do you know it?" asked Devin.

"My step-dad plays it every time he gets high."

"This-is-really-good-shit," said Blair, melodically.

Devin took a toke, and said, "Here's a question. Suppose you could go back in time, let's say, one year ago when you were sixteen. Would there be two of you? Could you meet your sixteen-year-old self, or would you just go back to who you were then?"

"That depends," said Blair. "If you, and you alone went back, then yes, there would be two of you. But if the whole world went back, then yeah, you'd just be you, one year ago."

"Would you know you went back?" asked Devin. "Or, since you're going back to before you left for the past, would you just be who you were at that point—meaning—without knowledge of your future trip back in time?"

Mike and Chrissy looked like they just finished shopping at "Lobotomies R Us."

"Or," said Blair, glassy-eyed, "if you went back and there were two of you, how would you tell yourself who you are and what happened?"

Mike chuckled. "What if you had a sex change, then went back in time and hooked up with yourself?"

"Is that how you were born?" asked Blair.

"At least I came out of a person."

"Really? I heard some bird shit on a rock and the sun hatched you."

"Suck my dick."

"You're a degenerate," said Blair.

Mike lit a fifth joint, took a puff, and passed it to Chrissy.

"What was that?" said Chrissy.

"What was what?" asked Mike.

"That noise."

"What noise?" asked Devin.

Chrissy, still holding the joint, stared at the darkness over her left shoulder. "I thought I heard something."

102

"If you're not going to smoke that, you wanna pass it?" said Devin.

"Take another toke," said Mike.

Chrissy took a hit, passed it to Blair, and peered into the black. She exhaled and said, "I heard something move."

"You probably did," said Blair. "A raccoon, a 'possum, or some other nocturnal animal."

"Nocturnal?" said Chrissy.

"Animals that are only active at night," said Blair, shooting Devin a "what-a-dumbass" look.

Chrissy grabbed her flashlight, turned it on, and scanned the woods.

"Don't start!" said Mike, grabbing the flashlight and turning it off. "There's nothing out there but animals. We'll finish this joint and go."

"Maybe it wasn't an animal," said Devin.

"What do you mean?" said Chrissy, eyes enlarging.

"Maybe it was a cacodemon," he replied.

"A what?"

"A kak-uh-demon," enunciated Devin slowly.

"What the fuck's a cacodemon?" asked Mike.

Blair had a sly glint in her eye.

"It's a type of demon," said Devin, throwing a few more sticks on the fire. "An evil spirit with malevolent intentions." He passed the joint to Mike.

"Let's start walking back," said Chrissy. "We can finish that on the way."

"Hold up, babe," said Mike. "I wanna hear this shit. So what's the deal with these cacodemons?"

"They roam the Earth," said Devin, "causing evil, killing people and stuff."

"Some of them are forest dwellers," said Blair, focusing on Chrissy. "They even haunt Crestwood Lake."

"Are you serious?" asked Chrissy.

"C'mon," said Blair. "You've lived here your whole life. You've never heard the rumors about this place?"

"They're all bullshit," said Mike, adjusting his crotch.

"I haven't heard them," said Devin.

"That's 'cause you just moved here," said Mike.

Devin waited for Blair to explain.

"There are legends about witches and demons haunting Crestwood Lake since the colonial times. There's been a lot of bizarre deaths, and missing people."

"You mean other than the two you mentioned before?" said Devin, more intrigued than scared.

"Yeah. This doctor and his wife killed each other. Another guy got stabbed to death in his house. And there's people who were on, or around the lake, who went missing. They found one girl's body floating under a dock. And then there's the suicides: a teacher and a nun."

"And the guy who owned the liquor store," said Chrissy.

"Oh yeah," said Blair. "He threw himself in front of a train."

"And all of them were psychos," said Mike, "or victims of psychos—not ghosts and goblins." Mike spit and snorted.

"Let's get out of here," said Chrissy.

"I wouldn't dismiss the occult too quickly," said Blair. "My dad's friend works in the coroner's office, and I overheard them talking one night. He told my dad all kinds of weird shit. They still don't know what killed the people in the woods. And they've come across corpses in Crestwood Lake with satanic tattoos on them."

"Oh, well that confirms it," said Mike. "Some whacko drug-addict got a satanic tattoo. That *proves* Crestwood Lake is haunted."

"Can we go now?" demanded Chrissy.

Mike turned to Devin. "So how do you know about these—what'd you call them—cacodemons?"

"I found this cool book in an old, used-book store in New Hampshire where I used to live—it's like an encyclopedia of evil spirits. Cacodemons are these hideous monsters: claws and fangs and shit. Sometimes they work in packs, commanded by an archwitch."

"What's an *archwitch*?" asked Chrissy, her right thigh jiggling.

"It's a head witch, like the opposite of an archangel."

"So, they're like the worst?" asked Blair.

"Oh yeah," said Devin. "They're Satan's chief henchmen. Totally evil, the most powerful. An archwitch's gang of cacodemons will ambush people and slaughter them. Then they harvest their organs."

"That's enough!" said Chrissy jolting up. "Let's get out of here."

"Ooooooooooooh," bellowed Mike like a ghost, extending his arms toward Chrissy. "The cacodemons are coming."

"Stop it you asshole!"

"Ooooooooooooh," he said, standing up, curling his fingers to resemble claws.

Blood burst from Mike's mouth, as the demon's talons plunged into his back, clutching his spine. He tried to call out but choked on another surge of blood.

Chrissy screamed.

Devin gaped in shock.

The creature lifted Mike off the ground, reached around, and slashed open his torso from his sternum to his genitals.

Devin got up to run. Two black things materialized, snatched his arms, and pulled them from their sockets. He wailed like a banshee. Then they dismembered his legs.

A fourth demon grabbed Chrissy's head from behind and twisted it. She died facing it backwards.

The two demons that killed Devin lunged at Blair, shoving her onto her back, and holding her down. Chrissy's assailant slashed at Blair's torso, ripping open her clothes, but only scratching the skin.

"What are you doing?" cried Blair.

The demon straddled her legs, completely pinning her. Growling, he slowly scraped his claw across her breasts, pure evil raging from his bright red eyes.

"No! Stop!" Blair shouted. She tried to fight but was overpowered.

The four demons twitched their heads in the same direction. The entire forest became unnervingly silent.

A shadowy figure, clad in a black capuchin, flowed from the darkness. When it reached Blair's feet it stopped. Two hands, tipped by pointed, black fingernails, thrust back the cowl. Her plush, brown mane spread over her shoulders.

"Release her," Adriana commanded.

The demons withdrew.

Blair grabbed her severed blouse and covered her breasts.

Adriana extended an open hand.

Blair's body sprung up, throat-first, into Adriana's grip.

"You've done well my child, but now your time has come as well."

"What are you talking about? I brought them here as you asked."

"You have my gratitude. In exchange, your death will be swift." She tightened her clasp on Blair's throat.

106

"But you promised to spare my life," choked Blair.

"I am . . . I could have taken your soul."

Adriana's eyes burned yellow.

Blair's vertebrae crackled.

The Alliance

It was 6:20 a.m. and Morgan was in the bathroom when the phone rang. He heard Vicki stumble out of bed, sleepily say "Hello," and then approach.

Vicki knocked. "Baby, it's Gil. He says it's important."

"Goddammit! Always when I'm on the crapper. Tell 'im I'll call 'im back."

"He'll call ya back, he's in the can," said Vicki.

"Oh great," said Gil. "I'm going to hear about this all day."

Fifteen minutes later Morgan entered the kitchen.

Vicki embraced him, kissed his cheek and said, "Coffee's ready."

"Thanks, hon." Morgan filled a large mug and picked up the phone.

"Hey, Butch," said Gil.

"What?" snapped Morgan.

"Well good morning to you too." The icy silence told Gil that he had expended his sarcasm allowance. "Aaronson just called me."

"At six thirty in the morning?"

"He's in Italy—it's twelve thirty there. He's about to get on a flight. He wants to meet with us first thing tomorrow morning."

"Did you tell him about what's happening?"

"Yes, he knows. He says it's vital that we meet. Why don't we visit Father Sean today?"

"OK, but we gotta do it first thing this morning; I got shit to do. Ya know Sammy, at the garage?"

"Yeah," said Gil.

"He's been reported missing. I got a lead to follow up on."

"You think it's related to what's going on?"

"I don't know yet," said Morgan. "I'll pick you up after breakfast; be outside your house at eight."

"Right," said Gil.

"What's happening?" asked Vicki, as Morgan hung up the phone.

"You're calling in sick tomorrow. We're going to Cambridge."

Morgan pulled into Gil's driveway at 7:59 and blew the horn. He waited two more minutes and blew it again. Drumming the steering wheel with his fingertips, he debated getting out of his vehicle. Instead, he called Gil on his cell phone. No answer. A few minutes later Gil stepped out of his house and scooted in the passenger side.

"Why is it so fucking hard for you to be on time?"

"It's only a few minutes," said Gil.

"Then why didn't you start getting ready a few minutes earlier?"

"Because I love it when you yell at me." Gil massaged his chest. In a sexy voice he said, "It turns me on, big boy."

"Eat my ass," said Morgan.

"I can't, we're running late."

Morgan sneered.

Gil grinned.

Saint Matthew's Roman Catholic Church was small and austere, with an attached rectory. Aging and built of wood, Saint Matthew's frequently had something in need of repair. A fresh coat of white paint wouldn't have hurt either. But the diocese was always short on funds, and the pastor was always short on volunteers.

After Father Mark was killed by one of Van Haden's acolytes, Saint Matthew's had a succession of transient pastors. Two were reassigned for administrative reasons, but three had left under discreditable circumstances: one ran off with his paramour, a second was arrested for child pornography, and a third died of a questionable overdose.

Only Morgan and his confidants knew how Father Mark met his demise. The lack of a body spurred a bevy of rumors, the most popular being that he abandoned the priesthood for a woman.

Father Sean, the latest replacement, was an Irishman, with curly chestnut hair, brown eyes, and a boyish face. Like Father Mark, he hailed from Boston. He was only twenty-three years old, and fresh out of the seminary when the Bishop offered him his own parish, but in the boonies of northern Vermont. It was unusual to give a fledgling priest such responsibility, but the bishop was desperate, and Father Sean was eager.

Morgan and Gil had met Father Sean when he arrived three months ago, but hadn't seen him since. Neither were churchgoers, and Morgan saw no point in establishing a more meaningful relationship until the game of "musical pastors" had run its course.

Morgan parked on the side of the church, almost in the exact spot as that fateful night in 2013. Motionless, he squinted at the building.

"Getting the creeps?" asked Gil.

"Do you hear something?"

Gil poked his hearing aid. "No."

"Someone's yelling. C'mon." Morgan withdrew his .357 magnum, jumped out of the truck, and reached into his shirt pocket.

They sprinted toward the rectory. Now Gil could hear it: wails of pain. Morgan ran shoulder first into the door—a veritable explosion.

The witches snarled, yellow eyes glaring.

"Help me!" cried Father Sean, hanging from the ceiling by his bound wrists, bruised and bleeding.

Morgan bit the cork off the vial of holy water and tossed its contents at the male witch.

The warlock shrieked in agony.

The other witch launched herself through the window. Morgan fired but missed. She was gone.

The warlock decomposed, a decrescendo of screaks and whines, his body collapsing into a smoldering pile of ooze, exuding noxious, gray smoke.

"Any others?" asked Morgan.

"No," said Father Sean.

Morgan holstered his weapon, pulled out his knife, and cut the bindings from the priest's wrists.

Father Sean dropped to his feet, then collapsed into Gil's arms.

"Call an ambulance," said Morgan.

"No," said Father Sean. "I don't need it. I don't think anything's broken."

Morgan said to Gil, "Take care of him. I want to check the place out."

Gil wiped the blood off Father Sean's face. "You got any ice?"

Father Sean gawked at the warlock's remains. "What the hell were those things?"

"That's what we're here to see you about."

Morgan canvassed the rectory and the church, finding nothing. When he returned, Gil and Father Sean were sitting in the parlor sipping Irish whiskey.

Morgan snorted and shook his head.

"I don't usually imbibe," said Father Sean.

"You weren't the one I was scoffing at."

Gil made a "what's-your-problem" face.

"What were those things?" asked Father Sean.

"They were witches," said Morgan.

"Witches?" said Father Sean.

Morgan motioned to Gil to proceed.

Gil took a long swig of his drink. "Do you believe in the Devil, Father?"

"The Bible says there's one. I'm not sure if I actually believe in him. Many clergy assume the *Devil* is merely a metaphor for our sins."

"He exists," said Gil. "We've met him face to face."

Father Sean looked bewildered.

"There were real witches in Salem," said Gil. "People who actually traded their souls to the Devil. A subgroup of the Salem Puritans broke away and established their own colony here in Crestwood Lake."

"Yes," said Father Sean. "The lost colony of Scalford."

"They didn't die out," said Gil. "They were slaughtered by Satan's witches and demons in 1713. The area was left abandoned and basically uninhabited until the town of Crestwood Lake was formed in the early twentieth century. In 2013, on the three hundredth anniversary of the destruction of Scalford, a renewed coven attempted to reestablish a foothold in Crestwood Lake. Many people were killed, some of them eviscerated, their organs removed for the coven's rituals. A few were driven to suicide. And some of them joined the Devil and became witches. Butch and I stopped them."

"How?"

"The souls of any particular coven are kept in a receptacle by Satan. Destroying the vessel and releasing the souls on hallowed ground allows the repentant among them to be freed. *If they are penitent*, the witches are reverted to normal humans. Demons, who are dead witches, are returned to heaven. The unrepentant, be them witch or demon, are banished directly to hell and thus, excised from the earth."

"Only we ain't gonna be able to do that this time," said Morgan.

"Why?"

"Last time," said Gil, "the Devil, under the guise of a merchant named Luther Van Haden, opened a wine store in Crestwood Lake. In his shop was a large, unique bottle of wine that contained the coven's souls. We were able to break it open on Saint Matthew's altar."

"But now," said Morgan, "we know who Van Haden is and how he operates. Before, he could be a brazen son of a bitch. Now he has to work on the sly. He ain't gonna make the same mistakes twice."

Father Sean finished his whiskey, still a little dazed. "What did you throw on that witch?"

"Holy water," said Morgan. "The last vial I had."

"That's part of why we're here," said Gil. "To get you to bless more."

"And that's the only way to kill a witch?"

"No," said Morgan. "Holy water is the only thing that kills them permanently. Any other death and they'll return as a demon."

"A demon?"

"Yeah," said Morgan. "They can be killed by holy water *or* fire."

"Demons actually exist?" asked Father Sean.

"Yes," said Gil. "Horrible monsters with even more powers than witches. They can't cloak themselves as humans."

"Unlike witches?"

"Yes," said Gil. "Witches are still human. You wouldn't be able to tell, unless they reveal themselves to you."

"What happened here today, Father?" asked Morgan.

"My bell rang. This couple . . . Robin and Zach, I didn't catch the last name, they wanted to discuss pre-marital counseling. I let them in and they assaulted me. They were looking for something. Tied me up and threatened to kill me if I didn't tell them where."

"Where *what* was?" asked Morgan.

"Some kind of objects, not people. They didn't say what, but insisted I knew."

"Think, Father," said Gil. "Do you have even the slightest idea? It could be crucial."

"I honestly don't know. They kept hitting me. Then, as they became angered, their eyes turned yellow. It was terrifying. I thought for sure they'd kill me."

"They would have," said Morgan, "if we didn't show up."

Father Sean removed the ice pack from the side of his face.

"You sure you don't want a doctor?" asked Morgan.

"I'll be OK. Why did they think I knew what they were looking for?"

"Because this is where we stopped them last time," said Gil. "The priest at that time, Father Mark, joined forces with Butch and me. They assumed you'd be involved."

"What happened to Father Mark?" asked Father Sean.

Gil glanced at Morgan and said, "He was beheaded by one of the witches."

Father Sean poured himself another whiskey.

"Listen, Father," said Morgan. "Tomorrow we're going to Cambridge to see Professor Doug Aaronson." Morgan turned to Gil, "Tell him who he is."

"He's a professor at Boston University. He specializes in parapsychology and the history of the occult. Aaronson's the foremost authority on Crestwood Lake and its haunted past. He helped us the last time."

"I think you should come with us," said Morgan.

"I know this is a lot to take in," said Gil, "but we need all the help we can get, especially spiritual help. The Devil's back, and we're sure he wants to reclaim his territory."

114

Morgan leaned closer to Father Sean. "I destroyed the bottle of souls on the altar of *your* church, with the entire goddamn coven inside. The Devil was standing in *your* pulpit."

"All right," said Father Sean, sitting up straight. "I'll go to hell myself, before I let Lucifer take over my church."

Gil refilled his glass and held it up. "That's the spirit."

They clinked their glasses and drank.

Morgan retrieved a bag of containers and vials from his pickup. They filled them with water, which Father Sean sanctified.

"So, this will kill anyone with the Devil?" asked Father Sean.

"No," said Morgan. "Only witches and demons."

"A witch," said Gil, "has bartered his or her soul to the Devil, in exchange for supernatural powers. But there are people working for Lucifer who haven't sold their soul, at least not yet. Holy water does nothing to them. They're still regular humans, so don't confide in anyone. You don't know who's who."

"They don't teach you this shit in priest school, huh?" said Morgan.

"No," said Father Sean, squinting at him. "Did your mother ever wash your mouth out with soap?"

"Yeah," said Morgan. "It didn't do any fucking good."

The Chronicle

My name is Carolyn Pentlock, and I enjoy watching people suffer. Nobody from this worthless realm—the Earthly one—has ever done anything for me. People only care about themselves, and when they do intercede on your behalf, it's inevitably because it serves them. This is exquisitely true for family members. Oh, they'll profess their devotion, always in the name of that noblest of motives: love—but this is willful deceit. Virtue is merely the Devil's Sunday clothes.

I was born in 1888 in Danville, Pennsylvania, a sleepy hamlet on the Susquehanna River. I was the last born of four, and the only girl. Danville was home to several iron mills, the chief employers in the region. Most of the men not working in the mills were farmers. Danville's population peaked at just over eight thousand in my birth year, and then declined during the early twentieth century as the iron industry shriveled.

My father wasn't an iron employee or a farmer. He was a custodian at Danville State Hospital, a state-run institution for the mentally ill that had opened in 1869. Most of his peers were envious, as his toil paled to that of a farm or factory worker. My father certainly didn't feel privileged, as his earnings were less than his back-breaking counterparts.

We lived in perpetual penury. With six mouths to feed, we were lucky to receive two meals a day, the second often never more than broth and bread. Our clothes were hand-me-downs, birthday presents were unheard of, and death had to be looming for a doctor visit.

When my mother wasn't mired in domestic servitude, she sporadically worked as a charwoman, to which my father took umbrage. He asserted that "her place was in the home." And while that now-sexist belief was the norm in the nineteenth century, the real reason for his rebuke was his ego. It irked him that he couldn't provide for his family—not enough to apply for a better job at the mills, mind you—but enough to displace his indolent self-loathing onto everyone else. One day my uncle called my father a "slack-ass." My father responded by relieving him of his two front teeth. From that day on, the aspersions kept flying, only behind my father's back.

My father was a mercurial disciplinarian. At times, true to his listless nature, he would ignore my brothers' roughhousing. But if he were in a mood, or had been drinking—watch out. Sometimes he'd line my brothers up naked, on their hands and knees, and thrash their behinds with his belt till they bled.

He rarely struck me. He didn't believe little girls should be hit. Instead, the gallant bastard would break one of my toys. I'll never forget the day he pulled my pink teddy bear's arms off. That wounded me more than his belt ever could.

Throughout my childhood, my brothers tortured me mercilessly. Children are inherently sadistic, and when left to their own devices, their base inhumanity blossoms into sheer cruelty. Early on, my siblings' pestering amounted to name-calling, hiding my things, and pelting me with snowballs. As they entered adolescence however, their abusiveness took a darker turn.

Their language toward me became more hostile, and laden with sexual overtones or vulgarities. They relished pulling up my skirt in public. Sometimes this was augmented by pulling my panties down. My middle brother liked to sneak up behind me, dirty underwear in hand, and force the crotch of his briefs over my face. All three of them thought nothing of barging in on me in my bedroom, or worse yet, the bathroom.

And where were my parents through all of this? My mother was frail and small-boned, the perfect shell for her weak-willed and ineffectual constitution. She suffered from episodes of depression, but even between her megrims, she was melancholic and languid. Moreover, she was afraid of my father, and eventually, my brothers. When she did muster the strength to scold them, she was disregarded, or hectored into submission. Appealing to her usually generated excuses for my brothers' behaviors, excuses packaged in honorable motives, such as, "They care about you, dear . . . that's just the way boys show it." I found crying into my pillow at night to be more comforting than beseeching her.

As for my father, my brothers' terrorizing of me never caused him to react. I suffered in silence: my father ignoring it, and my mother whitewashing it.

Eventually however, my father became my defender—as long as I became his paramour. It began when I was twelve. If my brothers harassed me, my father would step in—the only time they would back off. Then he would plop me onto his lap—directly onto the center of his lap—and hug me, kiss

117

me, and rub my thighs. At first, it felt safe and wonderful. Someone was protecting me from my tormentors, and lavishing me with displays of affection. But over time, as his hands rubbed further up my thighs, and more of his kisses found my mouth, a sickening sense of violation comingled with the comfort. What a strange and confusing mix of feelings.

Around this time my mother had taken to drinking. The escalation of her intemperance and my father's lechery seemed to coincide. My father drank irregularly, but like his temper, when he indulged he would go to extremes. One night when I was fourteen, he came home very drunk. My mother, besotted herself, was passed out on the couch. I was in the upstairs bathroom taking a bath. My brothers were banging on the door, taunting me with obscenities. My father went berserk. He assaulted my brothers, punching them, until they ran out of the house. My mother, unconscious downstairs, never awoke.

After my brothers escaped, my father returned to the bathroom, gently asking me to open the door. I slipped out of the tub and put on my robe. My father hugged me and asked if I was all right. I said yes, but then he undid my robe, buried his mouth in my neck, and squeezed my buttocks. I squealed.

"Be my little baby," he whispered.

"No!" I yelled, pushing him away.

He stumbled back and tripped into the tub. "You little bitch!" he hollered, arms flailing, water splashing.

I tore into the hallway, half-crazed, trying to think. I heard him sloshing to his feet. My bedroom was the closest refuge. I ran into it, slamming and locking the door behind me. I frantically scanned the room. My window. Could I get out through there? From the second story?

My father pounded on the door. "You open this door right now or you'll get the beating of your life!"

I sprang to the window and unlocked it, but it was stuck.

As I pulled on it my father threw himself against the door, cracking the wood around the latch. "Open up now!"

118

I pushed back against the door to no avail. He lunged again, cracking the wood further. One more shove and he'd be in. I turned to run back to the window and gasped . . .

"Don't be alarmed," he said. "I'm here to help you."

I gawked: a tall, elderly gentleman, clad in a black suit, with a bright red tie and pocket handkerchief, and profoundly deep-brown eyes.

"I will not let him hurt you, Carolyn."

"Who . . . who . . .?"

"Relax," he said, holding up one palm. "I wish to save you from this madness."

I turned toward the door. The hallway was silent, as if time had stopped. I snapped my head back. "Who are you?"

"I am Luther Van Haden," he said, as if proclaiming something magnificent.

"How did you get in here?"

"How I arrived is not significant. What I can do for you *is*. I can ensure that your father, and your brothers for that matter, will never harm you again. Would you like that?"

"But who are you? What do you want?"

His eyes narrowed. "I want to protect you."

"Why?"

"Because I want you to join *my* family. We do not take advantage of each other. You will be loved. You will be safe." He extended his hand. "Will you join me?"

"What are you going to do?"

"*I'm* not going to do anything." A revolver appeared in his hand. "You are."

My heart thumped. I looked at the bedroom door again, then back at him.

"I cannot kill your father. I can only help you to save yourself." Still offering the gun, he placed his other hand on my shoulder.

A strange, but wondrous sensation rushed over me. My fear subsided, my heartbeat waned, I felt calm . . . confident . . . vitalized!

"Take the weapon and join me."

I stared at the gun, then into his eyes. I wanted to keep feeling the way I did.

There was a pound against the door. "Open up you bitch!"

"It's now or never," he said.

I took the gun.

He vanished.

The door burst open.

I fired . . .

~~~~~~

My mother and I were both sent to institutions. I went to a reformatory and she, having had a complete breakdown, went to the asylum where my father had worked. One month later she hanged herself there. My three brothers were unloaded to various relatives.

My oldest brother, after a distinguished criminal career, was found guilty of murder and executed. My second (the worst of the three toward me), became a corrupt politician. Despite his unscrupulousness—or maybe because of it—he was successful for a time. While vying for the governorship, he was arrested for sexually abusing a twelve-year-old girl. I like to think that the last thing that went through his mind, before his own bullet, was remorse for how he treated me. My youngest brother dropped out of high school and joined the army. He died at the Second Battle of the Marne in July 1918.

120

Thanks to my new Master, I wasn't at the reformatory long. He had powerful associates everywhere, and they finagled the system to discharge me to the care of my new "mother," Darlene Thorn. She had been with the coven since the Great Chicago Fire of 1871. I assure you, it was not caused by Mrs. O'Leary's cow.

Darlene was more than a mother to me. She became my closest friend and mentor. She groomed me for witchhood, teaching me everything I needed to know about the dark forces.

Witches' powers vary greatly. Each individual's necromancy is a function of our Master's overall plan, and his specific needs at the time of our metempsychosis, i.e., the transfer of our soul to him, or what we call, our rebirth. None of us, not even our Master, can read the minds of others, mortal or not. However, I was awarded an uncanny ability for sensing others' emotions and weaknesses. It rendered me the perfect psychological predator.

In addition to the powers our Master bestows upon us, a variety of additional gifts may be bargained for in exchange for our souls. My personal desire was to always be beautiful, a somewhat moot request, as witches are virtually immortal, and retain their appearance from the day of their rebirth. I say "virtually" immortal, because aside from holy water, only our Master can *permanently* terminate a witch's life. Allow me to explain further.

There are primordial, immutable laws to Earth's realms that transcend time, and supersede the powers of all of its inhabitants, be they mortal or mystical. For all his might, our Master can only terminate those who have relinquished their souls, namely witches and demons. He cannot directly take the lives of mortals; he can only eliminate them via his agents. Hence, one of his primary motivations for recruiting covens of inductees.

Immortality and supernatural capabilities are the most cherished gifts, and therefore, come at a high cost. The benefactor is indentured to serve our Master for their entire existence. Should one fail in his or her duties—or worse yet—turn against him, their soul in his possession can be obliterated, normally after suffering mercilessly first.

Returning to my blossoming into witchhood—my Master insisted that I receive higher education. "One cannot control this world without knowing it," he would say. My Master facilitated my entrance into Pembroke, the women's college of Brown University, and enjoined me to focus my studies on history, the antiquities, political science, theology and psychology.

121

Despite my academic burdens, I always made time for predation. Social events, such as cotillions, enabled us to fraternize with the male students of Brown. These were the proving grounds where I honed my skills of luring gullible men into misfortune, and sometimes worse.

I now had the power. I was no longer that frightened little girl, victimized by my older brothers and father. I was a beautiful young woman: petite, shapely, with delicate features, dark eyes, and long dirty-blonde hair that I wore in a chignon. Only now my femininity housed a vengeful bloodlust, empowered by the mettle of the Antichrist. I was the consummate femme fatale.

Underneath their physicality and bravado, men are all pathetic little dupes. Even the strongest is no match for a charming seductress, stroking his ego, dangling the prospect of unbridled passion. I had three or four of them in limbo at any one time. I dated each one intermittently: just enough to keep his desires burning, yet far from satisfied. If we bumped into his friends I fawned and doted upon him, bolstering his pride upon the shores of their jealousy. I wore perfectly-tailored dresses, laughed at their jokes, and always—always—agreed with them. I hinted at pleasures to come, teased them coquettishly, and allowed them to feverishly kiss me before concluding the night. I found it titillating to imagine them masturbating about me afterwards. And if one started losing patience with my delaying the ultimate prize, then I made sure he saw me in the company of one of his rivals. And they say women are jealous? Ha! Nothing brings a man back into the game like the fear of someone else winning it. I spurred numerous fights between competing suitors. It enlivened me to watch them beat each other bloody for a woman they could never win. What a wonderous tableau. So deeply gratifying.

I told them all that I would not surrender my virginity until I had a ring on my finger. (I of course, was not a virgin. I had fornicated innumerable times with my Master and other members of the coven.) Nevertheless, I convinced them that an engagement band bought them exclusive rights to my garden of delight. That's when I went in for the kill.

I timed it just right to have Clark walk in as I orally satisfied Terrance. Clark went to prison for attempted murder, while Terrance was left with permanent injuries.

I maneuvered Samuel into leaving his fiancée and giving me her ring, only to tell him I was pregnant by another man and breaking it off. Two weeks later he shot himself.

Bret bought me a whole new wardrobe before I falsified information that he was cheating on his exams. He got expelled.

Alfred went as far as to put me in his will to prove his love for me. What chumps! Men will do even more for the promise of sex, than the actual sex itself. I planted evidence, inculpating him, inside the bedroom of a thirteen-year-old girl who had been inexplicably raped. Alfred's corpse was found on the bank of the Providence River. The girl's brothers were suspected but never charged. Yes, college was a glorious time. In addition to my treacherous successes, I amassed quite an impressive diamond collection. How wonderfully evil!

I finished my master's degree in 1913. I was done trifling with love-struck college boys. It was time for bigger game. In October of that year, I was called to Crestwood Lake for the bicentennial celebration of the coven's destruction of Scalford, Crestwood's predecessor. In 1713, after years of bewitching Scalford, the coven burned the colony to the ground. All of the remaining colonists were killed or inducted. The decimated settlement lay dormant for nearly two hundred years until Crestwood Lake was founded.

We held our ceremony in the woods surrounding the lake, presided over of course, by our Master. Three dozen witches and demons attended, including the legendary and reclusive archwitch, Adriana Barberi. In some ways, she was even more imposing than our Master.

We chanted, sang hymns in his honor, and listened to his riveting sermons about spirituality and the conquest of this world. Then we gathered around our bonfire, with the slaughtered remains of various animals and people, consumed their organs, and burned their carcasses in the flames. Our rituals conclude with the conferring of additional powers upon members eligible for necromantical elevation.

My Master, overjoyed with my development thus far, and sensing my readiness, awarded me a very special power: *usurpation*, the ability to assume the body of others. Usurpation is normally performed after a witch kills her victim. But a witch could certainly possess the person while they are still alive. Once the merger is complete however, should the subject die, only one soul can remain. The witch can remain in the deceased—the person appearing alive and normal—but possessed. Once the witch vacates the body, it would return to death. Or—and I can't imagine why—the witch could restore the subject's life, at the cost of her own.

With my latest weapon at my disposal, my Master presented me with a new challenge. My mission: inject myself into international affairs to prolong the first world war. My target: Margaretha Zelle. I was to become Mata Hari.

Margaretha Zelle was born in the Netherlands in 1876. By the time she was a teenager, her life was in shambles from her father's bankruptcy, parents' divorce, and mother's death. Sent to live with her godfather, she was sexually molested by a teacher. At eighteen she married a physically abusive, unfaithful, alcoholic army captain. He gave Margaretha syphilis, which was transmitted to her children, killing her son at age two, and her daughter at age twenty-one.

In 1903 she left her husband (who never paid her alimony and kidnapped their daughter), and began her descent into debauchery. She moved to Paris, rebranded herself Mata Hari, and became an exotic dancer, pushing conventional limits. Her act culminated in a progressive shedding of her clothing until she was clad in only a bra and jewels. She was hailed for her intriguing beauty, graceful dancing, and wild spirit. Openly promiscuous, she captivated audiences, especially the opposite sex. She mingled in wealthy circles and attracted powerful men on both sides of the impending world conflict. That's where I came in.

I poisoned Margaretha in January 1914 in her apartment in Paris. I spent the next two years hedonistically exploiting her career and wanton escapades. I had a marvelous time, luring sundry men into my bed. Those with power or important connections, who could fulfill my ultimate goal, were spared from any immediate consequences. Those without influence, the "toys amongst the big boys," as I called them, were nothing more than fresh game. I sated my sexual cravings, basked in their admiration, and then raped their world. Bank accounts, marriages, reputations, and quite often, lives were lost.

In 1916 I began a torrid affair with Captain Vadim Maslov, a Russian pilot working for the French. He had ties to prominent officials in his government's upper echelon. I actually fancied him, one of the extremely few whom I had any affection for. Thus, once I had milked him for his contacts, I spared his life, blinding him instead of killing him, yet still rendering him feckless.

Through Maslov, I colluded with the intelligence services of the French and the Germans. Be it with my body, brain, or magic, I wheedled my way into their confidence, influencing them to enlist me for their purposes. They expected me to use my notoriety and wiles to glean vital information from their adversaries, and I did—for both sides.

I slept with generals, politicians, and spies. It was almost like college. One general wanted to leave his wife for me—buying me expensive jewelry and clothes. It doesn't matter if they're a bed-wetting teenager or a seasoned military commander. When it comes to women, they're all the same. The mature ones however, in addition to women and sex, also vie for money and power. They engage in magnificent schemes, political ploys, and even wars, to control the world. I do it by simply lying on my back.

For three years I manipulated the French and German governments, alternating the dissemination of secrets in a see-saw fashion, so neither side could fully grasp the upper hand. But even the obtuse dogs of war eventually caught on. One German spy in Madrid suspected I was a double agent. He sent a message to Berlin about me, in a code he knew the allies had already cracked. When the French intercepted the message, the game was over.

In 1917 I was arrested, tried, and sentenced to death. Even as I awaited execution, a gooey-eyed French attaché with whom I had a dalliance, was lobbying for my release. So pitiful. I watched him cry as I stood before the firing squad sans blindfold. I vacated Margaretha's body before the shots were fired, or else I would have been transformed into a demon. That may be my Master's intent someday, but for the present, he basked in the untold number of war causalities achieved from the perpetuated conflict.

My modus operandi was resoundingly established: I would zero in on a troubled, corrupt, or psychologically compromised woman, kill her, assume her body, and spin my web. Over the years I have had many identities. As Eva Braun (Hitler's mistress), I prolonged World War II; as Madame Nhu (de facto first Lady of Vietnam), I instigated the Vietnam War; and as serial killer Aileen Wuornos, I shot seven men while working as a prostitute (seven that they know about).

My powers were also intensifying. The longer a witch lives, the stronger he or she becomes. There is a gradual accumulation of spiritual energy, but also supplemental abilities awarded for successful performance.

Because of my accomplishments, my Master summoned me back to Crestwood Lake in 2016 for a mission of utmost importance: the demise of Captain Butch Morgan. In 2013 Morgan annihilated our coven. It has been an arduous task, discreetly restoring it to its former glory. My Master intends on retaking Crestwood Lake, obliterating it if necessary. Crestwood Lake is a nexus of evil in this Earthly domain and strategically important for the conquest of this realm.

One day I came across this mechanic—Sammy I think his name was. I offered him sexual favors in exchange for marijuana. After I clawed off his manhood, I killed him and dragged his body into the woods. His organs were used in one of our ceremonies. There must have been an eyewitness, because I received a visit from the captain. Just as well. I like to study my prey before making my move.

I was working in a spa owned by a Chinese woman named Mia, that offered special massages for its male clients. I was merely a plant, using the position to eavesdrop on Crestwood Lake, gather information, and wreck an occasional marriage or two. Every mission has its perks.

I had just opened the shop one morning and was making coffee. It was Mia's day off and my first appointment wasn't for a half hour. That's when the Marlboro Man strode in.

"Can I help you?" I asked.

He looked me up and down before saying a word. But he didn't eyeball me as most men do: like a famished dog ogling a piece of meat. Instead, his eyes icily streamed over my dainty frame, clad in my usual short skirt, nylons and pumps.

"Are you Carolyn Pentlock?"

"Yes."

"I'm Captain Butch Morgan of the Crestwood Lake Police. Is that your yellow Porsche in the parking lot?"

"Yes. Why?"

"Where were you Sunday, September fourth?"

"I don't know—"

"The Sunday of Labor Day weekend."

"I must have been home."

"No, you weren't. Where did you go?"

"If it was a Sunday, I was home. We're closed on Sundays. Maybe I ran an errand or two, I don't remember."

"I got a witness who does remember. She remembers a bright yellow Porsche parked outside Sammy's Garage that day. Sammy, the owner, appears to be missing."

"I wouldn't know anything about that."

"Well excuse me, Ms. Pentlock, but I think you're full of shit."

I didn't know what to say. I wasn't used to dealing with men like this. My instinct was to schmooze him, maybe even offer him a service, but that clearly wasn't going to work.

"Do you know how many yellow Porsches there are in Crestwood Lake, Ms. Pentlock?"

"No, I don't."

"Just yours. Now do you want to rethink your answer before things get worse?"

"Captain, I don't know this person or this garage. I'm new to Crestwood Lake. Perhaps your witness is mistaken."

"Why are you here?"

"What kind of question is that?"

"Why are you here? Crestwood Lake ain't the kind of place people move to."

"Uh . . . I broke up with my boyfriend and moved out."

127

"From where?"

"What?"

"Stop stalling and give me a straight answer. From where?"

"Burlington."

"What's your boyfriend's name?"

"Uh, Jimmy Gertz."

"What was your address in Burlington?"

"Uh, fourteen Maple Street."

"You got any ID?"

I handed the captain my driver's license.

He scribbled down the information on a pad. "What do you do here, Ms. Pentlock?"

"Manicures, pedicures—"

"Massages and hand jobs?"

"Who the hell do you think you are?"

"Your license is a fake." Morgan reached into his shirt pocket. "Sorry, but I have to do this . . ."

I saw the tip of the water vial when the radio on his hip crackled: "Butch, it's Edwards, it's urgent!"

The captain glanced at the radio.

"Butch, answer the goddamned radio, your house is on fire!"

The captain grabbed the radio and snapped "What?"

"We just got a call from your neighbor; your house is on fire. I got units on the way."

The captain exclaimed "Vicki!" Then he pointed at me and said, "I'm not finished with you," and ran out of the building. I've never seen a pickup truck move so fast.

Van Haden placed his hand on my shoulder. "I thought you could use some help, dear. Probably wasn't necessary, but you never know. You know what you must do now?"

"Yes, I do."

Morgan was doing eighty miles per hour on the single-lane, gravel road that led to his house. He pulled out his cell phone and called Vicki.

"Hey, baby," she said.

"Are you OK?"

"I'm fine, why?"

"Are you home?"

"Yes."

"The house is OK?"

"Yeah, everything's fine. What's wrong?" Morgan could hear the dread in her voice.

"I just got a call from the station saying our house is on fire."

"Everything's fine. What's happening?"

"Get out of the house. Go to Gil's, or the station. Just get out of there."

"What's going on?" her voice rising.

"I don't have time to explain." Morgan slammed the brakes and spun his truck around. "I'll call you back in a little while."

Carolyn was racing toward Morgan. So were her thoughts:

129

If my Master was right, and he usually was, the captain would be headed right back. On my passenger seat lay a sawed-off shotgun. The captain couldn't get within splashing distance of me before I fired. And, he couldn't match the speed of a 128-year-old witch. After I shot him, I would kill his wife.

I careened around a curve. In the distance I saw a figure standing in the middle of the road. A red figure. It was a woman. A woman with long brown hair in a red robe. Was it one of us? She just stood there and stared. I accelerated.

I was about one hundred feet away when she raised her hand. The car completely died, coming to a stop, faster and smoother than if I had applied the brakes. I grabbed the gun and marched toward her. I fired. Her hand still raised, she stopped the projectiles. They fell to the ground like raindrops.

"Who the hell are you?" I growled.

I darted to the side, faster than any mortal could move, but she shoved me onto my back, strangling my throat, strong, and determined. Her brilliant hazel eyes punctured me. I was stupefied. *What* was she?

"I don't know what you are, but my Master will kill you," I half growled, half choked. I unleashed my talons, swiping at her as hard as I could.

"Your father didn't act alone," she said, unrelenting in her grip.

"What?"

"Don't you know how Lucifer works?"

"What do you mean?"

"You fool," she said, withdrawing a small glass bottle from underneath her robe, holding it over me.

"No!"

The bottle burst, spraying its contents upon me—a fulmination of smoke and steam and searing pain! My flesh was boiling—

Gravel shot out of the back of Morgan's furiously spinning tires. He undid his seatbelt and cocked his .357. He saw the yellow Porsche in the

130

distance, idle, driver-side door open, no one in sight. Morgan hit the brakes and jumped out, vial in his left hand, magnum in his right. He scanned the area, then slowly approached the car.

On the ground was a smoldering silhouette.

The Professor

Morgan's dark-blue Chevy Silverado barreled south on Interstate 93, bound for Cambridge, Vicki at his side, Gil and Father Sean in the back. Morgan had just finished telling the men about the previous day's events.

"My God," said Gil. "Who the hell else is running around Crestwood Lake with holy water, killing witches?"

"That's what I'd like to know," said Morgan.

"Vicki, you got any ideas?" asked Gil.

"It could be anyone. When I was in the coven, Van Haden always warned us that our enemies were everywhere."

"You were in the coven?" asked Father Sean.

Vicki exhaled heavily, a slight gloss to her eyes. "Yes."

A long silence followed. Vicki could feel Father Sean's questions. She turned and faced him. "My ex-husband beat me for years until Butch arrested him. He went to prison, but I was a mess. Couldn't sleep—had nightmares when I did—always on edge. At my lowest point, Van Haden came to me, promising to relieve my suffering. That's how he works: entices you when you're most vulnerable. Sometimes he's the cause of that vulnerability. Anyway, all I saw was a way out. I didn't consider the evil I would eventually be a part of. I just wanted my pain to end. I ended up in even more pain from the guilt."

Morgan reached over and held Vicki's hand.

"When Butch and me destroyed the bottle of souls," said Gil, "Vicki's soul was freed. But we lost Father Mark and Cassandra, a white witch."

"A *white* witch?" said Father Sean.

"A witch who uses his or her supernatural abilities for the good of mankind," said Gil.

"I've never heard of anything like this. How does one even become a white witch?"

"We don't know exactly," said Gil.

"We were too busy trying to stop Van Jerk-off," said Morgan. "Didn't exactly have time for a history lesson."

Father Sean stared off to the side.

Morgan looked at him through the rear-view mirror. "You still got the guts to handle all this shit, Father?"

"Yes . . . I'm just trying to take it all in."

"We should probably tell him about Derrick," said Gil.

"Who's Derrick?" asked Father Sean.

"Vicki's ex-husband."

"Derrick got out of prison," said Morgan. "Came to Toby's where Vicki works and started harassing her. I beat the piss out of him. Now he's pressing charges, and the mayor and county prosecutor are trying to railroad me."

"Are they with Lucifer?" asked Father Sean.

"Could be," said Morgan. "Hard to tell a regular asshole from an asshole working for the Devil." Morgan squeezed Vicki's knee. "You sure you're OK, hon?"

"I'm all right, baby."

"Father," said Morgan, "you ever been to that new book store in town, The Good Book?"

"No, I haven't."

"Ever meet the owner? His name's Guerin. Scott Guerin."

"No, why?"

"Just curious. I'd bet my balls there's something up with him."

Morgan's cell phone rang. It was the station. He pressed the Bluetooth button on the dashboard and said, "Hello."

"Butch, it's Carl. We got four missing teenagers. Their parents just came in and reported it."

"Which teens?"

"Blair Underhill, Mike Kachinsky, Devin O'Connor, and Chrissy Truax. All seniors at the high school. Do you know them?"

"Don't know the kids, but I know a couple of the families. How long they been missing? Where were they last seen?"

"They were together yesterday. Kachinsky's brother told us they were headed to the woods, the usual trail on the north side. None of them came home last night."

"All right, you know what to do. Get the dogs, organize a search party, and comb the woods. Tell the state boys too. We could use the extra men. I'll be gone all day so keep me informed."

"OK, Butch."

Morgan hung up and punched the steering wheel. "Goddammit."

Vicki's eyes swelled with tears.

"Maybe they just took off somewhere," said Father Sean.

"Unlikely," said Gil. "Like we told you, the coven kills people and uses their organs in their rituals. This is the same thing that happened in 2013. People would start disappearing."

"We found three mutilated corpses in the woods last time," said Morgan.

"And earlier this month," said Gil, "we found my neighbor dead with missing organs."

"Holy Mother of God," said Father Sean.

It was just before noon, as the group concluded their three-hour trip in the cobblestone driveway of Douglas Aaronson's palatial Victorian home.

Father Sean gazed upward, beholding the building like a country boy in the big city for the first time. "All this from being a professor?"

"He's a silver-spooner," said Morgan.

Gil leaned toward Father Sean. "Butch has a bee in his bonnet about wealth."

"I don't have a *bee* in my *bonnet*," said Morgan.

"You're right, it's more like a bug up your ass."

"My foot's gonna be up *your* ass in about three seconds."

"It is easier for a camel to go through the eye of a needle," said Father Sean, "than for a rich man to enter into the kingdom of God. Matthew 19:24."

"There ya go," said Morgan.

"Yeah, right," said Gil. "Your issue with wealth is due to *religion*. How about we just call you Father Butch."

"I could've been *your* father—but the dog beat me over the fence."

"Troglodyte."

"Douchebag."

"All right, boys," said Vicki. "How about we just focus on why we're here."

The group exited the car and approached the house. In the doorway stood Aaronson, attired in an olive-green tweed jacket, button-down shirt, and wool pants. His neatly coiffed brown hair extended halfway down his neck. A pair of frameless designer eyeglasses shielded his warm brown eyes. "Welcome, everybody."

"Hi, Doug," said Gil. "It's so good to see you."

"Indeed. Hello, Vicki."

"How are you?" she replied.

"I'm fine. And of course, it's always a pleasure, Captain."

"Professor," said Morgan shaking his hand. "Still got the girly hairdo, huh?"

Aaronson smiled widely. "It's comforting to know there are a few constants in this ever-changing universe." Aaronson turned and said, "And you must be Father Sean."

"I am."

"Gil told me you'd be coming. Welcome. Come on, let's go inside. I've prepared us some lunch."

Aaronson led the group into his smaller dining room; it was only a thousand square feet. In the middle of the room, upon the hardwood floor, stood an eight-foot, teak dining table sporting numerous platters. The offerings included a panoply of tea sandwiches, smoked salmon, tomato and arugula salad, pâté, crudités, crostini, and a selection of cheeses. Decanters of red and white Burgundy complemented the food.

As the group took their seats, Aaronson reached into an ice bucket and retrieved a can of beer. "Captain, I have this for you, unless you would prefer your usual bourbon?"

"The beer will be just fine, thanks."

"Where's your housekeeper?" asked Gil. "Mrs. Clarkson, right?"

"Mildred's in Kent, visiting her family." Aaronson held out his hands. "Please, help yourselves."

"What a beautiful spread," said Vicki. "So gracious of you."

"It is my pleasure. I just wish we were here under better circumstances."

"What's that?" said Morgan pointing at the pâté.

"Foie gras, Captain."

"Frog what?"

Gil rolled his eyes.

136

"Foie gras," said Aaronson slowly. "Goose liver from France."

Morgan grimaced and pointed at the sandwiches. "Anything weird in these?"

Aaronson chuckled. "No. Those are tuna, ham salad, cucumber and basil, and these, especially for you, Captain, are roast beef with a horseradish mayonnaise."

"I appreciate it, Professor."

"Pearls before swine," said Gil.

Morgan gave Gil the finger, then popped open his beer.

Aaronson waited for everyone to fill their plates and glasses. Then he took note of Father Sean's bruises. "Gil told me about your run-in with the witches."

"I owe my life to the captain and Gil. They said you might know what they were looking for."

"I know exactly what they were looking for. That's why we're here."

All eyes fell upon Aaronson. Even Morgan stopped chewing.

"Let us enjoy our meal first," said Aaronson. "They'll be plenty of time for more serious discourse."

Vicki took another sip of her wine. "This white is wonderful. What is it?"

"It's Vaudésir, considered the best grand cru in Chablis."

"Where's Chablis?" asked Morgan.

"In the northern Burgundy region of France," said Aaronson.

"Butch is taking me to Paris," said Vicki, with an impish smile.

"That's splendid," said Aaronson. "Have you been to France before, Captain?"

"No."

"Well I can give you plenty of recommendations of sites to see and places to eat. France is fantastic."

"I want to stroll down the Champs-Élysées and buy some expensive French perfume," said Vicki, as pert as ever.

"That should be no problem," said Aaronson. "And how about you Father, have you been to Europe?"

"Just a trip to the Vatican while I was in the seminary."

"When was that?"

"The summer of 2013."

"Ah, when Pope Francis blessed the sculpture of Saint Michael, consecrating all of Vatican City to him."

"Yes, I was there for that."

"Two thousand thirteen was a banner year in the struggle between good and evil," said Aaronson. "Francis's actions and words were noteworthy that day."

"Why is that?" asked Gil.

"Because he specifically mentioned the Devil. The secular press accused him of religious mania, or at the very least, using old-fashioned language. But the Pope actually believes the Devil is a living being who endeavors to undermine the Church. To quote Dr. William Oddie, a renowned Catholic writer and editor, 'The demonic undermining of those who lead the Church at all levels, has been through the ages, an obvious Satanic tactic.'"

Aaronson continued, "The Pope cites the corruption in the Roman Curia as evidence of the Devil's influence. He suspects Satan of infiltrating the Vatican itself, hence his appeal to Saint Michael. What do you think, Father?"

Father Sean placed his wine glass on the table. "Uh . . . I don't know what to think, Professor. Until recently, I probably would have said that all this talk of the Devil is just a bunch of fire and brimstone. But after what happened to me the other day . . ."

138

Morgan finished his last sandwich, followed by a long swig of beer. "All right, Professor. Let's get down to business."

"Certainly," said Aaronson. "Well, our discussion of Saint Michael is no coincidence. In fact, he plays a vital role in what I'm about to convey"—Aaronson leaned toward Morgan—"in how *you're* going to save Crestwood Lake, once and for all."

"How?" asked Morgan.

"I'm a member of a secret society. We call ourselves The Camorra."

"What's a Camorra?" asked Father Sean.

"The original one," said Gil, "was a clandestine criminal organization, based in Naples. They've been around for centuries, but the term Camorra dates to about 1820."

Father Sean looked at Gil curiously.

"Gil was a history teacher and a librarian," said Vicki. "He wrote a good book on the Salem Witch Trials too."

"Our Camorra," said Aaronson, "is composed of scholars, and religious leaders of divergent faiths, from all over the globe. Our mission is straightforward: to counter the Devil's evildoing on Earth."

"You said it was a *secret* society?" asked Gil.

"Yes, very few people know we exist."

"Van Haden knows," said Vicki.

"Indeed," said Aaronson. "We're aware that he is cognizant of us. He has made several attempts to thwart us over the years."

"Van Haden's definitely back in Crestwood Lake," said Morgan. "The body count's starting already."

"Yes, Captain, we know that Satan has returned."

"You said there's a way to get rid of him, once and for all," said Gil.

"From Crestwood Lake, not the Earth," replied Aaronson.

"Let's have it," said Morgan.

"Are any of you familiar with the Castel Sant'Angelo in Rome?"

"Sure," said Gil.

"I know of it, but have never been there," said Father Sean.

Aaronson turned toward Morgan and Vicki. "The Castel Sant'Angelo is currently a museum on the Tiber River, just outside the Vatican. It was built between 123 and 139 AD by the Roman Emperor Hadrian, to serve as his mausoleum, which it did until being plundered by the Visigoths in 410.

"In 590, a plague was decimating Rome. Pope Gregory I beseeched the people to pray. Purportedly, Saint Michael, the archangel who had exiled Lucifer from heaven, appeared atop the mausoleum, brandishing his iconic sword, and terminating the plague. Thenceforth, the building was denominated the Castel Sant'Angelo. In 1536 a statue of Saint Michael was sculpted, and surmounts the structure to this day."

Aaronson turned to Father Sean. "I assume you are familiar with the Prayer of Saint Michael?"

"Of course. It was written by Pope Leo XIII in the late 1800s. It's known as the exorcism, prayer. He composed it after allegedly having a vision of demons threatening Rome."

"Yes," said Aaronson, "but that version is mostly apocryphal."

"How so?"

"Leo may have been beleaguered by demons, but the original prayer was written by Emperor Hadrian."

"Hadrian?" said Gil. "He wasn't even a Christian."

"Not at first," said Aaronson. "Initially, he was sympathetic to the Christians, prohibiting them from being persecuted because of their theology. History recounts Hadrian as sickly in his final years, but it wasn't from disease; he was being terrorized by demons. After his Roman gods failed to bring relief, Hadrian summoned Christian priests, who urged him to appeal to Saint Michael. Hadrian held a vigil in the saint's honor, ordering his entire staff to pray to the archangel. It was at this time—not the plague of 590—where Saint Michael materialized upon the roof of the mausoleum, driving the evil spirits away."

140

"How do you know this?" asked Father Sean.

"There are accounts from the ancient world, but many hailed from dubious sources. However, in 2015, an archeological excavation in Turkey, in what used to be the Roman province of Bithynia, uncovered texts from the Greek historian Arrian of Nicomedia. Arrian lived during Hadrian's reign and documented these events."

"That don't prove they happened," said Morgan.

"I'm not finished, Captain."

"Sorry. Go on."

"After the exorcism of his demons, Hadrian composed the prayer to Saint Michael. He etched the original prayer, in Latin of course, on a stone tablet. He then proclaimed his mausoleum a shrine to Saint Michael. It is said that angels appeared and enshrined the tablet, as well as Saint Michael's sword, the same one used to dispel Lucifer, in Hadrian's mausoleum.

"It's unclear when or by who, but the sword and tablet were buried deep beneath the mausoleum. They were not discovered when the Visigoths sacked it in 410 or the Goths in 537. The centuries elapsed, and the truths about the original events faded into obscurity. Even some of the Camorra's members had doubts about their veracity—until now."

"What happened?" asked Vicki.

"Do you remember the earthquake that struck Italy last month? The epicenter wasn't far from Rome. The Castel Sant'Angelo's cellar sustained the most damage, where the quake ripped open a massive fissure. At the base of the ravine, the original stone tablet upon which Hadrian etched Saint Michael's prayer—and the sword—were discovered."

Father Sean made the sign of the cross.

"How can you be sure of their provenance?" said Gil.

"Our experts," said Aaronson, "have already carbon dated the stone to the century of Hadrian's reign, but the sword is even more intriguing. The handle is made of pure gold, which as you all know, is highly malleable. This one however, is not. It was placed in a hydraulic press, which exerted a force of ten thousand pounds per square inch to no effect. Moreover, the composition of the sword's blade cannot be identified."

141

"What?" asked Gil.

"The blade is white—*pure* white. I've never seen anything in this world so impeccably white. We brought it to the Italian Institute of Technology in Genoa, one of the leading scientific centers in the world, and they could not identify its molecular structure."

"Are you serious?" said Gil.

"Gravely serious."

"You took a big chance exposing it to the world," said Morgan.

"You're quite right, Captain, but we had to know for sure."

"Why?"

"According to the legend, whoever is in possession of the tablet and sword, if they recite the prayer in its original Latin, can evoke the spirit of Saint Michael to defeat the Devil."

"So why didn't you?" said Morgan.

Aaronson hunched forward and met Morgan's eyes. "It must be done in Lucifer's presence, from wherever you're trying to banish him."

"Mother of God," said Father Sean.

"What are you getting at, Professor?" asked Morgan.

"I think you know, Captain. Van Haden has indubitably returned to your town. Armed with these artifacts, *you* must drive him out—in person."

"And just how the hell do you expect me to do that? Invite him over for tea?"

"No, Captain. You're going to have to go to him."

"Where?"

"In his lair beneath Crestwood Lake."

"What?"

"I've been there," said Vicki.

"What?" said Morgan, snapping his head toward her.

"It's where I was transformed into a witch."

"How come you never mentioned this hideout?" asked Morgan.

"I was only there a few times. The coven usually met in the woods or somewhere else. I didn't even think of it until just now." Vicki looked at Aaronson. "How do you know of it?"

"Lucifer is not the only one with spies."

"So let me get this straight," said Morgan. "I'm supposed to march into Van Haden's joint, tablet and sword in hand, and get medieval on his ass?"

"Unless," said Aaronson, "you know where he's keeping the receptacle containing the current coven's souls."

"Fat chance," said Morgan. "How big is this tablet?"

"About the size of a laptop."

"And just how do I get into Van Haden's hideout?"

"We believe there's a passageway to his subterranean chamber in the woods on the north side of the lake."

"Exactly where on the north side?" asked Morgan.

"I'm sorry, I can't be more specific than that. Vicki, Do you have any idea?"

"No. I never walked into his den. We were transposed there."

"The north side would make sense," said Morgan. "Many of the incidents over the years happened there. Brian Delmore was slaughtered there back in 2013. This morning, I got a call about four missing teenagers, reportedly heading into the northern woods. There's a well-known trail there where they go to party."

"Where is the tablet and sword now?" asked Father Sean.

"On a private vessel heading for Portland, Maine, from Italy," said Aaronson. "It'll take ten days. One of my colleagues is on board. From Portland, a courier will bring them to us. I have not given him a specific address yet. We must decide here and now, where to have them sent."

"Why not my church?" asked Father Sean.

"No way," said Morgan. "Van Haden obviously suspects your involvement. And one of the witches that attacked you got away. Surely, she'll report that Gil and I were there. Plus, like we told you, Saint Matthew's was where our last showdown with Van Haden occurred."

"I agree," said Aaronson. "The Devil already has his eye on you, Father."

"It has to be somewhere that Van Haden would never suspect," said Vicki. "A place that has absolutely no connection with us or the previous events."

"Agreed," said Aaronson. "But, Captain, you still must find Lucifer's chambers by the time the artifacts arrive. No matter where we have them delivered, it will not be safe to hold them indefinitely. Ideally, you must be ready to use them the moment they arrive."

"But where?" said Gil, "Certainly not a public place. We can't risk anybody seeing us."

"The cemetery," said Morgan. "In the middle of the night."

"You can't be serious," said Vicki.

"Why not? The Crestwood Cemetery. It's not even in Crestwood Lake. It's out in the middle of nowhere on a dead-end road next to the state forest. No one's going to be there at three in the morning."

Gil scoffed.

"What?" said Morgan indignantly.

"Sounds like something right out of a horror novel."

"You got a better idea?"

"Not at the moment," said Gil.

Vicki wrung her hands. "But what if we haven't found Van Haden's lair in time. Where do we bring the artifacts then?"

"We got ten days to come up with a backup plan," said Morgan. "What do you think, Professor?"

"A cemetery in the dead of night. Why not? Give me the exact location before you go, and I'll relay it to my courier."

Gil poured another glass of wine. "So, you've got the *actual* sword used by Saint Michael to eject the Devil from heaven?"

"I'm sure of it," said Aaronson. "And the original exorcism prayer."

"How does the prayer go?" asked Gil.

Aaronson opened a folder on the table and handed everyone a sheet of paper. "I've made copies." He read from his:

> *"Saint Michael Archangel, defend us in battle,*
> *be our protection against the wickedness and snares of the Devil.*
> *May God rebuke him, we humbly pray,*
> *and do thou, O Prince of the heavenly host,*
> *by the power of God, cast into hell,*
> *Satan and all the evil spirits,*
> *who prowl through the world seeking the ruin of souls.*
> *Amen."*

"So I recite this to Van Haden," said Morgan. "What happens then?"

"I don't know," said Aaronson.

"And what if it doesn't work?" asked Vicki.

Aaronson looked like a doctor about to tell a patient she was terminal.

"It means I'm a dead man," said Morgan.

Aaronson stroked his beard, darted his eyes, and finally said, "I suppose so."

Vicki wiped her eye and said, "Baby, you can't do this. I can't lose you."

"If we don't stop him, we're gonna lose each other anyway. For sure Van Haden wants both of us dead."

"I've never heard of any of this," said Father Sean. "Of Saint Michael's sword being preserved, or driving away the Devil with this prayer. No offense, Professor, I'm sure you found a tablet and a sword, but how do you know for certain what they are, or what they can do?"

Aaronson stiffened. "The curator of the Castel Sant'Angelo, Bernardo Iannucci, is a member of our society. Adriana Barberi appeared before him in his office and tried to kill him for the artifacts."

"What?" said Gil, almost knocking over his wine.

"He was thrown out of his office window with a force no Earthly human could muster, and impaled on the gate below. One of the security guards in the courtyard locked eyes with Barberi and went blind. Iannucci identified her; there's a famous portrait of her in the museum."

"Oh my God, it's true," said Vicki.

"What's true?" asked Aaronson.

"When I was in the coven, there was talk about an archwitch named Adriana. We never met her." Vicki turned to Morgan. "An archwitch is the second in command, just under the Devil. She is very powerful, and ruthless. If she's involved, then Satan is bringing all his forces to bear."

"Who is this bitch?" asked Morgan.

"Adriana Barberi was descended from the Borgias," said Gil.

"And who are the Borgias?" asked Morgan.

"A powerful and villainous family in Italy during the fifteenth and sixteenth centuries. Remember me asking Casandra about them? She confirmed their clan was infected with witches."

Aaronson glimpsed at Father Sean, who was rubbing his right temple. "Well, Father?"

"God have mercy on us," he said, reaching for another glass of wine. "Why? Why is Crestwood Lake so important to Lucifer?"

"It's not just Crestwood Lake," said Aaronson. "Do you know the history of all this?"

"Yes. The captain and Gil told me."

"The Devil's greatest weakness is his ego—his pride," said Aaronson. "Van Haden had Crestwood Lake, and he lost it. Vicki betrayed him, the captain and Gil defeated him, and his coven was wiped out. He will not rest until he is vindicated."

"Professor," said Father Sean, "can you explain something to me?"

"I'll try."

"What is a white witch?"

"A supernatural entity at odds with Satan."

"Where do they come from? How does someone become a white witch?"

"We're not positive. Casandra, who aided the captain and Gil last time, gave us some insights. She was a descendent of an angel, but that doesn't mean they all are. There may be other routes to becoming a white witch. Like evil witches, they can be killed, otherwise, they appear to live indefinitely, gaining supernatural strength with time."

Aaronson surveyed the table. "Would anyone like some dessert? I have a lovely coconut cake. Maybe some coffee?"

"I'll have some more wine," said Gil.

"Me too," said Vicki.

Aaronson chuckled. "By all means. Captain, another beer?"

"Just one more. I have to drive."

"Is there anything more of importance we should discuss?" asked Aaronson.

Everyone shook their head.

"Captain, I'll contact Gil when the ship makes port. I assume you'll keep me abreast of your progress in the interim." Aaronson turned toward Vicki. "Shall we talk about Paris?"

Vicki brightened. "Yes, I'd love to."

Aaronson went into a lengthy commentary about Paris's multitudinous offerings: the art museums, the architecture, French culture, and of course, the gastronomic delights. Gil was engrossed by the historical sites, Father Sean by the cathedrals, and Vicki by everything.

Morgan sat there quietly, barely listening, sipping his beer . . . plotting.

The Epicure

I dragged myself out of bed, hungover of course, and fixed my favorite breakfast: coffee and cigarettes. I smoked my cigarette on the toilet. I like to smoke when I take a shit. Most people read—I smoke.

My head felt ponderous and thick. I don't even remember driving home. Last thing I recall is a fuzzy image of being in the bar with my cooks and waiters, and the three women from table two. I think one of them gave me head. God knows how many Jack Daniels I had. I know I popped at least two Oxy. Whatever. It was a good night. I grossed over three grand, which is decent for a Sunday. It'll enable me to make payroll.

I bought Pierre's in Crestwood Lake five years ago with the proceeds from my deceased parents' house. I turned it into a French bistro, and it's been a struggle to stay afloat ever since. Not exactly a lot of gourmands in Jerkwater Vermont. But, I'm the only upscale restaurant within thirty miles, have good food—and most importantly—serve alcohol. Without booze, I would have been sucking dirt by now.

And yeah, my food is good. People have no idea how much work and sacrifice I put in to it. After high school I joined the army where I became a cook. My sergeant was a professionally trained chef and taught me a lot, until I got kicked out for drugs. I returned to my home town in New Hampshire, which had a vocational school. I got student loans and enrolled in their culinary program. Then I reneged on the loans.

Afterwards, I spent five years working grueling jobs in kitchens all over New England. Let me tell you: chefs are assholes. They're all a bunch of angry, narcissistic, control freaks. They berate their staff, who eventually open their own place, and continue the cycle of abuse. Every chef thinks his way of doing things is right, and everyone else's is wrong. I had one dipshit scold me for whipping my cream in a circular fashion as opposed to sideways. Ever see anyone whip cream sideways in a circular bowl? Me neither. Fucking dickwad.

I however, do not mistreat my employees. If anything, I'm too nice— let the parasites take advantage of me. You won't find many restauranteurs giving their staff free drinks after hours. Truthfully, I don't mind. At least I'm the boss. I don't have to answer to nobody but me.

I flushed the toilet, peeked out the window, and seesawed into the living room. On the coffee table was an empty can of refried beans, a glass of Jack Daniels, and a bottle of Oxy. It really was a good night. I lit another cigarette and put on the news.

"Another person has been reported missing, in the seemingly never-ending slew of disappearances that have been plaguing northern Vermont since 2010. Although it's unknown whether all the incidents are the work of one person, locals have dubbed the perpetrator the "Body-Snatcher." The latest is twenty-two-year-old Debra Kendricks of Lancaster, New Hampshire, who was last seen leaving Bogey's Tavern in St. Johnsbury Friday night. Debra was with a group of friends, who claim she hadn't drank excessively, and left for home afterwards. Debra is a student at White Mountains Community College and lives with her parents and younger brother. Anyone with information about Debra should contact the St. Johnsbury Police.

"We now go to WCAX reporter Megan Donnelly, at the headquarters of the Vermont State Police in Waterbury, with more on these disappearances."

"Thank you, Mary. Good morning everyone. I'm here with Lieutenant Masterson of the Vermont State Police. Lieutenant, Debra Kendricks is now the thirty-fifth person to be reported missing in northern Vermont in the last six years. Are these cases related?"

"No, we don't think so, only because of the variety of the subjects: males and females of every age."

"Some question whether one or more serial killers are at work, especially in light of some of the horrific murders that have also happened in the region over this time."

"At this point there's no evidence that any of the missing people were apprehended by a serial killer. We don't even know if they were the victims of foul play. The investigation is still ongoing."

"Any connection between the missing people and the murders?"

"Not at this time."

"Are there any persons of interest?"

"I can't comment on the details of an ongoing investigation. But I would like to reassure the public that we are looking into each and every case, with the aid of local law enforcement."

"Thank you, Lieutenant. This is Megan Donnelly, WCAX news."

I poured myself another cup of coffee, popped three Advil, and channel surfed until the funk in my head eased. I had to get to the restaurant. We were closed on Mondays, but there's always shit to do: product deliveries, cleaning, making stock, the list goes on and on. I stubbed out my cigarette and got ready for work.

While taking a shower, I heard a noise. I imagined the shower scene from the movie *Psycho*. That freaked me out as a kid. While shampooing, I perceived a dark figure on the other side of the curtain. I squinted as the soap dripped into my eyes. "Fuck!" I shouted, flailing at the curtain with one hand, rubbing soap off my face with the other. No one was there. I quickly rinsed and dried, grabbed my 9mm, and checked my house, finding nothing but the remnants of my paranoia. I recalled my army buddy's favorite saying: "Just because you're paranoid doesn't mean people aren't out to get you."

My disgust with my foolishness took charge. I had to get to the restaurant. I had a new cook to break in: a wimpy nineteen-year-old named Kyle, fresh out of cooking school. He had thin, blond hair, and lips that looked like a woman's. Newbies are a mixed bag. They usually don't know shit and need close supervision. On the other hand, they're eager as hell and start at minimum wage.

As I walked into the kitchen I could smell the pots of chicken and veal stock simmering. My one chef was blanching fava beans while another was rolling out sheets of dough. Kyle was making my signature hors' d'oeuvre: goat cheese and white truffle pastries.

"Finish that later," I said. "I want to show you how to make the boudin noir."

"The what?" asked Kyle.

"Boudin noir. Blood sausages."

"Gross."

"Never heard of them?"

"I heard of them, just never made them."

"Well you are now."

"Are they actually made with blood?"

I went to the walk-in fridge, retrieved a large, plastic storage container holding a red liquid, and placed it on the counter in front of Kyle.

"Oh, man. That's real blood?"

"It's pig's blood," I said.

"Where do you get that shit?"

"From my meat guy. You mix it in with the ground pork and seasonings to make the sausage." Ignoring Kyle's grimaces, I demonstrated all the steps to fabricate the sausage. Then I retreated to my office, lit a cigarette, and got lost in clerical work.

I called Tony, my meat supplier, as I searched the internet for other butchers. Of all my vendors I owed Tony the most money. Two reasons. First, being an ardent carnivore, my menu was laden with meat, and second, my alcohol distributor got priority since liquor was my most profitable item.

"Hello," he said.

"Tony, it's Dave."

"Who?"

"Dave Nyman from Pierre's."

"Oh."

I could hear the dismay in his voice. "I'd like to place an order."

"You already owe me fourteen hundred and you want more stuff?"

"I had a good weekend. I can pay you half."

"When I get the seven hundred, then I'll take your order, but not until then."

"All right, I'll drive over today and give you the cash. In the meantime, can I give you my list?" I hastily clacked away at the keyboard.

"Fine, but you better show today. What do you want?"

"Give me fifteen pounds of lamb loin, and twenty-five pounds of the rack of lamb,"—clack-clack-clack-clack—"and I need"—clack-clack—"Aaaaagh!"

I almost fell out of my chair. I dropped the phone as I thrust away from the computer. On the screen was an image of me being restrained by two black creatures, while a third slit open my gut. Then it vanished. What the hell? Was I going crazy? Was it a sick prank?

I grabbed my chest, caught my breath, and peered at the screen. All I saw was my google search. I retrieved the phone. "Tony, you still there? . . . Tony? . . . Goddammit!" Instead of calling him back I decided to just drive over, pay him his money, and get my supplies. What I really needed was a drink.

I checked on Kyle's progress, went to Tony's, returned, and made sure everything was ready for business tomorrow. I went home and opened a bottle of Jack. I didn't usually get sauced two nights in a row, but today was definitely an exception. I sipped my booze and contemplated my life.

Here I was, a thirty-two-year-old chef. Yes, I had my own restaurant, but that was shaky at best. Even when I was on top of my bills, I wasn't making a lot of money. People think restaurants are gold mines. What a joke. They see a thirty-dollar salmon entrée, compare it to the supermarket price, and think I'm making a killing. They have no clue. They don't consider the never-ending unforeseen costs: taxes, salaries, equipment, utilities, insurance, maintenance, pest control, snow removal, the list is endless.

Nor do they appreciate how much food I throw out because it didn't sell. If I buy less, the per unit cost goes up, and if I run out of an item, customers get irked. Buy too much, and there's inevitably waste. And you never can predict the weekends you'll sell twenty-four salmon entrees and the ones you'll sell only eight.

Not to mention the food that gets tossed because some nimrod thinks it's too salty, or too oily, or too this, or too that. Frigging people. I even had one moron return the tuna tartare because they wanted, "the real tuna, ya know, like from a can."

Anyway, I digress. The Jack makes my brain wander. What was I talking about? Oh, yeah, the perilous nature of the restaurant business. What would happen if I went out of business? I could never work for someone else again. I had to find a way to continue the grind. I made a steak, checked the windows, and had another drink. The phone rang.

"Hello?"

"Hey, baby, it's me."

It was Nikki, a doping skank who'd offer me a booty call when she was out of Oxy. Basically, she was a hooker, only I paid her in drugs instead of cash. But because she needed the Oxy more than I needed the tail, I had all the power in the relationship.

"What's up?" I said.

"Oh, just wanted to see how you were doing, thought maybe we could get together."

"This week's kind of hectic for me."

"Aw, c'mon Davey. What's the point of having a squeeze, if ya can't squeeze her in?"

"Maybe this weekend."

"Oh, I can't wait that long to see ya, baby."

I tightened my grip on the receiver. "I don't have any Oxy to spare right now."

"Well, why didn't you just say that to begin with, ya dick?"

"Goodbye, Nikki." I jammed the phone into the charger. Then I had another drink, took an Oxy (I had four bottles), and passed out on the couch. I awoke at three in the morning and fumbled for my keys.

A few days later I was reviewing the wine list with Cliff, my head waiter and sommelier. Whoever coined the phrase "It takes money to make money," must have sold wine. The more preeminent your cellar, the more you can attract affluent oenophiles who order expensive bottles. A restricted

154

inventory saves money, but at the cost of sales. It's yet another balancing act in the restaurant business.

"We only have two bottles of the Vosne-Romanée premier cru left," said Cliff.

"Well don't promote it, because I can't afford to buy more now. If we run out, we either have to disappoint customers or reprint the list."

"Then we should at least acquire more of the Vosne-Romanée Village, or we'll have nothing from that commune."

"Let's see how we do this weekend. You need to up-sell more. If a customer is contemplating a hundred-dollar-bottle, then they can afford another fifty for a better vintage or producer."

"I'll try, but I don't want to come off as pushy."

"And we're selling too many wines by the glass. Point out how it's cheaper per glass to buy a bottle. And try to unload that Prunotto Barolo. I bought too much of it."

Cliff raised his palms. "Italian wine at a French bistro."

"Yes, Cliff, I'm quite aware. But it's a good Barolo and will go with any of our meat dishes just as well as Bordeaux. Dazzle the customers with how good the price is for an older vintage. Feed'em some bull shit about how versatile my dishes are in terms of their wine-friendliness."

"OK."

"This weekend the special is monkfish. Here's chance to up-sell the Puligny-Montrachet. Promote it to anyone who orders a cheaper Chardonnay. If we can sell six bottles of the Montrachet this weekend, then I can order a case of the Vosne-Romanée."

"OK, Chef."

I left my office and entered the bar, where my staff had congregated in front of the TV. "I'm not paying you people to watch television."

Paul, my bartender said, "The Body-Snatcher struck again."

I looked up at the TV, catching the news story already in progress.

155

"Kirby Police found blood, and evidence of a struggle in Justin Barclay's home on Kirby Mountain Road. When his girlfriend hadn't heard from him in days, she let herself in and discovered the crime scene. Barclay, a forty-one-year-old plumber, was self-employed. Police are investigating any possible links between what appears to be Barclay's abduction and the series of disappearances—"

"That's it," I said, turning off the TV. "Back to work. Kyle, what are you doing right now?"

"Prepping the cassoulet."

"I need you to make the liver terrine as well."

Kyle recoiled.

"Don't worry, I'll show you. C'mon." I went to my filing cabinet, retrieved a copy of my recipe and handed it to Kyle. "Follow these measurements to the letter." In the interest of time, I helped Kyle gather the ingredients. I went to the meat fridge and plopped the plastic-wrapped liver in front of Kyle.

Kyle squinted.

"You ever make liver in cooking school?"

"Uh, actually, no we never did."

"This is pig's liver."

"Chefs are really in to pig parts, huh?"

"The Andalusians have a saying, 'The only thing you cannot eat of a pig, is its squeak.'"

"Andalusians?"

"Andalusia is a region in Southern Spain. We're going to make a forcemeat. You know what that is, right?"

"Yes," said Kyle meekly.

"Well, go get the food processor and open up the liver."

156

I proceeded to show Kyle how to make the terrine. When we finished I said, "OK, get back to your cassoulet prep and then work on the family meal."

In better restaurants, before the dinner rush, all the employees will have a meal together that the kitchen staff has prepared. We call it family meal, and I think it's very important. People need a break, and they need to eat. It's also time for staff to bond and discuss any last-minute issues.

I had one room in the back that we used for family meal and small parties. The entire staff gathered and chowed down on braised pork shoulder, mashed potatoes, and glazed carrots.

"The pork is pretty tasty Kyle. You did a good job today," I said.

"Thanks, Chef."

"Anybody know the guy who got kidnapped?" asked Chad, one of my line cooks.

"I've seen his plumbing truck," said Miguel, one of the busboys, "but I didn't know him."

"Who do you think this psycho is?" asked Julien, my burly sous chef.

"It's probably the same freak that killed all those people a couple of years ago. They never found him," said Stefan, one of the waiters, followed by a raspy burp.

"You're disgusting," said Ashley, my stunningly attractive hostess and general manager.

"I'm passionate about what I *eat*," said Stefan, his lecherous smile engulfed by his seedy beard.

Ashley scoffed.

"It could be alien abductions," said Paul.

"Get the fuck outta here," said Thomás, my other line cook. "It ain't no aliens from outer space. Stop watching Star Trek and get a life."

"I'm telling ya," said Stefan. "It's the same freak."

"Some people think it's witchcraft," said Ellie, a normally shy, diminutive waitress.

157

"What are you saying?" asked Julien. "You talking about Wicca, or actual witches, like Halloween shit?"

"Real witches," Ellie replied.

Half the group rolled their eyes, the other half stared at her like she was mental.

"Why are you looking at me like that?"

"You're crazier than Paul," said Cliff. "At least there probably *are* aliens."

"Like you've never heard the rumors about Crestwood Lake," said Ellie.

"We heard them," said Stefan. "We just don't believe that crap."

"Well I do," said Ellie. "That nun who drowned herself in the lake three years ago told my cousin, her friend, about this coven of witches."

"Oh, well that settles it," said Stefan. "Your cousin's suicidal friend talked about witches, so it *must* be true, 'cause people who croak themselves are always so rational."

"You're such a jerk," said Ashley.

"Jerk this," replied Stefan.

"Knock it off," I said. "Enough talk about witches and psychos. Anything we need to discuss about business?"

"Your fish guy left a message," said Ashley. "It's about your bill."

"He'll have to take a number. Anything else?"

"The dishwasher's acting up again," said Miguel. "I think it's time to replace it."

"That's not gonna happen. Do the best you can until we get the repairman out here again. Any issues with the food? What happened with table twelve last night?"

Stefan cleared his throat. These two women returned the braised lamb shank. They said it didn't taste right."

"What does *not taste right* mean?" I asked.

"Don't know, Chef. They just said it didn't taste like it normally does."

"Was the lamb shank from Tony?" asked Thomás.

"No," I said. "I had to use Green Mountain Meatpackers. The stuff we got now is from Tony, so we should be OK. Anything else?"

Nobody spoke up.

"All right then. Let's get going, we got a full house tonight. Kyle, come with me."

I led Kyle to the prep table. "I need you to prep the kidneys."

"Pig's?"

"No, these are veal kidneys. Calves' to be specific. You ever do this before?"

"Just once in cooking school."

"Well let me show you again." I retrieved a kidney from the container and placed it on the cutting board. "First you have to remove this outer membrane and the fat. Then cut them in half and remove this white sinew inside. Got it?"

Kyle nodded.

"OK, finish those up and then make sure your station's ready for dinner."

About two hours later, in the middle of the dinner rush, I was working the line when Ashley burst into the kitchen.

"Dave, there's some woman here who doesn't have a reservation, demanding a table. I told her I didn't have any until after eight. She says she knows you—insists on speaking with you."

I wiped my hands, cursed under my breath, and marched to the hostess stand. My stomach flinched. "What are you doing here?" I asked.

"Do you want to discuss it *here*?" A foursome was coming through the front door.

I grabbed her elbow and ushered her into the coat room. "What do you want?"

"We had an agreement."

"I *know* we have an agreement."

"You're not living up to your end."

"What are you talking about?" I asked.

Her brow furrowed. "You've been holding out on me."

"Bull shit."

"The numbers don't add up."

"Then you need a new calculator."

Her eyes bored into mine.

"Look, I only keep my cut, so if you're coming up short, it's one of your other suppliers."

She clutched the back of my neck and kissed me, passionately—then sunk her teeth into my bottom lip.

"Ow! You fucking bitch!"

She licked the blood off her mouth, said "Goodbye, David," and walked away.

I teetered back to the kitchen, holding my lip. "Get back to work!" I shouted at the employees gawking at me.

I had a miserable night. I cooked like a neophyte at his first job. I made mistakes and barely kept up with the pace. Yelling at my staff, I fought my way through the dinner rush. As soon as it ebbed, I let my cooks take over. I told Ashley to lock up, drove home, and popped an Oxy with some Jack. The alcohol burned my wound, so I popped another Oxy. Makes sense to me.

At some point I passed out. I awoke just after two in the morning—I think—or was I dreaming? An incessant buzz penetrated the room. My head felt clouded, in a different way than it normally does. "Aaagh!" A sharp pain between my right hip and testicle. I flailed my arms. Where was I? The buzzing increased. My left hand hit the corner of my couch. I was on the floor.

I heaved myself onto the couch, reached to my right, knocked over a bottle of something, found the table lamp, and turned the switch. A pitch-black creature with pointed ears and white eyes approached. The walls were covered with wasps, buzzing and twitching. I screamed and sprang off the couch, crashing into my coffee table, a cacophony of shattering glass accentuating the relentless buzz. I spun around in the shards—everything was gone: the creature, the wasps, the sound. I lay there for a minute, listening and scanning. Nothing. I stumbled to my feet, retrieved my pistol, and canvassed the house. It must have been a dream. Or the pills. Or both.

I lit a smoke, chugged some Jack, and took an Oxy. Then I staggered to my car and sped off into the night. Time to resupply.

The next day I slept till noon. The night before seemed like a blur. Strangely, I felt normal, despite the booze, pills, and nightmarish visions. I went downstairs, strode into the living room and winced. The coffee table was still in a million pieces. It wasn't all a dream. The hell with it; I'd worry about it later. I had to get to the restaurant.

I wolfed down some ham and cheese, sans bread, and took a quick shower. Then I went to my basement, lugged my 75-quart cooler out to the driveway, and dropped it in the back of my pickup.

Arriving at the restaurant, I again found my staff gathered around the TV. "What's going on here?"

"Look, Chef," said Thomás. "He attacked two women this time. Stabbed one, kidnapped the other."

"Where?" I asked.

"Shhhhhhhhh," hushed Ashley, trying to hear the news report. "Some bar in Northumberland." She turned her attention back to the TV.

Kelly Griswold is in stable condition at Weeks Medical Center after sustaining multiple lacerations. She was able to give police a description of the assailant, which matches this image from the tavern's video surveillance. The police are asking anyone who recognizes this man to contact . . .

"That's you, Chef," said Julien.

"No it's not!"

"Yeah, it is," said Chad.

Everyone turned around and stared at me.

"I don't pay you people to watch TV."

"*You're* the Body-Snatcher!" said Stefan.

"Get back to work or you're fired!"

"Oh I don't think so," said Ashley.

Julien raised his chef's knife and took a step forward. The rest of the staff followed suit. They all glared at me, a mob of eyeballs, inching forward.

I stepped back. "What the hell is wrong with you people?"

"Someone call the police," cried Ellie.

Miguel withdrew his phone.

Julien inched closer.

I bolted out the back door, rushed to my truck, and peeled out of the parking lot. My mind was rabid. The police would be coming; my house was the first place they'd check. I had to get there first. I tried to think of everything I'd need: cash, credit cards, laptop, Oxy, gun. No time for clothes. I could buy new ones later.

Where to go? Canada was an hour away. The police would alert the border patrol by then. I could be in New Hampshire in a half hour. Still, more than enough time for the cops to be watching the interstates.

I know. Of course! I'd go to Barclay's house, the plumber I killed. He lived alone. The police already searched it. And if his girlfriend showed up, well, no problem. I'd hide out there until I could think of an exit plan.

I screeched into my driveway, dashed into my house, grabbed my necessities, and left. I hightailed it to Barclay's, parked in his garage, and broke in through the back door. I turned on the heat and swallowed an Oxy. I tried to collect my thoughts. I should check the house first. No one should be there, but my paranoia demanded certainty. I grabbed my gun and crept from room to room. The downstairs was clear. I went upstairs and inspected every room. Nothing. Ok, that's done. I went to the kitchen to find some food when I noticed a door in the corner. *The basement.* I had to put my mind at ease. I opened the door, found the light, and followed my pistol down the stairs.

It was a typical basement: unfinished, dusty, and cobwebbed. I saw a furnace, hot water heater, and assorted piles of junk. Nobody was there. I started back to the kitchen when the light went out and the door slammed shut.

Searing pain shot through my shoulders. I yelped. Its nails dug in, slamming me backward onto the floor. Something sliced through the backs of my knees, severing the tendons. Something else snatched my groin, piercing and twisting it. I wailed in unimaginable pain. The light came back on.

It was the same black demons with stark-white eyes from my nightmare. Two of them held my arms, their talons impaling my flesh. A third restrained my crippled legs. I was oozing blood all over.

Kyle came forth.

"What the hell are you doing?" I shouted.

"Shut up," said Kyle, seizing my throat. He turned toward the stairs.

Darlene Thorn sauntered down, almost as if gliding on air—clad in a black cape, keenly contrasted by her blonde hair and cadmium yellow eyes.

"We had a covenant, David . . . and you broke it."

"No."

Darlene scowled. "You still continue to deny it?" She raised her voice. "You think I don't know about how many you slew? Our agreement was simple: you keep the carcasses, we receive the blood and organs. But you got greedy."

Kyle scoffed. "Did you really think I believed those were *pig's* organs?"

"I wasn't greedy. I couldn't pay my vendors. I needed product."

"Then you should have come to me," said Darlene gritting her teeth, "not betrayed me."

"Give me another chance. I've got a cooler full of fresh meat in my truck. All yours, please!"

"It's too late," said Darlene. "There's no recourse for treachery."

One of the demons jammed his talons into my eyeball, yanking it from its socket.

I screamed as he popped it into his mouth.

Another demon slit open my belly.

Blood shot up my throat.

The entire group descended.

"Everything but the squeak," said Kyle.

The Avengement

"Where the fuck is he?" snarled Burrows. "I thought he was supposed to be here at noon."

"I don't know," said Jameson. "He set the time."

"Who ya lookin' for?" asked Cindy, a raffish, brunette barmaid at Toby's, as she placed their drinks on the table.

"Butch," said Burrows. "Have you seen him?"

"No. He usually don't come here on Vicki's day off. Ya guys want some chow, or ya just having drinks?"

"Just drinks," said Jameson.

Cindy scratched her right breast and bounced away, sneaking into the back room for another one-hitter of weed.

"You sure he's coming?" asked Burrows.

"Yes. He was quite emphatic. Said he wanted to get this over with. Said he was willing to plead it out now before Derrick goes to trial. That he and his wife wanted to get away."

"That don't sound like Butch, although . . . maybe he does want to leave town. Vicki could've talked him into splitting."

"Why?"

"I'll check with my sources—maybe *they* persuaded him to leave."

"Your sources?"

"Don't worry about that right now," said Burrows. "All I care about is getting rid of him. The sooner the better. I assume you put Derrick in the county pen?"

"What do you mean? He's out."

"Huh?"

"He made bail."

"You arrested him, right?"

"Yes."

"For a parole violation?"

"Yeah."

"So why isn't he back in the slammer?"

"Because," said Jameson, "we still have something called due process. Derrick pled not guilty to the parole violation. Like any other crime, he must stand trial. And he was only in prison for domestic assault, not something like murder. Then we could've held him until trial."

"But still—"

"The judge set one hundred thousand dollars bail. His mother put up her house. He got out three days ago. I thought you knew."

"No, I didn't."

"Is that a problem?"

"No, it's not a *problem*, it's just that . . ."

"Just what?"

"Nothing, nothing. It just complicates certain things."

"I thought you and Derrick were friends."

"We're not *friends*," said Burrows, contorting his face. "I don't give a dead rat for his worthless ass. He's a means to an end—an end to Butch Morgan."

Jameson stared.

"What?" said Burrows.

"You don't like anybody, do you?"

"Oh you should talk. All you want is another headline on your wall."

"Sure, I want a conviction, but that doesn't mean . . . son of a bitch." Jameson raised his eyes.

166

"What?" said Burrows.

"It's Derrick, he's got a gun."

Burrows twirled around in his chair as people gasped.

"How ya doing guys?" said Derrick, holding his 9mm at arm's length.

Various patrons squirmed or took cover.

Derrick waved his gun around the room. "Don't anybody move, or I'll blow you away." Then he redirected his weapon at Burrows and Jameson.

"What are you doing?" asked Burrows. "We're on the same side."

"Oh really?" Derrick swung his pistol into Burrows's face, drawing blood.

Burrows grunted as the right side of his body bounced off the table. He grabbed his cheek and defensively raised his other arm.

Derrick pulled out his phone and tapped it. A recording came on:

"You want to get rid of me, or do you want to protect your kissing cousin?"

"OK, Butch, you have a deal."

"And Derrick?"

"Fuck him. A small price to pay for your arrogant ass."

Derrick turned off the recording. "Does this sound like the same side to you, jerk-off?"

"I just said that to trap Butch," said Burrows, looking around the room, realizing what he just admitted.

Derrick turned toward Jameson. "And you're a dirtbag too. You were ready to send me back in the joint."

"Talk to him," said Jameson pointing at Burrows.

"Fuck you! You slimeball shyster."

"No Clyde," said Derrick squeezing the trigger, "Fuck *you*!"

Burrows's brains splattered across Jameson and the floor. The patrons shrieked.

Jameson's eyes were as wide open as his mouth, pieces of flesh and blood dripping off his cheeks. He held up his hands and muttered, "I can get you off. I'm the prosecutor. I can drop the charges."

"Drop this," said Derrick, shooting Jameson in the left eye, brain and blood bursting out of his skull.

The front door flew open. "Drop the gun or die, Derrick!" shouted Morgan, holding his magnum with both hands, aiming at Derrick's head.

Derrick turned, gun in hand.

Morgan fired.

Derrick's body reeled to the floor, the three men now sharing a meeting of the minds.

Morgan looked around. "Anybody hurt?"

Most of the people were too shocked to respond. A few shook their heads. One woman was crying.

Cindy held up a beer. "That was bitchin' man!"

Morgan smirked and called the station.

The Parley

Morgan stopped his pickup along the north shore of Crestwood Lake, just before the infamous trail leading into the woods. The same spot he parked in three years prior, when investigating Brian Delmore's murder. Morgan recollected the moment he first viewed Brian's mutilated corpse. Now he was afraid of reliving that experience—times four. Morgan's officers had already searched for the missing teens, but he still had this odd feeling that the cadavers were waiting for *him*.

Like a wet dog shaking off water, Morgan joggled his head of his irrationalities and refocused. He was the only officer who knew the teens' fate, and thus, needed to examine the area himself. Even more important, it was imperative to find the entrance to Van Haden's chambers, and Morgan had a hunch where to start. The trek through the forest would also give him solitude to mull over his next move. So, with magnum and holy water ready, Morgan wended his way into the northern woods.

Morgan was being lauded as a hero by the press and the populace for gunning down Derrick. Even the slightest rumblings of impropriety regarding his previous assault of Derrick, were now transformed into accolades for meting out well-deserved justice.

The plaudits for their police chief, however, were but a temporary diversion from the community's growing unrest. For a second time in three years, deaths were accumulating: the gunman at the supermarket, Peter Hadley, Lori Oliver and her victims, and now Derrick Larson, Clyde Burrows, and Wilfred Jameson. And that was in addition to the missing people such as Sammy Martin and the four teenagers.

The head of the Crestwood Lake Town Council, Adley Turner, had been named interim mayor. He was already being implored by the citizenry to augment the police force. A few residents, despite Morgan's heroism, felt the entire department should be revamped. Parents were tightening their children's curfews, schools had increased security, and the community's suspiciousness of non-locals had intensified. Meanwhile, a subgroup of anti-gun supporters exploited the recent events to lobby against Vermont's permissive gun-carrying law.

All of these concerns and more, whizzed through Morgan's head as he hiked along the trail, eyes surveilling all around him. It was a cloudy, fifty-nine-degree day, the last of September, and the foliage was at its peak. Nature, however, was wasting its splendor on Morgan.

Despite the multitude of vexations on Morgan's mind, his thoughts still drifted to Vicki. Morgan loved her even more than his deceased wife Connie, which provoked pangs of guilt. It was one of the few havens in his soul where remorse could find any refuge—not because Morgan didn't have a conscience, but rather because he didn't have much conflict *about* his conscience. Morgan had a clear-cut idea of right and wrong. He didn't harbor any compunction about killing Derrick. In Morgan's mind, Derrick was a worthless waste product who got what he deserved—end of story. Yes, Morgan's black and white view of morality was simplistic, but on the other hand, he rarely lost sleep at night.

Morgan feared for Vicki's safety. He couldn't protect her twenty-four-seven, and she rejected having a bodyguard, or hiding until the current dilemma was resolved. She refused to live a sheltered life: withdrawing would only be a step backward in the struggle to transcend her trauma. Morgan's respect for her fortitude came at the cost of his peace of mind.

Morgan also worried about Gil, inevitably on the Devil's radar as well. Seventy-five years old and living alone—he was an easy target. All their banter and character differences didn't change the fact that Morgan loved Gil too, even though he would never use that word regarding another man. Gil had been his best friend for over thirty years. Other than Vicki, no one else was privy to Morgan's inner world.

Morgan reached Brian Delmore's murder site: a nondescript patch of brush, just off the trail. He pictured Brian's mangled body, and his inconsolable parents. Reliving the memory, Morgan's stomach felt like it was crawling up his throat. He growled at the image of Van Haden in his mind, "Damn you to hell."

"Damn who, Captain?"

Morgan whipped around.

There he stood, imperious as ever, sporting his customary black suit and fiery red accoutrements.

170

Morgan drew his .357 and unloaded all six chambers into Van Haden's face.

"Now what was that for, Captain?"

Morgan hit the cylinder release button, emptied the shells and popped in a speed loader.

"Feel safer now?" asked Van Haden.

Morgan quickly looked over both of his shoulders, never taking his finger off the trigger.

"I'm immune to holy water as well, Captain."

Maintaining a firing stance, Morgan took one sidestep so he could see behind Van Haden.

"Captain, let me save us some time. You have my word that no harm shall befall you today." Van Haden raised his index finger and eyebrows. "*Today.*"

"What do you want, you piece of filth?"

Van Haden extended his palms. "I simply want to talk to you."

Morgan was a block of glaring ice, frozen around the handle of his magnum.

Van Haden lowered his hands and stiffened. "Captain, your firearm is useless. Please put it away and hear me out."

Morgan slowly holstered his weapon. "Get on with it. I don't have all day."

"Well, first of all, allow me to compliment you on that wonderful trap you set for Derrick and Clyde. I couldn't have done better myself."

"All three of them work for you, I suspect."

"Not Jameson. He was just a bonus."

"Still as scummy as the rest of you."

"Oh yes, he was delightfully unscrupulous. I like that in a person."

171

"What do you want?" asked Morgan.

"Oh, Captain, I think we both know that—I want Crestwood Lake. And, just like my fallen comrades, I want you out of the way."

"Ain't gonna happen."

"Now, now . . . before you beat your chest—"

"I took you down once you prick, and by God, I'll do it again."

"Captain, the conquest of Crestwood Lake is inevitable."

"Over my dead body."

"Your terms are acceptable, but I was hoping for a less drastic solution."

Morgan stared at Van Haden as if he was murdering him with his eyes.

"Captain, underneath your bravado and boorish affectations, you are a reasonable man, a logical man. It is this man I wish to appeal to."

"I'm telling you right now you son of a—"

"Humor me, Captain." Van Haden waved his arm. The forest disappeared. They stood in a white desert: a barren panorama of snow-like sand, extending to the horizon. It was as bright as a clear summer day, yet there was no sun in the sky.

Morgan grabbed the handle of his magnum and spun around.

When he completed his circle, he flinched. Standing before him was Connie, his wife of twenty-one years who died in 2012 from cancer. She appeared in her prime: radiant, her honey-blonde hair, curving around the contour of her face.

"Hello, Bart," said Connie, calling Morgan by his given first name.

Morgan tilted his head and squinted.

"I miss you dear," she said.

"You're . . .you're not real."

172

"I know you miss me too."

"*You're* not real."

"I'm glad you married Vicki."

Morgan felt a heaviness in his chest.

"I know you felt guilt about remarrying, unsure if you were acting out of love or grief. But you *do* love her. And she loves you."

Morgan glanced to his side. Van Haden stood silently.

"He brought me here to talk to you." Connie reached out her hand.

Morgan took a step back.

"Bart, please. Listen to me. I can rest easily knowing you're alive and well. Let it go, dear. Leave him be."

Morgan turned toward Van Haden and gritted his teeth. "How dare you."

Connie's eyes filled with sorrow. "Bart, please. It will bring me peace."

Morgan bristled, and pointed at Van Haden. "I've had enough of your bullshit parlor tricks."

Connie disappeared.

"Fine, Captain. No more apparitions. Instead I will show you reality. How do you wish to spend the rest of your life? Happily, with Vicki, I imagine. I know you're planning to retire, see the world. That can still happen. Observe . . ."

Morgan beheld his future, as if watching it from the front row of a movie theatre. On the "screen" he and Vicki strolled down the Champs-Élysées, the Arc de Triomphe in the distance. It was an invigorating spring day and Paris was bubbling with life. Vicki was smiling and bouncing like a giddy schoolgirl. Her left hand held a shopping bag of treasures, her right held Morgan's. She pulled him toward her and kissed him.

Then, the Grand Canyon . . . the couple stood on an observation ledge, enraptured by its magnificence. Miles of majestic rock formations lay before them, their iridescent hues contrasted by a stark-blue sky—a dream come true for Morgan. An eagle soared through the warm air. Behind them, next to the RV, awaited a table for two, and their picnic lunch.

The spectacle switched to Crestwood Lake, years later, a gray-haired Morgan, recumbent in his favorite chair, next to the glowing fireplace, watching his beloved football. Vicki, her long red hair, now somewhat grizzled, placed a cup on the table next to him. "Here's your coffee, baby."

Morgan took her hand and kissed it.

"Hungry, baby?"

Morgan nodded.

"The pot roast is almost ready."

The doorbell rings and Gil, now well in his eighties, arrives, bottle in hand. He and Morgan drink and exchange witticisms as they watch the game.

"This can be your future," said Van Haden, as the scene reverted to the alabaster landscape. "I can ensure it. You and Vicki will live in contentment for the rest of your days. You will never be troubled by me again—so long as you don't trouble me. I'm not foolish enough to ask you to join me. I'm merely asking that you step aside."

Morgan clenched his jaw.

"It's pointless to resist me, Captain. You can't win. I am eternal; I will be here until the end of time. Just leave me be and live a long, comfortable life. I promise it will unfold as shown."

"And I'm supposed to trust a piece of shit like you?"

Van Haden frowned. "As deplorable as you may find me, I *am* a man of my word. If I, or one of my colleagues forges a pact, we honor it. We value loyalty and integrity, Captain."

"Integrity? Don't make me laugh. You don't know the meaning of the word."

"And you do?" said Van Haden. "You unabashed hypocrite. While I admire the ruse you entrapped Clyde and Derrick with, it nevertheless belies your self-righteousness. You abuse your authority by assaulting Derrick, then manipulate him to murder Burrows and Jameson, thus creating a pretense for killing him. Tell me, *Captain* Morgan, does that sound like integrity to you?"

"Yes, it does. I did what I had to do—to stop scumbags like you. I don't hurt innocent people."

"Oh, so that's your justification? Integrity, Captain, is the adherence to one's moral principles. Abandoning those principles to combat corruption, is not integrity, that's moral relativism. And by the way, your actions were about saving your own skin, to avoid imprisonment for your misdeeds. And that my good man, is the essence of hypocrisy."

"You contemptable bastard."

"I grow weary, Captain. I can guarantee you and Vicki a long, happy life." Van Haden glowered and spoke emphatically. "I will even forgive Vicki's betrayal, something I *never* do. But you must stay clear of me forever. Now what is your answer, Captain?"

"Go fuck yourself."

Van Haden's eyes turned dark red. His voice deepened. "Fine. You won't listen to reason, then maybe you'll listen to fear. Behold your new future . . ."

Morgan was surrounded by Van Haden's dungeon. He saw himself, and Gil, naked, bloodied, hanging from the ceiling by shackled wrists, backs against the wall. Vicki, also naked, was shackled, legs and arms spread, to a massive stone slab in the center of the room.

A gruesome red demon entered the chamber. His skin was leathery, talons extending from his hands and feet. He had a bald, mottled scalp, pointed ears, and fangs. He approached Gil.

"No . . .no . . ." mumbled Gil, trembling, blood streaming from his nose and ears.

The demon growled, then inserted one talon into Gil's right shoulder. He slowly slid it diagonally across Gil's torso, stopping at his left hip.

Gil screamed, every muscle in his body contracting.

"You bastard!" hollered the chained Morgan.

Vicki bawled.

The demon reached into Gil's abdomen, clasped his intestines, and retreated to the far wall, disemboweling him along the way.

Vicki squealed.

Gil shrieked and writhed . . . and then succumbed.

Morgan tugged at his chains. "You fucking coward! Killing an old man who's bound. Unchain me and take me on. Or are you afraid?"

"I'm saving you for last," snarled the demon. He approached Vicki.

"No!" shouted Morgan.

The demon etched a shallow laceration around each of Vicki's breasts, then licked his talon.

Vicki cried and panted.

Morgan twisted, fighting the chains.

The demon climbed upon the slab and knelt before Vicki. He waved his hand; the shackles around Vicki's ankles clanked open. He seized her knees and hoisted her spread legs.

Vicki tried to squirm out of his grasp, but it was futile.

The demon inched his pelvis toward Vicki. His penis was monstrous, and lined with barbs, certain to shred flesh on its backward strokes. The demon thrust forward . . .

"No!" screamed Morgan, yanking his chains. "No!"

Morgan was back in the forest, his heart about to burst from his chest. He was drenched in sweat.

Van Haden restrained a perverse smile. Then he scowled and gripped the back of Morgan's neck, faster than Morgan could see—paralyzing him. Van Haden moved his face to within a foot of Morgan's and drilled into his eyes. In a morbidly grave voice, he said, "Believe me, Captain. I've just shown you your futures. Which one will hinge on whether you defy me or not."

The red demon from the dungeon appeared immediately behind Van Haden. His one claw rested on Van Haden's right shoulder. His menacing face glared over Van Haden's left."

"I believe you know Clyde Burrows," said Van Haden.

Burrows glared, his eyes a blistering red. "Derrick wasn't a witch—but I was."

Morgan grunted and tried to break free, but he was frozen.

"You know the terms, Captain," said Van Haden.

Burrows licked his fangs. "I can't wait to taste Vicki's blood."

Van Haden released Morgan and stepped back.

Burrows vanished.

"I'll see you in hell, you son of a bitch," said Morgan.

"So you shall," said Van Haden disappearing.

Morgan stepped off the trail and onto the spot where Brian Delmore's body was found. He crouched and touched the ground.

It was warm.

The Progenitor

"We will torture you to death. We will consume your organs and drink your blood. We will kill your children—destroy your lineage . . . We will ravage your very existence."

Such were the words etched into my husband's twelve-inch crucifix as we sailed to the New World in September 1712. Three years prior, when I was seventeen, I married Myles and moved into his cottage in Guilford, England. I found the cross while organizing our new domicile, horrified by the inscription.

Myles explained it had belonged to his mother, and was vandalized by her neighbor, a demented old hag. The two women had maintained a contentious relationship for years. He wasn't cognizant of the catalyst, but nevertheless; their animosity escalated over time. Myles's mother was very religious. Convinced that the crone was a witch, his mother hung the crucifix outside, facing the old woman's shack. One day his mother came home to find her house smeared with blood, and the crucifix defaced with the grim engraving. Because of the sanctity of the cross, she retained it, and passed it on to her son. Out of the same reverence, Myles wouldn't think of discarding it.

Myles's mother was found brutally murdered late last year: throat slit and disemboweled. Interestingly, the old woman had disappeared, and was never seen again. Myles feared that he was next. He told our friends he was venturing to the colonies for economic reasons, but the truth was he believed his family had been cursed.

I didn't want to leave England. Nor did I believe in witchcraft, but Myles, and my father, William Phelps, who was accompanying us to the New World, did. Only one man is required to trump a woman's feelings in 1712. With two men it's a landslide.

And so I, Mrs. Elizabeth Latham, a proper English lady, swallowed my trepidation and heartache. I relinquished my homeland, and dutifully followed my husband into a forbidding and uncertain future.

Myles considered settling in Salem, since his friend had emigrated there. But, given the witch trials, that notion was summarily dismissed. Myles wanted nothing to do with any place having even a remote connection to witchcraft, and thus, opted for Scalford instead.

The Salem witch hysteria claimed the life of twenty-four people: twenty by execution, and four who died in prison awaiting trial. Massachusetts governor Sir William Phips interceded and abolished the trials in October 1692. Despite the extirpation of the devilment, a subgroup of ninety feverishly devoted Puritans believed that evil still infected Salem. Led by their harsh and hidebound minister Alexander Pitt, this faction vacated Salem and established the settlement of Scalford, so named after Pitt's birthplace in England.

Our minister in Guildford was a cousin of Pitt's and maintained contact with him. Pitt's last communiqué, over a year ago, reported that Scalford was flourishing. Myles, being a more fervent devotee himself, was delighted to hear about Pitt's zealous and ultra-pious outpost. My father concurred, and that sealed our fates. Myles booked passage the very next day.

What a horrendous journey! Six weeks aboard a cramped and fetid vessel, teaming with rats. The stench alone left me nauseated, let alone the perpetual rocking of the ship. Next to my creaking bunk I had two chamber pots, one for each end. It was the most sickening and insufferable experience of my young life.

We finally arrived in Boston. I pleaded with Myles to allow us a few days before traveling to Scalford. I desperately needed a respite to rest and hold down some solid food. But he and my father wouldn't hear of it. They had no intention of "squandering" the meager funds we had on accommodations. We spent the night in the cheapest room available. The next day, accompanied by thirteen other settlers from the ship, we collectively purchased horses, wagons, and provisions, and set off on a painstaking two-hundred-mile journey.

Because of the terrain, we could only manage twelve to fifteen miles a day. The trek was as cold as the ship, but not as crowded or putrid. Our food was strictly rationed. We augmented it by shooting wild turkeys and other small game. My hunger was so acute, even disemboweling a rabbit couldn't subdue it.

The worst part of the trip was the nights. On the ship, the greatest demons after dark were insomnia and vomiting. But after nightfall, in the unforgiving wilderness, that's where real demons came to life.

We heard horrid screeches, howls, and wails. It sounded as if a swarm of animals and people were slaughtering each other. One night, just outside our tent, I heard an ominous growling.

"It is the beast incarnated as a werewolf!" cried my father.

"What beast?" I asked.

My father ignored me and scrambled to his feet. Working swiftly, he took a shovel, scooped up heaps of burning ashes from our fire, and deposited them just outside our tent. Then he grabbed a pouch, retrieved a batch of dried stems and flowers, and distributed them on the embers. They crackled as they burned, the wind dispersing the smoke. We heard a yelp, and then what sounded like a large animal bounding away through the woods. The howling ceased.

"What did you do?" I asked.

"Wolfsbane," he said.

"Wolfsbane?"

"A plant that drives away evil spirits, particularly wolves."

"Was that a wolf?"

"No," said my father. "It was a werewolf."

"There's no such thing as werewolves."

"The Devil can command the souls he possesses to assume any form."

I was speechless. Here I was, thousands of miles from my home, which I'd never see again, in the middle of nowhere, being threatened by wolves, as my father went mad.

Myles put his arm around me and guided me back to our makeshift bed. "It'll be all right my dear. Only a few more days, and we'll be in Scalford."

I didn't say a word. Inside, my myriad emotions roiled. I lay awake all night, listening . . .until daybreak, when . . .

"He's dead! He's dead! Noooooo!"

Alice Minter's tortured cries awoke the entire camp. Inside her tent, her husband Elias lay in three pieces. The fourth was missing. Two of the other women grappled with Alice, who was distraught and thrashing, leading her away into another tent.

"It is the work of the Devil," proclaimed Minister Isaac Winslow, the spiritual leader of our group.

"But I drove the wolf away with wolfsbane last night," said my father.

Isaac kneeled down to inspect the dismembered corpse more closely. "This is not the work of a wolf. There are no teeth marks. The flesh is cleanly separated. This is the work of a demon, harvesting organs. Your wolfsbane would have been useless."

Our band was on the verge of panic. A fervid debate ensued about whether to return to Boston or forge on to Scalford. Myles and my father were in favor of the latter.

Finally, Isaac raised his arms and shouted, "Enough! The Devil is everywhere, not just here in the woods. You can find his evil hand in Boston as surely as anywhere else. We did not come all this way to turn back now. Have you forgotten what our savior enjoins about remaining resolute? James 1:12: blessed is the man who remains steadfast under trial, for when he has stood the test, he will receive the crown of life." Isaac pivoted his head, meeting each pair of eyes in turn, pointing and said, "Ye who quail in the face of our Lord's enemies, will *not* earn his favor."

Isaac's impassioned speech restored the group's composure—and their submission. The only thing that frightened a Puritan more than the Devil, was displeasing God. We buried Elias's body, performed the perfunctory religious rites, and then endured another of Isaac's cants about remaining faithful in the face of adversity.

On a more practical note, we decamped expeditiously, and trudged as far as possible until nightfall. One of the horses died, our food supply was exhausted, and Alice decompensated into a catatonic state.

181

Two days later we arrived in Scalford, ravenous, weak and weary. The residents welcomed us and tended to our needs. Myles, my father, and I, were set up in a small cottage. As much as I loved my father, I didn't want to live with him, but we couldn't afford two dwellings.

The next day, Alexander Pitt came calling. A tall man, with thin, dark hair, that wormed its way out of his hat to his earlobes. Stern and rigid, his salutations and questions felt more like an interview than an introduction. I mentioned that his cousin in Guildford was our minister, but he reacted indifferently.

Then, as if he were relaying some mundane piece of trivia, he impassively informed us that Scalford was beset by bubonic plague. Nine colonists had perished since we began our transatlantic crossing. I was appalled. According to our minister, Pitt's last correspondence beamed with applause for Scalford, depicting it as a thriving and devout community. Even though that was a year before the epidemic struck, I nevertheless felt deceived.

In a further contradiction of his most recent missive, Pitt professed that evil was in our midst, and that the plague was the work of the Devil, or a punishment from God. Either way, Scalford was failing in its devotion to our Lord. Pitt lectured us about sin, and proffered a bitter warning for anyone rejecting the Almighty. Even my father was left in awe.

Before Pitt left, he alluded to an event, two days hence, that would demonstrate the consequences for sinners. He admonished us to take heed, then stoically concluded with, "Welcome to Scalford."

I immediately suggested we return to England, but I was rebuffed by Myles and my father. They felt it was ridiculous to come all this way just to capitulate and return. Moreover, as my father pointed out, we needn't fear the plague, so long as our souls remained pure and our fealty to the Lord unyielding. I scoffed. The only thing that was "unyielding" was his reasoning, especially to female persuasiveness.

That night I slept fitfully. Early in the morning, someone knocked on our door. Already caught off guard by the hour, I was further taken back by our guest. Holding a basket of apples, an intriguingly comely young woman, with long, curly black hair and crystal-blue eyes, confronted me. She didn't speak—she discerned.

"Good . . . morning," I said.

"Welcome to Scalford," she said coolly. "I'm Dorothea Blackmore."

"I'm Elizabeth Latham. A pleasure to make your acquaintance." I extended my hand, she shook my fingers. "Do come in, please." As she stepped through the door I said, "Myles, Father, we have a visitor."

The men came forward.

"This is my father, William Phelps, and my husband Myles."

Dorothea cracked a smile while shaking my father's hand, which widened upon grasping Myles's. Holding his hand longer than a customary greeting, she locked eyes with my husband. "It's so nice to meet you. Welcome to Scalford." She handed him the basket. "I understand you had a terrible journey here."

"Yes," said Myles. "Somewhat traumatic."

"I'm caring for Alice Minter," said Dorothea.

"How is the poor girl doing?" asked my father.

"She's still in shock. Not eating. But she'll come around."

"It must be emotionally trying for you and your husband," I said.

"Oh, I'm not married," said Dorothea, returning her gaze to Myles.

I grabbed the basket from Myles and stepped between him and Dorothea. "Thank you for the apples. I shall make a lovely pie out of them."

"Do let me know if I can assist with your settling in," said Dorothea, turning toward the door.

"Ma'am," said my father, "before you go may I ask you a question?"

I turned and sneered at him.

"Of course," said Dorothea.

"I noticed a large stake surrounded by kindling and firewood in the church's courtyard. Whatever is that for?"

"They're putting a witch to death tomorrow."

183

"What?" said Myles.

"My God in heaven," said my father. "Who is it?"

"Jane Brewster," said Dorothea.

"And how do they know she's a witch?" I asked.

"Two women with whom she cavorts now have the plague. Her next-door neighbor's pigs died of a strange affliction, she missed Sunday services, and she lost her temper and used profanities with another woman."

"That doesn't prove she's a witch," I said.

"Is that so?" said Dorothea tilting her head, an adversarial gleam in her eye.

"So we're going to burn everyone to death who knows someone with the plague, or has a neighbor whose livestock died?"

"Enough," said my father.

"No," I said. "That's not right."

"Please, dear," said Myles, putting his arm around me. He turned toward Dorothea. "It was a strenuous journey; you must excuse her. There will be no questioning of the Lord's judgment from us." Myles looked at me. His eyes said, "Not another word out of you, woman."

Dorothea touched Myles's arm and said, "I understand. Let me know if you need anything."

The moment Dorothea left I pushed Myles away and faced him and my father. "Look at what the two of you have done. We gave up our home for *this*? Rotting on a stinking ship for six weeks, attacked by wolves in the wilderness, only to be delivered to the plague, and people being burned alive. Have the two of you lost your senses?"

"Now, dear," said Myles reaching out.

I knocked his hand away. "Don't *dear* me. Especially after the way you let that harlot fawn upon you. Or is that why you want to stay here?"

"How dare you," said Myles.

184

"How dare I? How dare *you* belittle me in front of that vixen. I question their reasonableness for burning a woman to death, and you attribute my behavior to the hardships that you yourself wrought? Goddamn you!"

My father smacked me off my feet, rendering me senseless.

"Don't you ever blaspheme in this house! How dare *you* invoke God's name in vain to condemn your husband. You've forgotten your place, woman." My father grabbed a club-like piece of firewood, stormed over to me, pulled my skirts over my buttocks and said, "You obviously need a reminder about respect for your family and the Lord."

"No!" cried Myles, grasping my father's wrist.

"Your wife needs to be disciplined."

"It is *my* responsibility to discipline her. She belongs to me now."

My father dropped the wood. "Fine. She is yours, but beware. Her insolence could call our faith into question." My father slammed the door as he left.

I lay on the floor, whimpering. I looked at Myles, wondering what he would do. He picked me up, escorted me to the bed, and held me.

"Winter is approaching," said Myles. "It's too late in the year to head back. Come spring, if we are unhappy here, we can return to England, OK?"

I nodded and wiped my eyes. "Do you promise?"

"With God as my witness."

I let out a sigh of relief and embraced my husband.

"In the meantime, you better control your tongue. Your father is right. Such displays could cast doubts about our propriety. It may already be too late."

"Why do you say that?"

"We've been here only two days, and already you're questioning the system. If this Blackmore woman is as devious as you say, surely she will share your comments with others. Possibly use them against you."

"Oh, Myles, I don't think—"

"They're putting a woman to death, in part for losing her temper with a citizen. What do you think they'll do to someone who challenges the authorities?"

"You're right. I'm sorry. And I'm sorry for how I spoke to you."

"All is forgiven, my love."

The next day my father attended the execution. Myles and I remained home . . . but still could hear the screams.

I tried to focus on Myles's promise to return to England in the spring. Knowing I only needed to persevere until then gave me hope. The three of us proceeded to acclimate to life in Scalford. What else could we do? Myles, an able carpenter, was immediately put to work. My father, an insufferably hard worker, began chopping a winter's worth of firewood. I of course, tended to the interminable household chores.

Myles's concerns about Dorothea nagged at my mind. A few days later I decided to conciliate and bring her a pie. It would also give me a chance to see how poor Alice Minter was doing.

As I walked to Dorothea's dwelling, I noticed a small, shabby cottage, all by itself in the distance. I saw a long-brown-haired woman puttering outside. How odd that all the homes were clustered around the center of the village but one. Who lived there?

Pie in hand I knocked on Dorothea's door. I heard people fumbling inside and something being knocked over. I waited and knocked again. The door flung open. Dorothea peered at me like I was an insect. Alice came out of the bedroom, fastening the top two buttons of her blouse.

"Good day," I said. "I wanted to thank you for the lovely apples you brought us. I made you a pie."

"Well how thoughtful," said Dorothea, her demeanor warming to tepid.

"May I come in?"

". . . Yes."

186

"Alice, how are you doing?"

"Much better," she said, smiling, a bounce in her step. She gave me a warm hug.

"Your grief must be unbearable."

"Oh no. I'm fine. Dorothea's friendship has eased my burden."

"Is that so?"

"Oh yes. She has deepened my spirituality by helping me understand my suffering, and how welcome I am here in Scalford."

"That sounds . . .lovely. But you must miss your husband."

"He's in a better place, and so am I."

"Thank you for the pie," said Dorothea. "I assume we'll see you at church tomorrow?" She motioned toward the door.

"Uh . . .yes. Have a nice day. Are you sure you're all right, Alice?"

"I'm fine. Don't worry about me. A woman in your condition has enough to attend to."

"Good day," said Dorothea, closing the door.

What in God's name did she mean by a woman in my condition? And what did Dorothea do to Alice? Less than a week ago she finds her husband in pieces and now she has spiritual tranquility? Hmmmph. In a pig's ass. I may be only twenty, but that's long enough to know God doesn't work that way.

As I walked back to my house I passed a neighbor's home. Minister Pitt, three men, and one woman, stood outside, as two other men carried a blanket-covered body out of the house on a stretcher. "What happened?" I asked.

"Henry Tillman," said Pitt. "The plague has delivered him to the Lord. Go home, child."

"I'm *not* a child."

Pitt bristled. "Do as you're told."

The woman in the group said, "I'll walk her home." She was a little over five feet, thin, with graying hair, and large, but gentle brown eyes. "You're Elizabeth Latham, right?"

"Yes."

"It's so nice to finally meet you. I'm Mary Pickford. How are you, honey?"

"Not good."

"I heard about what your group went through on the way here. I'm sorry for your troubles." Mary looked at the stretcher, turned to me and said, "Let's go. Pitt is bad enough. Add a corpse and I'm at the end of my tether."

"You don't like him either?"

"Nobody does, honey. But he's our leader, and the senior minister. God gives with one hand and takes with the other."

Mary put her arm around mine as we walked. "What brings you to Scalford?"

"Pitt is a cousin of our minister back in Guildford. Pitt wrote to him, telling him about how wonderful Scalford was. But we come here only to find the plague, and people being burned at the stake."

"If they don't drown them," said Mary.

"What?"

"People convicted of witchcraft are either drowned in the lake or burned to death."

"How many people have been executed?"

"I'm not sure. Lost count. More than twenty since Scalford was founded in 1693."

"Do you believe in witchcraft, Mary?"

"I believe in the Lord our God, and his nemesis Satan, and his followers, whom we call witches. Don't you?"

"Of course. My husband's mother was tormented by a witch back home in Guildford."

"How is your husband?"

"He's fine. Seems to be adjusting."

"Has he been visited by Dorothea yet?"

"What?"

"She visits all the new men. Did she come by your house with some bread, or maybe a basket of apples?"

I gaped at Mary.

"I'd keep an eye on her, honey. Today it's apples, tomorrow it's forbidden fruit."

"I'm surprised she hasn't been accused of witchcraft."

"Oh she has, but the elders looked the other way. They don't want to bite the hand that feeds'em. She visits them too."

"In a community as reverent as Scalford?"

"Hypocrisy is a cornerstone of Christianity," said Mary.

"I thought you said you believe in God."

"I do. I don't believe in man."

Mary's misanthropic admission stunned me. We walked for another minute or two without speaking. I pointed and asked, "Who lives in that shanty, all by itself over there?"

"Oh, that's Velma. I'd keep my distance from her as well."

"Why?"

"She's a leper. Came here a year after Scalford was founded. They isolate her, so she doesn't infect the rest of us. She's the only one excused from having to attend church."

"How does she survive?"

"She plants her vegetables and raises chickens and goats. Every so often a few of the townsfolk drop off supplies outside her house, so long as she stays inside."

"The poor dear. Perhaps I could bring her some provisions."

"Be careful, honey. Some people think she's a witch. I suspect if it wasn't for the leprosy, she would have been hauled in and questioned by now."

"Good Lord. Is there anyone here who hasn't been suspected of witchcraft?"

"You haven't . . . yet."

When we reached my house, I invited Mary in, but she declined, saying she had chores to do. Her comments about Dorothea were unsettling. Myles is a man of integrity, and I trusted him. But no woman in her right mind would be indifferent to some strumpet's advances toward her husband. I had no idea what to do about it. As a young, female newcomer, I was at the bottom of a Draconian, and increasingly complicated pecking order.

I didn't share my true thoughts about spirituality with Mary. I hardly believed in heaven, let alone hell. Gossip was a driving force in Puritanical society, and as Myles had pointed out, any lack of faith could come back to haunt you. Strangely, it wasn't good enough for the Puritans to believe in God. Disavowing the existence of the Devil and witchcraft was also considered heresy, and impeachable. In an ignorant, dogmatic culture, deviation from any part of the narrative is a threat.

As I opened my door I heard voices. My father, Myles, and another man in his mid-twenties with dark hair were seated at our table talking.

Myles stood up. "Elizabeth, I'd like you to meet Tom Ramsey. Tom, this is my wife, Elizabeth."

Ramsey rose. "How do you do ma'am? I live two doors down."

"Nice to meet you."

"Tom here," said Myles, "splits his time between blacksmithing and carpentry. He's helping us build the new stables."

"I see. Maybe you could bring your wife on your next visit?"

"I'm afraid that won't be possible, ma'am. She's suffering from the plague. Already killed my father, now it's set its sights on her. I just hope my daughter is spared."

"Oh, I'm terribly sorry. If there's anything we can do, let us know."

"Thank you, ma'am."

"Tom's from London," said my father. "Came to Salem when he was a boy."

"Oh, so you were there for the trials?"

"Indeed I was, ma'am. Not much different from what's going on now."

There was so much I wanted to ask him: about the societal order, the people accused of witchcraft, the legal system, the strictures on the inhabitants. But, it can seem impudent to ask too many questions, especially from a woman. I scoffed inside my head. Merely inquiring about the intricacies of the system could cause one to fall victim to it. So I suppressed my natural curiosity and yielded to my role. "Could I offer you something to eat, Mr. Ramsey?"

"No, I'm fine, but thank you."

"Very well then. I will leave you gentlemen to your business."

Later that night I lay in bed with Myles, stewing. If Ramsey's family had been afflicted with the plague, could he have infected us? Myles argued it wasn't catching unless the person was symptomatic. Fears aside, I remained curious about what Ramsey knew about this strange new world. I questioned Myles about Ramsey, but it soon became clear we had different concerns. Myles didn't care about how our society functioned, the perverse religiosity, or the horrid incriminations. He was preoccupied with practical matters, such as buying supplies, preparing for the winter, and transporting goods. My father was the same.

Myles became tired of talking and wished to satisfy his cravings before retiring. With so many worries on my mind, the last thing I felt was amorous, but my feelings were not germane to the marital obligations.

Myles lumbered on top of me, thrusting. I dug my nails into his back. My feigned desire intensified his, and I longed to escape into sleep as soon as possible. The rhythm of his breaths became rapid and choppy. He moaned as he started to climax—his eyes turned black—fangs bared—I shrieked.

Myles wheezed, "Are you OK?"

His eyes and mouth were normal. I was mystified.

"Dear?"

I remained addled.

"Did I hurt you?" he asked, regaining his breath.

"No, no. It was just intense."

"Oh," he said, with a jaunty smile, rolling off to his side of the bed.

I turned away from him, clutched myself, and tried to make sense of what I saw. Was I losing my mind?

Myles was asleep in minutes. I lay awake all night.

The next morning, I was nauseated and retching. Did I have the plague? It was Thomas Ramsey; he must have given it to me. My father downplayed my queasiness, attributing it to something I ate, but Myles insisted I see the doctor. I reminded him that we had church later that morning, but Myles argued that if it were the plague, I shouldn't be infecting the entire community. He brought me straight to the home of Solomon Prower, a physician from Boston.

While the doctor examined me, his wife kept Myles company, offering him breakfast and inundating him with her lamentations about missing Boston. When Dr. Prower finished, he summoned Myles.

"Is it the plague, Doctor?" asked Myles, even before Prower closed the door.

"No, it's morning sickness."

"Morning sickness?" said Myles wide-eyed, turning to me.

"I'm pregnant, love."

Myles's shock turned to glee. "That's wonderful, darling. God has blessed us."

I don't know if I was happier about not having the plague, or having a child, but I embraced my husband with relief. Myles walked me home, bopping with delight, even as we passed a small procession, escorting the latest victim to Scalford's cemetery.

My father, overjoyed, prompted us to get ready for church. "We have much to thank the Lord for today," he proclaimed.

My initial elation was giving way to new consternations, such as all the anxieties of birthing and caring for a child. My mother died bearing me. Would I meet the same fate? I fretted about the previous night's hallucination. Could pregnancy cause that? Was I going mad? And then, on top of all that, was the distressing realization that my pregnancy would delay our return to England for at least a year. It was nearly December and the baby wouldn't arrive till July. Unquestionably, it would be unwise to trudge back to Boston, and then sail across the Atlantic with a newborn. But the prospect of staying another year in this godforsaken place gave me thoughts too dark to mention.

The three of us sat in church, with me between the men, waiting for Pitt to commence the service. I looked over my left shoulder and saw Dorothea and Alice entering. Every pew had vacant spots, two were entirely empty. But that brazen hussy, sidekick in tow, ignored them all, crept up the side aisle, and seated herself right next to Myles.

"Why hello, Myles," she beamed. "Elizabeth," she said coldly.

Alice greeted Myles, then gave me a half-hearted wave.

I scooched over in the pew closer to my father, took Myles's hand and pulled him toward me. Dorothea countered by wiggling her buttocks closer to Myles. I was fuming. Had we not been in a house of God I would have reacted. I couldn't wait until the service was over to give Dorothea a piece of my mind.

During Pitt's service a series of gasps erupted from the congregation. Turning in the direction of the cries I was thunderstruck to see a woman waltzing down the center aisle stark naked!

"Good God!" my father said. "She must be possessed."

"Behold!" shouted Pitt. "Such is the work of the Devil!"

One of the men took off his coat, charged the woman, and wrapped it around her.

"Take her to the pillory," ordered Pitt.

With all the commotion, I never got the chance to confront Dorothea.

The poor woman was dragged to the pillory where her head and hands were locked into the openings. Pitt removed the coat declaring, "You want the world to see you naked? So be it." He took a leather strap and proceeded to beat her bloody. After every few lashes he interrogated her, demanding to know who inspired her to behave in such a manner. She pled ignorance and begged for mercy. But Pitt continued to flog her until blood dripped down her legs.

Why she wasn't accused of being a witch herself is beyond me. People were inculpated for far lesser offenses. But Pitt was undeterred that she was a victim of sorcery. The logic of his incriminations was often arcane and mercurial.

A few days later, a man by the name of Peter defecated in public. The same scenario ensued, only he didn't receive as many lashes. Apparently, men's genitals are not as morally repugnant as women's.

Four days later, Ramsey's wife died. By then, his six-year-old daughter had become infected. I felt terrible for him, even a little guilty. I was married and expecting, while Ramsey had lost his father and wife, with his daughter soon to follow.

As we gathered around the grave, watching his wife's body descending into the ground, I noticed a lone figure standing in the distance. I think it was Velma, the leper. I don't know why exactly, probably my sympathy, but I felt compelled to engage her. I imagined how I would feel, beset by a horrid disease, shunned by my community.

"Where are you going?" asked Myles.

"To introduce myself to Velma." I gestured toward her.

"Are you out of your mind? The plague isn't enough for you? You want to expose yourself to leprosy as well?"

"I'll be fine."

"You're carrying my child."

"I won't get that close."

I turned and marched off before Myles could retort. Velma stood motionless as I approached. I stopped about twelve feet from her. She indeed had leprosy. Her face was disfigured: wrinkled, rough, and dappled with misshapen lesions. Conversely, her eyes were beautiful: lustrously hazel. She wore a gray dress and bonnet.

"Good morning. I'm Elizabeth Latham. Mary Pickford told me about you. I wanted to say hello, see if you needed anything."

"That's very kind of you."

"Can I bring you some food?"

"No thank you, but you're a good soul."

I didn't know what else to say. Well I did, but couldn't. I felt stupid making small talk.

"I sense you want to ask me something," said Velma.

"Scalford troubles me. Frightens me actually. I want to return to England but . . ."

"But you're with child."

"How do you know?"

"Word travels fast in Scalford, even to outcasts. I'm sure you've heard rumors about me."

"They say you're a witch, but I don't believe such things."

"You better start," said Velma.

"Why?"

"Because you're in grave danger. Especially since you're expecting."

"What does my child have to do with it?"

"The death or conversion of a pregnant woman is particularly valued."

"Conversion?"

"To the dark side."

"Or death?"

"Lucifer relishes the slaughtering of infants."

"You're mad. Or you're one of them."

"I've seen it firsthand! This place is a bastion of evil. You and your husband are still pure of heart. Get out of here while you can."

"I'm sorry to have troubled you." I turned to leave.

"Mary Pickford is a witch," said Velma.

I turned back.

"Do not be deceived by her genteel demeanor. The mantle of evil is benevolence."

Oh, the agony. I had felt pity for this woman and wanted to help her. In exchange for my compassion, I'm told that my life, and my unborn child's life, is in danger, from witches no less. Was there *any* truth to what Velma said, or was it all insanity? Either way, I was in a perilous situation: an isolated colony of lunatics or monsters. I ran back to Myles and collapsed in his arms, crying as he dispensed his "I told you so's."

Within a week, Ramsey's daughter was dead. Pitt, ignoramus that he was, excoriated him for betraying God, believing it was the only plausible reason why the Lord would take his father, wife, and daughter. Ramsey, in his grief, attacked Pitt, snapping his neck. Ramsey was found guilty of willful murder, accused of being a witch, and burned at the stake.

Mary Pickford encouraged me to attend the execution with her, but I refused. Mary seemed all too willing to view the grim festivities, almost as if she were restraining jubilation. She didn't harbor any malice toward Ramsey that I knew of. Why would she revel at his death? Flashes of what Velma said about Mary continued to nettle me.

Isaac Winslow, the most vociferous and iron-fisted of the elders, became our new head minister. He vowed to "root out the evil that was severing our relationship with God." I remember thinking he could start by hanging himself.

After Ramsey's execution, there was an uptick in distressing events. It seemed like every week something outlandish would happen: a couple fornicating in public, a man stabbing his dog to death, a few suicides. We found mutilated animals, strange wolf-like tracks, and upside-down crosses scribbled on the sides of houses. Most disturbingly, the plague continued to claim lives, as did executions for witchcraft. Every enormity brought new accusations, some of which resulted in convictions. Winslow's judgment appeared to be just as despotic as Pitt's.

Myles acceded to leave Scalford the following spring. At this point, even my father concurred. By July, as I was about to give birth, the colony had dwindled to forty-one people.

My labor was brutal: excruciating pain. Dr. Prower and Alice Minter, who had been a midwife in Guildford, attended me. Eight hours in, I was almost depleted. Exhausted from pain, saturated in sweat, I felt on the verge of unconsciousness. Prower and Alice were bleary as well. Prower took Alice aside and mumbled to her, but I could still overhear.

"The baby's no closer to arriving. This could take hours more. I'm not sure she'll survive it. I must get some food and rest. When I return you may take nourishment."

The doctor left. I whimpered, looking to Alice for comfort.

Alice took a wet cloth and wiped my brow. "There there, dear. You'll pull through. I can assure it."

Alice clutched my arms. Her face turned gray as her features distorted. Her eyes enlarged, sinking into her skull into two dark, amorphous orbs. In a deep, ghost-like voice she uttered:

"We will torture you to death. We will consume your organs and drink your blood. We will kill your children—destroy your lineage . . . We will ravage your very existence."

I screamed as loud as my waning strength would allow. A shooting pain tore through my abdomen. I screamed again.

Alice, appearing normal, scampered to the door and flung it open. Myles and my father rose. "Go fetch the doctor. The baby's coming!"

Fifteen minutes later, my daughter Sarah entered this world. What a harrowing rush of emotion. My greatest joy, and my greatest horror, comingled into a bewildering experience. The joy won out, but not by much. As Myles and my father cheered, and praised God, I was bedeviled by my hallucination. Or was it? Velma's warning reverberated through my brain.

Three days later I became horribly ill: fatigue, vomiting, and fever. My body ached, and I couldn't keep food down. Eventually the fever subsided, but the nausea, pain, and weakness persisted. I was barely able to nurse. My sleep was disrupted by nightmares. It wasn't much consolation, but I was deemed a target of witchcraft, as opposed to a perpetrator. The afflicted are generally perceived as victims, unless their suffering becomes egregious, as with Ramsey, then one is decried unholy for inciting God's wrath. Puritanical compassion certainly has its limits.

Winslow came every day, and along with Myles and my father, recited prayers at my bedside. I felt like some kind of martyr for Christianity. I held Sarah virtually non-stop, using what little strength I had to attend to her needs. I would allow Myles and my father to hold her but would not permit her out of my sight. I would die if necessary to protect her.

Summer turned to fall. My illness finally abated, but things in Scalford were getting out of control. The village was embroiled in full-blown witch hysteria. Macabre and bizarre phenomena persisted. Even I was starting to become a believer—not in God, but the Devil. Fierce debates raged daily about vacating the settlement and returning to Salem.

It was the last Sunday in October. I was well enough to attend church and could no longer be excused due to infirmity. I remained fearful of exposing Sarah to the world, but forgoing the liturgy could cause other complications. Moreover, Winslow had made it clear that he expected all of the remaining twenty-eight citizens of Scalford to be present. After the services, he planned on holding a final and peremptory discussion about deserting the colony.

We took our customary pew in church, my father seated on the center-aisle side, then me, followed by Myles. Winslow was in the middle of his sermon, droning on with the barefaced intention of convincing the citizenry to remain in Scalford. Windows shattered, a door slammed, people shrieked, a group of grotesque demons stormed the building! One was tall and muscular, with gray-brown skin, a skull-like head and the horns of a ram. Another was red and slimy, a snake for a tongue slithered in and out of his mouth. A third was a mottled black and green, with sharp talons extending from his feet and hands. And they all had monstrously red eyes. Smoke billowed from behind the altar.

People were gasping and screaming. I looked around the frenzied congregation. A third of them, yellow eyes glistening, encircled the pews, blocking escape. Mary Pickford was one of them. Flames engulfed the church. I wrapped my arms around Sarah.

The demon with the ram horns bounded to the center aisle and emitted a monstrous roar. Then, in a voice so deep it sounded like it echoed from hell itself, said, "Mark my words. This is your only chance. Join us or die!"

"Don't listen to him!" shouted Winslow. "Away with you, Satan!"

One of the witches raised a flintlock pistol and fired, striking Winslow in the center of the chest. He collapsed on the altar, dead.

Pandemonium ensued. Most of the congregants tried to run. A few trembled in their pews. The witches and demons descended on the ones trying to escape.

Myles grabbed my arm. "Let's go!"

I pressed Sarah against my chest and jumped up. I turned to my father.

He sat there, a tortured expression on his face, accentuated by his yellow eyes. "Go now," he growled.

"Father! No!"

"It's too late for him," cried Myles. "We must go."

We dashed into the side aisle. From the rear, Alice Minter was storming toward us, hatchet in hand. Two pews ahead of us, Dorothea, brandishing a large knife, moved to cut us off. The front of the aisle, adjacent to the altar, was engulfed in smoke.

"Go," said Myles. "It's our only chance."

We ran forward, directly into the smoke. There was a door, partially afire, that led to a small ancillary room with a window. Myles crashed into the door and dragged me and Sarah through. Flames crackled up two of the walls. It was hard to breathe. I choked as Sarah wailed.

"Hurry!" I yelled.

Myles, coughing, found a broom. He jabbed at the window with the handle, breaking the glass piecemeal, but it was too late.

Dorothea charged, stabbing Myles in the back. He fell to the floor. She straddled him, stabbing repeatedly.

"No!" I yelled, trying to protect Sarah with my arms.

Alice entered, darted between me and the window, and raised her hatchet.

"Give her to us," said Dorothea, "or you both shall die."

The black and green demon slinked in behind Dorothea, extending his talons.

"Never," I snarled.

Alice started to swing, but something swooped in through the window, clutched her head and twisted it, snapping her neck.

Velma waved her hand. The fire shot off the wall, enveloping Dorothea and the demon. They screaked and writhed.

Velma threw her arms around me and Sarah, transported the three of us through the window, and to the beginning of the forest, on the edge of Scalford. I was still coughing out remnants of smoke. Sarah seemed to be choking.

Velma placed her hand on Sarah's head, restoring her breathing and calming her. I could see the church surrendering to the flames. Fifty yards or so into the forest I saw three wagons, horses, and a group of men.

Velma's leprosy was gone. Her skin was radiant, her long brown hair flowed, and her hazel eyes sparkled unlike any I have ever seen before. I was in awe.

"These men will get you to Boston. You can decide where to go from there."

Once again, my mind was a tempest of emotions: shock, horror, and relief. "Myles?" I asked?

"I'm sorry," said Velma. "I can't save everyone."

"Are you a witch?"

"I'm a white witch."

"What's that?"

"I don't serve Satan."

"Velma," I said more to myself than her. "Your name means 'determined protector.'"

"Yes, but that's not my real name."

"What's your—"

"Don't ask. My identity must remain secret."

"What are you doing here?"

"I am on a mission. I can't discuss the details. You should get going."

Velma bade me farewell. The men made me comfortable and wrapped Sarah in blankets. As we rolled away, Velma's figure receded, the distant smoke intensified, and my grief compounded. I mourned, cradling Sarah, as we trundled forth into an incomprehensible new world.

~~~~~~

I elected to remain in Boston. One of the men who delivered me from Scalford hired me as his live-in housekeeper and nanny. He and his wife have been most kind to me, as has the entire city. Sarah is a vibrant and carefree two-year-old, utterly oblivious to her tragic beginnings.

While permanently scarred by the past, I have managed to regain my emotional bearings. Until the other day, when I received a letter from my father, devoid of a return address, and brimful with sorrow.

He had taken his own life. Racked with insurmountable guilt for turning to the Devil, his only recourse was to terminate his life and accept the fires of perdition. He didn't explain how he planned to kill himself, or why he turned his back on God. He simply reiterated his regret, pleading for me to forgive him.

After two days of sporadic crying, I was able to restore my equanimity. I have much to live for: Sarah of course, but also, the new man in my life. We met at church, which I now attend faithfully. After courting for five months he asked me to marry him. My answer was a resounding yes. We are madly in love and will wed before winter. I can't wait to move into his home and rebuild a family, maybe give Sarah a brother. I can't wait to become the wife of Bartholomew Morgan.

The Machinations

Morgan pulled up in front of Gil's house on the west side of Crestwood Lake. The small driveway was already at capacity with Gil's Escort and Vicki's lightning-blue Mustang. Morgan got out, spit, and banged on the front door. Betsy, Gil's aging terrier, barked.

Vicki opened the door and hugged him. "Hey, baby."

Morgan kissed her cheek.

"What's that?" Vicki asked, pointing at the two-foot-long cardboard tube in his hand.

"You'll see," said Morgan, plopping onto the brown leather couch.

Vicki sat next to him.

Gil was in his usual spot: the loveseat perpendicular to the couch. "Wanna bourbon?"

"No," said Morgan. "I gotta go to the grammar school and see the kids."

"Weren't you just there last month?" asked Gil.

"Yeah, with the firemen, reviewing fire safety. Today I want to talk to them about strangers approaching them, in person and on the internet."

"Where's Father Sean?" asked Vicki.

"In Boston," said Morgan. "At the ceremony for the new cardinal they're appointing, or anointing, or whatever it is they do. He'll be back by Sunday."

"So what's the plan?" asked Gil.

"Before we get into that, I have to tell you guys something."

"What?" asked Vicki.

Morgan relayed his encounter with Van Haden in the woods. He explained the two futures that Van Haden had shown him. And even though he feared retraumatizing Vicki, he shared with her the lurid details of the bad one. He did it because he wanted her to make an informed decision. If she chose not to fight, he would respect her, even though it went against every molecule of his being.

When Morgan finished, Gil took a long swig of his rye.

Vicki stared at the crackling flames in the fireplace.

"Honey," said Morgan, "if you want to say the hell with this shit and get out of here, I'll understand. I'll retire, we'll sell the house, we'll head to—"

"No," said Vicki, shaking her head. "I know how he works. He presented it as if there are *only* two outcomes. He damn sure isn't going to show you a scenario where you've defeated him. I will not spend the rest of my life knowing we gave in . . . feeling guilty for lives lost that we might have saved. No. I will not run away."

Morgan smiled. "That's my gal." Then he looked at Gil.

"I'm in. What's our strategy?"

"Aaronson's supposed to contact you when his courier has the artifacts," said Morgan. "That night we'll meet the courier at the cemetery."

"Where we going to hide them?" asked Vicki.

"We're not. We're going straight to Van Haden's from the cemetery."

"You found it?" asked Gil.

"I think so."

Vicki grabbed Morgan's forearm. "Are you serious, baby?"

"After Van Haden vanished, I felt something. I touched the ground where we found Delmore's body . . . It was *warm*."

"Intriguing," said Gil.

"It makes sense," said Morgan. "Most of the weird shit has taken place on the north side."

Gil squinted. "But even if the entrance to his underground den is there, how do we get in?"

"I remembered there was an old copper mine in the hills there, about a mile or so away." Morgan opened the cardboard tube, pulled out a rolled-up paper, and spread it out on Gil's coffee table. He placed the TV remote on one end and Gil's drink on the other to keep it flat.

Gil gave him a look.

"You can't go on the wagon for three stinking minutes?" said Morgan.

"What is it, baby?" asked Vicki.

"It's an old geological survey map of Essex County. I got it from the town archives." Morgan pointed. "Here's the mine, and ya see this line; it was one of the shafts. Notice where it goes."

"I'll be damned," said Gil.

"Right toward the spot where Delmore was killed," said Morgan. "It goes down on a thirty-degree angle. I've been to what's left of the mine, at the entrance to this shaft. Years ago, some kids were partying there, and one fell and broke his leg."

Gil took a deep breath and raised his eyebrows.

"What?" asked Morgan.

"I guess the reality of this is setting in. I see where you were coming from at Aaronson's. We're going to hike down a mile-long mine shaft, in the dark, with the tablet and sword, into the Devil's hideout, probably take on a bunch of witches and demons along the way, and throw the Devil out of Crestwood Lake."

"This shit ain't gonna be easy," said Morgan.

Gil grabbed his glass and swigged, as the map rolled closed.

Morgan turned to Vicki. "This is obviously very dangerous. We don't have much chance. I know you don't want to give up, but that doesn't mean you have to be in the thick of it. You could stay back here and—"

"No! I'm not having this conversation again. I will not cower in the shadows, worrying about whether you're dead or alive. We're in this together no matter what happens."

205

"Yes, dear," said Morgan.

"What if that shaft doesn't lead to Van Haden's den?" asked Gil.

"Then we dynamite the spot where the ground was warm."

"What?"

"You heard me. I'm bringing dynamite. And conventional weapons. And of course, all the holy water from Father Sean."

"Uh, Butch, don't ya think dynamite will kind of alert them to our presence?"

"That's what we want. We gotta read that prayer in front of Van Haden."

"It won't make a difference any way," said Vicki. "Believe me, they'll know we're there."

"But let's just say we don't get in, and have to retreat," said Gil. "What do we do with the artifacts? How do we keep them safe?"

"We get out of Crestwood Lake, temporarily," said Morgan. "We head back to Cambridge. Regroup and plan our next move with Aaronson. In the meantime, we'll meet Father Sean this weekend, fill him in on what we discussed, and finalize the details."

Gil replenished his drink. "Did you hear that they ID'd the Body-Snatcher?"

"Of course," said Morgan.

"Who is he?" asked Vicki.

"David Nyman, the chef who owns Pierre's," said Gil. "They got him on video. Only problem is he's missing."

"Van Haden used to go to Pierre's," said Vicki.

"I'm not surprised," said Morgan. "I'm sure Nyman's one of his flunkies."

206

"Oh, you can count on it," said Vicki. "He may not be an actual witch, but I'm sure he was enlisted to kidnap people. Keep up the coven's supply of organs and blood."

Morgan glimpsed at his watch. "I gotta go. Don't want to be late for the kids. Doesn't set a good example."

"You really like the kids, don't you?" asked Gil.

"Does that surprise you?" asked Morgan.

"You? Yeah it does. Just want to understand why."

"Children are totally innocent. Only innocent human beings on the planet. And they're honest. They don't fuss about peoples' feelings or political correctness, or any of that bullshit. If you smell, they'll tell you. Not because they're trying to hurt you. Just because they think it's normal to talk about the obvious. I find it fucking refreshing."

"Now I understand," said Gil.

The Specter

Two hundred and forty miles from the coast, the SS Raphael entered the Gulf of Maine, headed for Portland Harbor. It bore the namesake of the archangel renowned for his defiance of the Devil, and his protection of sailors. Built in Norway in the 1950s, the 180-foot cargo ship was soon to be scrapped. Fog enshrouded the vessel, limiting visibility to six hundred feet. Dusk was imminent, and would seal the ship's surrender to the foreboding murk.

On the bridge, Italian Captain Aldo Conterno, paced, bouncing his eyes between the instruments and the invading gloom.

Nigel Poole casually sipped his port. "Nervous, Captain?"

"I don't like it when I can't see the horizon."

"That's what radar's for," said Poole.

"Gadgetry is no match for a seadog's senses."

"Have a wee spot of me port. It'll take the edge off."

Conterno sneered. "*I* don't drink when I'm on duty."

"Maybe you should."

"And what's that supposed to mean, Mr. Poole?"

"Nothing, mate. You just seem a little tense."

Conterno stepped toward Poole. Looking down at the six-foot Englishman he said, "I'm tense, *mate*, because I don't approve of hauling secret cargo. I'm the captain of this ship and I should know everything that's within it, including that crate of yours."

"We discussed this with your employer before we left."

"I don't give a shit. My employer isn't the one sailing through thick fog with unknown cargo, and thirteen people's lives."

"We're almost there."

"No, we're not. We're doing less than ten knots because of the fog."

Poole sipped his port.

"What's in that crate?"

"I'm afraid I'm not at liberty to say."

"Then get the hell off my bridge."

"Captain!" shouted the first officer. "A ship, dead ahead!"

"What?" said Conterno. "Why didn't the radar pick it up? Hard to starboard!"

"Aye, sir. Hard to starboard."

"This is why I don't trust gadgets, Poole."

The Raphael lurched, as if it had hit an iceberg. The navigator and second officer, seated at the con, bounced off their screens. Poole and the first officer grabbed the edge of a fixed table. Conterno fell, landing on his knee and outstretched hand. Poole went to help him up.

"Get off of me." Conterno stood up and sprang to the con. "What happened?"

"I don't know," said the navigator. "We've come to a complete stop."

"How could we just stop? A ship this size doesn't just stop. Hard to starboard, then ahead full."

"The controls won't respond, sir."

"What the hell is going on?" said Conterno.

"The other ship is coming," said the first officer.

"What is that?" asked the second officer.

"It's a brigantine," said Conterno. He reached for his binoculars and held them to his eyes. "What in God's name? It's an early eighteenth century brigantine, flying a jolly roger. But there's no one on deck. There seems to be . . . dammit, I can't see."

209

The fog thickened as the brigantine approached, obscuring the ship's details.

"Sound the horn! Signal collision!" yelled Conterno.

The second officer blared the ship's horn. The brigantine was unfazed. The navigator tried to work the controls, but they were unresponsive.

"We're gonna hit," said the second officer.

"Look," said Poole.

The brigantine turned at the last minute, easing alongside. Everyone on the Raphael's bridge bolted out onto the deck and gawked.

"What in blazes?" said Poole.

The brigantine seemed to fade in and out of reality. Not a soul was present. And yet, something was powering it. It maintained its position, a mere ten yards from the Raphael. Despite its fluctuating corporeality, the men could discern a row of canons, the wheel, the two masts, and rigging. Curiously, it did not appear to be a replica, or even a refurbished original. It was unpainted and decrepit, as if it had been roaming the seas for centuries. The jolly roger flapped in the wind.

"A pirate ship?" said Conterno.

"A ghost ship," said Poole.

Multiple pairs of yellow and red eyes illuminated along the deck of the brigantine.

"Run!" shouted Poole, dashing back toward the bridge. Before entering, he stopped and looked back.

The other men were more astonished than frightened, still trying to grasp what they were beholding.

"Run!" yelled Poole, but it was too late.

The witches and demons pounced, leaping through the air, descending on the men like starving vampire bats. A red demon with a horned skull, swung its talons and sliced off the top of Conterno's head. The witches, armed with hatchets, swords, and knives, slashed and hacked the remainder of the officers.

Poole's initial impulse was to radio for help, but there was no time. He smashed open the weapons cabinet and grabbed a .45 automatic. Bullets could only kill the witches, but he took it nonetheless. Then he charged toward his cabin in the ship's bow.

One engineer stayed in the engine room, but the remainder of the crew came topside, hearing the ship's alarms and commotion.

Poole ran past two crew members and hollered "Abandon ship!" Screams could be heard behind him. He reached his cabin, flung open the door, and threw on a life preserver. Then he collected his wallet, and holy water. He removed the rubber seal from one vial, and held it in his left hand, thumb over the top. With the .45 in his right hand, he raced forward toward the cargo hold doors, in the center of the ship.

He saw a witch hacking a crewman into pieces with her axe. He charged. She raised her weapon. He discharged his .45 into one of her yellow eyes, producing a future demon, but killing her for now.

Shrill cries and screams came from every direction. Just beyond the cargo hold, Poole saw a witch decapitating a crewman with a sword, while an indiscernible creature ripped the limbs from another crewman's torso. Something growled behind Poole. Whipping around, he was confronted by a demon in a white shroud, a black abyss for a visage. It slowly raised its arms, talons ready to strike.

Poole jerked his vial forward, splashing its contents on the faceless demon. It howled and writhed, collapsing into a roiling heap of smoking muck.

Poole ran toward the cargo hold. His chances of saving the artifacts were miniscule, but maybe he could eliminate more of hell's apostles. He reached the center of the ship. The cargo hold had been breached. Five demons and witches stood around it. The demon that killed Conterno was cradling the sheered head.

A tall warlock said, "It's over Poole. You can't save them. You can't even save yourself. Surrender peacefully, and you'll die without pain."

A tremendous explosion erupted from the engine room, sending a ball of flame into the sky. The ship rocked violently, knocking everyone over. Conterno's empty cranium rolled across the deck. Poole and the evildoers floundered back to their feet.

"How do you want to die?" asked the witch.

Poole heard a noise behind him. Another witch and demon were stalking toward him. The ship was starting to list.

"This is your last chance," said the witch.

Poole shot the witch in the chest, darted to the railing and jumped, furiously swimming away. A second explosion rocked the vessel. The fog enveloped him, but he could still make out the fiery outline of the Raphael, beginning its descent. He couldn't see the brigantine, nor did he want to. Swimming on his back, buoyed by the life preserver, he paddled his arms and kicked his feet until exhausted. Then he allowed his head and limbs to go limp, and pondered the wisdom of his choice.

The Hellhound

Mrs. Clarkson poured the Sauternes into the Riedel glass, then returned the bottle to the cabinet. Noticing herself in the mirrored back panel, she adjusted her gray bun. She ambled down the long hallway, adorned with paintings and plaques, and entered the study. Professor Aaronson sat next to the fireplace, immersed in a book about medieval witchcraft.

"Your Sauternes, sir." She placed the glass on the table next to him.

"Thank you, Mildred."

"May I get you anything else?"

"No, that's fine. Why don't you retire early? I'm sure you still have some jet lag."

"Thank you, sir. Have a good evening." She returned to the hallway, which terminated at her bedroom door.

Aaronson's eyes bounced off his watch, then back to his book. He sipped and read, but the wine was the only thing he could digest. He closed the book and checked his e-mail: no new messages. He paced, sipped, and checked. Finally, he called.

"Hello, Professor."

"Daniel, it's me, what's happening?"

"Nothing's happening. There's no word from them."

"What do you mean there's no word from them? They were due in this morning."

"The last message was two days ago."

"But they have a satellite connection, did you call—"

"Professor, we've called their cell phones, the satellite phone, the ship's radio . . . I even e-mailed them. There's nothing, sir."

"Did you check with our contacts in Italy?"

"Of course I did. They haven't heard anything either."

"My God man, when were you going to tell me this?"

"Tonight. I was giving them a little more time."

"We don't have time you imbecile! That ship didn't just disappear. A loss of communication can only mean one thing."

"Don't take it out on me. I'll try them one more time, then we can alert the Coast Guard . . .hold on a second, we might have something . . ."

Aaronson heard a muffled grunt and a crash.

"Daniel? Daniel!" Aaronson waited . . .

"Professor?" asked a creepy voice.

"Who is this?"

"You're next."

Aaronson's throat closed. He tried to collect his thoughts. He exhaled, repeatedly pressing the call button on his cordless phone until he had a dial tone. He keyed in Gil's number. It rang three times.

"You're next," answered the same voice.

His horror mounting, he threw the phone down, took out his cell phone, and dialed Morgan.

"We will consume your organs and drink your blood."

Aaronson wheezed. He darted to his desk, gathered his things, and then scrambled to Mildred's door. He knocked frenziedly. "Mildred. I'm sorry to disturb you." He knocked harder. "Mildred, I have to leave for Vermont. You can't stay here." He pounded. "Mildred!"

He opened the door. The room was black. "Mildred?" Aaronson flipped the light switch.

Mildred dangled from the ceiling, eyes and tongue bulging, a noose around her neck.

Aaronson wailed. He ran down the hallway, dashed out of the house and jumped into his Mercedes. Screeching the tires, he floored it out of the driveway, his mind a beehive. He dialed Morgan's number again. The ringing resonated through the car's speakers, followed by a click.

"You're next."

Aaronson hung up and dialed 911. One ring and then . . .

"We will ravage your very existence."

Aaronson groaned, bouncing his cell phone off the passenger seat. Grasping the wheel with both hands, he dodged and weaved his way to Interstate 93. He got on the highway and revved it up to eighty-five. He tried to collect his thoughts . . .

He'd drive straight to Crestwood Lake, find Gil and Morgan, and try to figure out their next move. Although, if the demonic forces had the artifacts, he wasn't sure there was one. Perhaps the Devil would win this round. Crestwood Lake might have to be ceded. Aaronson scoffed. Telling Morgan to forfeit his town would be like asking the Devil to be baptized.

Aaronson thought about himself. What would he do with his house? He couldn't live there anymore. If the Devil took Crestwood Lake, would Lucifer still come after him? Or was he doomed no matter what? Aaronson scoffed again. He already knew that answer.

His mind continued to swirl. How did they find him? How did they know he was involved? What about the rest of the Camorra? Were they onto them as well? Aaronson decided to try one more call. He'd ring Cardinal Rossi at his home in Rome. It was 3:30 in the morning in Italy. Rossi had to be home, unless . . .

It rang three times before being answered by a chorus of cackles . . . then silence . . . then his dead mother's voice: *"There's nowhere to run, Douglas . . ."*

Panicked and flustered, Aaronson veered toward the median. He yanked the wheel, careening across the highway to the far right lane. Panting, he checked his rear-view mirror, as if that would make a difference now. Luckily, he was the only car within a quarter mile.

Aaronson composed himself and resumed a steady eighty-five. He still had another two and a half hours to drive. Every few miles he checked the back seat.

It was a partly cloudy night, the clear patches of sky faintly illuminated by the waxing crescent moon. There were less cars on the highway than usual. He didn't know if that was good or bad. The droning of the car and monotonous scenery allowed his mind to wander.

Aaronson reflected on his life, contemplating what he had forfeited by pursuing his academic and supernatural pursuits. He had relinquished his share of his deceased parents' manufacturing business to his brothers, albeit for a sizeable compensation. He hadn't forged many close friendships. And, he was still a bachelor at fifty-one, a growing source of discontent.

Still, he had embarked on an unparalleled journey, delving into a realm that few even knew existed. Furthermore, his knowledge and exploits could contribute to the world's salvation. *Whatever you have to tell yourself*, he thought. None of it would bring back poor Mrs. Clarkson. And how many others would have to die? Aaronson's uneasiness re-escalated. He checked the backseat. He thought about trying to call Morgan or the Cardinal again, but decided against it.

He was now only forty minutes from Crestwood Lake. What would he do if Satan's forces had already overrun it? That thought only exacerbated his apprehension.

A sharp thunderclap jolted Aaronson out of his head. He looked up. The sky was occluded. A streak of lightening illuminated the turbid clouds. Another thunderclap ushered in the first sheet of rain, a surging patter across his windshield. The automatic wipers sprang to life, furiously whipping to-and-fro.

The car hydroplaned; Aaronson decelerated. Another flash of lightening, and detonation of thunder. The wind pelted the rain laterally across his car.

Visibility worsened; Aaronson leaned forward and peered. He noticed a small, fuzzy, spot of light. Was it a headlight? It morphed into the face of a white-haired man, with menacing, dark eyes. It lunged at Aaronson, bearing its teeth, vanishing when it smacked his windshield. Aaronson yelled and lurched back. He clenched the wheel, forearms flexing.

Aaronson approached the I-93 bridge over the Connecticut River, the border of New Hampshire and Vermont. He couldn't see any other cars. He eased the accelerator and hugged the right lane, flashes overhead, rain unrelenting.

Passing the center of the bridge, a bolt of lightning struck the road ahead. The roadway burst, a twenty-foot section crumbled, falling a hundred feet into the river below. Aaronson jammed the brakes, fishtailing left and right, as he twisted the wheel. The car skidded sideways, stopping on the edge of the shattered pavement, perilously balanced. Were it not for Aaronson's weight on the driver side, the vehicle would have plunged into the cold rushing water.

Aaronson was consumed in fear. The car teetered. He leaned to the left, barely swaying the wobble in his direction. He couldn't open the door. The outer edge was jammed against an upheaved segment of asphalt. His side window was his only hope. Aaronson pressed the button; it slid down. About to exhale a sigh of relief, he sucked in a gasp instead.

"Good evening, Professor."

Aaronson flinched away. The weight shifted. The car started to topple.

A hand clamped down on the door, above the retracted window. "Relax, Professor. You're not going anywhere."

Aaronson was agape. It was the same face that had just assailed him, only now, it was attached to a six-foot-five-inch frame, donned in a black three-piece suit and red tie. His large eyes were oppressively dark brown, irises and pupils virtually fused into singular black orbs. The rain and the wind faded. The man was completely dry.

"Who are you?" asked Aaronson.

"Who do you think?" asked Van Haden, as his Stygian eyes flickered to red and then back. Above his shoulder, the now visible crescent moon was crimson.

Aaronson noticed Van Haden's hand, effortlessly steadying the car. His fingernails were immaculate. He wore an onyx ring, topped by three gold dog heads, each with rubies for eyes.

217

"Cerberus," said Aaronson. "The three-headed dog that guards the gates of Hades."

"Very good, Professor. I would have expected nothing less."

A shudder went through Aaronson's torso.

Van Haden's countenance was unyielding.

"You must be Luther Van Haden." His voice quivered.

"Nice to make your acquaintance, Professor."

"Whatever you want, I'm not interested."

"Oh really?" Van Haden relaxed his grip. The car tipped.

"All right, all right," cried Aaronson.

Van Haden snatched Aaronson by his shirt, pulling him through the window. The Mercedes plummeted, smashing into the river in an explosion of water. Van Haden, standing on the edge of the broken roadway, held Aaronson at arm's length, dangling him over the river.

Aaronson looked down, watching his car sink.

Behind Van Haden, the actual Cerberus materialized. Twice the size of a wolf, it had shiny black fur and talons on its paws. The three scarlet-eyed heads growled, baring their fangs.

"Beguile me with your acumen, Professor. Do you know Cerberus's duty?"

Aaronson was terrified.

Van Haden jerked his fist, snapping Aaronson's head back. "I asked you a question."

"Cerberus prevents the damned from escaping hell."

Van Haden smiled sinfully, eyes shining. "That's right, Professor." He tightened his grip. "*You* cannot escape."

Wiggling his legs, Aaronson said, "What do you want from me?"

218

"Another feeble human playing coy. You *know* what I want."

"You're not getting the artifacts. I'd die first. Besides, you can't kill me anyway. I know the rules you're bound by."

"You think so, huh, Professor? Ready to stake your life on that?"

Cerberus snarled.

Aaronson squirmed.

Van Haden let go.

The Connivance

The chair smashed into the TV, shattering the screen. Nathan swung it again. "Goddamn you!" And again. "Shut the hell up!" And again. And again. And again.

The other patients in the community room bolted into the hallway. Some went back to their rooms, a few stood around aimlessly. Linda headed toward the nurse's station to alert the staff, but they were already streaming toward the commotion. Crashing blows continued to resound from the community room.

The intercom blared, "Dr. Strong to Four West, Dr. Strong to Four West." Dr. Strong was the Berlin Medical Center's code for immediate assistance due to an out of control individual. Any available staff in the vicinity were expected to respond.

"Nathan's destroying the TV," cried Linda to Terry, the charge nurse leading the troop of staff converging on the scene.

"Go back to your room, everybody," said Terry. "We'll take care of it."

The lost souls in the hallway complied. Linda stood her ground. "I thought there was supposed to be a staff member present at all times."

"Not now, Linda."

Linda pointed at her. "You shouldn't allow him to be out of his room. He's violent. What if he attacked one of us?"

"This is not the time for this discussion. Go back to your room. Now!"

Miriam, one of the other nurses, placed her hand on Linda's arm. Edging her away, she gently said, "We can talk about this later. Please just go to your room for now."

Linda yanked her arm away and marched off. "Bunch of morons. You're gonna get one of us killed."

Standing in front of the entrance to the community room, Terry addressed the employees. "OK everybody, you know the drill. We're going to place him in restraints. We'll talk to him first and give him the option of walking to his room. If not"—Terry pointed to four staff members in a row— "you take the left arm, right arm, left leg, and right leg. If I say, 'We're done talking,' that's the code to move in. Got it?"

Everyone nodded.

Terry and her team entered the community room.

Nathan was pacing, kicking pieces of the TV with each pass, mumbling obscenities.

"Hi, Nathan," said Terry casually. "What's wrong?"

"You *know* what's wrong." Nathan knocked over a chair.

"The Devil's talking to you through the TV again, huh?"

Nathan paced and muttered.

"Nathan, I'm sorry he's troubling you. Why don't we go to your room? This way you won't be anywhere near the TV."

Nathan's eyes darted randomly, suggestive of visual hallucinations.

"Nathan, can we please go to your room? I want to get you away from the TV."

Nathan picked up a piece of the TV and threw it at Terry. "Fuck you!"

"We're done talking."

The group descended, seized Nathan's limbs, and carried him toward one of the seclusion rooms. Nathan, five-foot-seven, and one hundred and thirty malnourished pounds, was easily overpowered. Nevertheless, he thrashed as hard as his scrawny frame allowed, calling the team every scurrilous invective he could think of.

The staff plopped Nathan on the bed and restrained his wrists and ankles. As he vulgarly invited them to orally gratify his nether regions, another nurse arrived with two needles: Haldol, an anti-psychotic drug, and Ativan, a fast-acting tranquilizer.

"Turn him over," the nurse said.

Two of the employees rolled him on his side, two others pulled down his pants.

The nurse injected his buttocks with the needles.

Nathan growled "You bitch!"

They returned him to his back and retreated. Nathan slowly slipped into placidity.

Two hours later I went in to talk to him.

"Nathan, May I come in?"

"Oh, Dr. Conway, yeah . . . come in."

Nathan was sedated, but not incoherent, so hopefully we could have a meaningful interaction. "What happened today?"

"It was the Devil, Doc."

"Was he insulting you again . . . telling you to do stuff?"

"Both. He calls me a faggot. Tells me I'm not a man. Tells me I have to kill people to prove my manhood."

"I'm sorry, Nathan. That must be tortuous."

"I'm not a homo, Doc."

"I know you're not. Nathan, listen to me. This is very important. You don't have to prove to anyone—people, the Devil, whomever—that you're a man. If anyone doubts you, that's *their* problem. We know who you really are."

"I know, Doc."

"Did anything happen today that upset you, that made the Devil talk to you?"

"No."

"Why didn't you come to me, or one of the staff when it started?"

222

"He told me not to. He said the staff think I'm a pussy."

"We do *not* think that. We're here to help you. Please, Nathan, if you start to get upset, or if the Devil talks to you, come to my office. If I'm not there, get another staff member."

"OK. Can I get out of here now?"

"It's probably a little too soon. We want to make sure you're calm and won't break anything or hurt anyone."

"I won't."

"You know the routine. They'll take you out of the restraints, but then they'll keep you locked in the room for a while. And if you're still calm, then they'll let you back out on into the unit, OK?"

"All right, Doc."

"Tomorrow, I'll see you in my office and we can chat some more."

I was halfway toward the door when Nathan said, "The Devil knows about you, Doc."

"What do you mean by that?"

"He knows about you. Knows you're trying to stop him from talking to me. He doesn't like it."

"I don't care what the Devil thinks about me. I just want you to be safe and not hurt anyone. We'll talk more tomorrow."

Nathan was a thirty-one-year-old paranoid schizophrenic. This was his fifth admission to Berlin's psychiatric unit. The patients called it the "Hitler Hotel," since the town was named after the German capital.

Nathan's symptoms were textbook: paranoia, delusions, and hallucinations, particularly what professionals call command hallucinations, whereby the voices order the person to do things, often to hurt themselves or others. Sexual and religious themes are quite common, as is thinking the voices or messages are being transmitted from the television or similar devices.

Schizophrenia is primarily due to anomalies in the brain and neural pathways, but stress and psychological factors play a role as well. For Nathan, I was sure his "devil" was his deceased father, who beat and belittled him for not "acting like a man." Aberrant biology may cause hallucinations, but *what* one hallucinates arises from that individual's issues and psychodynamics.

Such is Nathan's background. My own history is much more boring. My younger sister and I were born and raised in Crestwood Lake. My father was a psychiatrist and my mother a nurse. They both worked at the Berlin Medical Center. My relationship with them was unremarkable. In fact, my entire childhood was mundane. Growing up in the hinterland of northern Vermont is like being exiled to Siberia. For some adults, such as my current self, it provides peaceful solitude. But for an adolescent, it's about as much fun as watching your toenails grow.

I excelled academically in high school, partly due to intellect, partly because I didn't play sports or have a girlfriend to distract me. I couldn't wait to go out of state for college and escape the desolate boondocks. I remember receiving my acceptance letter to NYU. It felt as if I were being paroled. My parents wanted me to stay close to home, but I needed to stretch my wings and be part of the real world. New York City was the answer.

I didn't know what I wanted to do occupationally, just where I wanted to do it. During the course of my studies, psychology intrigued me. I always had a curiosity about what made people tick. Midway through my bachelor's, I decided to become a psychologist, later completing my Ph.D. at Fordham. I spent the next decade working in Manhattan hospitals and maintaining a small private practice in the evenings for extra cash.

One of my reasons for opting for the big city, was to improve my odds for meeting a future wife. I always had bad luck with women. I tried to console myself that it was due to living in a remote area with limited opportunities. But I knew it went deeper than that. Women just didn't like me. I wasn't ugly, obnoxious, or anything overtly repulsive. As far as I could tell, I always acted like a gentleman and was easy to get along with. Yet there was still something ineffable about me that didn't pique female interest. I would get some dates, but one of two things would happen: the relationship would fizzle prematurely, or she would wind up pursuing someone else. I've had my heart wrecked more times than I care to remember.

And so, pushing forty, no better off romantically, and tiring of the downfalls of city life, I decided to return to my roots. I relocated back to Crestwood Lake, and with my father's influence, obtained my current position as the psychologist on the psychiatric unit of the Berlin Medical Center. That was four years ago. I still have a private practice, but only two evenings a week. With the sparse population, and even sparser affluency, there isn't much demand for private psychotherapy. Not to mention that rural areas have no shortage of stigmatization for those seeking such services.

My private patients were basically a handful of high-functioning, moneyed neurotics: a lawyer with marital problems, an anxious banker, and a few depressed wives of doctors from the Medical Center. And then there was Wendy. Oh—my—God. Wendy Alexander was one of the most ravishing women I've ever seen. A petite, long-haired blonde in her mid-twenties, with the face of a model. I am certain Wendy could waltz into the headquarters of Victoria's Secret and get hired on the spot. But, as I've learned both personally and professionally, exceptional exterior beauty rarely exists without inner disfigurement.

I met Wendy four months ago when she was admitted to the psych unit after her second suicide attempt. She had swallowed a bottle of sleeping pills just before her degenerate boyfriend arrived home from work. He saved her life but terminated the relationship. After being discharged, she started seeing me privately for therapy.

Wendy had a menial clerical job with piss-poor insurance. They only authorized a dozen sessions. So when the insurance lapsed, I reduced my fee substantially, charging her only a trifle. I justified my altruism by attributing it to her clinical needs, but that wasn't the real reason. I couldn't bear to never see Wendy again. Even if I was indirectly gratifying my unfulfilled longings by remaining her therapist, I was still helping her. How's that for a world-class rationalization?

Not surprisingly, Wendy came from a dysfunctional household. Her father had abandoned her mother and older sisters when she was only eight. Wendy's mother drank, had a parade of suitors, and worked as a stripper. Wendy was basically raised by her indifferent sisters, as her mother was usually preoccupied with riding her boyfriend, a pole, or the Jack Daniels express.

Wendy muddled through high school, had one abortion, and smoked a lot of pot. She had no problem attracting men, but inevitably derelicts and druggies. I suspect, on an unconscious level, she was trying to reenact and repair the broken relationship with her father. I hate admitting this, but

225

somewhere in my psyche was a white horse, whose rider thought he could heal Wendy with unconditional love.

And then my rational side would temporarily hold sway. The psychologist in me knew you can't love someone out of their pathology. What was missing in Wendy was not love, but the underlying personality structure that is capable of receiving and giving love. Like a house on unstable ground, all the cleaning and painting in the world won't stop it from buckling. But then I would become enthralled with her tender lips, or the way her calves sensually merged into her high heels, and the white horse would neigh with desire.

I recall a pivotal exchange in a recent session where we were exploring Wendy's suicidal reactions to men who didn't love her.

"Well how would you feel, Doc, if your girlfriend cheated on you, or didn't want to commit to you?"

"I would feel terrible. Anybody would. But most people wouldn't become suicidal. There's something about you that makes you want to die when your partner fails to love you. What do you think that is?"

"I don't know. I guess I feel like what's the point. Here we go again. Another man who can't be there for me. Why can't I meet a decent guy?"

"What is your definition of a *decent* guy?"

"You know, a guy who doesn't want you only for sex, but actually loves you. A guy who's not a loser, who has some brains and a good job. You know, a guy like you."

Did you hear the record needle just screech to a halt? This is what psychoanalysts call "transference," whereby the patient projects their yearnings, unconscious conflicts, and other assorted baggage onto the therapist. Wendy was beginning to idealize me. A patient is only privy to part of their therapist's personality. However, it's a warm and fuzzy part: it empathizes with their pain, doesn't judge them, and seeks to save them from their misery. That feels nice, especially when your life has been devoid of such compassion. A deprived soul like Wendy can come to view that singular aspect of my professional demeanor as the entire package. They fall in "love" with that inflated image, unconsciously struggling to mend the privations of the past, and fill their current emotional voids.

226

Pffffft! So much for the psychobabble. My white knight was ready for a crusade. I told Wendy we were out of time, and we'd discuss it further in our next session. Then I wrestled with my own demons. I was in agony—an excruciating conflict between my ethics and my needs—a war in my mind. I opened a bottle of vodka and drank myself into unconsciousness, fantasizing about Wendy the entire time.

The next day I was in my office on the unit when I received a call from Gavin Reid, the assistant county district attorney (now acting DA due to Wilfred Jameson's murder). To augment my private practice, I provided psychological services for the county and state: child custody evaluations, criminal assessments, and therapy for the occasional court-ordered offender. They're always such a joy.

"Doc, we need you to do an evaluation."

"Sure, what's the case?"

"His name is Stan Lupinski," said Reid. "Single, forty-five-year-old welder originally from Burlington, now living in Crestwood Lake. No psych history, but he's had a few scrapes with the law. Has an ex-girlfriend, total junkie, who has custody of their ten-year-old daughter. Well, the girlfriend just got arrested for possession for the third time. She's facing prison. So Lupinski is petitioning the court for custody of his daughter. We'd like you to check him out to see if he's suitable."

"Why are you getting involved? Shouldn't this request be coming from Lupinski's lawyer?"

"His lawyer's a friend of mine, and I owe him one. I told him I knew a good shrink who would give his client a fair shake."

"Fine. My usual fee applies. Is this guy safe to come to my place, or should I see him at his lawyer's office?"

"No, he's fine."

"You said he had a few scrapes with the law."

"Nothing serious. When can you see him? Can you do it this week?"

"Uh . . . I guess I could see him Thursday after work. Maybe like six o'clock?"

"Good. I'll set it up," said Reid.

"Meantime, can you overnight me his file, arrest record, all that."

"No problem, Doc. Thanks."

I was circumspect about the individuals I accepted into my private practice, because it was in my home. My office was at the far end of my house, with its own separate entrance. One of my college professors had a similar set-up, and I recall asking him about the potential dangers. He replied that he didn't see very disturbed individuals. However, there are plenty of people who seem normal on the surface, yet underneath lurks madness. Only after the relationship progresses—when it becomes more intimate—does the true psychopathology emerge. Six months into therapy, and you realize you're treating Jeffrey Dahmer. This happens all the time in romantic unions. I knew the risks, but I couldn't afford to rent a separate office for a small caseload. And, the home office was a great tax deduction.

Anyway, I got off the phone with Reid and went straight to morning report. Seated in the meeting room was the psychiatrist, Dr. Fazarro, the charge nurse Terry, and other nurses and aids.

"Sorry I'm late guys, I got tied up on the phone." I shook loose a Styrofoam cup from the stack and filled it with coffee.

"Morning, Ted," said Dr. Fazarro. "We were just discussing Nathan."

"He's in restraints again," said Terry.

"What'd he do now?"

"Attacked one of the night nurses," said Dr. Fazarro.

"*Attacked* her?"

"Shattered her orbital bone."

"What set him off?"

"Who cares?" said Terry. "He assaulted one of my nurses. On top of all of the other times he's lost control. He needs long-term care; he's not responding to treatment."

"I turned to Dr. Fazarro who said, "I agree. We should transfer him to the state facility.""

I sighed. Everyone looked at me like they expected a rebuttal, but I knew it was the right thing to do. I begrudgingly nodded my approval.

I hadn't known Nathan long, but I was starting to make a therapeutic connection with him. Most schizophrenics are impervious to any serious psychotherapy. But Nathan, despite periods of severe psychosis, had lucid intervals where he was reachable. He had shared with me some of the abuse he endured as a child. In theory, if I could help him deal with that emotional pain, it might reduce the number of psychotic breaks. In theory.

Coffee in hand, I went to the seclusion room to see Nathan one last time. Again, he was heavily sedated, but not delirious or unresponsive.

"Hi, Nathan, it's Dr. Conway. Just want to see how you're doing."

"I know who you are, Doc. You don't have to announce yourself."

"I'm sorry. I know they gave you some medication, just making sure."

Nathan, wearing a hospital gown, was strapped to the bed by all fours. A semi-filled urine bottle rested on the floor beside him. His hair was oily. He needed a shower and a shave. Three of his toenails were exchanging fungus recipes.

"What happened last night?" I asked.

"I punched a nurse."

"Why?"

"She's with the Devil."

"How do you know?"

"Ya just *know* these things. I know about her, she knows about me— The Devil knows about *you*."

"Me?"

"Yeah, Doc. He knows about all of us."

"Nathan, remember we discussed your father and all the things he did to you? And how abuse like that can affect a person?"

229

"Saving me won't bring Paula back."

"What?"

"You heard me."

"Paula who?"

"C'mon, Doc. Paula Swindlehurst. Your patient who hung herself three years ago."

Thunderstruck, I swallowed hard as Nathan peered at me with careworn eyes.

"How did you know she was my patient?"

"Because the Devil told me the same thing would happen to me. Unless of course, I joined him."

"Nathan, the same thing is not going to happen—wait—forget the Devil—how did you know she was my patient?"

"You can't save Wendy either, Doc."

"Wendy?"

Nathan sighed. "Can we cut the bullshit, Doc?"

"Are you saying Wendy is going to kill herself?"

"No. I'm saying she doesn't have to."

"Why?" I asked shaking my head.

"Because she'll kill you instead . . ."

"And you're asking *me* to cut the bullshit?"

Nathan's entire body sharply contracted, as if receiving a paralyzing jolt of electricity. He appeared to levitate a few inches off the bed. His head creaked sideways as his eyes rolled up into his head—two barren orbs confronting me. Then, in Wendy's voice: "Why can't I meet a decent guy, ya know, a guy like you."

I dropped my coffee and flew out of the room. Two patients gawked as I stumbled into the hallway, half-crazed. I walked briskly to my office, shut the door and collapsed into my chair. I squeezed my temples, striving to make sense of what just happened.

It had to be his psychosis. But how would that make him levitate? Maybe he wasn't levitating. Maybe part of him that I couldn't see was touching the bed. But that was Wendy's voice. The psychosis couldn't explain that. Did he know Wendy? She left the unit before he came in. Maybe they crossed paths in the past. Maybe he met her—a knock at my door.

It was Hannah, one of the nurse's aides. "Ted, are you doing group? It's 9:15 and the patients are waiting."

"Oh shit." I looked at my watch. "Uh . . . yes, I am." I walked to the group room in a dazed state. For the entire hour, I barely listened to the patients, an endless loop of the interaction with Nathan replaying in my head.

He was transferred to the state psychiatric facility the next day.

Thursday evening arrived. I had been obsessing about Wendy and Nathan all week. Gazing out my home office window, I watched Stan Lupinski pull into the driveway. It was then I realized Reid had never sent his file. He appeared somewhat younger than forty-five, with a medium build and stubby gray hair. Even from my window I could see his recessed, disturbed eyes. We hadn't even begun the interview and I was already creeped out.

Stan had an icy, robotic demeanor, devoid of humanity, with thinly veiled rage. He was more of a *thing* than a person, and he interreacted with me like I was the same. I had the distinct feeling that he could kill me, with no more consideration than one spits away an errant food particle. His face was expressionless, yet contempt raged in his sunken eyes. He was a festering corpse.

He described a horrendously abusive childhood as if relaying the weather, impassively sharing that his uncle and father would take turns sodomizing him. He freely revealed equally cruel behaviors on his part toward small animals and other boys. The only moment he enlivened, was when he described burying a cat up to its neck, then running over it with a lawn mower.

He described an extensive criminal record, with no insight as to how that would influence my opinion about his parental suitability. He spoke of his daughter as if she were an object, with abject detachment in his countenance and verbiage. Indeed, his perception of people in general, was an antisocial tangle of projected malevolencies and disdain. He referred to women with profane anatomical epithets, particularly his daughter's mother, whom he hoped would rot in jail. My churning stomach reached its conclusions on this monster even before my brain.

Finally, I had heard enough. "OK, Mr. Lupinski, we're done."

"So what do you think, Doc?"

I didn't know which was worse: his presentation, or his cluelessness about what it exposed. "I haven't received your records yet. I don't form any opinions until I have all the information."

I waited until Stan's jalopy was out of sight, locked all my doors, and opened a bottle of vodka. After my second drink, I decided to call in sick the next day. As I finished my third, headlights streamed into my driveway. "Oh, God no," I said. The car stopped, someone got out, and footsteps trampled toward my office door, followed by a series of pounds. My stomach sank. The psycho was back.

I went into my office and hit the light switch. "Who is it?"

"Dr. Conway, it's Wendy."

She sounded distraught. I opened the door.

"Tears rolled down her cheeks. "I know we don't have an appointment, but can I please speak with you?"

She wore a tight, short black dress, stockings, and black stilettos. To say she looked sexy would be like saying Mozart was musically inclined.

I ogled her up and down.

She noticed and said, "I was about to go to a party and my mother called." She sobbed. "She called me a whore!"

"Come in. Have a seat. I'll be right with you, OK?"

I went to my kitchen, took a couple gulps of vodka, and returned to my office.

Wendy gushed about the conversation with her whacko mother. She only saw her mom sporadically. Most of their relationship transpired on the phone, when her mother would drink and dial, complain about her miserable life, and then vilify Wendy.

I didn't say much. Didn't need to. Fifteen minutes of virtually uninterrupted purging and Wendy was recomposed. She rose and said, "I'm sorry. I've taken enough of your time."

"No, it's OK. I'm glad you're feeling better." I stood up.

Wendy stepped toward me, the closest she's ever been, and took my hand. "Thank you, Doc. I don't know what I would do without you."

"It's my pleasure."

"You're the only one who cares about me." She leaned in.

I succumbed.

We were locked in the most passionate kiss I've ever known. My God what a feeling! I could have just simply held her forever, dying a happy man in her arms. But of course, we both wanted more. Our lips still pressing, I led her to the couch. And on the same cushions from whence she bared her soul, Wendy surrendered her flesh, loving me more rapturously than any fantasy I could envision. It was the zenith of my life.

We drank, cuddled, and talked for hours. We made our way to the bedroom where we made love again. She fell asleep with her head on my chest. I lay awake for hours . . . it was wonderful.

We awoke the next morning and indulged our passions again. I called in sick and made coffee. Wendy had to go to work, as her small employer afforded minimal sick time. I wanted to plan our first official date. Wendy wanted to go to Pierre's, the hoity-toity French place. I had never been there but didn't really care. I would eat dog food in the ghetto just to be with her.

I was in the happiest mood of my life. I didn't even feel guilty about abandoning my professionalism with Wendy. We were right together, and I wouldn't let anything in the world compromise that. I used my newfound energy to clean the house and write the report on Stan. I didn't need his unsent

233

file. I opined unequivocally that Stan was unfit to be a custodial parent. I hoped to never have anything to do with that miscreant again. I e-mailed Reid my report that afternoon.

Saturday night, Wendy and I were seated in front of the fireplace at Pierre's, when our waitress approached.

"Hey guys, I'm Kim, I'll be your server tonight. Would you like some wine to start off?"

I studied Kim as Wendy ordered a $140 bottle. What the hell, it was our first date.

"Aren't you a nurse at Crestwood Manor, the nursing home?" I asked.

"Yes, this is my weekend job. You look familiar."

"I'm Dr. Ted Conway. I'm the psychologist from Berlin Medical Center. I think we met last year at that seminar the hospital held about geriatric psychiatry."

"Oh yeah. Ugh." Kim rolled her eyes. "What a snooze-fest that was."

"So what's the deal with the chef here? I heard something about him being reported missing."

"Yeah, nobody knows. The manager keeps running the place and paying us, that's all I care about. I'll get your wine."

Dinner went well, the food was generally superior—although the liver terrine tasted funky. Wendy and I chatted about our backgrounds, mostly mine. Wendy seemed fascinated with me, asking all the questions about my life that she never could ask before.

Kim brought us the check. "Excuse me, Dr, Conway. I don't mean to interrupt your evening, but do you have a private practice?"

"Yes, I do."

"Could I have your card and maybe give you a call? There's some issues I need to talk about."

"Sure, here."

"Are Monday nights good? I'm always off on Mondays."

"Yeah, just give me a call."

As Kim departed, Wendy leaned in and said, "Don't get too close, Doc. You seem to have a thing for young blondes."

"Baby, nobody could replace you."

Wendy gulped the rest of her wine, and with a mischievous smile said, "Let's go home."

We spent the remainder of that night and most of Sunday in bed. She was an animal. And I was her chew toy. It was sublime.

As I opened up the blinds to Monday morning, Wendy gently moaned, stretching and swirling in the blue flannel sheets. "What are you doing?" she asked.

"I have to get ready for work."

"Oh no. I'm off today. Why don't you stay home with me?"

"Baby, I'd love to, but I already called in sick Friday."

"So take one more day. This way it'll look like you're really sick and didn't just want a three-day weekend."

"Ohhhhhhhh," I whined, conflicted.

Wendy threw the sheets off her, spread her legs and licked her lips. "I'll make it worth your while."

Sold! To the shrink in the black briefs by the bedroom window.

First we made love, then we made breakfast. We took a long walk in the woods, had lunch, and crashed in my living room.

"I'm in the mood for a drink," said Wendy. "What do you have?"

"I've got a few bottles of wine."

Wendy grimaced. "Nah, something stronger, I feel frisky."

"There's two bottles of vodka in the kitchen. One's already started."

Wendy retrieved the opened bottle and two glasses with ice. As we sipped our Russian elixir, Wendy asked me questions about the psych unit. She was titillated by my insider view. She poured us more drinks. I made her laugh with amusing stories involving the escapades of some of the crazier patients. We continued to imbibe.

Things were starting to get fuzzy, but at some point in the late afternoon, we polished off the bottle of vodka.

"I'll get the other," said Wendy

"We better slow down," I said.

"Honey, we're just getting started." Wendy went to the bedroom, collected her purse and returned to the kitchen, followed by silence.

"What are you doing?" I asked.

"Just checking my phone, be right there."

I heard Wendy open a bottle, some indistinct noises, then ice cubes plopping into two glasses. She walked into the living room and handed me one. "Finish that and then let's go to bed."

I sipped the vodka.

"Finish it while I'm still horny," said Wendy playfully.

I chugged it.

Wendy led me to the bedroom and stripped off her clothes. I followed suit. Then she gave me voracious head. I exploded like a wildcat.

"Now I want you to do something for me," she said.

"Sure." My head began to spin. I felt like I was going to pass out.

Wendy took out a pair of handcuffs from her bag. "I want you to do me while I'm cuffed to the bed. It turns me on."

"O . . . K," I said. I would have agreed to anything at that point.

Wendy hopped onto the bed, bent over on her knees, face down, rear up, and stretched out her arms. Her incredible derriere beckoned me with untamed lust. "C'mon, cuff me."

I handcuffed each of her wrists to the bed railing. Then I got behind her and rubbed myself against her. Despite feeling like I'd been given anesthesia, I managed an erection.

The last thing I remember was my climax . . .

Stan and Kim marched into the room, both wearing gloves. Kim carried a duffle bag.

"Ya sure he's out?" asked Kim, eyeballing Conway's prone, unresponsive body next to Wendy.

"He's out," said Wendy, still cuffed to the bed. "I crushed two Xanax in his vodka." She turned her head toward Stan. "C'mon. Let's get this over with."

"This will prove your loyalty," said Stan. "You'll be rewarded generously for this."

"I know," said Wendy, breathing heavier.

"Ready?" asked Stan.

"Just do it," said Kim.

Stan punched Wendy in the face, breaking her nose, discharging blood all over the head of the bed. Wendy grunted and moaned.

Stan opened up the duffle bag and took out a black paddle. He swung it repeatedly into Wendy's buttocks. Wendy yelped after each strike. When her skin was inflamed and starting to bleed, Stan stopped.

Stan placed the paddle in Conway's hand, ensuring the psychologist's fingerprints were left in the proper places, then dropped it on the floor. He grabbed Conway by the ankles, eased his body off the bed, dragged him to center of the room, and placed him on the floor next to the paddle. Then he left.

Kim called the state police.

~~~~~~

The world came into view. I had a humongous headache.

"Good evening, Doc," said Prosecutor Reid.

Handcuffed to a bed, I gazed around. "Where am I?"

"You're in Northeastern Regional Hospital."

"What happened?"

"You tell me."

I yanked at the cuffs. "Why am I restrained?"

"Because you kidnapped, bound, and raped a woman."

"What?"

"Doc, please don't waste my time."

"Wendy?"

"Yes, Wendy Alexander. *Your patient.* You cuffed her to your bed, broke her nose, thrashed her behind, and raped her."

"She's not my patient anymore, she's my girlfriend. She asked me to handcuff her. Our sex was consensual."

"Was her broken nose consensual?"

"I didn't break her nose!"

Reid held up Wendy's picture. "I suppose it broke itself?"

"No! I didn't do that. What's happening?"

"Your BAL was 2.5, and you had tranquilizers in your system."

"We had a few drinks, but I didn't take any drugs."

"So your blood test is a fabrication too?"

"What's going on here?"

"Look, Doc, I'll give you the benefit of the doubt. I'll assume you were so fucked up you don't recall the details. But I'm only going through this once. Another one of your patients, Kim Wagner, came to your office for her appointment—"

"She's not my patient, not yet, and she didn't have an appointment."

"Shut up. Kim came to your office and heard a woman screaming. She ran inside and saw you raping Wendy. You went after Kim with the same paddle you assaulted Wendy with, but passed out. Wendy's and Kim's stories match. Your fingerprints are on the paddle and the handcuffs."

"Check my house. You'll find Wendy's fingerprints all over the place. She was my girlfriend!"

"That doesn't mean you didn't restrain and rape her."

"No! I didn't—"

"You're dead in the water, Doc. You're going before a judge in the morning. You won't get bail, you'll rot in jail until trial and end up in prison. Or you can play ball and I can turn this into simple assault, a misdemeanor. No jail time, just a fine."

"You got me on kidnapping, rape and assault, and you're just gonna turn all that into a *misdemeanor*?"

"That's right."

"OK, I'm not stupid. What do you want from me other than a guilty plea?"

"A more favorable report on Stan Lupinski."

"What? You want me to falsify a report? Why?"

"I told you. I owe his lawyer a favor. And *you* don't want to go to jail."

"Are you serious? That man is a psychopath."

"You'll lose your license, pay tens of thousands of dollars in fines, and go to the state pen for twenty years. Or, you can keep your license, stay out of jail, and pay about a grand. Your call, Doc."

I tried to think. My head throbbed. I could hire a lawyer. That would cost more than a grand, and could he get me a better deal? Doubtful. "Fine, I said. I'll do it."

Reid reached into his leather bag and retrieved a laptop. He opened it and plopped it on my lap. "Type."

"Now?"

"Right now."

The next morning, I was led into the Essex County Courthouse. When it was my turn the bailiff read my name, the docket number, and the charges.

"How do you plead Dr. Conway?" asked the judge.

"Your honor," said Reid. "We've reached a plea agreement. The defendant will plead guilty to simple assault. Considering this is his only arrest, the state is not recommending jail time."

"The judge scanned the arrest report. "Are you out of your mind, Mr. Reid?"

"Sir?"

"The defendant restrained, beat, and raped a woman, and you're letting him walk free on simple assault?"

"Your honor, the defendant is a clinical psychologist who has performed work for this court, this is his only offense, and—"

"Stop!" said the judge. "I don't want to hear it. This is the most ludicrous plea agreement I've ever seen. I don't know what day and age you're from, Mr. Reid, but in these times, we do *not* take sexual offenses lightly."

Reid opened his mouth.

"Not another word. The defendant is to be remitted for trial. No bail." The judge slammed his gavel into the sound block. "Next case."

The officers shuffled me out of court. I tried to protest, but they ignored me, shoving me into a solitary cell.

"No! You can't do this to me. I'm innocent!"

They walked away.

I turned away from the bars, gasped, and jumped back in horror.

Paula Swindlehurst hung from the corner, head slumped. Her wavy, midnight-brown hair enveloped her face. She slowly raised her chin. Her skin was a grayish-green, with thin black cracks etching their way across it. Her eyes were dark and caved in. "You said you loved me, Ted."

I trembled, aghast.

"Why, Ted? Why did you hurt me?"

"I . . . I didn't mean to hurt you."

"You did this to me . . ."

"No, no."

"You did this to me!"

"No!"

~~~~~~

Wendy knocked on the door.

"Who is it?"

"It's me, Wendy. Stan is with me."

"Come in my dear."

Wendy, Stan, and a pre-adolescent girl entered.

"You have done well, young lady."

"Thank you, Master," said Wendy.

Van Haden placed his hand on Wendy's cheek. Her nose completely healed. "You will find I am magnanimous to those who suffer in my name. Welcome to the coven. Darlene here will attend to you shortly."

"Yes, Master."

"Welcome," said Darlene, extending her hand.

"Thank you, ma'am."

"You may leave us for now."

Wendy departed.

Van Haden nodded at Stan, then bent over and smiled at the little girl. "I'll bet you're Olivia."

She nodded.

"We're one big happy family here. *We* will never leave you. Darlene would like to spend some time with you. She bought you a whole bunch of new dresses, and some pretty jewelry. Later you can try it all on. Would you like that?"

Olivia nodded, a thin smile forming.

"Go with Daddy now, and Darlene will fetch you later."

Stan and Olivia left.

Darlene picked up their glasses of champagne, handing one to Van Haden. "Conway hung himself in his cell this morning."

Van Haden sniggered.

"I thought that would amuse you."

"And Reid?"

"Nathan's dismembering him as we speak."

"How wonderfully evil," said Van Haden.

242

The Peripeteia

Morgan sat at the bar, checking his watch.

"Want another bourbon, baby?" asked Vicki.

"No. One's enough. I gotta stay sharp. How about a coffee?"

"Sure thing."

It was a typical Sunday afternoon at Toby's: about ten patrons, mostly men, watching football. Morgan caught snippets of the game but couldn't concentrate on it.

Vicki brought his coffee.

Morgan looked at his watch again. "Where is that douchebag?"

"Oh, baby. You should know by now he's always late."

Five minutes later, Gil pranced in. On his way to the bar he saw two women he knew sitting at a table. He exchanged a few words and then sat down with them.

"Jesus Christ," mumbled Morgan. He finished his coffee, then marched over to the trio. Morgan scowled at Gil and tapped his watch.

"Hi, Butch," said Gil. "This is Joanie, and her daughter Melissa."

"Good afternoon, ladies," said Morgan, grabbing the collar of Gil's jacket and tugging. "Please excuse Gil here, but he's late for a meeting with me."

"No problem," said Melissa.

"I'll call you later," said Gil.

"OK," said Joanie.

When they were out of earshot, Gil said, "Geesh, Butch, what's your problem?"

"You're like a fucking dog in heat. And you're late."

"I just wanted to say hi."

"What's up with Aaronson?" demanded Morgan.

"Don't know. The ship was supposed to be in yesterday. I called him last night and this morning. Haven't heard back from him."

"So tell me, what exactly about that scenario gave you the impression that you could stop and go skirt-chasing?"

"All right already."

"Want a drink, Gil?" asked Vicki.

Gil glimpsed at Morgan and said, "I'm gonna need a few." Gil took out his cell phone. "I'll try him again now."

"Don't bother," said Morgan. "Storm last night took out the cell tower."

Vicki placed a glass of rye in front of Gil.

"Honey," said Morgan, "Can you please hand me the cordless phone."

"Calling Aaronson?" asked Gil.

"I'm calling Father Sean. Haven't heard from his ass either."

"Hello," said the priest.

"It's Morgan."

"I was gonna call you. Got back a little while ago."

"We gotta talk."

"Yes. Can you come here? I'm in the church. There's a big leak in the roof, and I'm cleaning up the altar. There's water everywhere."

"On my way." Morgan turned to Gil. "Finish your drink. We're going to Saint Matthew's." Morgan motioned to Vicki.

"Can I have one more before we go?" asked Gil.

"Why don't you just stick your dick in the glass and solve both problems at once?"

244

Vicki approached.

"Honey, we're headed over to see Father Sean."

"You're coming back here right after?" asked Vicki.

"Yeah. You OK?" asked Morgan.

"With the cell phones out, it just makes me a little nervous that I can't reach you."

"We won't be long," said Morgan.

"I could stay here with Vicki if you want," said Gil.

"Nice try, slick. Let's go."

Morgan swung open the front door of Saint Matthew's. The vestibule was dark, and the only light emanating from inside the church were the racks of red votive candles on the side of the altar.

"Father," called Morgan, heading down the center aisle. "Father?"

They stopped just before the altar.

"Butch, let's get out of here. Something's wrong."

"I agree," said Morgan.

They turned toward the front door.

The lights came on.

One of the black demons with white eyes blocked their path. Snarling, it extended its talons.

"Hello, Captain."

Gil and Morgan spun around.

Adriana stood on the altar, clad in her black capuchin, flanked by two robed figures, their cowls obscuring their faces. To their left was a coffin, from within which could be heard muffled cries.

Morgan drew his magnum and pulled the trigger, but it wouldn't fire.

245

"Alas, Captain," said Adriana. "Consider that the first step in your emasculation."

"And exactly which asshole are you?" Morgan reached into his pants pocket.

"I am Adriana Barberi."

"You're Adriana?" said Gil, his eyes broadening.

"I see my reputation precedes me."

Morgan popped the cork from the vial in his pocket, twirled around and splashed it on the black demon.

The demon was unfazed.

Adriana and the two hooded figures snickered.

"It's not holy water," said Adriana, "unless it's blessed by a priest."

The first figure pulled back his cowl. Father Sean glowered at Morgan with his yellow eyes.

"You piece of shit," growled Morgan.

Gil looked for an escape route, but a shrouded, faceless demon guarded their right flank, while Stan, wielding the same knife he killed Peter Hadley with, blocked their left.

The second hooded figure retracted his cowl. "Pathetic humans," said Van Haden. "Your trusting nature renders you such easy prey." From inside his robe Van Haden withdrew Saint Michael's sword, holding it up for all to see. Its brilliant white blade was blinding. "I'm always one step ahead of you, Captain."

"It's over," mumbled Gil.

"No, it's not," muttered Morgan out of the corner of his mouth. "They want something, or we'd be dead by now."

"Yes, you are correct, Captain. I do indeed want something. Where is the tablet?"

"I don't know."

Van Haden rolled his eyes and motioned for Adriana and Father Sean to step aside. Upon the altar was a long, purple cloth, draped over something running the length of the table. Van Haden yanked the cloth away. Underneath were the decapitated heads of Cardinal Rossi, Cardinal Salvador, Bishop Mwamba, Rabbi Azaria, and Maharaj Magesh.

"Allow me to introduce the Camorra," said Van Haden. "Well, most of it. I have a few heads to add. I'd be happy to include yours, Captain."

"You know I'll die before helping you."

"Yes, indeed. Men like you require other forms of persuasion." Van Haden pointed at the coffin.

Father Sean flipped it open and hoisted up Aaronson, bound, gagged, and squirming. His face was bruised and bloodied.

"Tell me where the tablet is, and I'll spare his life. In fact, I'll spare the three of you."

"I don't know where it is," said Morgan. "And even if I did, I wouldn't tell you."

Father Sean withdrew a large knife and held it against Aaronson's throat.

"Last chance," said Van Haden.

Aaronson grunted and shook his head no.

"The professor's as willing to die to stop you as I am," said Morgan.

"As I assumed," said Van Haden, gesturing to Adriana.

Adriana clapped her hands twice.

Two men dragged in a struggling person in a brown sack.

"Enough!" said the one man, striking the person in the head.

The men untied the top of the sack and pulled it down.

Vicki was also bound and gagged.

"I'll fucking kill you!" screamed Morgan, lurching toward the altar. Adriana extended her hand. Morgan jolted back as if hit by lightning.

"I'm tired of these games, Captain," said Van Haden. "Now tell me where the tablet is, or I swear to you on everything I hold unholy, you will watch your friends and wife die."

"But I really don't know where it is."

"I do!" cried a voice from the back of the church.

The black demon squealed and wrenched, disintegrating into a sizzling, vile muck.

Nigel Poole stepped forward, holding multiple containers of holy water. "You want the tablet, Lucifer, then let my comrades go."

"Who are you?" asked Morgan.

"Oh," said Van Haden. "You haven't met? Perhaps you were being truthful, Captain. Allow me to introduce Mr. Nigel Poole. A so-called demonologist from the insignificant island of Great Britain."

"Allow me to strike him down, Master," said Adriana, extending her black, pointed fingernails.

Sirens wailed in the distance.

Stan and the shrouded demon each took a step forward.

"Wait," said Van Haden raising his hand. "Where is the tablet?"

"Are you blinkin' deaf?" asked Poole. "I told ya, release my comrades."

"You know," said Van Haden, "I've never encountered a race as pompously naïve as the English. Do you really think I would relinquish my advantage? You, the captain, and his sidekick may retrieve the tablet. I'll keep the professor and the captain's wife until it's delivered, or they die."

"You heard my terms," said Poole.

Van Haden waved his hand. The professor and Vicki vanished. "And you've heard mine."

248

Vicki's voice echoed from a distance, "Butch, help me!"

Morgan bristled. "If you lay a hand—"

Van Haden and his entourage disappeared.

Poole recapped his water vials.

Morgan clutched Poole's shirt with both fists. "Where the hell is that tablet?"

"Butch," said Gil. "Not here."

Morgan shook Poole violently. "You tell me where that tablet is, or I'll kill you before he does."

"Butch! Please, stop." Gil put his arm between the two men. "Calm down. Let's get out of here while we can."

Morgan shoved Poole as he released him.

Poole stumbled but regained his balance. "What the hell is wrong with you, mate? We're on the same side."

Morgan stormed toward him.

Poole hurried out of the church and onto the sidewalk.

Morgan grabbed him again, shoving him onto the hood of a car. He withdrew his magnum and pushed it against Poole's forehead. "Start talking, or I'll blow you away."

"Butch, don't," said Gil. "This is exactly what Van Haden wants you to do."

"Shut up!"

"I'm in the Camorra with Aaronson and those dead men," said Poole. "I was on the bloody cargo ship with the sword. We suspected the Devil knew about the shipment, so we decided to send the tablet separately. We were right, because we were intercepted by a ghost ship of witches and demons. They killed everyone on board the cargo ship and blew it up. I grabbed a life preserver and jumped overboard. The next day I was picked up by a fishing vessel."

"How convenient," said Morgan. "You're the only one who survived."

249

"I'm not lying to you, mate,"

"I'm not your fucking *mate*." Morgan grabbed one of Poole's water vials, bit off the top and dumped it on Poole's chest. Nothing happened. "Where's the tablet?"

"Not here," said Poole. "They could still be watching."

"Butch," said Gil, "Van Haden knows you don't know where it is. You would have given it up for Vicki. Planting a spy won't get information out of you that you don't have."

Morgan relaxed, but still pointed his pistol at Poole.

The sirens continued. Smoke could be seen billowing from the center of town.

"Butch, something's happened."

"Get in my truck," said Morgan, not taking his eyes off Poole. "You're coming with us."

Morgan called the station from his truck radio.

"Toby's is on fire," said the dispatcher.

"Anyone hurt?" asked Morgan.

"Not that we know of."

"I'm on my way."

When they reached Toby's, they discovered the entire building was aflame. The firemen were doing what they could, but it was hopeless. They put most of their energy into stopping it from spreading. Thankfully, Toby's was a stand-alone building.

"Gotta be arson," said the fire chief to Morgan. "The rate it burned— had to be an accelerant."

Morgan made sure everyone was accounted for and safe. One of the patrons asked where Vicki was. Morgan said she was OK and walked away before he was asked more questions. Morgan placed Lieutenant Edwards in charge of the scene. Then he drove away with Gil and Poole.

"Where are we going?" asked Poole.

"My house," said Morgan.

"They used the fire to kidnap Vicki," said Gil.

Morgan punched the steering wheel. "Why wouldn't she listen to me. I could've hid her."

Seated in Morgan's living room, Gil shakily poured everyone a drink.

Poole recounted the Camorra's meetings and what happened on the ship in detail. He continued, "I had a car waiting for me in Portland. I tried calling Aaronson and you, Captain. Every time I dialed I got a sinister voice making threats. I went to a local church and collected some holy water. Then I drove straight here. I went to the police station. They said it was your day off, to try Toby's. I met your wife, told her who I was, and what happened. She said I just missed you, that you were at Saint Matthew's. They must have torched the pub just after I left."

"So where's this tablet?" asked Morgan.

"On its way to Boston, on one of Bernardo Iannucci's private vessels."

"Private vessel?" asked Gil.

"Iannucci's loaded," said Poole. "He owns a fleet of merchant ships. Inherited the business from his father. He pays others to manage it while he runs the museum."

"When's it arriving?" asked Morgan.

"Should be Wednesday. Iannucci's ship was leaving four days after mine. I'm supposed to meet him at the container terminal at the port of Boston."

"Gil and I are going with you," said Morgan.

"Of course," said Poole. "I'm going to need a place to stay in the meantime."

"There's a little hotel on Route Two in Concord," said Morgan.

"Butch," said Gil with pleading eyes.

"He ain't staying here," barked Morgan.

"You can stay with me," said Gil.

"Why thank you, mate, much appreciated. Hope you have something better to drink than this bloody Yank bourbon."

Morgan glared.

"I've got Scotch and Irish whiskey," said Gil.

"Now you're talking," said Poole. "Gentlemen, we have to figure out our next move."

"I already know our next move," said Morgan.

"What is it?" said Poole.

"You'll know if I decide to tell ya," said Morgan.

Poole stood up. "Now look, mate. I can understand why you don't trust me. But you have to decide whether you want my help or not. We either work together, or I might as well be off."

"I got to get to the station," said Morgan. "I got shit to do because of the fire. I'll meet you guys at Gil's tonight. I'll decide then. Got it?"

"Nigel," said Gil. "Let's go to my place while Butch does his thing. Give him time to digest everything. His wife was just kidnapped by the Devil."

"Right," said Poole. "I'm sorry, Captain."

"I gotta go," said Morgan. He went into the kitchen, returned, and threw a set of keys to Gil. "Take Vicki's car."

"We'll get your wife back, Captain," said Poole. "Lucifer won't don't anything to her as long as he doesn't have the tablet."

"And if he gets the tablet before we do?"

"Then I'm afraid we'll all come to a sticky end," said Poole.

"And what does that mean exactly?"

"It's a British phrase for a sudden and unpleasant death," said Gil.

252

As the men started to leave, Morgan tapped Poole on the shoulder. "Wait outside for a moment. I got to talk to Gil."

"Right," said Poole.

Morgan handed Gil his Smith and Wesson 9mm.

"He's not one of them," said Gil. "I told you, If Van Haden thought you knew where the tablet was, he would have never let us leave the church. And if it is arriving in Boston, and Poole's one of them, Van Haden would have simply killed us and sent him to get it."

"Shut up and listen to me. I understand your reasoning, but you can never let your guard down. If you have to, you blow him away."

"OK . . ."

"I mean it, Gil. Do you have the balls to do so if need be?"

"Yes, if I had to."

"I'll see you later."

Gil and Poole drove away. Morgan collapsed on his couch, buried his face in his hands, and did something he hadn't done since he was eight years old.

He wept.

The Deathsman

"They say that house is haunted," said Eve pointing to the creepy rattrap across the street. The words rolled off my realtor's tongue as if they were just another vacuous comment, the ones interspersed between the dollops of substance we speak each day. As if they had no bearing on whether I purchased the three-bedroom colonial overlooking the eerie eyesore. As if she knew me.

"Who lives there?" I asked.

"No one," said Eve. "At least not in the five years I've worked at the Crestwood Lake agency. I could dig up the tax records and see who owns it."

I shook my head. "I don't care. Better than having some asshole neighbor or noisy kids."

"If you want solitude, this is the right place." Eve's cell phone vibrated. She ignored it, but I could feel her eyes saying, "So what's the verdict? I have seven other clients and don't have time to jerk you off all day."

"Three fifty huh?"

"Yes. The home's relatively new and has over an acre of property."

"Fine. Let's do it. I'll pay cash."

"Splendid. I'll get the ball rolling."

I certainly did want solitude. I had just finished a job and needed some serious downtime with peace and quiet. I had stashed up plenty over the course of my career and could afford to take a break.

I didn't bother painting, or redecorating, or any of that fluff. I had the place cleaned, made a few minor repairs, and simply moved in. I parked my black leather recliner in front of the picture window. I wasn't interested in being part of the world, but I liked to keep an eye on it. From my recliner I had an unobstructed view of the road, and three of my neighbor's homes, especially the "haunted" one across the street. I referred to it as the *spooker*.

In addition to needing some relaxation, I also wanted a respite to mull over my goals. My forties have been an interesting decade thus far. For the first time in my life, I began to contemplate the future. When you first realize there are less years ahead than behind you, you've officially arrived at middle age.

How did I want to spend the remainder of my life? Certainly not working as much as I had. Maybe I'd pick up an occasional job here or there, but I yearned for something more meaningful, whatever that was. I toyed with the idea of getting married, a novel idea for me. I definitely didn't want kids. I'd rather have a tumor. But a wife? Hmmmm. Not sure on that one. I don't think I could actually tolerate having someone that entrenched in my life. She'd have to be an only child and an orphan. In-laws are multiple metastases.

And she would have to give me space—lots of space. No-questions-asked space. And have zero control issues. Don't be telling me what to do or how to do it. And we're not going antiquing on weekends, or salsa dancing, or volunteering at some stupid animal shelter. Who am I kidding? I don't need a wife. I need someone else's wife. Someone who just uses me for sex with no strings attached.

Ya know, come to think about it, Eve wasn't a bad package. She was about my age, thin, with curly red hair. She had a cute gleam in her brown eyes, when she wasn't looking at me like a paycheck. She didn't have a ring though. She'd want to build a nest. Probably already has kids from a previous marriage. Didn't strike me as the "lets-just-screw-but-not-screw-up-our-lives" kind of woman. Damn shame.

God, how long had it been since I was with a woman? About eight months, I think. Oh yeah, that hot little Asian nymphette I picked up in Hong Kong. Man, did she know how to fuck. But I was just there on business and had to move on to my next engagement. My work was such a double-edged sword. It brought me to all sorts of exotic places, and women. But, on the other hand—back to the middle-age thing—there's this feeling of not having any roots in my life. But then again, I *don't* want that. Jesus Christ, I don't know what the hell I want.

Believe it or not, I've dallied with writing a book. A tell-all story about my career. Maybe some hot-shot LA producer will turn it into a movie or something. I could make a fortune. Nah. That would bring exposure and nosey people. Ugh! That's the last thing I wanted. I'd need a ghost writer. Ha. Like whoever owns the freak show across the street. Speaking of which . . .

One afternoon, I was seated in my recliner drinking coffee. It was dusk, and the outlines of the trees were lazily surrendering to the night, the time of day when the haunted house looked most haunted. Midday, it was too bright to be really scary, and at night you could barely see it. But at twilight, with its features blending amorphously into the gloom, and its spiny projections contrasting against the shadowy sky, then the canvas was primed for horrific imagery.

The spooker was a narrow, three-story house with a tented roof, the four corners of which sported long spires, topped by a bizarre, ornate design. The house was composed of grungy, gray wood, cracked and weathered, and dotted with murky windows. The decrepit wraparound porch completed the ensemble. The house was surrounded by knee-high grass, and a rickety wood fence, even more dilapidated than the house.

As I sipped my coffee I pondered the spooker. My curiosity about its history piqued. Who lived there? What happened that they let it deteriorate? Did they still own it? If so, why? Why pay property taxes for a useless relic? Or did they abandon it and allow the town to appropriate it?

Cater-corner to my home, next to the spooker was a white wooden house similar to mine. The Taylors lived there with their two girls. I'm not good at guessing children's ages, but I'd say they were around ten or eleven. The father was a dentist, and the mother, an office worker in St. Johnsbury.

I know all this because the wife welcomed me to the neighborhood, cake in hand, the day after I moved in. I thought she'd never shut up talking about her family. Only good thing was she didn't ask too many questions about me. Everything was about her one daughter's this, and the other daughter's that. I had wanted to query her about the spooker, but ten minutes into her discourse I felt like shoving a pencil in my eye. I feared that asking her anything could initiate another ten minutes of blather. So, I just politely thanked her for the cake and explained that I had housework to do. She did have a nice ass, though.

Finishing my coffee, I glimpsed at the spooker. I saw a gangly man shambling across the porch. I blinked and did a double take, but it was gone. I went to the kitchen, placed my cup in the sink, and returned to the window. I crouched down, chin almost resting on the sill, watching, but saw nothing more. I don't imagine shit. Someone *was* there.

That night I couldn't sleep. That's not me either. Nothing on my mind; just couldn't knock off. I lay there in bed debating whether a glass of whiskey would help. Sometimes it relaxed me, sometimes it made me edgy. Somewhere around the seventh "should-I-or-shouldn't-I," a harrowing moan emanated from the spooker. An unearthly moan. Trust me, I've heard people holler and whine all kinds of things. But I never heard anything like that.

I got out of bed and peered out the window. There was a dim red glow coming from the spooker. What in the world? Did someone break in? Maybe it was some kids partying—smoking weed or something. Should I do something? Like what? I just stood there watching. Eventually the light faded. That's when I noticed my heart palpitating. And that was definitely not me. Nothing frightens me. *Nothing.*

The next day I decided to call Eve. Two reasons. First, to see who owned the spooker, and second, to ask her out. What the hell? Might get lucky. Maybe I'd get real lucky and she'd just want a casual thing too. I'd make it clear from the start that I wasn't looking to pick out china patterns. I did believe in being honest with women. It saves you a lot of bullshit and noisy confrontations later on.

So I called Eve and asked if she could find out about the spooker. She questioned what prompted my sudden curiosity. I told her some kids were playing inside it the other night, and wanted to know who was responsible for the property. She was in the middle of showing a house and said she'd research it later and call me.

I knew she was preoccupied, but nevertheless suggested we have dinner Saturday night. I wanted to catch her off guard and get a flustered "yes," as opposed to a contemplated "no." It worked. She said OK, and I told her we'd talk later about the details. I peeked out the window at the spooker and made some lunch.

Later that evening I called Eve back. When I asked her where she wanted to go, she suggested Pierre's. Frigging hifalutin French. What was I going to say—no? The next morning I'd be taking the most expensive crap of my life. We agreed to meet at seven. Then the conversation got real interesting.

"I found out about the haunted house," said Eve. "Two of my older coworkers gave me an earful."

"Oh yeah? What'd they tell you?"

"The house used to belong to *Ned Guttman*."

"Who's that?"

"You never heard of Ned Guttman? Oh, that's right. You're not from around here. He was an infamous serial killer. Murdered a whole slew of people in northern Vermont back in the sixties. He was an executioner in Texas."

"An executioner?"

"Yeah. He worked at the Texas State Penitentiary in Huntsville. He was the one who flipped the switch on Old Sparky."

"Old Sparky?"

"The famous electric chair. They tell me it's now in the prison museum. Anyway, Guttman fried dozens of convicts over the years. I guess it got to him, because he quit the job and moved here. But something in him snapped; he went psycho and killed twenty-something people. I don't know all the details, but eventually the police figured out it was him. They surrounded his house and he blew his brains out. They found bodies, some skeletons I think, buried under the floor of his basement."

"Holy shit."

"He had a son who paid the property taxes for years. He tried to sell it but—no surprise—couldn't find a buyer. Eventually the son died, or just abandoned it, and the town took it over. Obviously, they haven't been able to unload it either. I understand they're debating whether to spend the money to demolish it, and just sell the property alone."

How could Eve not already have known this before selling me my house? She said she'd been at the Crestwood Lake agency for five years. Anyway, I was looking to get into her pants, not her ethics, so I didn't say anything.

I got off the phone, fetched a glass of whiskey, stepped out onto my front porch, and lit a cigarette. As I blew out that glorious first puff, I could see the silhouette of the spooker against the night sky. I pondered the previous owner. A demented lunatic, indiscriminately killing innocent people. It doesn't get much worse than that. I was practically a saint compared to him.

As I smoked my butt I heard what sounded like a beast growling. That's right—*a beast*. It didn't sound like a dog. It was a low growling, coming from the back of the spooker. Then I heard multiple voices whispering over one another—some kind of foreign language—maybe Latin? Then a few words of English slowly mixed in, as if it were in the process of being translated. Then, all the voices converged into one unmistakable presage:

"Deathsman—we come for you!"

What the fuck? Who was talking, and who were they talking to? The voices and growling stopped. I stared at the spooker but didn't see anything. I crushed out my cigarette and stepped inside. Someone was messing with me. Probably the same kids from last night, smoking weed and getting their jollies freaking people out. Three drinks later, the growling started again. I grabbed my .45 auto, slipped out my back door, and skulked toward the spooker.

The house was disturbingly dark. Despite treading lightly, the crunching leaves would have given away my presence to anyone within earshot. I stepped inconsistently, thinking it would sound less like a person walking. I brought a flashlight but hadn't turned it on. The cloudy sky obscured any moonlight. The lights from the Taylor's house cast a faint glow onto the spooker.

I ascended the porch steps. Creaks snapped through the limpid night air. I tried the knob on the front door, but it was locked. I shone my flashlight into the window, but still couldn't see inside clearly. I discerned an old chair and a small table, cobwebbed and filthy. No ghosts.

Something touched my shoulder. I spun around so fast I almost lost balance. Nothing was there. I heard footsteps and snickering off to the side. Now I was getting pissed. They had no idea who they were messing with.

I bounded off the porch, flashlight now blazing, and headed toward the sounds. Marching around the side of the house, I slipped in something squishy and fell on my right side. I sat up and rubbed my upper arm. Rising to my feet, I scanned the ground with the light and flinched: a festering, red, steaming pile of innards. I shined the light on my shoes; they were splattered with blood. Another snicker from the back of the house.

I darted around the rear and waved the flashlight wildly. Above the back door, nailed to the house, was an eviscerated German Shepard, crucified,

259

upside-down. Written next to it, in what must have been its blood, were the words:

Deathsman—we come for you!

I didn't know what to make of it. What a sick joke. This was beyond what a bunch of teenagers partying and playing tricks would do. Someone in need of some serious psycho-mental help was loose in the neighborhood. Hmmmph. Come to my house and try that shit. I'll put one right between your eyes. I shined my light around one more time and headed back home.

Crossing the street, I noticed my bedroom light was on, even though I hadn't been in my bedroom all evening. I snuck up on my back door, tiptoed inside, and canvassed my house gun-first. I didn't find anything other than the light I *know* I never flicked on.

I poured myself a drink, pulled my 1984 Webster's II Dictionary off the shelf, and sat in my recliner. I flipped to the word deathsman:

(dĕths´mən) n. *Archaic.* An executioner.

I slept with my .45 in my hand that night.

Saturday came. I picked up Eve and drove to Pierre's. She looked fantastic. She obviously had her hair done that day. She wore compelling eye makeup, a short, tight, red dress, stockings, and come-fuck-me pumps. I would've crawled across a field of broken glass and through a pool of lemonade to get to her.

But I was going to pay for it another way. All men have to pay for it in one form or another. She ordered a three-hundred-dollar bottle of wine. Did she think I was made of money? Well, I sort of was, but she didn't know that.

Eve ordered blood sausages as an appetizer. Fucking gross if you ask me. I nibbled at the greens they came with. For dinner we had the lamb chops with some weird root vegetable I never heard of. It was pretty good though. I don't think any lamb chop dinner is worth forty-nine bucks, but this one came close. We elected to skip dessert for an after-dinner drink. Eve ordered us two cognacs, at twenty-five bucks a pop. The waiter bragged about the splendors of this cognac, and how long it was aged. Age this—it all pees out the same.

All I knew, is I was dumping over five hundred for a meal. I better come out of this with more than just a hard-on.

Halfway through our pretentious French swill Eve leaned forward and gazed intently into my eyes. I was hoping she'd say: *let's go back to my place.* Instead, she says . . .

"I have a job for you."

"A job for me?"

Eve reached into her purse and handed me a letter-sized envelope, one inch thick.

I opened it to find a wad of bills. I whizzed my thumb across them: all hundreds. I'd say twenty-five grand. "What's this for?"

Eve finished her cognac. "Cut the crap. We know what you do, and we know your terms. Half now, half when the job is done."

"Who's we?" I asked.

"My boss and I."

"Your boss at the real estate agency?"

"No, that's just a front that makes a little side money. My *real* boss."

"And who is that?"

"You don't know him. And it's better you didn't. He doesn't want anything leading back to him." Eve motioned to the waiter.

I ran my finger over the bills again. She better still put out tonight.

The waiter approached.

"Two more cognacs," said Eve.

"What are the details?" I asked.

"It's in there with the money. Your contact is Malcolm Rittenberger."

"*The* Malcolm Rittenberger? The billionaire financier?"

"Does that intimidate you?"

I frowned. "No one intimidates me, lady."

"Good. His penthouse and corporate office are both in Manhattan. He'll be in New York all next week. He's in deliberations with European bankers regarding his next venture."

"What's Rittenberger's connection to your boss?"

"Let's just say that Rittenberger and my employer are at an impasse. We need your skills to resolve the matter."

"How am I supposed to fix things without knowing the specifics?"

"Everything you need to know is in the envelope. You resolve this and there will be more work for you in the future. So do you want the job or not?"

"I get expenses on top of my fee: travel, meals, etc."

"No problem," said Eve.

The waiter returned with our cognacs.

Eve held out her glass. "To our new partnership?"

I reached to clink her glass but hesitated. "That's not how I christen a deal with a woman like you . . . or are you not part of the package?"

"Oh honey, that was always in the offing."

~~~~~~

Three days later I checked into my hotel on Manhattan's fifth avenue. I could see Rittenberger's office across the street from my window. I scoped out the neighborhood, got lunch at some hole-in-the-wall Mexican joint, and called my driver.

I returned to my room and opened my suitcase. Then I went to the window and slid apart the drapes. I retrieved my glass cutter from my case and adhered it to the window with the suction cups. I etched out an eight-inch-wide circle, pulled the handle, and withdrew the glass disc.

Then I set up the tripod and loaded my Tango 51 sniper rifle. I set the rifle in the tripod, adjusted the scope, and aimed it at Rittenberger's office. I waited . . . and waited . . . and waited. I knew he was in the building, and had meetings scheduled throughout the day.

My thoughts wandered to Eve, who I could envision a future with. She already knew what I did for a living, and she certainly wasn't the Susie Homemaker type. Plus, she was unbelievable in the sack—insatiable—a one-woman porn flick.

I wasn't ready to start a serious relationship, however. I still needed some time off. That was my whole point of moving to East Jabib, or what the inhabitants of this corner of Vermont call "The Northeast Kingdom." Now that's a laugh. *Kingdom.* More like miles and miles of woods, sparsely populated by yokels, sprinkled with weirdos like Ned Guttman. Not to mention whatever whack job was playing pin-the-tail-on-the-autopsy over at the house of horrors.

And yet people would condemn me for what I do. Yeah right. Ninety percent of the people I eliminate are scum. How do you think pricks like Rittenberger got so rich, by buying Girl Scout cookies and helping nuns cross the street? I provide a much-needed service. I've taken out every kind of trash from wife beaters, to corporate swindlers, to murderers. I even wasted an Albanian maggot who kidnapped young girls and sold them into the sex trade. So before you judge me . . .

Rittenberger walked into his office, followed by a leggy blonde secretary. He was going on and on about something. Jesus, this guy never shuts up. Ditch the bitch and sit down. I ain't got all day.

Finally, the blonde walked out of the room. Rittenberger picked up the phone. Oh shit. He held the receiver on the side of his head facing me. C'mon jerk-off, I need a clear shot. Finally, he switched hands. I squeezed the trigger. His head exploded like a cantaloupe.

I left everything, scurried out of the room and down the stairs. They'd never trace the equipment to me. It was all stolen and I only touched it with gloves. I bolted out of the hotel and into my waiting car. By the time the police arrived I'd almost be out of the city. I dumped my hat, glasses and fake beard a half mile away. My driver pulled into a private garage where I switched cars.

The next one took me out of the city and on to Paterson, NJ. What a shithole. I had an Arab associate there, Hami Akah. He owned a car repair joint, among other businesses. I switched cars again. Hami would ensure the last one ended up as scrap metal within hours. I gave him ten grand. The last car drove me to Vermont; planes are too traceable. The job was done. Time to collect my money and see if *Eve* wanted to play with my *serpent.*

The next morning, I was waiting for Eve to arrive. I was anxious to get my hands on the rest of the dough. The problem with "half now, half when the job is done," is they can screw you out of the second half. I was pacing in my living room, peeking out the window every minute for her car.

During one of my trips to the window I saw the Taylor girls walking to their bus stop. They were passing the spooker when on the side of the house, out of their view, I saw the gangly man, with a large knife, crouching, as if ready to pounce.

I stuck my .45 in my belt under my shirt and dashed out of the house. "Girls! Girls!" I yelled, as the man ran behind the back of the house.

The girls were startled and cringed.

"It's OK, girls. Go to your bus stop. Stay away from this house."

The girls ran, more freaked out by me than anything else.

I drew my weapon and sprinted to the rear of the spooker. The back door was ajar. I kicked it open. "All right, motherfucker. You're mine now!"

The inside was a disaster: layers and layers of dust, dirt, and cobwebs. It smelled like a damp dog's ass. I stood in what had to be the kitchen, based on the corroded sink and rusted old stove. I was motionless, listening, but it was silent. To my right was a small room, possibly a walk-in pantry. I stuck my head in but found nothing but shelves, grime, and dead bugs.

From the kitchen I entered the living room. I saw a few old chairs, broken light fixtures, and swaths of cobwebs. In the one corner was a door. I flung it open. It was a decrepit bathroom: cracked sink, missing toilet, and a grody, brown bathtub. I inched forward to find a cat's skeleton inside the tub.

"Deathsman, we come for you," echoed a ghostly voice from upstairs.

264

My heart fluttered, but my anger won out.

In the corner of the foyer was the staircase to the second floor. Slowly I made my ascent. I hate climbing stairs in search of prey. Having the height advantage, they can easily waylay you. I held my weapon steady with outstretched hands, watching above me with intense vigilance.

I reached the top of the stairs. The second floor was just as scuzzy as the first. There was a hallway with three closed doors: likely two bedrooms and a bathroom. I observed a door in the ceiling leading to an attic.

I kicked open the first door. A shower of dust descended on my head. It was a half bath, highlighted by a damaged, mucky toilet. A faded Hustler Magazine languished in the corner.

The second door was slightly ajar. I pushed it open. Aside from the filth, there was nothing in it but an old dresser with a cracked mirror. It was so soiled, I could barely see my reflection. I did see the man raising his knife, however.

I whipped around and fired—at a blank wall. What the hell was going on? That was it. I was fed up. There was only one hiding place left. I stormed over to the final door and slammed my weight against it. It bounced off the wall and creaked to a stop.

In the center of the room was an electric chair—a prison electric chair. It was old, but strangely, not covered with dust. I stepped forward to inspect it. The last thing I remember is the blow to the back of my head.

Grunting, I tugged at my bindings. He was hideous: pallid skin flecked with irregular moles, tall and lanky, bony hands, and shoulder-length, thin gray hair. His hollowed eyes were almost black. He wore some type of uniform. My gun was on the floor at his feet.

I yanked but had little leeway. My ankles and wrists were locked in the chair's steel cuffs. A wide leather belt tightly encircled my chest, rendering me virtually immobile.

"What do you want from me?" I snarled.

On the wall was a lever. He rested his hand on it.

"No! What do you want?"

"We come for you, deathsman," he said, in a thin, faltering voice.

"Who's *we?*"

"Your crimes are heinous. Your penalty is death."

"No! I don't kill innocent—"

He pulled the lever.

Searing, excruciating pain surged through my body. Every single nerve I had was afire. Paralyzing me, I couldn't scream—only suffer.

He pushed the lever up.

My breathing was labored. My eyes felt like they were bulging. My heart zoomed.

I looked for mercy.

"I want you to enjoy it before you die," he said.

"I'll pay you whatever you want."

He pulled the lever.

I bit through my tongue. My left eye popped out of its socket.

Lever up.

Lever down.

Lever up

Lever down . . .

~~~~~~

"Well?" asked Eve.

"I'm almost there," said Kim, clacking away steadily on her keyboard.

"You there yet?"

"Yes! I've hacked his account. Oh, looky what we got here. We're going to get much more than our twenty-five thousand back."

"That's fabulous," said Eve.

"Transferring now . . . just waiting for the confirmation . . . aha, there we go. The money's in our Cayman Islands account." Kim closed the laptop.

"Great. Now I can call our client." Eve picked up her desk phone and dialed. "Hello, Mr. Pizer. It's Eve."

"Everything go as planned?"

"Yes, Mr. Pizer. I am very pleased to inform you that everything went *exactly* as planned. Mr. Rittenberger will not be interfering with your financial plans anymore."

"Splendid. And the final payment?"

"You may remit a certified check to Van Haden Holdings Inc."

The Stigma

Morgan spent the remainder of the afternoon doing paperwork and attending to miscellaneous details involving the fire at Toby's. He swigged his tepid coffee and called Gil.

"Hey, Butch."

"What's up with Poole?"

"Everything's fine. He's a fascinating individual. Knows a lot about the supernatural. Been fighting the Devil for years."

"Just wanted to check before I arrived. Be right over."

Morgan strode into Gil's living room where a glass of bourbon awaited him.

"Good evening, Captain," said Poole.

Morgan nodded.

"Are you OK, Butch?" asked Gil.

"No, I'm not fucking OK. And I won't be until I get Vicki back. Do you know what I'm going through? Thinking about what *she* must be going through? What if he's torturing her? And now I have to sit on my ass for three days until I can do something about it."

"Lucifer won't do anything to her until he has what he wants," said Poole.

"Yeah, you said that before. How do you know?"

"Because that's the way he works. First of all, he won't jeopardize his bargaining chip. He'll leave her unharmed until he gets the tablet—let everyone think that he's playing by the rules. But once he has it, games up, mate. He'll kill all of us—slowly."

"But we can't defeat him with the tablet alone, right?" said Gil.

"No, you'll also need the sword," said Poole.

Morgan placed his glass on the table. "He's probably got Vicki and Aaronson in his hideout under Crestwood Lake. You know about that?"

"Yes, I am quite aware," said Poole. "Aaronson and I spoke the day I set sail. Have you found the entrance in the woods?"

Morgan looked at Gil, hesitatingly.

"You either trust him or you don't," said Gil.

Morgan turned back to Poole. "There's an abandoned mine about a mile from the lake. There's an old shaft that leads directly to the water. We get the tablet, arm ourselves to the teeth, and go in."

"Not much of a plan," said Poole. "But I suppose there's no better one."

"I wonder how Van Haden got Aaronson?' asked Gil.

"The I-93 bridge on the border of New Hampshire and Vermont collapsed Saturday night in the storm," said Morgan. "They fished his Mercedes out of the river."

"How did you find out?" asked Gil.

"You recall that I'm the chief of a police department, right?"

"So, Aaronson knew something happened to the ship, couldn't call us for some reason, and drove here to warn us."

"That's what I figure," said Morgan, helping himself to another bourbon. He looked at Poole. "What time does the ship come in Wednesday?"

"They're due in early in the morning."

"Here's what I propose," said Morgan. "We leave here in time to meet the ship when it arrives. We do this as discreetly as possible because Van Haden's operatives could be anywhere. I'll be dressed in civilian clothes. We'll take Gil's car to a car rental joint—not my police truck—pick up a new vehicle, and take that to Boston. We get the tablet and go directly to the woods."

Gil replenished his rye. "We need more holy water. I know the priest at Saint Elizabeth's in Lyndonville. I'll get some."

Morgan turned to Poole. "Have you been to Crestwood Lake before today?"

"No. Been to America many times, but never here. Why?"

"A couple weeks ago I was investigating this woman I suspected of being a witch. I found her dissolved remains. Someone killed her with holy water. Unless Van Haden got rid of one of his own."

"He'd never do it with holy water," said Poole. "You have a silent partner, Captain."

"That don't make me feel better. Does the name Scott Guerin ring a bell?"

"No, who's he?"

"A book store owner in town that I'm suspicious about."

"My, my," said Poole. "You certainly have some loose ends."

Morgan finished his bourbon. "So what's your deal, Poole?"

"My deal?"

"Yeah. Who exactly are you and how did you get into this shit?"

"We got all night," said Gil. "And lots more whiskey. Tell him what you told me."

Poole refilled his glass of Scotch. "I'm from Wolverhampton, England. Studied archaeology at Oxford. I'm a digger."

"What does that mean?" asked Morgan.

"I don't spend my time in classrooms. Give me an ancient burial site, a shovel, and a grant, and I'm happy. I spent ten years excavating all kinds of historical sites, mostly in the Middle East. I was part of the teams that found the Zayit Stone in 2005 and the tomb of Herod the Great in 2007, both in Israel."

"I understand there's debate about the alphabet on the Zayit Stone," said Gil.

"Yes," said Poole. "Some scholars think it's Phoenician, while—"

270

"Oh please, spare me" said Morgan. "Just get back to your story."

"Very well, mate. Demonology has always fascinated me. Over the course of my career I've found many artifacts related to it. The more items I came across, the more I studied it.

Then in 2010 I was at an excavation in Syria when we discovered an unknown cave. Deep inside it we found drawings on the walls about Belial."

"Who?" asked Morgan.

"Belial," said Gil. "An infamous and powerful demon. Some think he was the original Satan."

"That's right," said Poole. "Some theologians believe it was he, not Lucifer, who initiated the original uprising against God. Supposedly, there was an ongoing conflict between Belial and Lucifer as to who would exert control. In any event, after the discovery, almost all of our workers, mostly indigenous peoples, deserted. They were petrified. They believed anything associated with Belial was cursed. We had to terminate the excavation.

"Three days later an earthquake rocked the region, collapsing the cave. Unearthing the site would have taken considerable resources and machinery, not to mention men. And no one in the region would go near it. The next year the Syrian Civil War broke out so any hope of recovering it was lost."

"Why is this significant?" asked Morgan.

"Until this time I was an atheist, a scholar. I didn't believe in God and the Devil. But the aftermath of that excavation made a believer out of me. After the quake and the loss of our workers, the rest of us, mostly archeologists and scientists, departed. A plane carrying most of the remaining personnel crashed into the Mediterranean. I lost seven friends and associates in that disaster.

"Aside from me, there were four other people who worked at the site and weren't on the plane. All four of them died tragically within the year. One drowned in Lake Cuomo under suspicious circumstances. Another was decapitated by an out of control bulldozer in Koblentz. A third was mutilated in a combine on his family's farm in Russia, and the fourth ended up in miniscule pieces, in over thirteen hundred cans of dog food."

Gil shook his head and added more rye to his glass.

"The one killed by the bulldozer was my good friend Fletcher. He called me just before he died, telling me that he woke up one morning with a tattoo on his chest: the seal of Belial. It's a circle with an intricate design inside it, with a series of upside-down crosses. In 2011, shortly after all of them had perished, I woke up one morning and found this . . ."

Poole unbuttoned his left shirt sleeve and pulled it up. He displayed the underside of his forearm to Gil and Morgan.

"The seal of Belial," said Poole.

"Goddamn," said Morgan.

"I knew Rabbi Azaria on the Camorra, from my work in Israel," said Poole. "His head was one of the ones on the altar in Saint Matthew's. I went to him and explained everything that happened. He introduced me to the Camorra, and I've been a member ever since. They've helped shield me to some extent, but I can't spend my life looking over my blinking shoulder. I don't have a woman I love at stake, Captain, but like you, I'm fighting for my life. That's my deal."

"That's not all you and Butch have in common," said Gil.

"What do you mean, mate?"

"Your strength of character. Aaronson told us years ago that some people seem to be relatively immune to evil. They possess an inner fortitude. Conversely, many who fall prey to the dark side, either as a victim or an ally, suffer from a constitutional weakness, be it psychological or moral. Butch and I have found this to be true. People with emotional vulnerabilities, or shady ethics, are much more susceptible to evil."

"That's a nice idea, mate, but that's no guarantee. A number of the people from the dig in Syria who died weren't daft or corrupt."

"Nothing's one hundred percent," said Gil. "But some personalities are more resistant."

Morgan turned to Poole. "How is driving the Devil out of Crestwood Lake going to help your situation," asked Morgan.

"I don't know for sure that it will. But if the mythos is true, and we can expel Lucifer, I'm hoping the cleansing will extend to me. Even if it doesn't, I'm already a marked man. And I'm not going down without a fight."

"I can respect that," said Morgan.

"Let me tell you blokes, something big is going on here."

Gil refreshed Poole's Scotch. "That's what Vicki said, because of Adriana Barberi being involved."

"That's right," said Poole. "It's thought she became a witch during the Piedmont Massacre in 1655."

Gil turned to Morgan. "That's when the Duke of Savoy's army slaughtered seventeen hundred Waldensians, a Protestant sect, in what is now the province of Piedmont in Italy."

"There's suspicion the Duke of Savoy was in bed with Lucifer," said Poole. "Anyway, Adriana always seems to turn up during pivotal clashes between God and the Devil. There have been other "Crestwood Lakes" in history and reports of her participation in them."

"So what exactly is going on here?" asked Morgan.

"You want my opinion?" asked Poole.

"No, I want the Easter Bunny's," said Morgan.

Poole smirked. "Viewpoints are mixed on the Camorra. Based on my research, I think Lucifer wishes to establish outposts, satellite hells if you will. Much like an invading army builds beachheads or strongholds along their routes of conquest. Lucifer wants to take over the world. You don't accomplish that willy-nilly. You have to create fortified positions from which you can garner recruits and organize your efforts. Crestwood Lake is one of those sites."

"Yeah," said Morgan. "He basically said that to me in the woods."

"He appeared before you in the woods?"

"Yeah."

"And what did he say?"

"He said he wanted Crestwood Lake."

273

Gil scoffed. "Butch has a gift for parsimony."

Morgan reached for the bourbon.

Gil opened a small box on the coffee table and handed Poole a set of rosary beads. "We discussed psychological ways of warding off evil, here's something more tangible."

Poole held them up and looked at them quizzically.

"Butch and I were given these by a priest. They're blessed. Put them on."

Poole put them over his head and slipped them under his shirt. "What priest?"

"His name was Father Mark," said Gil. "He helped us defeat the Devil last time."

"What happened to him?" asked Poole.

"He was decapitated," said Gil.

"Bloody hell. You call that warding off evil?"

"Like I said, nothing's one hundred percent."

"I'm gonna crash on your couch tonight," said Morgan. "I won't be able to drive."

"No problem." Gil topped off all their glasses. "Anything else we need to discuss about our plans?"

Morgan and Poole shook their heads.

Gil raised his glass. "Then here's to not coming to a sticky end."

Gil and Poole then became engrossed in a protracted conversation about archaeology and history.

Staring at the fire, Morgan didn't hear a word. All he could think about was Vicki.

A mere half mile away, but more than a half mile under the frigid surface of Crestwood Lake, all Vicki could think about was Morgan.

274

The Mayhem

"What do you want from me?" cried Alan, hands tied behind his back.

"Shut up and move," said Stan, poking his .380 auto against Alan's back, prodding him up the steps of the Crestwood Lake water tower.

"Is it money? I'll pay you as much as I have."

"Shut up or I'll put one in your lower back and drag you up."

Alan trudged upward, heart and mind racing: what to say, what to do. Forty-five minutes ago, he was sitting in his living room watching TV when his cellar door burst open. Stan pistol whipped him into submission and tied his wrists. Then he marched him with impunity, in the bright morning sun, to the water tower.

Alan had never met Stan, that he knew of. He replayed his scotch-soaked memories of Toby's through his mind, scanning for Stan's face, but came up blank.

"Who sent you?" asked Alan. "My ex-wife?"

"Keep going," growled Stan.

Alan had been a successful entrepreneur. He previously owned three gas stations, a hardware store, and a pizzeria. Then his wife decided to leave for Florida with her new boyfriend. She found a vindictive lawyer whom she paid handsomely, in cash and flesh. Armed with years of Alan's shady tax returns, they coerced him into a devastating financial settlement. He was left with one gas station, which netted him about seventy thousand a year, a fraction of his former earnings, but enough that he could sit at Toby's every day and drink.

They reached the top of the tower. Stan grabbed Alan by his collar and pointed the gun at his head. "Step over the railing."

"Please, don't do this. I'll give you whatever you want."

Stan cocked his pistol. "I want you to step over the railing."

275

With his hands bound behind his back, Alan threw his right leg over the waist high railing, yelped as he pinched his testicle, then steadied himself by bracing his left leg against the metal. He gingerly lifted his left leg over, teetered momentarily, and regained his balance on the thirty-inch catwalk, one hundred and twenty feet above the ground.

"What do you want?" whined Alan.

"Jump," said Stan.

A quarter mile away, in the bell tower of the Trinity Baptist Church, Darlene Thorn watched Jill Lerman drink her wormwood tea. Jill's hands trembled, jostling spurts out of the vibrating cup.

"Easy, my dear," said Darlene, steadying Jill's hands with hers. "Finish the rest."

Jill gulped the remainder.

Darlene took the cup and said, "You understand why we're doing this?"

"Yes," said Jill's quivering voice.

Darlene placed the noose around Jill's neck and tightened it. "Our master, unlike his counterpart, rewards sacrifice. You will be afforded untold gifts in his realm." She led Jill to the window, then securely fastened the rope to the bell's wooden support structure. "Why don't you sit on the ledge? I'll help you."

Jill was born and raised in Cincinnati, and never quite fit into small town, America. Jill was adopted by her mother, a civil court judge and compulsive gambler, and her father, an underboss in the Cincinnati mob. It was a symbiotic union. Her mother helped her father avoid legal reprisals, while he provided the funds for her profligate habits.

Her parents were never outright abusive, but Jill was more of an afterthought than a daughter. She had a nanny until age thirteen, and then was basically left to raise herself. Mom spent her free time at the track, or with her alcoholic girlfriends; dad was too busy overseeing a criminal empire.

276

When Jill was seventeen, she was date-raped by one of her high-school classmates, the son of a senior mob boss. Her attacker's behavior was excused; Jill's trauma was ignored. Her mother minimized the experience, while her father bordered on suggesting she'd caused it. Jill had never felt so isolated and betrayed in her life.

Jill wanted to flee the big city, and her parent's invalidation. She went to college in Maine and majored in education. She loved children and longed to have her own. After graduating, she had two job offers, one in Portland and one in Crestwood Lake. She assumed a small town would help heal old wounds. Sadly, emotional bleeding attracts other kinds of sharks.

Darlene assisted Jill onto the ledge in front of the bell. "Slide your legs around, dear."

Jill was now perched in the bell tower window, two and a half stories high. She could see virtually all the businesses along the two main roads that formed Crestwood Lake's town center. People ambled along, assorted cars and trucks wove their way through the streets. In the distance she could see the water tower . . .

"Jump," said Stan.

"What?" said Alan.

"I said jump."

"Why are you doing this?"

Stan pressed his pistol against Alan's forehead. "Jump, or I'll blow you away."

"It's time," said Darlene.

Jill's breathing became labored. Her chest pounded.

"It's OK, my dear. This will only take a few seconds and then everything will be fine. I promise."

A tear dripped down Jill's cheek.

277

"Go ahead," said Darlene.

"Now," yelled Stan.

Alan and Jill plummeted.

~~~~~~

At the police station, a flood of phone calls inundated the dispatcher. Morgan, hearing the unusual number of whirs and police chatter, entered the dispatcher's enclosure.

"What the hell is going on?"

"I don't know, sir," said the dispatcher. "The town's going nuts. All kinds of calls: car accidents, suicides and other deaths, gunshots, a dog attack. We need help."

"Get the night shift to come back in. Call the state boys as well, see if they can spare a few men. Send the firemen to help with the car crashes. What suicides?"

"Crazy old Edith Banks was found dead in her bed, surrounded by empty pill bottles. Diane Farley on Crestwood Road heard a gunshot in her garage. Found someone dead inside it. And get this, they found a school teacher, Jill Lerman, swinging from the Baptist Church's bell tower."

The phone rang again.

"Crestwood Lake Police," Officer Irwin.

Morgan waited as Irwin listened through his headphones.

"OK, hold on." He turned to Morgan. "We got a situation in the bank. Someone with a gun has the employees and customers hostage. Don't know if he shot any of them."

"Just one gunman?" asked Morgan.

"That's what the caller says."

"I'm going to the bank. Where's Edwards?"

"He went to the church."

"Tell him to meet me at the bank. Then get the extra men and triage them out accordingly."

Morgan hopped in his truck and sped out of the parking lot. He knew exactly what was happening. Van Haden was indulging his vindictiveness, and Crestwood Lake was going to pay. Probably assumed the commotion would keep Morgan off balance as well.

Morgan called Gil.

"Hello," said Gil groggily.

"Wake up. The town's going bonkers."

Gil heard sirens in the distance. "What's happening?"

"All kinds of shit: accidents, suicides; I got a gunman with hostages at the bank. Where's Poole?"

"Asleep, I guess."

"Listen, you better go to that church and get some holy water. Take Poole with you."

"OK," said Gil.

"Call me later and let me know."

~~~~~~

Arlene Pasternak was sitting in an Adirondack chair at the end of her dock, sipping her morning coffee and beholding the lake. It was chilly, but she bundled up, and relished the waterside tranquility. Arlene was working on her third novel, a thriller/romance about German and French spies during World

War II. Her plot was stymied and whenever she hit a creative roadblock, she would retreat to her dock, stare blankly at the water, and allow her imagination to run free.

Arlene was semi-retired, living on the revenue from her local gift shop, the pittance she earned from writing, and her spouse's life insurance. Her husband Neil, a postal worker, disappeared three years prior on the lake under mysterious circumstances. He was fishing from his boat one weekend while Arlene and her daughter were at a wedding in Rhode Island. His boat washed up on shore with blood stains. That was all that was ever found of Neil Pasternak.

Arlene dealt with her pain by immersing herself in writing. But the mental gymnastics only partially kept the grief at bay. Still living in the house they had shared for decades, reminders of Neil's presence were everywhere, especially the lake. Vexingly dichotomous, sitting by the lake soothed and provoked Arlene's heartache. It was where she lost her husband, yet being near the water somehow made him seem closer. But sometimes the balancing act tipped in favor of the heartache. That's when Arlene would wrap herself in a blanket and vegetate in front of the TV.

Watching the morning mist rise, Arlene was deep in thought: if the French spy killed the German colonel on the train, then the colonel wouldn't be available for the reception at the embassy. Maybe if the spy sneaked into the embassy and killed the colonel there, maybe by poisoning his drink. But then, how to explain how the French spy got across the border to get into the embassy? Maybe if the spy posed as a German officer he could—Splash!

Arlene spilled her coffee on her lap. She twisted her neck and gasped. Her husband Neil stood before her. His skin was ashen, eyes dark and morose, clothes drooping from his scraggy frame. He embodied living death.

Arlene jumped out of her chair. "Neil?"

Neil stretched out an emaciated hand. "Help me," he said, in a slow, eerie voice.

Arlene was agape.

"Help me. I need you."

"Honey?"

280

"Please, I'm lonely. Help me."

"What . . . what do you want?"

Neil glided closer. "Don't leave me alone. I can't take it." His eyes teared. He stretched his bony hand a little further.

Arlene took his hand. It was ice cold.

Neil's eyes glowed red. Transforming into a black demon, his hands became claws. He dug them into Arlene's neck, and plunged the two of them into the frigid depths.

~~~~~~

Morgan screeched to a stop outside the bank. One of his officers, Phil Hanbury was already on the scene.

"What's going on?" asked Morgan.

"Some psycho with a pump-action shot gun has the bank employees and some customers hostage. He's fired a few warning shots. I tried to talk to him, but he yelled at me to stay back or he'd start killing people. I was just about to—someone's coming out!"

A frightened young woman ran out of the bank, looked around wildly, saw the police car, and darted toward Morgan and Hanbury. It was Deidre Hamilton, one of the tellers. Morgan knew her.

"Are you OK?" asked Morgan.

"Yes. He wants to talk to you. He said that you, and only you, unarmed, had to go inside or he'd start shooting people."

"Has he hurt anyone yet?"

"He hit the manager with the butt of his rifle, but he hasn't shot anybody."

Morgan turned to Hanbury. "Take care of Deidre. I'm going in."

"Captain, are you nuts? He'll kill you."

"I don't think so."

"How can you know that?"

"Long story. Just take care of Deidre."

Morgan went to his truck, placed his magnum on the floor, then slipped his Colt .32 semi-automatic pistol in his belt behind his back.

Two other officers arrived on the scene, as had an increasing number of bystanders. Morgan ordered the officers to contain the crowd. Then he walked into the bank. Three employees and one customer were lying face down in the middle of the floor.

Stan emerged from a corner, pointing his shotgun. "One false move and I'll blow you away, got it?"

"No problem," said Morgan, holding up his hands. "What do you want?"

"You know what we want, Captain."

"I'm in the process of getting it. It's only been two days."

"We're running out of patience."

"If you kill me, you won't get it at all."

"I'm not gonna kill you, pig. I'm gonna kill them." He pointed his weapon at the people on the floor.

"All right," said Morgan. "I can deliver the goods. How do you wanna do this?"

"I'm giving you one hour. Every minute you're late—"

Morgan looked behind Stan and yelled "No!"

Stan turned. No one was there. He spun back, just in time to meet Morgan's bullet with his forehead. Stan collapsed like a limp piece of meat. The hostages shrieked.

"Everybody out," said Morgan.

The group scrambled to their feet and ran outside.

Morgan walked over to Stan's body and scoffed.

"Stupid fuck," he said.

~~~~~~

Vicki lay in a fetal position in her eight-foot-square cell. No light, no bed, and nothing but a hole in the corner to relieve herself, which hardly mattered given the paucity of food and water provided. Sporadic wails peppered the grim silence. Vicki's exterior discomfort paled in comparison to her internal misery. Even at the height of Derrick's physical abuse, she had never felt so despondent, so much despair.

Vicki had nothing to bargain, not even her soul. A traitorous apostate of hell, she would never be trusted again. She couldn't even hope for death, as Van Haden had been known to keep betrayers alive for years, inflicting unimaginable suffering. Her only potential recourse, was to discover a means to take her own life.

A soft orange glow illuminated the cell. Vicki nervously sat up, preparing herself for what only could be the first round of torture. Footsteps approached. A tall shadowy figure appeared in front of the cell. Van Haden stepped through the bars and stood before her. She hadn't spoken to him since she'd been captured.

"Hello, Vicki."

"I don't know where the tablet is. It was supposed to arrive with the sword. Aaronson doesn't know either."

"Yes, I'm quite sure that he doesn't." Van Haden tossed two objects on the floor next to her: Aaronson's pinky and testicle.

Vicki shrieked. "Damn you," she cried, tears erupting from her eyes.

"Why did you betray me?"

"Why did I betray *you*? You bastard. I know how you work. Derek was one of your minions. You ruin peoples' lives, then *rescue* them, only to take possession of their soul."

Van Haden crouched down in front of Vicki. She recoiled. "Vicki, my dear, I've never done this before, but I am going to give you an unprecedented chance to redeem yourself. We will welcome you back into the fold. I will even spare the life of your husband and his friends—once we have the tablet of course. But you must come back to me now."

Vicki wiped her eyes and took a deep breath.

"You'll save your husband's life," said Van Haden.

"I will never be a part of you again. Butch would rather die than see that happen. You might as well just kill me now."

"Oh no, my dear. You're not getting out that easy. As soon as I have the tablet, I will torture all of you together, so you can watch yourselves suffer before death." Van Haden clenched Vicki's chin. "I am going to do unspeakable things to your body."

Vicki struggled to break his grip but couldn't.

Van Haden rose. "Be back soon, my dear."

"I'll see you in hell," said Vicki.

Van Haden chuckled. "You already are."

Morgan strode out of the bank. Lieutenant Edwards approached him.

"I shot the perp," said Morgan. "How's the manager?"

"I think he'll be OK; ambulance is on the way. Butch, we got all kinds of calls involving suicides and strange deaths. What the hell is happening?"

"I don't know. We called in the night shift and the state police. The teacher that hung herself, was she from Crestwood Lake Elementary?"

"Yeah."

"Assign a man there. We have to guard the kids."

284

Their radios crackled to life. "This is dispatch, we got shots fired on Hillcrest Drive."

"I'll take that," said Morgan. "You clean up the scene here."

"OK, Butch."

Morgan was heading back to his truck when the large propane tank outside the hardware store exploded. A gaseous fireball erupted into the sky, setting the store and two adjacent buildings on fire.

"Jesus Christ!" yelled Morgan.

Seconds later, two car bombs detonated on Main Street, engulfing additional buildings in flames. Morgan contacted the station, ordering them to alert the neighboring fire departments. Another fire, of unknown cause, began on Vermont Avenue, the town's other major artery, bisecting Main Street.

People poured out of their homes and shops. A car struck one passerby as it swerved to avoid fleeing pedestrians. Sirens blared from all directions. Fire trucks, ambulances, and police cars from bordering municipalities converged on Crestwood Lake. The fires continued to spread, faster than the laws of physics would dictate.

Morgan hurried to the closest fire, at the hardware store. The entire building and adjoining structures were ablaze. Two doors down, an eatery was catching. Above the restaurant was an apartment. An elderly woman leaned out her window, calling for help.

Morgan ran to her building and shouted, "Is this your door?"

"Yes, but there's smoke in the stairway."

It was risky breaking open a door with fire on the other side, but Morgan had little choice. He threw his weight and busted it open. He could feel the heat permeating through the walls. Smoke was filtering into the stairwell, rising up to the apartment. Morgan charged up the stairs and broke the top door open. He dashed to the woman's bedroom, scooped her up in his arms and scurried back down the stairs.

Morgan carried her across the street and set her down. "Are you OK?"

"I think so," she said, between coughs.

Morgan called to a group of onlookers. "Hey, make sure she's OK. I have to go." Morgan hustled back to his truck and grabbed his shotgun. As he walked around the front of his truck, a large black dog with bright red eyes growled at him.

"I ain't got time for this bullshit."

The dog lunged.

Morgan fired both barrels, pulverizing the demonic mongrel. Then he headed toward the center of town where he could coordinate the rescue and firefighting efforts.

It took the fire departments of Crestwood Lake and three nearby towns most of the day to extinguish the fires. Half of the structures on Main Street and Vermont Ave were damaged or destroyed. One fire truck collided with an oil truck, creating an additional disaster. A tractor trailer had somehow lost control and skidded into the lake. A news helicopter had crashed in the woods. Thirty-five people lost their lives and another forty were injured in the day's events.

Morgan didn't get home until after midnight. He took a long swig of Bourbon and went straight to bed, sleeping with two guns.

He awoke four hours later. His mind was a cyclone. He lay there briefly, trying to becalm the internal storm. Tomorrow he'd be traveling to Boston to collect the tablet. Gil had made the arrangements for their excursion and acquired a supply of holy water—real holy water. There was nothing more to do on that front.

Morgan's immediate priority was helping his town recover from yesterday's tragedies. He hoped no new horrors would occur, not only for Crestwood Lake, but also for himself. If things simmered down, it would be easier to slip away to Boston, and then deal with Van Haden, or more to the point: save Vicki's life or die trying.

Morgan got up, made coffee, and called the station for the latest information. Crews had worked through the night, sifting through the rubble, searching for bodies. Thus far, everyone was accounted for.

Morgan heated up a large can of corned beef hash. He wolfed it down with some bread, finished his coffee, and showered. Thoughts of Vicki stabbed at his mind. He stopped by Gil's house, collected some holy water, and finalized their plans.

Morgan went to the station, which was already a frenzy of activity. A group of reporters and concerned citizens awaited him outside, anxious to bombard him with questions. Morgan had no time or patience for the mob, particularly the reporters, who in his mind, were nothing more than vultures feeding off the corpses of the disaster. But he feared that ignoring them would only incite them further. So he stopped, and allowed the jackals to encircle.

"Captain, was this an act of terrorism?"

"Who planted the car bombs?"

"Are the suicides related to the bombings?"

"Has a state of emergency been declared?"

"What are you doing to ensure the public's safety?"

Morgan raised his hands until the crowd simmered down. "Our first priority was searching for survivors. I'm happy to announce that no further victims were found overnight. At this point in time, there is no evidence of terrorism. Members of the state police and even the FBI have been sent to assist, and I want to thank them for their help. I've posted men at the local school as a precaution—"

"Was the school threatened?" asked a bumptious reporter.

"It's just a precaution, since a schoolteacher was one of the casualties yesterday. We're asking the public to stay in their homes and allow the authorities and emergency vehicles unobstructed access to the damage. The fire officials will be inspecting the burned areas and the police will be conducting their investigations as well. That's all I can tell you at this time."

The crowd fired off a barrage of additional questions, but Morgan retreated into the station. He met with Lieutenant Edwards, the second in command, and reviewed the police's activities. Of course, Morgan knew exactly who was behind the atrocities. Nevertheless, he had to go through the same motions he would take with any other non-demonic disaster.

Interim Mayor Turner arrived at the station and called a meeting with Morgan, the FBI agents assigned from the Burlington field office, the state police captain, the fire chief, and members of the town council. Morgan hated meetings. Nothing but a bunch of assholes discussing bullshit instead of taking action, which they were incompetent to do anyway.

A power struggle ensued between the town council, the state police captain, and the FBI agents, as to who would take over the investigation. Normally Morgan would have had a few choice words for all of them, but he didn't care whose turf it was. He knew what had to be done. All he wanted was to get out of the room, get through the day, and try to save his wife. Given the extent of the chaos, the FBI chose to pull rank, and take command. Morgan yessed everyone, told them what they wanted to hear, and didn't put up a fuss about anything. Edwards looked at him like he was a transplanted alien, fresh from his pod.

With the meeting concluded, Morgan wove his way through the awaiting reporters, ignored their firestorm, and got in his truck. He planned to cruise through town and inspect the aftermath for himself.

Morgan pulled onto Main Street, where most of the damage had occurred. It looked like a war zone. Numerous buildings were nothing but charred piles. Just as many were structurally intact, but damaged. Shopkeepers were rummaging through the debris, salvaging whatever they could. Morgan passed the shattered remains of one of the vehicles used as a bomb, parked in front of the devastated post office. He passed Mr. and Mrs. Underhill, standing in front of the burnt remains of their convenience store, which they had operated for over thirty years. She wept on her husband's shoulder.

In the distance, Morgan could see Scott Guerin's book store. A woman with long brown hair walked briskly out the front door and around the side. As Morgan got closer he noticed the buildings on each side of the bookstore were damaged, yet strangely, The Good Book was perfectly untouched. His curiosity aroused, Morgan parked his truck and approached. The lights were on and the "Yes, we're open," sign dangled in the window. Morgan marched in the front door.

Guerin stood there, dressed in gray wool pants, and an impeccable white shirt, almost as if he were expecting Morgan. "Good morning, Captain. Would you like a cup of coffee?"

288

"No thanks," said Morgan looking around. No one else was in the store.

"Can I help you with something?"

"Yeah, you can. You can explain to me why the buildings around you were affected by the fire, and yours doesn't even have a scratch."

"The Lord works in mysterious ways."

"Don't give me that crap."

"How do you expect me to answer your question? How am I to explain something as unpredictable as a fire?"

"I don't know, but it sure seems funny to me."

"Captain, I had nothing to do with the fire, or any of the other horrible things that happened. It saddens me deeply; you have no idea."

"Who was that woman with long brown hair I saw leaving here?"

"You don't know her."

"How would you know?"

"She's not from Crestwood Lake. Captain, I'm sensing there's more bothering you than some random customer of mine."

"I don't trust you, Guerin. And I'm not convinced you're innocent."

"I'm not your enemy, Captain."

"Then prove it to me. You said this town was an epicenter of evil. How do I get rid of it?"

"Do you know why God is sometimes referred to as the light of the world?"

"Something having to do with the light of truth."

"That's correct—the light of truth. The Devil operates from the shadows, cloaking his true nature, deceiving others. But when he is exposed, his power wanes. That's when he is most vulnerable. He must be revealed and renounced."

"And how do I know you're not deceiving me?" asked Morgan.

"Time will tell, Captain. In the meantime, you know what you have to do."

"Yeah? What's that?"

Guerin walked over to his counter, picked up a narrow, rectangular card, and handed it to Morgan.

"What's this?"

"It's a bookmark."

Morgan examined it more closely. On the bookmark was the famous 1636 painting of Saint Michael by Guido Reni, depicting the archangel stomping on Satan's head while brandishing his sword. Morgan scrutinized Guerin's face.

"Good luck to you, Captain."

Morgan walked out, with the strangest feeling he'd ever had in his life.

~~~~~~

Vicki, curled up in a corner of her cell, hadn't slept the entire night. Finally, the physical and mental exhaustion triumphed, and she drifted into a light sleep. A rat devoured the remainder of the stale bread that comprised her breakfast. It scurried through the bars as the witch appeared. Silently, she crouched, placing her hand on Vicki's forehead. Vicki gasped, every muscle in her body contorting.

The Rendezvous

It was exactly 3:00 a.m. as Morgan, holding a duffle bag, banged on Gil's door, setting off the Betsy alarm. Poole answered.

Morgan walked in and petted the dog. "Hey girl, how are ya?" He turned toward Poole and gruffly said, "Where's Gil?"

"In the loo."

"The what?"

"What you Yanks call the john."

Morgan took a 9mm out of his belt and handed it to Poole. "You know how to use this?"

"Yes, I do, Captain."

"I got a few other goodies which I'll give ya later."

"I got a message from Iannucci last evening," said Poole. "The ship is due in about seven in the morning."

"It's three hours and twenty minutes to Boston harbor," said Morgan. "Plus, we have to get the rental car, so we should be OK. That's assuming we get going." Morgan approached Gil's bathroom door and pounded on it. "Hey sweetheart, you wanna finish your makeup and get your ass out here?"

"Geesh," said Gil. "Gimmie a minute."

Morgan walked into the kitchen and made sure the dog's dish was full. Gil came out of the bathroom.

"Got your gun?" asked Morgan.

"Yeah," said Gil lifting up his jacket.

"Let's go."

The trio took Gil's car to St. Johnsbury where they rented a Chevy Equinox. From there, they headed straight to Boston. Morgan drove, Gil road shotgun, Poole sat in the back.

"Iannucci is meeting us at the port," said Poole.

"I thought he was recovering from his injuries," said Gil.

"He is. He's in a wheelchair. Has to have more surgery. But he insisted on accompanying the tablet himself."

"I admire his balls," said Morgan. "I'd do the same thing."

As they drove, Morgan relayed the previous day's events and once again reviewed their plan. Morgan always had a plan.

With business out of the way, Poole and Gil delved into a protracted discussion about the British government and its policies toward the American Colonies prior to the Revolution. Morgan tuned them out and thought about Vicki.

Speeding most of the way, Morgan made good time. He could always flash his badge if he got pulled over. They arrived at the port at 6:46 a.m.

They parked in the FedEx parking lot, with an unobstructed view of the long, rectangular channel where the cargo ships docked. Morgan poured himself a cup of coffee from his thermos. Gil withdrew a flask from his jacket and took a swig.

"Are you fucking kidding me?" asked Morgan.

"What?" said Gil innocently.

"With what we have to do today, you need to be sharp."

"Bollocks to that," said Poole. "Give me a sip too, mate."

"We're not gonna get drunk on one little flask," said Gil, handing it to Poole.

"You got a problem," said Morgan.

"Butch, this could very well be the last drink of my life."

Morgan shook his head and returned to his coffee.

"I think that's them, lads," said Poole, pointing straight ahead.

Morgan spied a black spot on the horizon, which slowly turned into a ship. He started the car and pulled along the south shore of the channel. Six huge cranes, used for loading and unloading ships, and rows upon rows of containers, stacked four high, lined the port.

Morgan went to the end of the road, then parked next to a small maintenance building. The three men got out and walked toward the water.

A passing worker said, "Can I help you gentlemen?"

Morgan pulled out his badge and said "No."

The man raised his hand and walked away.

The four-hundred-foot ship lumbered into the channel. When it came to a complete stop, the men proceeded to the gangway and waited.

Poole got on his cell phone. "He's coming now."

A motorized wheelchair emerged, operated by a dark-haired man with a moustache, in a blue pinstripe Armani suit. He was flanked by three burly men, sidearms on their hips, rosary beads around their necks.

"Bernardo," said Poole, extending his arms.

"Ciao, my friend," said Iannucci, embracing Poole.

With misty eyes Poole said, "Lucifer's got Aaronson. Everyone else in the Camorra's dead."

"Yes," said Iannucci. "If I wasn't on the ship, I'd be one of them."

"How did this happen?" asked Poole.

"Satan has spies everywhere. Three days ago, the Camorra had a meeting. According to my sources, each of the members were followed as they left, murdered in different ways . . ." Iannucci quivered, "and then decapitated."

"I know," said Poole. "Lucifer has their heads in a church in Crestwood Lake."

Iannucci made the sign of the cross. "By God's hand we will exact retribution."

Poole pointed to the wheelchair. "How are you doing?"

"Ahhhhhh," said Iannucci waiving his hand. "A lot of pain, but nothing that some vino and one of those pills can't cure. Who do we have here?"

"This is Gil Pearson."

"Nice to meet you," said Gil, shaking his hand.

"And this," said Poole. "This is Captain Morgan."

"Ah," said Iannucci, "The cowboy."

"How do you do," said Morgan with a smirk.

"Come," said Iannucci. "Let's get out of the light. We can use that small building over there. I know the owner."

Iannucci led the group to a small structure housing an office and storage room. "The workers won't be here till eight," he said. He handed the key to one of his bodyguards who let them in. Iannucci, Poole, Gil, Morgan, and one bodyguard went inside. The other two men stood watch outside.

"So where is it?" asked Poole.

"I'm sitting on it." Iannucci motioned to his bodyguard who grasped him under his arms and pulled him up. Iannucci grunted in pain. While the guard held him he said to Poole, "Lift up my seat.

Poole complied, removing a rectangular-shaped package wrapped in a white linen cloth, embroidered with a gold crucifix. The guard lowered Iannucci back to his seat.

"May I see it," said Poole, barely containing his excitement.

"Please," said Iannucci.

Poole removed the cloth, exposing a dark gray, inch-thick granite tablet, ten inches wide by thirteen inches long, weighing thirteen pounds. Etched in white lettering in Latin was the Prayer of Saint Michael.

"This is magnificent," said Poole.

Gil nudged in front of Morgan to get a better view. "It doesn't look like it's been buried for centuries."

294

"We cleaned it up a bit," said Iannucci, "but you're right. Even when first exhumed, it looked amazingly fresh."

"Mr. Iannucci," said Morgan.

"Call me Bernardo."

"OK, Bernardo. What exactly is the deal here? Aaronson said if the sword and tablet are together, and someone reads the prayer, it will conjure up Saint Michael, or something to that effect, somehow getting rid of the Devil?"

"Well," said Iannucci, "first, I wouldn't use the word *conjure*. It's supposed to invoke the spirit of Saint Michael."

"Meaning what? Like he'll appear?" asked Morgan.

"We don't know exactly, but I suspect that the actual archangel can't be summoned like a genie from a lamp. His spirit—somehow his power—can be beckoned and used to expel evil. I know that's vague, but no one has ever done this before."

"So we don't know for sure this will actually work," said Morgan.

"I'm afraid not," said Iannucci.

"So I can end up standing there like an idiot, reciting some Latin shit, which I can't speak to begin with, while Van Haden laughs his ass off?"

"I can recite it," said Poole.

"So can I," said Gil. "Plus, we got three hours' drive to teach you how. Even you could learn it in that time."

Morgan sneered.

"Listen to me," said Iannucci. "I understand the Devil already possesses the sword. You cannot allow him to confiscate the tablet as well. If he acquires both, he will be virtually unstoppable."

"But if all this hocus pocus shit is bogus," said Morgan. "then we're all dead, and Van Haden gets a worthless souvenir."

"Bogus?" asked Iannucci.

"That's American for bullshit," said Morgan.

"There must be something to it, Captain, or Adriana wouldn't have tried to kill me for it."

"That's right," said Poole. "And Van Haden would have already killed us all in the church."

"All the same," said Morgan, "I like to have more going for me than superstition."

Poole turned to Iannucci. "How long will you be in port?"

"Two days."

"We're heading back now. If you don't hear from us by then, you'll know what happened."

"God be with you," said Iannucci.

Morgan scoffed. "If he ain't, you know who will."

The Apocalypse

Darlene Thorn added the blood and wine to the decanter, swirled it, and poured the mixture into her glass. "Do you want some?"

"No," said Adriana, seated in front of the fireplace, peering into the flames as if staring into another dimension.

Darlene sat opposite the archwitch and sipped her bloodied Bordeaux. "You seem pensive."

Adriana slowly turned her head. "I am."

Darlene drank, awaiting her elaboration, not daring to ask further.

"Foreboding," said Adriana.

"I don't understand."

"I sense a presence, strange, yet familiar . . . archaic . . . uncertain."

"A presence?"

"You don't feel it?"

"I don't have your powers of clairvoyance," said Darlene. "Is it the tablet?"

"No."

"Our enemies?"

"I can't be certain."

"Perhaps you should inform our Master."

"No. One does not burden him with spurious presentiments."

"If you're right and don't tell him, there will be reprisal."

"If I'm right, it won't matter."

Gil drove back from Boston. The plan was to proceed straight to the north shore of Crestwood Lake, into the woods, and toward the abandoned mine. Morgan was uneasy about implementing their strategy in daylight. It made him feel more exposed, even though he knew they could be detected at any time. And he'd never find the mine in the dark anyway, even with flashlights. From what he remembered, it wasn't even on the trail, but nestled within the brush a quarter mile off the path.

Morgan sat in the back with Poole. He opened two large duffle bags, from which he withdrew and distributed their equipment: backpacks, several vials of holy water, ammunition, knives, flashlights, water-proof flares, cigarette lighters, rope, and three grenades.

"Incendiary grenades?" asked Poole.

"That's right," said Morgan.

"Are you serious?" said Poole.

"Damn straight," said Morgan. "We can put a bullet in a witch. But we can only kill demons with holy water and fire. You know how to use these?"

"Yeah, I did a stint in the army," said Poole.

"Fine. You take one."

"How did you get these?"

"I know a lieutenant colonel at the Army Mountain Warfare School in Jericho, Vermont. Not all the ordnance used in their exercises gets detonated, if you know what I mean."

"Butch has friends in some useful places," said Gil.

Morgan pulled out three bullet-proof vests from the one duffel bag. "We'll put these on before we head into the woods. Everyone's wearing their rosary beads?"

Gil and Poole nodded.

"And each man gets one of these." Morgan held up three sticks of dynamite.

"Good Lord," said Poole. "Did you bring a blinking nuclear bomb as well?"

"In case the mine entrance is sealed off," said Morgan. "Plus, I'm not one hundred percent certain that the old shaft leads to Van Haden's hideout. We might have to go back to the other spot in the woods I told you about. There's no clear opening there, so we'll have to make one."

"What exactly is our goal?" asked Poole?

"My goal is to save my wife. If I can save Aaronson too, fine. But Vicki is my primary concern."

"Not stopping Lucifer?" asked Poole.

"And how am I supposed to do that? He's already got the sword. If this myth of yours is true, we need both, right?"

"Yes," said Poole. "But you don't plan on just handing him the tablet, do you?"

"I'm gonna do whatever it takes to get my wife back."

"But don't you see, man. Once Lucifer has his hands on the tablet, we're all doomed."

"I ain't thinking that far ahead. I'm just focused on Vicki."

"Well you better bloody think about it. Even *if* you pull off a miracle and get her out, if the Devil gets the tablet, you won't have her for long. And a lot of other innocent people will die."

Gil took a deep breath and braced himself.

"Pull over," ordered Morgan.

"Butch, we're in the middle of nowhere—"

"Pull over now!"

Gil complied.

Morgan faced Poole. "Listen you limey bug, I'm in charge here, and my priority is saving Vicki. If I can take out Van Haden in the process, I will. But *nothing* is more important than my wife. Now if you have a problem with that, get the fuck out right now."

"Captain, five of my friends were killed. One is crippled for life, and one is being held prisoner with your wife. I'll help you get Vicki back, but I want that bloody bastard as well."

Morgan stared silently.

"Can we go now?" asked Gil.

"Move," said Morgan. He slid the tablet into his backpack. Pointing to himself with his thumb he said, "The tablet goes with me."

"Fair enough," said Poole.

The trio reached the north end of Crestwood Lake. They donned their bullet-proof vests and equipment-laden back packs. They trekked into the woods, Morgan leading the way.

It was an inviting October day, not too cool, with a few clouds floating across the picturesque sky. The kind of day that under normal circumstances, would have been perfect for an invigorating hike.

They arrived at the site where Brian Delmore was murdered. Morgan crouched down and touched the ground. "Guys, feel this."

Gil and Poole did the same.

"Damn," said Gil. "It's like there's an oven buried underneath."

"It's even warmer than the first time I felt it," said Morgan. He looked at Poole. "Based on the maps I have, the mine shaft goes right through this area."

They continued on the trail for another hundred yards when Morgan stopped and scanned the vicinity. "This way," he said, leading the men off the path, northwest through the trees.

A fiendish screech tore through the forest, causing the three of them to flinch.

"What the bloody hell was that?" asked Poole.

"Just the beginning," said Gil.

The men trudged on, sidestepping felled trees, boulders, and brush. Morgan stopped and combed the trees.

"You sure where it is?" asked Poole.

"It's been a year since I was there, but yeah, I'm fairly certain it's this way."

The gradient increased. Gil wheezed sporadically.

"You OK?" asked Morgan.

"Don't worry about me," said Gil. He opened his flask and took a swig.

Morgan rolled his eyes.

"I need the calories," said Gil.

"You need your head examined, that's what you need."

"My aunt Tilly," said Poole, "drank like a fish. Lived to be ninety-two."

"So what are you saying?" asked Morgan. "That I got to put up with his ass another seventeen years?"

"When did you learn to do math?" asked Gil.

"Ha ha," said Morgan.

"You do need the calories," said Poole to Gil. "Wouldn't hurt you to put on a few pounds."

"More than a few," said Morgan.

"And you could stand to lose some," said Gil.

"My mate back home lost one hundred and twenty pounds," said Poole.

"How'd he do that?" asked Gil.

"He broke up with his girlfriend."

Gil and Poole chuckled.

"Shut up," barked Morgan, coming to a stop.

"What?" said Gil.

"That's it." Morgan pointed to an outcropping of rock and boulders, largely concealed by vines and brush. "On the other side of that slab of rock jutting out."

The men plodded through thick brush. Poole got stuck on the thorns of a prickly vine. "Damn these buggers," he said.

Next to the large slab was an opening, partially occluded by the moss-covered trunk of an old fallen tree, a pile of large rocks, and a jumble of vines. Morgan yanked away the vines, then proceeded to heave the rocks.

Poole stepped forward, grabbed a rock, hoisted it as far as his knees, grunted, and dropped it. "I'll let you do it, Captain. These Yankee stones don't take kindly to Englishmen."

Morgan smirked and removed the remaining rocks. He shined his flashlight into the cavity. "Yeah, this is it. We're gonna have to crouch down for a while, but then it opens up further in."

Morgan hunched over and said to Poole, "Normally I'd say ladies first, but in this case, I think I better lead." He stepped inside.

Poole turned to Gil. "Charming blighter, isn't he?"

"He's the best man to have on your side, and the worst man not to."

"Why don't you go next. I got your back, mate."

Gil bent over, turned on his flashlight, and headed in, followed by Poole.

Morgan shined his light forward; two rats scurried away. The ground was rocky and damp, the air musty. A jagged boulder, too cumbersome even for Morgan, blocked their path. "Poole, get your ass up here. I'm gonna need your help."

Poole edged in front of Gil and shined his light on the boulder. It was shaped like a giant anvil.

"If we both pull on the narrow end," said Morgan, "I think we can slide it just enough."

302

Morgan and Poole, hunched side by side, gripped the end of the boulder with both of their hands.

"Pull," commanded Morgan.

The men heaved, the rock pivoted about forty-five degrees.

"Again," said Morgan.

The men tugged, the rock slid further.

"That should be enough," said Poole between breaths.

Still crouched, Morgan squeezed between the boulder and the cave wall. Gil and Poole did the same.

Shining his light, Morgan said, "It's gonna widen up."

Twenty feet later the passage enlarged to a height and width of eight feet. It became less dank, but darker, as they were beyond sight of the entrance. An unusual odor wafted through the air.

"What the hell is that smell?" asked Gil.

"You're behind the captain," said Poole.

Morgan turned around and in a hushed tone said, "Keep your voices down. We should try to be as inconspicuous as possible."

Gil and Poole nodded.

"Stay sharp," said Morgan. He pointed at Poole and said, "Every so often shine your light behind you." Morgan withdrew his sawed-off shotgun from his pack. Taped to the barrel was a long, narrow flashlight. "Take out your sidearms and have your water ready. Let's go."

Morgan crept forward, shotgun in hand. A slew of rats scampered toward them, darting in and around their feet.

"Aaaagh," cried Gil.

A red-eyed rat leapt from a crevice and landed on Morgan's shoulder. Morgan grabbed it and slung it into the wall, killing it instantly.

Poole stomped on another one. "Bloody rotters."

303

The ground declined, slightly steeper than Morgan's predicted thirty degrees. Treading became more arduous, as the men had to exert force to maintain balance. Fortunately, the rocks dappling the path became smaller and more scattered, smoothening the ground.

"How far have we gone?" whispered Morgan.

Gil shined his light on the pedometer strapped to his wrist and calculated. "Three quarters of a mile, at most."

Morgan touched the stone wall. "It's warm. I'll bet we're under the spot where Delmore was killed. In about a quarter mile, we should be under the lake."

A few minutes later Morgan stopped. "I think we're on the right track." He pointed at the ground. Two human skulls, jaws open, faced the trio. "C'mon," he said, stepping over them.

"They approach," said Adriana. "And they have the tablet."

"Splendid," said Van Haden.

"I cannot ascertain which one is carrying it."

"Oh, I have no doubt about that."

"We could kill them all now."

"No! They must suffer, especially Morgan. He will watch me eat his wife's heart before he breathes his last."

"But Master, the sooner we dispatch them, the sooner we can—"

"No! I will have my vengeance. *No one* betrays me. And no mortal makes a mockery of *me* without paying the price!" Van Haden smacked the candelabra into the wall. The entire room vibrated. "Do you understand, or do I need a new archwitch?"

"No, Master. Tell me what to do next."

"Prepare the anterooms and the central chamber."

The men plodded forth, swathed in a dim, scarlet glow. They rounded a bend, perceiving three distant lights. The ground became slippery.

Morgan shined his flashlight downward. "What the hell is that?"

"Guano," said Gil.

"Huh?" asked Morgan.

A legion of bats came flying at them, a cacophony of shrill screeches. Morgan fired both barrels—a burst of blood and shredded flesh—but they kept coming. Most flew around or above the men, but many did not.

Gil and Poole grunted as multiple bats landed on them, biting their way into any available flesh. The men dropped their flashlights and weapons, swiping furiously.

One bat sunk its fangs in Morgan's scalp while another bit his neck. He fumbled to reload the shotgun, pulled the bats off, and fired again into the unyielding swarm—another explosion of guts and blood.

Poole and Gil crouched, protecting their faces, yanking bats off their shoulders and necks. Morgan swatted as many as he could off Gil and Poole's posteriors until his back became overrun with the winged rodents. He threw himself back against the wall, crushing as many as he could.

"Bloody bastards!" yelled Poole, swiping, and flailing.

Gil yelped, A bat had lodged itself on his cheek. Morgan swatted it off and stomped it. Then he knocked the remainder off Gil's back and shoulders. Gil returned the favor. Then they helped Poole eradicate the last of his attackers. The bats finally dissipated.

Morgan grabbed Gil's shirt and growled, "Next time Mr. Webster, just say bat shit." He released Gil. "You guys all right?"

"Yeah," wheezed Poole.

Gil nodded.

"Grab your lights and pistols," said Morgan. "Expect another attack. They definitely know we're here now."

Morgan proceeded, carefully sneaking up on the three lights, which turned out to be torches. At the end of the tunnel, was a circular clearing abutted by three new tunnels, a torch blazing above each.

"Now what?" asked Gil.

"We could each take one," said Poole.

"No," said Morgan. "That's what they want. Divide and conquer. We stay together. I'm sure we'll find the welcoming committee no matter which way we go."

Morgan started toward the center tunnel when a large, black, three-headed dog, eyes and maws afire, emerged, growling.

"I'll be dammed," said Poole.

"It's Cerberus," said Gil.

"English," said Morgan, "Or I'll feed ya to the son of a bitch."

"It's the legendary three-headed mongrel that guards the gates of hell," said Gil.

Morgan aimed at the center head and fired one barrel from his shotgun.

Cerberus snarled even louder.

"Guns won't work," said Poole. "I got this." He placed his flashlight and pistol on the ground. Then he unstrapped his backpack and deposited it next to them.

"Pick those up," barked Morgan. "Never put your weapons on the ground. Stow them on your person if you need your hands."

"Not in this case," said Poole, stepping toward the beast.

"Are you mad?" asked Morgan. "Who the hell do you think you are?"

"Heracles," said Gil.

"Exactly," said Poole, slipping off his bullet-proof vest and holding it open in front of him, like a shield.

"What the fuck are you talking about?" asked Morgan.

306

Cerberus barked and growled, all three sets of eyes converging on Poole.

"We'll explain later," said Gil. Then he called to Poole, "You better hope it's not a myth."

Poole approached the three-headed monster.

Out of the corner of his mouth Gil said to Morgan, "Have your holy water ready, although it probably won't work."

When Poole was within a few feet, Cerberus reared back on his haunches, ready to pounce.

Poole lunged first, smothering the middle head with his vest, throwing his weight upon it.

The side heads howled. Then they turned, mouths open, as if to strike.

Pushing against the balls of his feet, Poole shoved the vest-covered central head as hard as his mortal strength would allow.

Cerberus snapped backward, yelping, fading into the center tunnel, a decrescendo of whimpers.

Poole walked back to Gil and Morgan, donned his vest, and retrieved his equipment.

"What just happened?" asked Morgan.

Pointing to his head, Poole said, "The brain is mightier than the sword."

"A fucking Englishman who can't speak English."

Gil shot Poole a knowing look and said to Morgan, "In Greek mythology, Heracles had to perform successive acts of penance for killing his wife and child. The final one was vanquishing Cerberus. Hades, the god of the underworld, told Heracles he could subdue Cerberus, but only if he could *master him without the weapons he carried.* Using a lion skin, Heracles squeezed the skin around Cerberus's head until it submitted."

"Hence me abandoning my weapons and using my bullet-proof vest," said Poole.

"Thanks Moneypenny," said Morgan. "I figured that part out." He turned to Gil. "Why did he kill his wife and child?"

"He was driven mad by Hera, the Goddess of women."

"Certainly gathers," said Poole. "Women been driving blokes potty since the dawn of time."

"OK, enough of this shit," said Morgan. "Which one of these tunnels are we going down?" He looked at Gil. "You got any ideas, Zeus?"

"Well, Cerberus went down the middle one, so we might as well—"

Everything shook, like an earthquake. The men tottered. Morgan and Gil reached out to steady themselves against the wall. Poole, standing in the center, simply extended both arms, wobbling to maintain his balance.

The ground became unstable. Stones and dirt fell from above. The ground cracked, fissuring like a splintering windshield. A loud rumbling echoed from below. The ground collapsed. The men plummeted, each through his own distinct cavity, splashing down into three separate aquifers, thirty feet below.

Gil swam to the surface, sucked in a gasp of air, and treaded water. Torches lit the perimeter of his subterranean chamber. He swam to the nearest shore and crawled out of the water. He scanned the area. The opposite end of the pool narrowed. It was difficult to see, but it appeared to converge into a stream exiting through a cleft in the rock. The earthquake had stopped. Looking up, he saw the hole from which he fell. It was out of reach. Surrounding the water lay a patchwork of boulders, stalagmites and stalactites.

Gil shouted for Morgan and Poole, but there was no response. Checking his equipment, he realized he'd lost his flashlight and pistol in the fall. He withdrew his lighter, flicked it repeatedly until he had a flame, and lit a flare. Three vials of holy water in one hand, flare in the other, he meandered his way to the other side, toward the possible exit.

"Gil," echoed a ghostly voice.

Gil stopped, confronted by a female figure. She wore a faint, light-blue, almost white, gown, the edges of which faded indistinctly into the air. She crept toward him, like a living corpse: sallow skin, concave eyes, bony

308

face, yet still recognizable. It was his deceased first wife Margaret. She died forty years after their divorce.

"Why did you abandon me?" Her words flowed together, a moaning, unearthly cadence.

Gil was aghast.

"Why, Gil, why?"

"Margaret?"

"Why did you abandon me?"

"I didn't abandon you. We were kids. Got married too young. It just didn't work."

"Why Gil?" she said, drawing nearer.

This is nuts, thought Gil. He turned to head back the other way but encountered another woman, same garb, just as garish, only this was his second wife, Ann. She passed away a year ago.

"You betrayed me," she whined in a similar voice.

"What?" wheezed Gil.

"You betrayed me for *her,*" she said, pointing her skeletal finger over Gil's shoulder.

He whipped around. A third wraith, his third wife Doreen, slinked forward next to the first. She appeared as cadaverous as the others.

"You're not dead," he said to her.

"You wounded me. I took my life because of you," she said, pointing her own bony digit accusingly.

Gil popped the cork off one of the vials of holy water. He moved toward the pair and splashed the contents onto Margret. Nothing happened. Gil uncorked a second, tossing it onto the other apparition. Again nothing.

"We are not Satan's demons," said Margret. "We are *yours.*"

Gil backed up and turned around. Ann was now carrying a grisly, distorted fetus. Its skin was dark red and wrinkled. Its face was compressed, scarred, and had one large eye, devoid of a lid. It glared at Gil.

"This is the child we aborted," said Ann.

"You killed me," wailed the fetus in a high-pitched voice.

Margaret and Doreen closed in from the one side, Ann and her offspring from the other. Gil felt on the verge of madness. A wave of terror surged through his torso. He clasped his chest. Was he having a heart attack?

The wraiths were almost on top of him. Gil bolted toward the water, jumped in, and began swimming toward the narrow end. His chest pain intensified.

Poole stood on the edge of his aquifer, in a similar cavern as Gil. He too had called out to his comrades, to no avail. Younger and hardier than Gil, he had maintained his grip on his weapon and flashlight. He readied two vials of holy water.

He circled the water's edge, weaving in and around the rock formations, hoping to find Morgan and Gil. He came across a human skeleton with a dagger sticking out of its eye socket.

A large, black dog, with fierce red eyes charged. Poole fired his pistol, but this demon-dog was immune. Poole turned to avoid the attack. The dog lunged, sinking its teeth into Poole's backpack. Viciously powerful, it tugged Poole, almost tackling him. Another dog rushed from the darkness, imbedding its teeth into Poole's calf, partially protected by his jeans and cowboy boots. Poole fired point blank into the dog's head with no effect.

Being yanked in opposite directions by the two beasts, Poole popped the top off his two vials, pouring the first on the dog assailing his leg. The dog emitted a shrill cry as it sizzled into a pile of cinders.

Poole squeezed the button releasing his back pack. It gave way as the other dog maintained its bite. Poole spun around, out of the straps. The dog pounced. Poole splashed it with the second vial. The dog howled as it disintegrated.

310

A third dog attacked. With no time to get to his pack, Poole was defenseless. He held out his forearm as the dog impaled his flesh. He grunted and tried to pull toward his pack, but the dog was too strong, and Poole feared losing his arm. Instead, he pushed toward the dog, hoping it might release its grip. It didn't. Poole darted in a semi-circle, with the dog clamped on his arm, spinning the mongrel around. The pack was now behind the dog. Poole lunged forward, trying to back the animal over the pack, where he'd at least have a chance of getting to his remaining holy water.

The dog pushed back even harder. Poole winced, his arm bleeding profusely. A fourth dog arrived, clutched the pack in its teeth, and scooted down a tunnel. A fifth dog rushed at Poole. Poole tried to kick it, but it caught his foot in his mouth.

The dogs forced Poole in opposite directions.

"You bloody motherfuckers!" Poole kicked the dog biting his one foot with the other.

The dog let go.

Poole fell on his back.

Both dogs leaped toward his neck, howling as they collapsed, smoking and melting upon his chest.

Poole pushed the decomposing bodies off and squirmed away.

Gil stood over him holding two empty vials of holy water.

"Thanks, mate," said Poole.

Gil immediately tended to Poole's arm, cutting away his sleeve, and tightly wrapping the wound with gauze and surgical tape.

"You look like shit," said Poole.

"To use your vernacular, I just had a row with my ex-wives."

"What?"

"Apparitions," said Gil. "Where's your pack?"

"One of the dog's got it. All I have is a flashlight, knife, and pistol."

"I have one vial of holy water left," said Gil. "It didn't work on the ghosts."

"You know what they're doing don't ya? They're getting us to use up our water on these pawns, so we're defenseless when the real threats come."

Gil nodded. "Have you seen Morgan?"

"No. We should head down that tunnel over there, where the dog went. Seems to be the only way out of here. Maybe we'll get lucky and find my pack."

The men approached the tunnel. It was utterly black.

"Maybe we could climb up and get one of those torches," said Poole.

"Let's just get out of here." Gil pulled a flare out of his backpack and lit it. Poole followed him into the tunnel.

Morgan's drop was closer to forty-five feet, into a deeper aquifer within the cave. Weighing three hundred pounds with his equipment, Morgan's splash was more like an explosion. He made his way to the surface, and onto the shore. His shotgun was lost, but all his other gear was intact; albeit, the dynamite was now useless.

Morgan's cavern was also bedecked with torches on the rocky overhangs and walls. He drew his magnum. The nearly water-tight cartridges should still fire. He yelled toward the hole he dropped from for Poole and Gil, but heard nothing.

Morgan surveyed his surroundings. Water trickled from a number of rocks. Stalagmites studded the cavern floor. Morgan assumed he was beneath Crestwood Lake.

He observed only one exit: a glimmering archway, carved into the rock wall. He snaked his way toward it, weaving around stalagmites, intermittently checking behind and above him. He crossed the archway, entered a short passage, and paused at its terminus. Before him was a round chamber, with a smooth base, encircled by numerous torches. It looked more like an arena than a cave. In the center was a stone slab, with an elongated object resting upon it.

Morgan exited the passageway. Holding his magnum in front of him, he reached into his pocket and uncorked a vial of holy water. A whip cracked, snagging his pistol and ripping it from his hands. Kim snapped her whip again. Morgan raised his arm. The leather smacked his skin and wrapped around his forearm with blazing speed. Morgan grunted and yanked, tripping Kim forward. Morgan splashed her with the holy water.

Kim scoffed. "I'm not a witch yet." She drew a pistol and shot Morgan in the chest.

Morgan collapsed on his back, motionless.

"I will be now," said Kim. She crouched over Morgan, and started to undo his backpack, when she noticed her flattened bullet protruding from the Kevlar.

Morgan seized her throat with both hands, choking her to death as the structures of her neck crackled. He tossed her aside, stepped toward his magnum, and bent over to pick it up. The point of a sword pressed against his neck, just short of breaking the skin.

"Pick it up and you're dead," said Darlene Thorn.

Morgan turned his head. At the other end of the silver rapier, Darlene, dressed in black pants and shirt, glowered at Morgan with her yellow eyes.

"Stand up," she said. "Slowly."

Darlene swung the sword across Morgan's upper thigh, nicking his flesh, slicing open his pocket, and spilling the vials of water within. Instantly returning the point to his neck she said, "I can't wait to watch you die, Captain."

"That's just like your boss. Sending his minions to do his dirty work."

Darlene pressed the sword harder, motioned toward the center of the arena, and said, "Move." She inched Morgan toward the large slab. Upon it rested another rapier. "I could kill you right now, Captain, but what fun would that be?" She pulled her sword back about a foot. "Go ahead, Captain. Pick it up."

Morgan contemplated the situation. He had more holy water in his backpack, and a .32 auto strapped to his ankle, but Darlene could kill him three times before he could get to either. He snatched the rapier and stepped back.

313

Darlene moved with him, staying within striking distance. "Are you much of a swordsman, Captain?"

"I'll rip your head off with bare hands or a blade. Don't matter to me."

Darlene whipped her sword just above Morgan's scalp, shearing a tuft of hair. "Good luck."

Morgan swung back, a crude, awkward swing. Darlene smirked, dodging it effortlessly. Morgan stepped away from the slab and held the sword in front of him with both hands, waiting for her to make her move, gauging her agility and strategy. Darlene approached casually, as if about to swat a fly.

Then she lunged forward, Morgan parried, his strength knocking Darlene off balance for a second. She whirled and back-handedly swung, nicking Morgan's elbow. She snickered. "I'll take you piece by piece if necessary."

Morgan charged, multiple swings, far from graceful, but wildly dangerous. Darlene countered each one, never losing her footing, her last parry followed by a thrust, which Morgan partially blocked, veering her blade along his belt. Morgan withdrew.

Darlene followed, waving her rapier like a magic wand, then lashing the air with two quick strokes. "En garde, Captain."

Darlene swayed from left to right, Morgan following her with his eyes. She flinched her free hand—he blinked—she thrust—he blocked—she swung—he blocked and swung—she ducked and swung again, just below his vest, cutting his belly. Morgan grunted and retreated.

Darlene stormed toward Morgan with repeated swings and thrusts. Morgan held his own, parrying each one, yet not being able to return the attack. He withdrew again, standing three feet from the rock wall, oozing blood and sweat.

"My master," said Darlene, "has ordered me to offer you this only once: give us the tablet and you and Vicki will be released unharmed."

"I'll discuss that with him after I kill you," said Morgan.

Darlene scoffed. "You're a fool."

Lilith, Darlene's cat, jumped from a ledge in the rocks, yowling as it landed on the back of Morgan's neck.

Morgan cringed and reached for the cat. Darlene lunged, Morgan twisted, her blade impaling his backpack. Morgan gripped the cat's neck. Darlene pulled her sword, but it snagged momentarily. Morgan swung the cat across her blade, severing it in two.

Darlene freed her sword. "You bastard!"

Darlene charged—so did Morgan. Their blades met, sliding down to the handles, the two enemies locked, pressing against one another with the cross-guards of their weapons. Darlene was a fraction of Morgan's size, but just as strong. Darlene's eyes were filled with rage.

Morgan elbowed her jaw, knocking her down to one knee. He swung downward. She jerked out of the way and swung, slicing his kneecap. Morgan lurched, Darlene returned to her feet.

Morgan scrambled away from the wall, toward the center of the arena. Darlene pursued, circling Morgan like a vulture, pointing her blade at Morgan's face. She went in for the kill. She swung and spun, slicing violently, as Morgan averted her strikes. She thrust, he countered, she kicked his wounded knee, then swung backwards hitting his cross-guard and knocking Morgan's sword onto the ground. Darlene, far more agile, scooped it up faster than Morgan could react.

Darlene held up both swords, and stalked toward Morgan, her face beaming with sick satisfaction.

Morgan held his one hand up in front of him, the other inched behind his back. "OK, I'll give you the tablet."

Darlene let out a smug snort. "You know, Captain. I knew I would defeat you, but I really expected more of you."

Morgan drew his throwing knife from his belt and whipped it into Darlene's heart. "You mean like that?"

She collapsed, blood gurgling from her mouth. Morgan quickly unsnapped his backpack, grabbed a vial of holy water and stood over her, watching her quiver and gasp. "No afterlife for you, bitch," he said, pouring the water on her.

315

Morgan collected the vials he lost earlier as Darlene dissolved and smoldered. One had shattered. Then he sealed his wounds with surgical tape and picked up his magnum. On the opposite side from whence he entered was another tunnel, narrower than the previous one. Morgan shined his flashlight into it, not seeing or hearing anything. He cocked his .357 and stepped inside.

This tunnel was completely dark and chilly. Morgan could detect a slight whiff of decomposition. The ceiling barely cleared his head. Something scurried past his feet. The ground was strewn with rocks, and occasional bones.

About fifty yards in, an adjacent tunnel ran perpendicular, forming a T-intersection. Morgan inspected it with his light, saw nothing, and decided to stay on course. Hearing a faint noise, he stopped and listened. Something was slogging toward him, but he couldn't locate the origin. It sounded like it was coming from all around him. He pointed his light forward, then backward, then forward, then backward, then . . .

Two large black demons with horns and spikes lumbered toward him. Morgan reversed, getting as far as the T-intersection. A multi-legged creature, as wide as the tunnel, wriggled forth, blocking his escape. Behind it followed Father Sean and another witch, armed with crossbows. There was only one option.

Morgan holstered his magnum, stuck the light in his pants, unclipped his two incendiary grenades from his belt, flipped the pins, and threw one in each direction. Then he ran as fast as he could down the perpendicular tunnel.

The combined explosion was immense. Even thirty feet into the side tunnel, the shock wave sent Morgan reeling. The air gushed past him like a cyclone, sucked into the freight-train of fire. Morgan got up, waited and watched, holy water in hand, to see if anything survived the blast. Nothing came. He checked his compass and retraced his previous bearings in his head. He was definitely underneath Crestwood Lake, and this side tunnel headed for its center. Morgan continued.

The tunnel became even narrower, its downward slope increasing. Morgan advanced cautiously, spiraling his light to scan the entire circumference of the path, pausing regularly to illuminate his rear. He didn't hear or see anything. Rather, it became eerily quiet.

316

Morgan tried not to think about Vicki. He needed every brain cell on guard duty, but it was futile. Horrid images of what could be happening to her flashed through his mind. Closing in to what he assumed would be the ultimate destination, his trepidation mounted. If Vicki was dead, he'd go down in a blaze of glory, taking as many of the bastards with him as he could.

Morgan heard a low rumbling behind him. The sound escalated rapidly. He shined his light. Charging toward him, a squadron of Baphomets: muscular, winged, goat-headed demons with raging red eyes. Hell's soldiers.

His water vials outnumbered, Morgan ran, but the Baphomets were faster. They barked and gnarred, like a frenzied pack of wild dogs, zeroing in on a kill. Morgan continued to run until—blackness—a totally dead vacuity. Morgan abruptly stopped and shined his light into it. The tunnel terminated into nothingness.

He uncorked his water vials. The Baphomets descended. Morgan sprayed as many of them as he could. The remainder trampled over their decomposing comrades, overtaking Morgan. They slammed him to the ground, clawing his thrashing frame. Three of them hoisted Morgan up, and hurled him into the void.

Morgan nosedived into the vacuum, completely helpless. *This is it*, he thought. This is the end . . . falling . . . falling . . .

In the distance was a bright aperture. As Morgan shot through it, he could see the ground approaching. Morgan twisted, hoping to avoid a facial collision. His velocity decreased. He crashed on his right side, stunned, but unbroken. Momentarily disoriented, Morgan sat up.

"Welcome, Captain. We've been expecting you," bellowed Van Haden, standing six feet away.

Morgan looked around. He sat on a twenty-foot circular stone slab, the top of a step-like structure of three progressively wider slabs, in the center of a sixty-foot chamber. Chains ran from the ground to his wrists, allowing only enough leeway to stand.

Torches burned on the onyx stone walls, alighting the entire space. Surrounding the center stage, stood an assortment of witches and demons. The witches held various weapons: crossbows, swords, and maces.

To Van Haden's left and right, ten feet up, on each wall perched a balcony. In the right one, Belial, Van Haden's archdemon, prevailed in his white shroud. His bright white eyes contrasted his black, and somewhat indistinguishable face. He rested his talons on the edge of his gallery.

In the left balcony stood Adriana, in a luxuriant purple gown, signifying her hellish royalty. Her lavish brown mane in full bloom—the archetype of villainous beauty.

Aaronson, Poole, and Gil hung from the ceiling by shackled wrists. Gil's nose streamed blood. Poole had a broken rib. The bandages from his dog-bitten arm were gone, and the wound further excoriated. Aaronson was in the worst shape: a combination of previous amputations and new contusions. He bled from his sides and legs. Despite their injuries, they were all conscious.

Standing to Van Haden's right, the demonic Clyde Burrows, holding the sword of Saint Michael, flaunting it like a prize.

Midway between Van Haden and Adriana, away from the other captives, but chained just the same, hung Vicki, panic in her eyes.

"Vicki!" blared Morgan leaping to his feet.

"Butch," she whined.

Morgan reached around his back. It was then he realized his pack was missing.

"Looking for this," said Van Haden, gesturing to his left, with a radiantly proud smile.

Adriana held up the tablet and cradled it in her arm. She too glowed with smug satisfaction.

Morgan drew his .357 magnum. It was the only weapon he had left.

Van Haden and the entire coven cackled. "Go ahead, Captain. Fire upon whomever you wish with your little pea shooter."

Morgan looked at Aaronson. "Professor?"

"It's over, Captain. There's nothing we can do."

Morgan pointed at Adriana, firing all six shots.

318

Moving as fast as the bullets, she blocked them all with the tablet.

The crowd cheered.

"You're pathetic," said Van Haden. "A woeful excuse for a man. Bravado and bullets mean nothing here."

"You've got the tablet and sword," said Morgan. "The least you could do is let my wife and friends go. I'll agree to your previous offer and leave you be."

"Oh no, Captain," said Van Haden, talking through his chuckle. "It's way too late for that." His face darkened. "You had your chance. I believe you enjoined me to fornicate with myself. Now you, your wife, and your friends are going to pay."

"Tell you what," said Morgan. "Take me. I'll join your coven. I'll do whatever you say. Just let my wife and the others go."

"No, Butch!" shouted Vicki. "You don't know what you're saying!"

"Silence!" hollered Adriana.

Van Haden cocked his head. A broad, devilish smile practically enveloped his face. "Well, well. I never thought I'd see the day that Butch Morgan would come groveling to me." Van Haden sniffed the air. "Smell that, everyone? That's the fragrance of desperation." Van Haden took a deep breath through his nose. "What a sweet aroma it is."

"Well, what's it gonna be?" said Morgan.

"No, Butch don't do it!" shouted Gil.

"Baby, no," cried Vicki. "I'd rather we die together."

"Oh, so touching," said Van Haden, mockingly holding his hands over his heart. "They want to die together. Now that's a proposition I think I can arrange."

The crowd approved.

"My offer stands," growled Morgan.

"My dear Captain, do you actually believe I am foolish enough to trust you? Do you think I would sacrifice the pleasure of your death—the pleasure of watching you see your wife and friends die—just for another coven member?" Van Haden raised his arms. "What do you think, everyone, should we admit this overblown brute into our ranks?"

The crowd erupted with jeers and catcalls.

Van Haden held up his palms.

The crowd fell silent.

"There you have it, Captain. The people say nay. Do you have any other offers to sell us?"

Morgan glared with eternal contempt.

"I didn't think so," said Van Haden. "You know, Captain, I've given much thought to your demise. I planned on slowly killing your friends, then your wife, and finally you. But if your wife was the penultimate victim, that wouldn't afford you as much time to bask in your grief. And I wouldn't want to deprive you of that. So let's begin with her."

"No!" shouted Morgan.

Van Haden pointed at Adriana. Now holding a crossbow, she fired into Vicki's heart.

Vicki gasped, her body falling limp in the chains.

"You fucking bastard!" screamed Morgan. He lunged at Van Haden, almost breaking his wrists in the chains.

Burrows snickered.

Van Haden guffawed.

The crowd cheered.

Vicki transformed.

Long, cascading brown hair, replaced her red locks. Illustrious hazel eyes sparkled like jewels. With the arrow still protruding from her chest, she turned toward Adriana and said, "Hello, mother."

Adriana dropped the crossbow. "Serafina?" She spied the sapphire amulet dangling from her neck.

"I'm a white witch. I've been searching for you for centuries." She pointed at Van Haden. "*He* orchestrated our family's demise. He masterminded the Piedmont Massacre. He killed your husband and your son, then used your suffering to convert you. You know how he works. Did you think you were an exception?"

"Don't listen to her!" growled Van Haden. "She is the deceiver!" Van Haden motioned to the congregation to storm the balcony.

Serafina leaned forward. "How many more innocent people will die because of *your* pain—which *he* caused."

"My God, what have I done?" whimpered Adriana.

"Save us now!" cried Serafina.

Adriana raised the tablet, and in Latin, quickly recited:

"Saint Michael Archangel, defend us in battle,
be our protection against the wickedness and snares of the Devil.
May God rebuke him, we humbly pray,
and do thou, O Prince of the heavenly host,
by the power of God, cast into hell,
Satan and all the evil spirits,
who prowl through the world seeking the ruin of souls.
Amen."

"NOOOOOO!" howled Van Haden.

The heavens rumbled, the cave shook, the waters of Crestwood Lake churned, Morgan's chains vanished. Saint Michael's sword burned like a welder's torch, molten fire shooting into Burrows's hands, scorching through his body, vaporizing him.

The sword fell toward Morgan. He grabbed it and swung it into Van Haden. The Devil wailed and writhed, his clothes and skin melting into a black skeleton. Teeth and fists clenched, he shook violently, shrieked, and burst into a cloud of putrid smoke.

All of the other witches and demons except Adriana, met the same fate. A chorus of screams resounded throughout the entire labyrinth, followed by dead silence. Serafina's chains had fallen away. Standing by Morgan she waved her hand, freeing Aaronson, Poole, & Gil, gliding them back to the ground.

"You're the one who killed Carolyn Pentlock," said Morgan.

"Yes," said Serafina. "I also saved the life of your great, nine times, grandmother in Scalford."

For the first time in his life, Morgan was speechless.

Adriana approached. She threw her arms around Serafina. "My dear child; I'm so sorry."

Poole turned to Aaronson. "What in bloody hell just happened?"

"Vicki was usurped by Serafina."

"Why is Adriana still here?" asked Gil.

"Because she repented, and summoned Saint Michael," said Aaronson.

Adriana let go of Serafina. Sobbing she said, "You've sought me all these centuries?"

"Yes," said Serafina. "From Europe, to Scalford, and back many times. Lucifer kept you well hidden."

"Can you even begin to forgive me?"

"You must make amends."

"How?" asked Adriana.

"By taking my place. You must help rebuild the Camorra. Your insights will be invaluable." She removed her necklace and fastened it around Adriana's neck.

Serafina placed her hand on Morgan, Aaronson, Poole and Gil, in turn, healing their wounds, restoring their bodies. Poole's demonic tattoo was gone. Serafina lingered with Gil, placing her hand above his heart. Gil took a sharp breath, as if injected with energy, instantly looking ten years younger.

322

"Those are the last acts I am permitted," said Serafina.

"What about Vicki?" pleaded Morgan.

"Oh no," said Adriana.

"Mother, you know it must be," said Serafina.

"What about Vicki?" demanded Morgan.

Adriana turned to Morgan. "I can't even begin to ask for your forgiveness, Captain. Perhaps my daughter's sacrifice will be a start."

"What's happening?" pleaded Morgan.

"Two souls can't occupy the same body," said Serafina. "I knew from the beginning it could mean my life."

"Serafina and Adriana embraced one last time. Then Serafina closed her eyes. A blinding white aura radiated from her body. It receded, leaving Vicki in its place.

Vicki threw herself into Morgan's arms. They didn't speak. They just held each other and cried.

There would only be one other time that Morgan would ever need to shed a tear. But that was decades away.

The Epilogue

Morgan, Vicki, Gil, Aaronson, and Poole, all sat in Morgan's living room, doing severe damage to various bottles of whiskey and wine. Gil was absolutely shit-faced.

"I'll tell ya," said Gil, "I nearly pissed my pants when I met all three of my ex-wives. Even Van Haden himself couldn't have scared me more."

"Have all three of them bought the plot?" asked Poole.

"No, the last one's still alive. That's when I knew it was bullshit."

"How's that exactly?" asked Vicki.

"Because even hell wouldn't let her in!"

"You're terrible," said Vicki, grinning.

"Oh yeah?" said Gil. "One time I said to her, 'tell me those three little words that make me walk on air.' She said, 'Go hang yourself.'"

Poole roared.

Aaronson said, "One of my psychology professors used to say that the problem with marriage is women expect men to change, and men expect women to stay the same."

"Damn, if that ain't true," said Poole.

"That's not true," said Vicki. "I don't want Butch to change." She met Morgan's eyes. "I love him just the way he is."

Morgan beamed.

"Well, there's always exceptions," said Poole. "In fact, ninety-nine percent of marriages give the rest a bad name."

The group laughed.

"Here's to your retirement," slurred Gil, holding up his glass toward Morgan.

324

Everyone clinked and sipped.

"We're leaving for Paris next week!" said Vicki.

"That's wonderful," said Aaronson.

"Tomorrow," said Vicki, "I'm getting online and booking everything. I can't wait to get away from here."

"You'll have to go to the Fontaine Saint-Michel," said Aaronson.

"What's that?" asked Morgan suspiciously.

"It's a monumental fountain with a statue of Saint Michael disposing the Devil."

"I think we've had enough of angels and devils for one lifetime," said Morgan.

Aaronson leaned toward Vicki and in a hushed tone said, "It's on the Boulevard Saint-Michel in the fifth arrondissement, left bank of the Seine. It's a bustling neighborhood with plenty of stores, cafes, and artistic venues. You'll love it"

"OK," said Vicki, winking.

Poole poured another whiskey and said, "Captain Butch Morgan waltzing through Paris. I'd kiss the Queen's arse to see that."

"Really?" said Morgan. "I'd figured you for kissing the *King's*."

Gil tapped Poole's arm. "Can you picture Butch in a French café?" Imitating Morgan's posture and voice, Gil said, "You got any fucking steak in this joint?"

Poole joined in, also in Morgan's voice, "And you got anything to drink, other than this sissy French wine, like American bourbon?"

Gil, playing the part of a French waiter, "Would monsieur like a glass with that, or will he be drinking it straight from the bottle?"

Poole and Gil guffawed. Aaronson and Vicki suppressed a snicker.

"Douchebags," said Morgan, cracking a smile. He turned to Aaronson. "So what are your plans now, Professor?"

325

"Nigel and I are heading back to Europe. We need to rebuild the Camorra."

Silence fell on the group.

"Well," said Aaronson, "it's just a matter of time before Satan . . ." Four pairs of eyes solemnly stared. "Ya know what, we can discuss that another time. What are you doing Gil?"

"Shit! Are you kidding me? I got a new lease on life."

"Yeah, you need a leash all right," said Morgan.

Gil ignored him. I got a date with Joanie tomorrow night. I'm not even gonna need any Viagra."

"How do you know?" asked Vicki.

"I tested it out myself."

Aaronson and Poole chortled.

"You walked right into that one," said Morgan to Vicki.

Vicki turned to Gil. "I always said you were a *handful*."

Morgan chuckled.

Aaronson uncorked another bottle of wine. "I'd like to make a toast."

Everyone lifted their glasses.

"In the words of Charles Caleb Colton, an English cleric, 'The firmest friendships have been formed in mutual adversity, as iron is most strongly united by the fiercest flame.'"

"Here, here" said the group in unison.

Then they drank and laughed the night away . . .

The sun radiated majestically in the cloudless sky. The wind swept gently across the pond, caressing delicate ripples toward the shore. Blue dragonflies hovered over a patch of lily pads, randomly setting down between the white flowers. A robin flittered along the water's edge, punctuating the tranquility with an occasional chirp.

On the path encircling the pond, an elderly man in high-watered khakis, cane in hand, ambled leisurely. A young mother pushed a pink stroller, her one-year-old girl, napping peacefully within its care.

Behind the young mother sauntered Van Haden, distinctly out of place in his broodingly-black suit and red accessories. He followed the woman and her baby half-way around the pond, stepping casually, almost aimlessly—one might even assume lost.

Van Haden reached the lone park bench on the eastern shore of the pond. Upon it sat Scott Guerin, in his flawlessly white shirt, navy linen pants, and brown penny loafers. His blue eyes beamed with clarity and composure.

"Mr. *Guerin*," said Van Haden. "I believe that's what you're calling yourself now?"

"It means guard," said Guerin.

"Yes, I am quite cognizant of the meaning of the name."

Guerin motioned for him to sit.

Van Haden slid his tongue slowly across his bottom lip, then deposited himself on the bench with one smooth movement.

The two sat quietly, facing forward, gazing at the water.

Finally, Van Haden broke the silence. "I imagine you're very proud of yourself."

"Proverbs 16:18," said Guerin. "'Pride goeth before destruction, and a haughty spirit before a fall.' I seem to recall that you've been admonished such before."

"Yours is a Pyrrhic victory at best."

"Even so, you're finished in Crestwood Lake . . . for all eternity."

"No matter," said Van Haden. "There will be other Crestwood Lakes."

"And other champions of heaven."

"*And* other fallen angels."

"Like Adriana?"

Van Haden scowled with seething contempt.

"You know, Lucifer, after all these millennia, you still haven't learned that evil is its own undoing. I bring the light of truth, and hope. You proffer empty promises, which is why your subjects eventually abandon you."

"Oh spare me the sanctimonious hypocrisy. They turn to me in the first place because they've lost faith in you. Is this the hope you speak of?"

"They lose faith *because* of you. When they realize you're the cause of their suffering, their faith is paradoxically renewed."

"Is that so?" asked Van Haden.

"Timothy 2:26: And they may come to their senses and escape from the snare of the Devil, after being captured by him to do his will."

"Yes, you can sit there and quote your little nursery rhymes all day, but the fact remains that you *allow* man to suffer, and that's what brings him to me."

"Man must have free will," said Guerin. "And suffering—I'll spare you the biblical citation—produces perseverance, character, and hope. Man can choose you, or he can accept his suffering, and fight you."

"Well," said Van Haden, "I'm sure you recall what Nietzsche—one of your detractors—said about fighting monsters?"

"Of course. He who fights monsters should be wary of becoming one. If you gaze long into the abyss, the abyss also gazes into you."

"That's right," said Van Haden, standing up. He leaned inward, eyes dark red, locking pupils with Guerin. "Beware, Messiah . . . I *am* the abyss."

328

Made in the USA
Middletown, DE
28 March 2019